PENGUIN CLASSICS

THE WAR IN THE AIR

H. G. WELLS, the third son of a small shopkeeper, was born in Bromley in 1866. After two years' apprenticeship in a draper's shop, he became a pupil-teacher at Midhurst Grammar School and won a scholarship to study under T. H. Huxley at the Normal School of Science, South Kensington. He taught biology before becoming a professional writer and journalist. He wrote more than a hundred books, including novels, essays, histories and programmes for world regeneration.

Wells, who rose from obscurity to world fame, had an emotionally and intellectually turbulent life. His prophetic imagination was first displayed in pioneering works of science fiction such as *The Time Machine* (1895), *The Island of Doctor Moreau* (1896), *The Invisible Man* (1897) and *The War of the Worlds* (1898). Later he became an apostle of socialism, science and progress, whose anticipations of a future world state include *The Shape of Things to Come* (1933). His controversial views on sexual equality and women's rights were expressed in the novels *Ann Veronica* (1909) and *The New Machiavelli* (1911). He was, in Bertrand Russell's words, 'an important liberator of thought and action'.

Wells drew on his own early struggles in many of his best novels, including *Love and Mr Lewisham* (1900), *Kipps* (1905), *Tono-Bungay* (1909) and *The History of Mr Polly* (1910). His educational works, some written in collaboration, include *The Outline of History* (1920) and *The Science of Life* (1930). His *Experiment in Autobiography* (2 vols., 1934) reviews his world. He died in London in 1946.

PATRICK PARRINDER took his MA and Ph.D at Cambridge University, where he held a Fellowship at King's College and published his first two books on Wells, *H. G. Wells* (1970) and *H. G. Wells: The Critical Heritage* (1972). He has been Chairman of the H. G. Wells Society and editor of the *Wellsian*, and has also written on James Joyce, science fiction, literary criticism and the history of the English novel. His book *Shadows of the Future* (1995) brings together his inte̶

literary prophecy. Since 1986 he has been Professor of English at the University of Reading.

JAY WINTER is Professor of History at Yale University. From 1979 to 2001 he was Reader in history at the University of Cambridge, and Fellow of Pembroke College, Cambridge. He is a specialist on the First World War, and the author of *The Great War and the British People* (2nd ed., 2002) and *Sites of Memory, Sites of Mourning: The Great War in European cultural history* (1995). He is one of the founders of the Historial de la grande guerre at Péronne, Somme, an international museum of the Great War.

ANDY SAWYER is the librarian of the Science Fiction Foundation Collection at the University of Liverpool Library, and Course Director of the MA in Science Fiction Studies offered by the School of English. He also teaches a science fiction module for undergraduates. He has published widely on science fiction and related literatures and co-edited the collection of essays *Speaking Science Fiction* (Liverpool University Press, 2000). He is also Reviews Editor of *Foundation: The International Review of Science Fiction* and Associate Editor of the forthcoming *Encyclopedia of Themes in Science Fiction and Fantasy* (Greenwood Press).

H. G. WELLS

The War in the Air

Edited by PATRICK PARRINDER
With an Introduction by JAY WINTER
and Notes by ANDY SAWYER

PENGUIN BOOKS

PENGUIN CLASSICS

Published by the Penguin Group
Penguin Books Ltd, 80 Strand, London WC2R ORL, England
Penguin Group (USA) Inc., 375 Hudson Street, New York, New York 10014, USA
Penguin Group (Canada), 10 Alcorn Avenue, Toronto, Ontario, Canada M4V 3B2
(a division of Pearson Penguin Canada Inc.)
Penguin Ireland, 25 St Stephen's Green, Dublin 2, Ireland
(a division of Penguin Books Ltd)
Penguin Group (Australia), 250 Camberwell Road,
Camberwell, Victoria 3124, Australia (a division of Pearson Australia Group Pty Ltd)
Penguin Books India Pvt Ltd, 11 Community Centre,
Panchsheel Park, New Delhi – 110 017, India
Penguin Group (NZ), cnr Airborne and Rosedale Roads, Albany,
Auckland 1310, New Zealand (a division of Pearson New Zealand Ltd)
Penguin Books (South Africa) (Pty) Ltd, 24 Sturdee Avenue,
Rosebank 2196, South Africa

Penguin Books Ltd, Registered Offices: 80 Strand, London WC2R ORL, England

www.penguin.com

First published 1908
This edition first published in Penguin Classics 2005
1

Text copyright © the Literary Executors of the Estate of H. G. Wells
Biographical Note, Further Reading, Note on the Text copyright © Patrick Parrinder, 2005
Introduction copyright © Jay Winter, 2005
Notes copyright © Andy Sawyer, 2005
All rights reserved

The moral right of the editors has been asserted

Set in 10.25/12.25 pt PostScript Adobe Sabon
Typeset by Rowland Phototypesetting Ltd, Bury St Edmunds, Suffolk
Printed in England by Clays Ltd, St Ives plc

CONTENTS

Biographical Note

Herbert George Wells was born on 21 September 1866 at Bromley, Kent, a small market town soon to be swallowed up by the suburban growth of outer London. His father, formerly a professional gardener and a county cricketer renowned for his fast bowling, owned a small business in Bromley High Street selling china goods and cricket bats. The house was grandly known as Atlas House, but the centre of family life was a cramped basement kitchen underneath the shop. Soon Joseph Wells's cricketing days were cut short by a broken leg, and the family fortunes looked bleak.

Young 'Bertie' Wells had already shown great academic promise, but when he was thirteen his family broke up and he was forced to earn his own living. His father was bankrupt, and his mother left home to become resident housekeeper at Uppark, the great Sussex country house where she had worked as a lady's maid before her marriage. Wells was taken out of school to follow his two elder brothers into the drapery trade. After serving briefly as a pupil-teacher and a pharmacist's assistant, in 1881 he was apprenticed to a department store in Southsea, working a thirteen-hour day and sleeping in a dormitory with his fellow-apprentices. This was the unhappiest period of his life, though he would later revisit it in comic romances such as *Kipps* (1905) and *The History of Mr Polly* (1910). Kipps and Polly both manage to escape from their servitude as drapers, and in 1883, helped by his long-suffering mother, Wells cancelled his indentures and obtained a post as teaching assistant at Midhurst Grammar School near Uppark. His intellectual development, long held back, now progressed astonishingly. He passed a series of examinations in science subjects and, in September 1884, entered the Normal School of Science, South Kensington (later to become part of Imperial College of Science and Technology) on a government scholarship.

Wells was a born teacher, as many of his books would show, and at first he was an enthusiastic student. He had the good fortune to be taught biology and zoology by one of the most influential scientific thinkers of the Victorian age, Darwin's friend and supporter T. H. Huxley. Wells never forgot Huxley's teaching, but the other professors were more humdrum, and his interest in their courses rapidly waned. He scraped through second-year physics, but failed his third-year geology exam and left South Kensington in 1887 without taking a degree. He was thrilled by the theoretical framework and imaginative horizons of natural science, but impatient of practical detail and the grinding, routine tasks of laboratory work. He cut his classes and spent his time reading literature and history, satisfying the curiosity he had earlier felt while exploring the long-neglected library at Uppark. He started a college magazine, the *Science Schools Journal*, and argued for socialism in student debates.

In the summer of 1887 Wells became science master at a small private school in North Wales, but a few weeks later he was knocked down and injured by one of his pupils on the football field. Sickly and undernourished as a result of three years of student poverty, he suffered severe kidney and lung damage. After months of convalescence at Uppark he was able to return to science teaching at Henley House School, Kilburn. In 1890 he passed his University of London B.Sc. (Hons.) with a first class in zoology and obtained a post as a biology tutor for the University Correspondence College. In 1891 he married his cousin Isabel Wells, but they had little in common and soon Wells fell in love with one of his students, Amy Catherine Robbins (usually known as 'Jane'). They started living together in 1893, and married two years later when his divorce came through.

During his years as a biology tutor Wells slowly began making his way as a writer and journalist. He wrote for the

Educational Times, edited the *University Correspondent*, and in 1891 published a philosophical essay, 'The Rediscovery of the Unique', in the prestigious *Fortnightly Review*. His first book was a *Textbook of Biology* (1893). But no sooner was it published than his health again collapsed, forcing him to give up teaching and rely entirely on his literary earnings. His future seemed highly precarious, yet soon he was in regular demand as a writer of short stories and humorous essays for the burgeoning newspapers and magazines of the period. He became a fiction reviewer and, for a short period in 1895, a theatre critic.

Ever since his student days Wells had worked intermittently on a story about time-travelling and the possible future of the human race. An early version was published in the *Science Schools Journal* as 'The Chronic Argonauts', but now, after numerous redrafts and much encouragement from the poet and editor W. E. Henley, it finally took shape as *The Time Machine* (1895). Its success was instantaneous, and while it was running as a magazine serial Wells was already being spoken of as a 'man of genius'. He was celebrated as the inventor of the 'scientific romance', a combination of adventure novel and philosophical tale in which the hero becomes involved in a life-and-death struggle resulting from some unforeseen scientific development. There was now a ready market for his fiction, and *The Island of Doctor Moreau* (1896), *The Invisible Man* (1897), *The War of the Worlds* (1898), *When the Sleeper Wakes* (1899; later revised as *The Sleeper Awakes*, 1910), *The First Men in the Moon* (1901) and several other volumes followed quickly from his pen.

By the turn of the twentieth century Wells was established as a popular author in England and America, and his books were rapidly being translated into French, German, Spanish, Russian and other European languages. Already his fame had begun to eclipse that of his predecessor in scientific romance, the French author Jules Verne, who had dominated the field since the 1860s. But Wells, an increasingly self-conscious artist, had larger ambitions than to go down in history as a boys' adventure novelist like Jules Verne. *Love and Mr Lewisham* (1900) was his first attempt at realistic fiction, comic in spirit and manifestly reflecting his own experiences as a student and teacher. By the end of the Edwardian decade, when he wrote his 'Condition of England' novels *Tono-Bungay* (1909) and *The New Machiavelli* (1911), Wells had become one of the leading novelists of his day, the friend and rival of such literary figures as Arnold Bennett, Joseph Conrad, Ford Madox Ford and Henry James.

But Wells was never a devotee of art for art's sake; he was a prophetic writer with a social and political message. His first major non-fictional work was *Anticipations* (1902), a book of futurological essays setting out the possible effects of scientific and technological progress in the twentieth century. *Anticipations* brought him into contact with the Fabian Society and launched his career as a political journalist and an influential voice of the British left. During his Fabian period Wells wrote *A Modern Utopia* (1905), but failed in his attempt to challenge the bureaucratic, reformist outlook of the Society's leaders such as Bernard Shaw (a lifelong friend and rival) and Beatrice Webb. Wells's Edwardian scientific romances such as *The Food of the Gods* (1904) and *The War in the Air* (1908), though full of humorous touches, are propagandist in intent. In other 'future war' stories of this period he predicted the tank and the atomic bomb.

Success as an author brought about great changes in his personal life. Ill-health had forced him to leave London for the Kent coast in 1898, but in the long run the only legacy of his footballing injury was the diabetes that affected him in old age. He commissioned a house, Spade House, overlooking the English Channel at Sandgate, from the architect C. F. A. Voysey, and here his and Jane's two sons were born – George Philip or 'Gip', who became a zoology professor and collaborated with his father and Julian Huxley on the biology encyclopedia *The Science of Life* (1930), and Frank, who worked in the film industry. Wells gave generous support to his parents and to his eldest brother, who was a fellow-fugitive from the drapery trade. Increasingly, however, he looked for emotional fulfilment outside the family, and his sexual affairs became notorious. He had a daughter in 1909 with Amber Reeves, a leading young Fabian economist, and in 1914 the novelist and critic Rebecca West gave birth to his son Anthony West, whose troubled childhood would later be reflected in his own novel *Heritage* (1955) and in his biography of his father.

As Wells's personal life became the gossip of literary London, his roles as imaginative writer and political journalist or prophet came increasingly into conflict. *Ann Veronica* (1909) was an example of topical, controversial fiction, dramatizing and commenting on such issues as women's rights, sexual equality and contemporary morals. It was the first of Wells's 'discussion novels' in which his personal relationships were often very thinly disguised. His later fiction takes a great variety of forms, but it all belongs to the broad category of the novel of ideas. At one extreme is the realistic reporting of *Mr Britling Sees It Through* (1916) – still valuable and unique as a portrayal of the English 'home front' in the First World War – while at the other extreme are brief fables such as *The Undying Fire* (1919) and *The Croquet Player* (1936), political allegories about world events each cast in the form of a prophetic dialogue.

Wells was by no means an experimental novelist like his younger contemporaries James Joyce and Virginia Woolf, but he was often technically innovative, and in some of his books the boundaries between fiction and non-fiction begin to break down. Sometimes he would take a classic from an earlier, pre-modern epoch as his literary model: *A Modern Utopia* (1905), for example, refers back to Sir Thomas More's *Utopia* and Plato's *Republic*. His bestselling historical works *The Outline of History* (1920) and *A Short History of the World* (1922) break with historical conventions by looking forward to the next stage in history. These works were written in order to draw the lessons of the First World War and to ensure that, if possible, its carnage would never be repeated; Wells saw history as a 'race between education and catastrophe'. The same concerns led to his future-history novel *The Shape of Things to Come* (1933), later rewritten for the cinema as *Things to Come*, an epic science-fiction film produced in 1936 by Alexander Korda. Both novel and film contain dire warnings about the inevitable outbreak and disastrous consequences of the Second World War.

By the 1920s, Wells was not only a famous author but a public figure whose name was rarely out of the newspapers. He briefly worked for the Ministry of Propaganda in 1918, producing a memorandum on war aims which anticipated the setting-up of the League of Nations. In 1922 and 1923 he stood for Parliament as a Labour candidate. He sought to influence world leaders, including two US Presidents, Theodore Roosevelt and Franklin D. Roosevelt. His meeting with Lenin in the Kremlin in 1920 and his interview in 1934 with Lenin's successor Josef Stalin were publicized all over the world. His high-pitched, piping voice was often heard on BBC radio. In 1933 he was elected president of International PEN, the writers' organization campaigning for intellectual freedom. In the same year his books were publicly burnt by the Nazis in Berlin, and he was banned from visiting Fascist Italy. His ideas strongly influenced the Pan-European Union, the pressure group advocating European unity between the wars.

But Wells became convinced that nothing less than global unity was needed if humanity was not to destroy itself. In *The Open Conspiracy* (1928) and other books he outlined his theories of world citizenship and world government. As the Second World War drew nearer he felt that his mission had been a failure and his warnings had gone unheeded. His last great campaign, for which he tried to obtain international support, was for human rights. The proposal set out in his Penguin Special *The Rights of Man* (1940) helped to bring about the United Nations declaration of 1948. He spent the war years at his house in Hanover Terrace, Regent's Park, and was awarded a D.Litt. by London University in 1943. His last book, *Mind at the End of Its Tether* (1945), was a despairing, pessimistic work, even bleaker in its prospects for mankind than *The Time Machine* fifty years earlier. He died at Hanover Terrace on 13 August 1946. He was restless and tireless to the end, a prophet eternally dissatisfied with himself and with humanity. 'Some day', he had written in a whimsical 'Auto-Obituary' three years earlier, 'I shall write a book, a *real* book.' He had published over fifty works of fiction and, in total, some 150 books and pamphlets.

Patrick Parrinder

Introduction

H. G. WELLS AND THE NIGHTMARE OF WAR

Nearly a century before the 11 September 2001 attack on the World Trade Center in Manhattan, the socialist iconoclast H. G. Wells conjured up the devastation of New York City by air attack. In *The War in the Air*, serialized in the London monthly *Pall Mall Magazine* in January 1908 and published with vivid illustrations later that year, Wells fashioned a warning, a premonition of what could happen when technology developed more rapidly than the capacity of statesmen to control its destructive potential.

And he was right. To a surprising degree, this dystopic novel anticipated much of the catastrophes to come in the two world wars. Wells foresaw the obliteration of the distinction between military and civilian targets in wartime. He captured the distance between those who bomb and those who are under the bombs, and the change in vision, and humanity, that follows. Air power looks down on a world where people are reduced to the size and insignificance of ants. Wells saw too the frailty of naval power, the weapon of choice in the nineteenth century in comparison to air power, the signature of the twentieth century. And he recognized long before the London Blitz the inability of air power alone to bring about the end of hostilities. Bombers can devastate, but they cannot occupy or control.

H. G. Wells was therefore a prophet of total war at the very moment of its birth. The notion of 'total war' is a term notoriously difficult to specify. Let me try. In its constituent parts, total war resembled other conflicts. The elements out of which it was forged were not at all new. But taken together, the concatenation of the elements of the mass mobilization of industrialized societies produced a new kind of war, total war. Its constitutive parts had existed separately before 1914, but had never before been fused together. Another way of making the same point is to say that the sum of the vectors of international violence was greater in 1914–18 than in any previous war. Here a difference in degree – an exponential increase in the lethality and reach of warfare – turned into a difference in kind. Total war is never 'total' or complete: some lives go on no matter what. Perhaps the term 'totalizing' is more accurate in describing the tendency of the technology of killing to draw into its orbit more and more of the resources of combatant societies and, by doing so, to make everyone at every single age a military target. In total war, no one is safe.

I will return below to the contours of his twentieth-century prophecy, but first it is important to see Wells less as a visionary than as a utopian, one with firm nineteenth-century roots.

Utopia and dystopia

Wells wrote self-consciously within a particular literary tradition. He occupied the space of dreamers who construct alternative worlds better than ours – utopias – or their mirror image – catastrophic dystopias – much worse than ours. From More to Swift, the literary conventions of utopian writing took on recognizable forms, which were developed in a number of ways in the nineteenth century.

A word or two about the kind of literary utopia Wells constructed is therefore in order. The best way to understand utopia is as a discourse in two contradictory parts. First, it is a narrative about discontinuity, a story through which men and women imagine a radical act of disjunction, which would enable the human subject, acting freely and in concert with others, to realize the creative potential imprisoned by the way we live now. But secondly, since the narrative is written by men and women rooted in contemporary conditions and language, it describes at times unwittingly where they are, perhaps even more than it shows where they want to be. Utopias force us to face the fact that we do not live there; we live here, and use the language of the here and now in all our imaginings.[1]

Utopia, in sum, is a fantasy about the limits of the possible, a staging in the imagination of the silences, of what is left unsaid about our social conventions and political cultures. Those who inhabit these silences play within them, begin to expose and disturb the contradictions in the way we live.[2] As Paul Ricoeur has argued, 'from this "no place" an exterior glance is cast on our reality, which suddenly looks strange, nothing more being taken for granted'.[3] What is strange, after all, may not last for ever.

Here is the second feature of utopian literature. It carries a message of warning, of admonition, and in one branch of the art, of apocalypse. This secular version of the end of things is one *The War in the Air* represents in particularly vivid colours. But it is important to note that this tale of doom is the prehistory of the world to come. Nineteenth-century apocalypticians like Wells believed firmly that first came the crash and then came the rebirth of a better world, rising phoenix-like out of the ashes of the old one. This turbulent optimism is visible in many nineteenth-century thinkers, like Marx and Engels, who believed in the inevitability of a crisis through which capitalism would collapse and a new order emerge in its place. This optimism dominated avant-garde painting throughout Europe. Groups like the Blaue Reiter in Munich, dominated by Kandinsky and Franz Marc, embraced visions of collapse and rebirth in many different forms. Wells, like most British thinkers, lived in an intellectual environment the climate of which registered a somewhat lower temperature, but affinities existed nonetheless. Wells did believe that the organization of society, both domestically and internationally, was fatally flawed, and that a more just, more rational order would replace it. His fiction dramatized these flaws and served as a warning to those who had naturalized the way things were into the way they had to be. The way to the future was through persuasion, not violence.

Who would lead the way to the new world? Intellectuals like Wells, to be sure, men and women who shed older notions of individualism to construct a social order based on reason, and practical reason at that. Intelligence and not the market or money or outmoded ideas of empire had to guide the state in its dealings with its citizens and with other states.

What was unique about Wells was that he brought to this set of convictions a knowledge of science which his fellow British socialists did not have. Science, applied to the creation of a more just society, was his dream. Wells, a man from a family of modest means, received a scientific education in part at the feet of the great Darwinian T. H. Huxley. He was an enthusiast for scientific progress, so long as it was guided by those with the vision to rise over the petty rivalries of states and empires. Without that conviction, politicians would use science to destroy and dominate the world. Wells went beyond most other British thinkers of the time, whose vision was overwhelmingly domestic. Here too is the link between *The War in the Air* and the decades of political work Wells put in on behalf of the idea of world government. Only by rising above the nation state, he believed, could the world avert the perils of militarized science, so evidently capable of destruction on a scale hitherto unimagined.

In this novel, Wells the Edwardian socialist, the radical polemicist of the pre-1914 years, provides a key to the transition of utopian ideas as between the nineteenth and the twentieth centuries. Saint-Simon, Fourier, Owen, William Morris and a host of other nineteenth-century socialists responded to the upheavals of the industrial revolution and the French revolution by imagining new and surprising forms of social organization. The rupture which precipitated their meditations was rooted in social and political revolution.

In the twentieth century, utopian visions have emerged out of the cataclysms of war, civil war and post-national violence. H. G. Wells is the first to announce this shift from what may be termed revolutionary utopias, characteristic of the nineteenth century, to war utopias, those which emerge out of the set of events we now term total war. Orwell's *Nineteen Eighty-Four*, published in 1949, is in this new tradition; so is Thomas Pynchon's *Gravity's Rainbow*, published in 1975. And so is much of the work of Gabriel García Márquez, whose magic realism is an offshoot of several utopian traditions.

García Márquez made this clear in his Nobel Prize acceptance speech of 1982. Here is how he put it:

> On a day like today, my master William Faulkner said, 'I decline to accept the end of man'. I would feel unworthy of standing in this place that was his, if I were not fully aware that the colossal tragedy he refused to recognize thirty-two years ago is now, for the first time since the beginning of humanity, nothing more than a simple scientific possibility. Faced with this awesome reality that must have seemed a mere utopia through all of human time, we, the inventors of tales, who will believe anything, feel entitled to believe that it is not yet too late to engage in the creation of the opposite utopia. A new and sweeping utopia of life, where no one will be able to decide for others how they die, where love will prove true and happiness be possible, and where the races condemned to one hundred years of solitude will have, at last and forever, a second opportunity on earth.[4]

Faulkner wrote in the shadow of the atomic bomb, while García Márquez wrote in the shadow of decades of massacre and suffering in Latin America. Both follow H. G. Wells, the novelist of the early twentieth century who conjured up the worst in order to imagine the opposite.

Edwardian socialism and the peace movement

Wells wrote a number of different utopias, reprinted in other volumes in this series. *The War in the Air* is unique in providing a focus on war and armaments as the enemies of civilization. In this respect, he was a typical British progressive of the early twentieth century. It was as much a liberal as a socialist belief that war was bad business. If nations thought they would enrich themselves through war, they had to think again. So Norman Angell argued in 1910 in his book *The Great Illusion: A study*

*of the relation of military power in nations to their economic
and social advantage.* So the British Foreign Secretary Lord
Grey predicted, at the outbreak of the Great War four years
later, that the commerce of the world would collapse and that
bread queues would be seen in London by Christmas.

These Edwardian certainties were shared by many in the
socialist movement. Their attention, though, was directed more
to domestic than to international problems. In Britain, with a
much smaller socialist element both in politics and in trade
unionism than on the Continent, the question of war and peace
was never central to socialist thinking. Britain had not engaged
in a major war for fifty years, and given the endemic racism
most socialists like Wells shared with his Edwardian contemporaries, the violence displayed by Britain in defence of her
empire in the Sudan, in Egypt, or in South Africa, counted for
little. For those who suffered most were neither British nor
Europeans.

At the time Wells wrote *The War in the Air*, he was a member
of the Fabian Society. This organization, formed in 1884, was
dominated by three people – George Bernard Shaw, Sidney
Webb and Beatrice Webb. Shaw was an Irishman, the predica-
ment of whose homeland dominated British politics in the
pre-1914 period. Only after the outbreak of war did Shaw
come round to Wells's point of view, penning in 1916 an
apocalyptic play *Heartbreak House*, at the end of which England is destroyed by Zeppelins. Before the war, the Webbs
focused on reforming and thereby ending the inequities of the
Victorian Poor Law. They had helped to found the London
School of Economics as a place where the administrators of the
rational state of the future would be trained. International
affairs were simply not in their field of vision.[5]

Wells was an entirely different kind of radical, one impatient
with the old guard of the Fabian Society, and prepared to
challenge conventions of sexual morality to which, like most
socialists, they were still attached. While writing *The War in
the Air*, Wells was trying to move the Fabian Society in a
direction he would find more congenial, but failing to do so, in
1907 he resigned.

He returned to fiction at this juncture and, by doing so, joined in a torrent of concern about the growing threat posed to Britain by Germany. It is easy to see how this fear came to capture so much public attention. German industrial and military power, and in particular her naval build-up, were clear challenges to Britain's domination of the north-west of Europe. But at the time Wells was concerned with *The War in the Air*, German ingenuity had found another vehicle for projecting her power and her sense of being a forward-looking nation, miles ahead of the decadent and conservative British. This was the Zeppelin, the giant dirigible developed through public subscriptions and with the support of the Kaiser. By 1907 Count von Zeppelin kept his craft in the air for more than eight hours, and covered 220 miles in the process.[6] A Zeppelin craze seized Germany; a cartoon in the satirical magazine *Simplicissimus* in early 1908 showed a sleeping England with a huge dirigible-shaped shadow covering it.[7]

What set Wells's novel apart was that the fantasy he wrote about Zeppelins and the decline of British power came not from the right but from the left.[8] His was no call to arms, but to domestic reform. What Wells brought to this equation was the sense that Britain was not educating its population, but instead wasting fortunes on weapons instead of schools.

Imagining war

The utopian elements in Wells's work are well known; so is his domestic political agenda. But what emerges from a reading of *The War in the Air* nearly a century after its publication is an uncanny sense of anticipation. The author of this novel knew technology and science, but he also knew how difficult it was to control them. The key to his ingenious story is the manner in which it shows that to wage war under conditions of industrialization is to open a Pandora's box, the contents of which are worse than anyone could realize.

In what ways worse? First, it is global and unending. Once war begins, Wells maintained, it spreads like wildfire. The reasons are multiple. Wells was a prophet of globalization, at a time before the term was invented but when the phenomenon was well known. There is nothing in the late twentieth-century concern with worldwide patterns of trade, investment and migration that was absent a century before. In a way, Wells is the novelist of the first of two globalizing moments, separated by the two world wars and their aftermath.

In this novel, there are five sets of international powers. The United States is one, 'a nation addicted to commerce, but roused to military necessities by the efforts of Germany to expand into South America, and by the natural consequences of her own unwary annexations of land in the very teeth of Japan' (p. 75). Germany is another; she aims at imperial expansion and the 'imposition of the German language upon a forcibly united Europe' (ibid.). The Asian Confederation of China and Japan is a third, totally underestimated by smug Europeans, with the manpower and resources to overwhelm them. Far more pacific is the British Empire, 'perilously scattered over the globe, and distracted now by insurrectionary movements in Ireland and among all its Subject Races' (ibid.). Even more pacific are France and her allies, the Latin powers, 'heavily armed states indeed but reluctant warriors' (p. 76). 'Russia was a pacific power perforce, divided within itself, torn between revolutionaries and reactionaries who were equally incapable of social reconstruction, and so sinking towards a tragic disorder of chronic political vendetta' (ibid.).

In this environment, a German airborne attack on the United States triggers a series of counter-attacks from both east and west which produces the end of Western civilization tout court. After destroying the American naval fleet defending the east coast, the German Zeppelin fleet reaches New York and by demonstrating the futility of defence, persuades the American government to surrender. This is so shocking to patriotic Americans that they continue the fight, thereby bringing down the destructive force of the German air-fleet on the city. Uncannily, German outrage that civilians fight on after terms have been agreed between military staffs and politicians anticipates the way they would react a bare seven years later to what they saw as unlawful civilian resistance in occupied Belgium. To find out what the *Schrecklichkeit* of the Great War would look like, there is no better introduction than the pages of Wells's *War in the Air*.

The German air attack provokes similar assaults which reduce to rubble the major capitals of Europe. London, Paris, Berlin are bombed in turn. The value of currency and international trade both fade away, and the problem of hunger returns to Europe as if the industrial and agricultural revolutions have never happened.

But then Wells adds an additional dimension to his imaginings of war which move in a direction dictated less by his understanding of science than by attitudes to racial difference commonplace in his culture. In this novel, the American defeat by Germany is simply the prelude to a vast airborne invasion of America by the Asian Confederation. After disposing of the German air-fleet, the Japanese, samurai swords in hand, seek out and destroy the survivors. Thus Asia supersedes Europe, and civilization recedes. But even this stroke of Asian military daring is not decisive; war becomes endemic. It rages like a bush fire, somewhere in the world, while civilian life is reduced to the level of peasants in the Dark Ages.

A new Dark Age indeed: this is where Wells leaves us in 1908. Here is Wells the pessimist, a man whose fiction evokes, in a critical and hortatory manner, a set of fears about the decline of Europe and the Yellow Peril which has traces of those dubbed 'Orientalist' by Edward Said.[9] The 'East', Said wrote, is a projection of the fears of the West. By conjuring up an 'East' of decadence, depravity and violence, Westerners could measure their 'civilization' against Oriental 'barbarism'. Wells plays with this set of views without endorsing them. There is clearly an element of respect and fascination, in particular for Japan: after all, the Asiatic air force overwhelms those of Europe and America. *The War in the Air* was published just three years after the victory of Japan in the Russo-Japanese war. The Chinese empire was then in the last stages of its dissolution, aided and abetted by European traders who treated the country like a colony to be exploited at will. By bringing them together in this novel in the form of an Asiatic confederation, Wells offered his readers a vision of British and European decline, which was his real destination. Wells, like his contemporary Conrad, was too intelligent to buy into the vulgar prejudices of his day about race. Wells used them to shock his readers into taking a hard look at the European world in which they lived.

Wells's novel on air war has another dimension to it, more positive and long-lasting. He is a novelist of dis-orientation. By entering the landscape of a new kind of war, air war, he challenges received wisdom about what we understand about both power and progress. He takes up the standard of those who see the nation state as both outmoded by international trade and communication, and mortally flawed by its own hubris, the belief in machines and a society constructed on their ever more efficient use. In *The War in the Air*, those machines destroy the world which created them.

Everyman at war

The narrative form that Wells adopted to shape his dystopia is essentially comic. In this way he constructs a counterpoint between the vast forces leading to doom and the ordinary, indeed banal, individuals whose sense of the world is bounded by petty commerce and romance. In the person of Bert Smallways, bicycle mechanic, Londoner and man of all trades, Wells found a small enough set of shoulders on which to set his global themes.

Wells drew this format out of earlier cultural forms and added to them some of his own distinctive style. The use of the fool to set in perspective the monumental foolishness of the world is a time-honoured device, particularly apt in portraying war. In nineteenth-century prose, the best instance of this strategy is the portrait of Fabrizio in Stendhal's *The Charterhouse of Parma*. Having no idea what is happening in the Battle of Waterloo, Fabrizio is nonetheless a witness to a history he singularly fails to comprehend. In a more serious vein, Tolstoy places Pierre at the centre of the battlefield of Borodino in *War and Peace*, and yet again our hero has little idea what is going on, but knows in his heart that great events are unfolding before him.

Similarly, Wells manages to land Smallways in a German Zeppelin during its mission to destroy the American fleet in the Atlantic and then to conquer and devastate Manhattan Island. Smallways's incomprehension is partly visual: in air war everything happens at a great distance; it is only when he sees an individual killed or executed that he begins to understand how monstrous war is. But in part Smallways's puzzlement over war is a function of what Wells terms his 'urbanized' temperament. In Smallways, Wells is able 'to express' what he terms 'the distinctive gentleness of the period. It was quite peculiar to the crowded townsmen of that time, and different altogether from the normal experience of any preceding age, that they never saw anything killed, never encountered, save through the mitigating media of book or picture, the fact of lethal violence that underlies all life' (p. 124). Here is the 'paradox' of modern life: 'The strength and heart of the nations was given to the thought of war', while the masses had become a 'teeming democracy' totally unfit in every way for fighting. The technology of war grew exponentially, while 'people grew less and less warlike' (p. 76–7).

The use of the comic to suggest the absurdity, the irrationality of war is now a commonplace of contemporary literature. Great War novelists used this device in a host of ways, and in doing so, they drew on cultural currents in Wells's fictional landscape. Some of these currents came out of the London music-hall tradition, filled with swagger, romance and buffoonery. Charlie Chaplin created his own blend of these ingredients, and in his 1918 film *Shoulder Arms* he returned to the themes Wells treated in a much more heavy-handed manner a decade before: the little guy, stuck in a military world of menace and danger, but who somehow manages to survive it all.

There is a touch of Kipling too in Wells's rhetoric. The inventor of a new kind of aircraft, Mr Alfred Butteridge, is hawking his secrets around the chancelleries of Europe, much as the Wright brothers did in the pre-war years. But unlike the Wrights, Butteridge is an 'Imperial Englishman' (p. 21), furious that the leaders of his own country do not leap to purchase his invention. After war breaks out and worldwide destruction commences, Smallways accidentally secures the plans to the Butteridge machine and gets them in the right hands. This helps Britain avoid conquest by the powerful Asian federation of China and Japan, or by any one of the other warring parties permanently in conflict.

At the end of the novel, the world has moved back a thousand years. Here Wells experiments in a kind of time travel where the future is profoundly regressive. Bert Smallways returns to England, devastated by a war which goes on and on without end. He finds his love, kills the man who would take her, and together they live a domestic life as peasants did in the ninth century.

The machines have won: they have destroyed the entire civilization which developed them. No worship of science here; instead we see an indictment of a social order in which there is no link between technology on the one hand and reason and social organization on the other. Wells the socialist, the believer in a rationally organized society remote from Edwardian England, meets Wells the pacifist, the man who knows enough about science to realize that once war begins, nemesis follows.

While much of Wells's fantasy about the future of warfare did indeed come about, he himself turned away from many of the positions advanced in *The War in the Air*. His sense of German barbarism, already evident in this 1907 novel, became dominant after war was declared in 1914. Wells supported the war, and turned his hand to propaganda, fashioning the term 'the war to end war' which became the byword of the Allied cause. He eventually became disillusioned with the war effort and, equally profoundly, with the post-war settlement, though he never gave up his belief in some kind of world state or supranational federation of nations.

The War in the Air is a tale of nations gone mad; of their insane bellicosity which brings disaster and ruin on them all. The stuff of fantasy, to be sure. And yet a century later, the image of death, indiscriminate mass death, coming from the air, is one we cannot escape. Wells's comic nightmare, banal and profound in equal parts, is one that simply will not go away.

Jay Winter

NOTES

1. Fredric Jameson, 'Of Islands and Trenches: Neutralization and the production of utopian discourse', in *The Ideologies of Theory: Essays 1971–1986. Volume 2: Syntax of history* (Minneapolis: University of Minnesota Press, 1988), p. 101.

2. Louis Marin, *Utopics: Spatial play*, trans. Robert A. Vollrath (Atlantic Highlands, New Jersey: Humanities Press, 1984), pp. xxii–xxiii.

3. Paul Ricoeur, *Lectures on Ideology and Utopia*, trans. George H. Taylor (New York: Columbia University Press, 1986), p. 17.

4. Gabriel García Márquez, 'The Solitude of Latin America', 8 December 1982. For the full text of the Nobel Prize acceptance speech, see: http://www.nobel.se/literature/laureates/1982/marquez-lecture.html

5. J. M. Winter, *Socialism and the Challenge of War* (London: Macmillan, 1974), ch. 2.

6. Robert Wohl, *A Passion for Wings: Aviation and the Western imagination 1908–1918* (New Haven: Yale University Press, 1994), p. 71.

7. Peter Fritzsche, *A Nation of Fliers: German aviation and the popular imagination* (Cambridge, Mass.: Harvard University Press, 1992), pp. 22ff, and esp. p. 39 for the cartoon.

8. Samuel Hynes, *The Edwardian Turn of Mind* (London: Heinemann, 1968), pp. 43–5.

9. Edward W. Said, *Orientalism* (New York: Pantheon Books, 1978).

Further Reading

The most vivid and memorable account of Wells's life and times is his own *Experiment in Autobiography* (2 vols., London: Gollancz and Cresset Press, 1934). It has been reprinted several times. A 'postscript' containing the previously suppressed narrative of his sexual liaisons was published as *H. G. Wells in Love*, edited by his son G. P. Wells (London: Faber & Faber, 1984). His more recent biographers draw on this material, as well as on the large body of letters and personal papers archived at the University of Illinois and elsewhere. The fullest and most scholarly biographies are *The Time Traveller* by Norman and Jeanne Mackenzie (2nd ed., London: Hogarth Press, 1987) and *H. G. Wells: Desperately Mortal* by David C. Smith (New Haven and London: Yale University Press, 1986). Smith has also edited a generous selection of Wells's *Correspondence* (4 vols., London: Pickering & Chatto, 1998). Another highly readable, if controversial and idiosyncratic, biography is *H. G. Wells: Aspects of a Life* (London: Hutchinson, 1984) by Wells's son Anthony West. Michael Foot's *H. G.: The History of Mr Wells* (London and New York: Doubleday, 1995) is enlivened by its author's personal knowledge of Wells and his circle.

Two illuminating general interpretations of Wells and his writings are Michael Draper's *H. G. Wells* (Basingstoke: Macmillan, 1987) and Brian Murray's *H. G. Wells* (New York: Continuum, 1990). Both are introductory in scope, but Draper's approach is critical and philosophical, while Murray packs a remarkable amount of biographical and historical detail into a short space. John Hammond's *An H. G. Wells Companion* (London and Basingstoke: Macmillan, 1979) and

H. G. Wells (Harlow and London: Longman, 2001) combine criticism with useful contextual material. *H. G. Wells: The Critical Heritage*, edited by Patrick Parrinder (London: Routledge, 1972), is a collection of reviews and essays of Wells published during his lifetime. A number of specialized critical and scholarly studies of Wells concentrate on his scientific romances. These include Bernard Bergonzi's pioneering study of *The Early H. G. Wells* (Manchester: Manchester University Press, 1961); John Huntington, *The Logic of Fantasy: H. G. Wells and Science Fiction* (New York: Columbia University Press, 1982); and Patrick Parrinder, *Shadows of the Future: H. G. Wells, Science Fiction and Prophecy* (Liverpool: Liverpool University Press, 1995). Peter Kemp's *H. G. Wells and the Culminating Ape* (London and Basingstoke: Macmillan, 1982) offers a lively and, at times, lurid tracing of Wells's 'biological themes and imaginative obsessions', while Roslynn D. Haynes's *H. G. Wells: Discoverer of the Future* (London and Basingstoke: Macmillan, 1980) surveys his use of scientific ideas. W. Warren Wagar, *H. G. Wells and the World State* (New Haven: Yale University Press, 1961) and John S. Partington, *Building Cosmopolis* (Aldershot: Ashgate, 2003) are studies of his political thought and his schemes for world government. John S. Partington has also edited *The Wellsian* (The Netherlands: Equilibris, 2003), a selection of essays from the H. G. Wells Society's annual critical journal of the same name. The American branch of the Wells Society maintains a highly informative website at http://hgwellsusa.50megs.com

P. P.

Note on the Text

H. G. Wells outlined his plans for *The War in the Air* in a letter dated 7 June 1907 to Frederick Macmillan, his usual British publisher. He described the projected book as a 'pot-boiler' which he intended to place with another publisher. He told Arnold Bennett that it took him four months to write (Bennett, *The Journals*, ed. Frank Swinnerton, entry for 5 March 1908). The American episodes, especially the description of the Niagara Falls, drew on his first visit to the United States in 1906. *The War in the Air* was serialized in the *Pall Mall Magazine*, beginning in January 1908, with illustrations by A. C. Michael. Michael's illustrations were also used in the first book publication (London: George Bell and Sons) in October 1908. The first American edition, illustrated by Eric Pape, was published in the same month by Macmillan in New York. *The War in the Air* enjoyed a popular success, and was reprinted many times. Wells added new prefaces for the 1921 Collins edition, for the 1926 Atlantic edition, and for the first Penguin edition, which was published in 1941.

Apart from the preliminary matter, the Collins and Penguin editions reproduced the original text published by Bell. The text of the Macmillan (New York) first edition is almost identical with that published by Bell, with spelling and punctuation in the British style, but this edition was later superseded by cheap reprints and at some point the text was copy-edited for American readers. Wells himself appears to have made no changes until he revised the text for inclusion in Volume 20 of the Atlantic Edition of the Works of H. G. Wells (London: T. Fisher Unwin, and New York: Scribner's, 1926).

The present edition follows the revised Atlantic text, modified as set out below. The two prefaces that appeared in the 1941 Penguin are also included as an Appendix. I have omitted Wells's preface to Volume 20 of the Atlantic edition, which includes a single paragraph on *The War in the Air*, largely summarizing the points he had made at greater length in his 1921 preface. Wells wrote in 1926 that, when his novel was published eighteen years earlier,

> Flying was still only in the hopping and gliding stage, and the navigable airship was a clumsy contrivance a few years old. [. . .] The reader may have some little difficulty in realizing that when this book was written the war was six and the Zeppelin four years away, and that the character of the German Crown Prince had still to shine upon the world. Many of the inevitable consequences of making war in three instead of two dimensions, the abolition of 'fronts,' the disappearance of the theoretical immunity of non-combatants, are stated quite clearly in this tale. (p. ix)

The remainder of the preface introduces the other material included in Volume 20, which was published under the title *The War in the Air and Other War Forebodings*.

The Atlantic edition, published simultaneously in London and New York, was printed in the United States using an earlier American edition as copy-text. Wells would have entered his revisions on the galleys. The Atlantic edition was intended to observe British spelling conventions, although in practice many American usages were retained. The present text aims to fully restore the 'British' character of the text. For this reason, 'aluminum' has been changed to 'aluminium', 'backward' to 'backwards', 'burned' to 'burnt', 'chints' to 'chintz', 'clinched' to 'clenched', 'cruelest' to 'cruellest', 'fetich' to 'fetish', 'inclosed' to 'enclosed', 'intrenchment' to 'entrenchment', 'intrusted' to 'entrusted', 'leaned' to 'leant', 'leaped' to 'leapt', 'learned' to 'learnt', 'rumored' to 'rumoured', 'smelled' to 'smelt', 'spelled' to 'spelt', 'spoiled' to 'spoilt', 'tire' to 'tyre', 'unforgetable' to 'unforgettable' and 'vender' to 'vendor' in accordance with the

UK and US first editions. Some 50 compound words, mostly hyphenated in the Atlantic text, have been modernized in accordance with British practice (e.g. 'everyone' for 'every one', 'flagship' for 'flag-ship', 'flying machine' for 'flying-machine', 'soda water' for 'soda-water'). A few place-names have been modernized.

Housestyling of punctuation and spelling has also been implemented to make the text more accessible to the reader: single quotation marks (for doubles) with doubles inside singles as needed; end punctuation placed outside end quotation marks when appropriate; spaced N-dashes (for the heavier, longer M-dash) and M-dashes (for double-length 2M-dash); 'iz' spellings (e.g. recognize, not recognise), and acknowledgements and judgement, not acknowledgments and judgment; no full stop after personal titles (Dr, Mr, Mrs) or chapter titles, which may not follow the capitalization of the copy-text. In addition, book titles are in italics, not quotation marks, and chapter numbers are in Arabic numbers, not roman.

SIGNIFICANT VARIANT READINGS

There are some 80 stylistic changes in the Atlantic text. A few of these (e.g. Long Island Sound, Green Island) introduce greater topographical accuracy into the American episodes and are most likely the product of American copy-editors. In all but one case, the original Bell and Macmillan readings are identical. Examples are given below:

Page/line	First edition reading	Atlantic reading
7:10	levelled that up	levelled it
8:23	employers for Bert	for Bert employers
22:31	of this affair	of this story
22:31–2	of . . . stability by the British Empire	by the British Empire of . . . stability
23:11–12	no uncle . . . baby ever harped upon it so relentlessly	he was as insistent as an uncle . . . baby

30:8	a plate-glass window	a big window
51:1	little wisps	cobwebby wisps
94:16–1	These are outside	Zese are outside
100:1	was a number of American maps	were American maps
139:28–9	from the east side, from these	from the East Side
142:28	Lower Island Sound	Long Island Sound
148:3	Oh! Blut und Eisen!	Ach! Blut und Eisen!
152:18	came the shrill ringing of the bells	came the shrill bugles
156:27	and his breath was suffocated	and he felt suffocated
160:23–4	squatted over his soup	consumed all his soup
161:11	squatted across the hinge	adjusted himself across the hinge
162:10	awestricken and perplexed beyond their power of words	awestricken and perplexed
176:23	by the time, that is, that mast	by the time that mast
197:20	hung a second consort,	hung a second;
201:33	Green Islet	Green Island
208:30	gets on one's nerves at last	gets on your nerves
247:8	chancy and irregular (Bell); change and irregular (Macmillan)	chance and irregular
248:25	as the races drew closer without concern or understanding	as the races drew closer
276:1	end the War?	stop the War?

A holograph manuscript and corrected typescript of *The War in the Air* are in the Wells Collection, Rare Book and Special Collections Library, University of Illinois at Urbana-Champaign. The whereabouts of the galley proofs of the Atlantic edition are unknown. Wells's letters to Frederick Macmillan are in the Macmillan Archive, British Library.

P. P.

THE WAR IN THE AIR

And Particularly How Mr Bert Smallways Fared While It Lasted

Contents

I

OF PROGRESS AND THE
SMALLWAYS FAMILY

'This here Progress,' said Mr Tom Smallways,[1] 'it keeps on.

'You'd hardly think it *could* keep on,' said Mr Tom Smallways.

It was long before the War in the Air began that Mr Smallways made this remark. He was sitting on the fence at the end of his garden and surveying the great Bun Hill[2] gas-works with an eye that neither praised nor blamed. Above the clustering gasometers three unfamiliar shapes appeared, thin, wallowing bladders that flapped and rolled about, and grew bigger and bigger and rounder and rounder – balloons[3] in course of inflation for the South of England Aero Club's Saturday-afternoon ascent.

'They goes up every Saturday,' said his neighbour, Mr Stringer, the milkman. 'It's only yestiday, so to speak, when all London turned out to see a balloon go over, and now every little place in the country has its weekly outings – uppings, rather. It's been the salvation of them gas companies.'

'Larst Satiday I got three barrer-loads of gravel off my petaters,' said Mr Tom Smallways. 'Three barrer-loads! What they dropped as ballase.[4] Some of the plants was broke, and some was buried.'

'Ladies, they say, goes up!'

'I suppose we got to call 'em ladies,' said Mr Tom Smallways. 'Still, it ain't hardly my idea of a lady – flying about in the air, and throwing gravel at people. It ain't what I been accustomed to consider ladylike, whether or no.'

Mr Stringer nodded his head approvingly, and for a time

they continued to regard the swelling bulks with expressions
that had changed from indifference to disapproval.

Mr Tom Smallways was a greengrocer by trade and a
gardener by disposition; his little wife Jessica saw to the shop,
and Heaven had planned him for a peaceful world. Unfortu-
nately Heaven had not planned a peaceful world for him.
He lived in a world of obstinate and incessant change, and
in parts where its operations were unsparingly conspicuous.
Vicissitude was in the very soil he tilled; even his garden was
upon a yearly tenancy, and overshadowed by a huge board that
proclaimed it not so much a garden as an eligible building-
site. He was horticulture under notice to quit, the last patch of
country in a district flooded by new and urban things. He did
his best to console himself, to imagine matters near the turn of
the tide.

'You'd hardly think it could keep on,' he said.

Mr Smallways' aged father could remember Bun Hill as an
idyllic Kentish village. He had driven Sir Peter Bone[5] until he
was fifty, and then he took to drink a little and driving the
station bus, which lasted him until he was seventy-eight. Then
he retired. He sat by the fireside, a shrivelled, very, very old
coachman, full charged with reminiscences and ready for any
careless stranger. He could tell you of the vanished estate of Sir
Peter Bone, long since cut up for building, and how that magnate ruled the countryside when it was countryside, of shooting
and hunting and of coaches along the high road, of how 'where
the gasworks is' was a cricket field, and of the coming of the
Crystal Palace.[6] The Crystal Palace was six miles away from
Bun Hill, a great façade that glittered in the morning and was
a clear blue outline against the sky in the afternoon, and at
night a source of gratuitous fireworks for all the population of
Bun Hill. And then had come the railway, and then villas and
villas, and then the gasworks and the waterworks and a great
ugly sea of workmen's houses, and then drainage, and the water
vanished out of the Otterbourne and left it a dreadful ditch,
and then a second railway station, Bun Hill South, and more
houses and more, more shops, more competition, plate-glass
shops, a board-school, rates, omnibuses, tramcars – going right

away into London itself – bicycles, motor-cars, and then more motor-cars, a Carnegie library.[7]

'You'd hardly think it could keep on,' said Mr Tom Smallways, growing up among these marvels.

But it kept on. Even from the first the greengrocer's shop which he had set up in one of the smallest of the old surviving village houses in the tail of the High Street had a submerged air, an air of hiding from something that was looking for it. When they had made up the pavement of the High Street, they levelled it so that one had to go down three steps into the shop. Tom did his best to sell only his own excellent but limited range of produce; but Progress came shoving things into his window, French artichokes and aubergines, foreign apples – apples from the State of New York, apples from California, apples from Canada, apples from New Zealand, 'pretty-lookin' fruit, but not what I should call English apples,' said Tom – bananas, unfamiliar nuts, grapefruits, mangoes.

The motor-cars that went by northward and southward grew more and more powerful and efficient, whizzed faster and smelt worse; there appeared great clangorous petrol trolleys delivering coal and parcels in the place of vanishing horse-vans; motor-omnibuses ousted the horse-omnibuses, even the Kentish strawberries going Londonward in the night took to machinery and clattered instead of creaking, and became affected in flavour by progress and petrol.

And then young Bert Smallways got a motor-bicycle. . . .[8]

§ 2

Bert, it is necessary to explain, was a progressive Smallways.

Nothing speaks more eloquently of the pitiless insistence of progress and expansion in our time than that it should get into the Smallways blood. But there was something advanced and enterprising about young Smallways before he was out of short frocks.[9] He was lost for a whole day when he was five, and nearly drowned in the reservoir of the new waterworks before he was seven. He had a real pistol[10] taken away from him by a real policeman when he was ten. And he learnt to smoke, not

with pipes and brown paper and cane as Tom had done, but
with a penny packet of Boys of England American cigarettes.[11]
His language shocked his father before he was twelve, and by
that age, what with touting for parcels at the station and selling
the Bun Hill *Weekly Express*, he was making three shillings
a week or more, and spending it on *Chips, Comic Cuts, Ally
Sloper's Half-holiday*,[12] cigarettes, and all the concomitants
of a life of pleasure and enlightenment. All of this without
hindrance to his literary studies, which carried him up to the
seventh standard[13] at an exceptionally early age. I mention these
things so that you may have no doubt at all concerning the sort
of stuff Bert had in him.

He was six years younger than Tom, and for a time there
was an attempt to utilize him in the greengrocer's shop when
Tom at twenty-one married Jessica – who was thirty and had
saved a little money in service. But it was not Bert's *forte*[14] to
be utilized. He hated digging, and when he was given a basket
of stuff to deliver, a nomadic instinct arose irresistibly, it
became his pack, and he did not seem to care how heavy it
was nor where he took it, so long as he did not take it to
its destination. Glamour filled the world, and he strayed after
it, basket and all. So Tom took his goods out himself, and
sought for Bert employers who did not know of this strain of
poetry in his nature. Bert touched the fringe of a number of
trades in succession – draper's porter, chemist's boy, doctor's
page, junior assistant gas-fitter, envelope addresser, milk-cart
assistant, golf-caddie, and at last helper in a bicycle shop. Here,
apparently, he found the progressive quality his nature had
craved. His employer was a pirate-souled young man named
Grubb, with a black-smeared face by day and a music-hall
side in the evening, who dreamt of a patent lever chain; and
it seemed to Bert that he was the perfect model of a gentleman
of spirit. He hired out quite the dirtiest and unsafest bicycles
in the whole south of England, and conducted the subsequent
discussions with astonishing verve. Bert and he settled down
very well together. Bert lived in, became almost a trick rider –
he could ride bicycles for miles that would have come to
pieces instantly under you or me – took to washing his face

after business and sometimes even his neck, and spent his sur-
plus money upon remarkable ties and collars, cigarettes and
shorthand classes at the Bun Hill Institute.

He would go round to Tom at times, and look and talk so
brilliantly that Tom and Jessica, who both had a natural tendency to be respectful to anybody or anything, looked up to him
immensely.

'He's a go-ahead chap, is Bert,' said Tom. 'He knows a thing
or two.'

'Let's hope he don't know too much,' said Jessica, who had
a fine sense of limitations.

'It's go-ahead Times,' said Tom. 'Noo petaters, and English
at that; we'll be having 'em in March if things go on as they do
go. I never see such Times. See his tie last night?'

'It wasn't suited to him, Tom. It was a gentleman's tie. He
wasn't up to it – not the rest of him. It wasn't becoming.' . . .

Then presently Bert got a cyclist's suit, cap, badge and all;
and to see him and Grubb going down to Brighton[15] (and back)
– heads down, handlebars down, backbones curved – was a
revelation in the possibilities of the Smallways blood.

Go-ahead Times!

Old Smallways would sit over the fire mumbling of the
greatness of other days, of old Sir Peter, who drove his coach
to Brighton and back in eight-and-twenty hours, of old Sir
Peter's white top-hats, of Lady Bone, who never set foot to
ground except to walk in the garden, of the great prize-fights
at Crawley.[16] He talked of pink and pigskin breeches, of foxes at
Ring's Bottom, where now the County Council pauper lunatics
were enclosed, of Lady Bone's chintzes and crinolines. Nobody
heeded him. The world had thrown up a new type of gentleman
altogether – a gentleman of most ungentlemanly energy, a
gentleman in dusty oilskins and motor-goggles and a wonderful
cap, a stink-making gentleman, a swift, high-class badger, who
fled perpetually along high roads from the dust and stink he
perpetually made. And his lady, as they were able to see her at
Bun Hill, was a weather-bitten goddess as free from refinement
as a gipsy – not so much dressed as packed for transit at a high
velocity.

So Bert grew up, filled with ideals of speed and enterprise, and became, so far as he became anything, a kind of bicycle engineer of the let's-'ave-a-look-at-it and enamel-chipping variety. Even a road-racer, geared to a hundred and twenty, failed to satisfy him, and for a time he pined in vain at twenty miles an hour along roads that were continually more dusty and more crowded with mechanical traffic. But at last his savings accumulated, and his chance came. The hire-purchase system bridged a financial gap, and one bright and memorable Sunday morning he wheeled his new possession through the shop into the road, got on to it with the advice and assistance of Grubb, and teuf-teuffed[17] off into the haze of the traffic-tortured high road, to add himself as one more voluntary public danger to the amenities of the south of England.

'Orf to Brighton!' said old Smallways, regarding his youngest son from the sitting-room window over the greengrocer's shop with something between pride and reprobation. 'When I was 'is age, I'd never bin to London, never bin south of Crawley – never bin anywhere on my own where I couldn't walk. And nobody didn't go. Not unless they was gentry. Now everybody's orf everywhere; the whole dratted country sims flying to pieces. Wonder they all get back. Orf to Brighton indeed! Anybody want to buy 'orses?'

'You can't say I bin to Brighton, father,' said Tom.

'Nor don't want to go,' said Jessica sharply; 'creering about and spendin' your money.'

§ 3

For a time the possibilities of the motor-bicycle so occupied Bert's mind that he remained regardless of the new direction in which the striving soul of man was finding exercise and refreshment. He failed to observe that the type of motor-car, like the type of bicycle, was settling down and losing its adventurous quality. Indeed, it is as true as it is remarkable that Tom was the first to observe the new development. But his gardening made him attentive to the heavens, and the proximity of the Bun Hill gasworks and the Crystal Palace, from which ascents were continually being made, and presently the descent of ballast upon his potatoes conspired to bear in upon his unwilling mind the fact that the Goddess of Change was turning her disturbing attention to the sky. The first great boom in aeronautics was beginning.

Grubb and Bert heard of it in a music-hall, then it was driven home to their minds by the cinematograph, then Bert's imagination was stimulated by a sixpenny edition of that aeronautic classic, Mr George Griffith's[18] *The Outlaws of the Air*, and so the thing really got hold of them.

At first the most obvious aspect was the multiplication of balloons. The sky of Bun Hill began to be infested by balloons! On Wednesday and Saturday afternoons particularly you could scarcely look skyward for a quarter of an hour without discovering a balloon somewhere. And then one bright day Bert, motoring towards Croydon, was arrested by the insurgence of a huge, bolster-shaped monster from the Crystal Palace grounds, and obliged to dismount and watch it. It was like a bolster with a broken nose, and below it, and comparatively small, was a stiff framework bearing a man and an engine with a screw that whizzed round in front and a sort of canvas rudder behind. The framework had an air of dragging the reluctant gas-cylinder after it like a brisk little terrier[19] towing a shy, gas-distended elephant into society. The combined monster certainly travelled and steered. It went overhead perhaps a thousand feet up (Bert heard the engine), sailed away southward, vanished over the hills, reappeared a little blue outline far off in the east, going now very fast before a gentle south-west gale, returned above the Crystal Palace towers, circled round them, chose a position for descent, and sank down out of sight.

Bert sighed deeply, and turned to his motor-bicycle again.

And that was only the beginning of a succession of strange phenomena in the heavens[20] – cylinders, cones, pear-shaped monsters, even at last a thing of aluminium[21] that glittered wonderfully, and that Grubb, through some confusion of ideas about armour-plates, was inclined to consider a war machine.

There followed actual flight.

This, however, was not an affair that was visible from Bun

Hill; it was something that occurred in private grounds or other enclosed places and under favourable conditions, and it was brought home to Grubb and Bert Smallways only by means of the magazine page of the halfpenny newspapers or by cinematograph records.[22] But it was brought home very insistently, and in those days if ever one heard a man saying in a public place in a loud, reassuring confident tone, 'It's bound to come,' the chances were ten to one he was talking of flying. And Bert got a box lid and wrote out in correct window-ticket style, and Grubb put in the window this inscription: 'Aeroplanes made and repaired.' It quite upset Tom – it seemed taking one's shop so lightly; but most of the neighbours, and all the sporting ones, approved of it as being very good indeed.

Everybody talked of flying, everybody repeated over and over again, 'Bound to come,' and then you know it didn't come. There was a hitch. They flew – that was all right; they flew in machines heavier than air. But they smashed. Sometimes they smashed the engine, sometimes they smashed the aeronaut, usually they smashed both. Machines that made flights of three or four miles and came down safely, went up the next time to headlong disaster. There seemed no possible trusting to them. The breeze upset them, the eddies near the ground upset them, a passing thought in the mind of the aeronaut upset them. Also they upset – simply.

'It's this "stability" does 'em,' said Grubb, repeating his newspaper. 'They pitch and they pitch, till they pitch themselves to pieces.'

Experiments fell away after two expectant years of this sort of success, the public and then the newspapers tired of the expensive photographic reproductions, the optimistic reports, the perpetual sequence of triumph and disaster and silence. Flying slumped, even ballooning fell away to some extent, though it remained a fairly popular sport, and continued to lift gravel from the wharf of the Bun Hill gasworks and drop it upon deserving people's lawns and gardens. There were half a dozen reassuring years for Tom – at least so far as flying was concerned. But that was the great time of monorail development, and his anxiety was only diverted from the high heavens by the most urgent threats and symptoms of change in the lower sky.

There had been talk of monorails[23] for several years. But the real mischief began when Brennan sprang his gyroscopic[24] monorail car upon the Royal Society. It was the leading sensation of the 1907 soirées; that celebrated demonstration-room was all too small for its exhibition. Brave soldiers, leading Zionists,[25] deserving novelists, noble ladies, congested the narrow passage, and thrust distinguished elbows into ribs the world would not willingly let break, deeming themselves fortunate if they could see 'just a little bit of the rail'. Inaudible but convincing, the great inventor expounded his discovery, and sent his obedient little model of the trains of the future up gradients, round curves and across a sagging wire. It ran along on its single rail, on its single wheels, simple and sufficient; it stopped, reversed, stood still, balancing perfectly. It maintained its astounding equilibrium amidst a thunder of applause. The audience dispersed at last, discussing how far they would enjoy crossing an abyss on a wire cable. 'Suppose the gyroscope stopped!' Few of them anticipated a tithe of what the Brennan monorail would do for their railway securities and the face of the world.

In a few years they realized better. In a little while no one thought anything of crossing an abyss on a wire, and the monorail was superseding the tramlines, railways and indeed every form of track for mechanical locomotion. Where land was cheap the rail ran along the ground, where it was dear the rail lifted up on iron standards and passed overhead; its swift, convenient cars went everywhere and did everything that had once been done along made tracks upon the ground.

When old Smallways died, Tom could think of nothing more striking to say of him than, 'When he was a boy, there wasn't nothing higher than your chimbleys – there wasn't a wire nor a cable in the sky!'

Old Smallways went to his grave under an intricate network of wires and cables, for Bun Hill became not only a sort of minor centre of power distribution – the Home Counties Power Distribution Company[26] set up transformers and a generating station close beside the old gasworks – but also a junction on the suburban monorail system. Moreover, every tradesman in the place, and indeed nearly every house, had its own telephone.

The monorail cable standards became a conspicuous fact in urban landscape, for the most part stout iron erections rather like tapering trestles, and painted a bright bluish green. One, it happened, bestrode Tom's house, which looked still more retiring and apologetic beneath its immensity; and another giant stood just inside the corner of his garden, which was still not built upon and unchanged except for a couple of advertisement boards, one recommending a two-and-sixpenny watch, and one a nerve restorer. These, by-the-by, were placed almost horizontally to catch the eye of the passing monorail passengers above, and so served admirably to roof over a tool shed and a mushroom shed for Tom. All day and all night the fast cars from Brighton and Hastings went murmuring by overhead – long broad comfortable-looking cars, that were brightly lit after dusk. As they flew by at night, transient flares of light and a rumbling sound of passage, they kept up a perpetual summer lightning and thunderstorm in the street below.

Presently the English Channel was bridged[27] – a series of great iron Eiffel Tower[28] pillars carrying monorail cables at a height of a hundred and fifty feet above the water, except near the middle, where they rose higher to allow the passage of the London and Antwerp shipping and the Hamburg-America liners.

Then heavy motor-cars began to run about on only a couple of wheels, one behind the other, which for some reason upset Tom dreadfully and made him gloomy for days after the first one passed the shop. . . .

All this gyroscopic and monorail development naturally absorbed a vast amount of public attention, and there was also a huge excitement consequent upon the amazing gold discoveries off the coast of Anglesey made by a submarine prospector, Miss Patricia Giddy. She had taken her degree in geology and mineralogy in the University of London, and while working upon the auriferous rocks of North Wales after a brief holiday spent in agitating for women's suffrage, she had been struck by the possibility of these reefs cropping up again under the water. She had set herself to verify this supposition by the use of the submarine crawler[29] invented by Doctor Alberto Cassini. By a happy mingling of reasoning and intuition peculiar to her sex she found gold at her first descent, and emerged after three hours' submersion with about two hundredweight of ore containing gold in the unparalleled quantity of seventeen ounces to the ton. But the whole story of her submarine mining, intensely interesting as it is, must be told at some other time; suffice it now to remark simply that it was during the consequent great rise of prices, confidence and enterprise that the revival of interest in flying occurred.

§ 4

It is curious how the final boom of flying began. It was like the coming of a breeze on a quiet day; nothing started it, it came. People began to talk of flying with an air of never having for one moment dropped the subject. Pictures of flying and flying machines returned to the newspapers; articles and allusions increased and multiplied in the serious magazines. People asked in monorail trains, 'When are we going to fly?' A new crop of inventors sprang up in a night or so like fungi. The Aero Club announced the project of a great Flying Exhibition in a large area of ground that the removal of slums in Whitechapel had rendered available.

The advancing wave soon produced a sympathetic ripple in the Bun Hill establishment. Grubb routed out his flying-machine model again, tried it in the yard behind the shop, got a kind of flight out of it, and broke seventeen panes of glass and nine flowerpots in the greenhouse that occupied the next yard but one.

And then, springing from nowhere, sustained one knew not how, came a persistent, disturbing rumour that the problem had been solved, that the secret was known. Bert met it one early-closing afternoon as he refreshed himself in an inn near Nutfield, whither his motor-bicycle had brought him. There smoked and meditated a person in khaki, an engineer, who presently took an interest in Bert's machine. It was a sturdy piece of apparatus, and it had acquired a kind of documentary value in these quick-changing times; it was now nearly eight years old. Its points discussed, the soldier broke into a new topic with, 'My next's going to be an aeroplane, so far as I can see. I've had enough of roads and ways.'

'They *tork*,' said Bert.

'They talk – and they do,' said the soldier. 'The thing's coming.'

'It keeps *on* coming,' said Bert; 'I shall believe when I see it.'

'That won't be long,' said the soldier.

The conversation seemed degenerating into an amiable wrangle of contradiction.

'I tell you they *are* flying,' the soldier insisted. 'I see it myself.'

'We've all seen it,' said Bert.

'I don't mean flap up and smash up; I mean real, safe, steady, controlled flying, against the wind, good and right.'

'You ain't seen that!'

'I *'ave*! Aldershot.[30] They try to keep it a secret. They got it right enough. You bet – our War Office isn't going to be caught napping this time.'

Bert's incredulity was shaken. He asked questions, and the soldier expanded.

'I tell you they got nearly a square mile fenced in – a sort of valley. Fences of barbed wire ten feet high, and inside that they do things. Chaps about the camp – now and then we get a peep. It isn't only us neither. There's the Japanese; you bet they got it too – and the Germans! And I never knowed anything of this sort yet that the Frenchies didn't get ahead with – after their manner! They started ironclads, they started submarines, they started navigables, and you bet they won't be far be'ind at this.'

The soldier stood with his legs very wide apart, and filled his pipe thoughtfully. Bert sat on the low wall against which his motor-bicycle was leaning.

'Funny thing fighting'll be,' he said.

'Flying's going to break out,' said the soldier. 'When it *does* come, when the curtain does go up, I tell you you'll find everyone on the stage – busy. . . . Such fighting, too! . . . I suppose you don't read the papers about this sort of thing?'

'I read 'em a bit,' said Bert.

'Well, have you noticed what one might call the remarkable case of the disappearing inventor – the inventor who turns up in a blaze of publicity, fires off a few successful experiments, and vanishes?'

'Can't say I 'ave,' said Bert.

'Well, I 'ave, anyhow. You get anybody come along who does anything striking in this line, and, you bet, he vanishes. Just goes off quietly out of sight. After a bit, you don't hear anything more of 'em at all. See? They disappear. Gone – no address. First – oh! it's an old story now – there was those Wright Brothers[31] out in America. They glided – they glided miles and miles. Finally they glided off stage. Why, it must be nineteen hundred and four, or five, *they* vanished! Then there was those people in Ireland[32] – no, I forget their names. Everybody said they could fly. *They* went. They ain't dead that I've heard tell; but you can't say they're alive. Not a feather of 'em can you see. Then that chap who flew round Paris and upset in the Seine. De Booley,[33] was it? I forget. That was a grand fly, in spite of the accident; but where's he got to? The accident didn't hurt him. Eh? *'E's* gone to cover.'

The soldier prepared to light his pipe.

'Looks like a secret society got hold of them,' said Bert.

'Secret society! *Naw!*'

The soldier lit his match, and drew. 'Secret society,' he repeated in response to these words, with his pipe between his teeth and the match flaring. 'War Departments; that's more like it.' He threw his match aside, and walked to his machine. 'I tell you, sir,' he said, 'there isn't a big Power in Europe, *or* Asia, *or* America, *or* Africa, that hasn't got at least one or two flying-machines hidden up its sleeve at the present time. Not one. Real, workable, flying-machines. And the spying! The spying and manoeuvring to find out what the others have got. I tell you, sir, a foreigner, or, for the matter of that, an unaccredited native, can't get within four miles of Lydd[34] nowadays –

not to mention our little circus at Aldershot, and the experimental camp in Galway.[35] No!'

'Well,' said Bert, 'I'd like to see one of them, anyhow. Jest to help believing. I'll believe when I see, that I'll promise you.'

'You'll see 'em, fast enough,' said the soldier, and led his machine out into the road.

He left Bert on his wall, grave and pensive, with his cap on the back of his head, and a cigarette smouldering in the corner of his mouth.

'If what he says is true,' said Bert, 'me and Grubb, we been wasting our blessed old time. Besides incurring expense with thet green'ouse.'

§ 5

It was while this mysterious talk with the soldier still stirred in Bert Smallways' imagination that the most astounding incident in the whole of that dramatic chapter of human history, the coming of flying, occurred. People talk glibly enough of epoch-making events; this *was* an epoch-making event. It was the unanticipated and entirely successful flight of Mr Alfred Butteridge[36] from the Crystal Palace to Glasgow and back in a small businesslike-looking machine heavier than air – an entirely manageable and controllable machine that could fly as well as a pigeon.

It wasn't, one felt, a fresh step forward in the matter so much as a giant stride, a leap. Mr Butteridge remained in the air altogether for about nine hours, and during that time he flew with the ease and assurance of a bird. His machine was, however, neither bird-like nor butterfly-like, nor had it the wide, lateral expansion of the ordinary aeroplane. The effect upon the observer was rather something in the nature of a bee or wasp. Parts of the apparatus were spinning very rapidly, and gave one a hazy effect of transparent wings; but parts, including two peculiarly curved 'wing-cases' – if one may borrow a figure from the flying beetles – remained expanded stiffly. In the middle was a long rounded body like the body of a moth, and on this Mr Butteridge could be seen sitting astride, much as a man bestrides a horse. The wasp-like resemblance was increased by the fact that the apparatus flew with a deep booming hum, exactly the sound made by a wasp at a window-pane.

Mr Butteridge took the world by surprise. He was one of those gentlemen from nowhere Fate still succeeds in producing for the stimulation of mankind. He came, it was variously said, from Australia and America and the South of France. He was also described quite incorrectly as the son of a man who had amassed a comfortable fortune in the manufacture of gold nibs and the Butteridge fountain pens. But this was an entirely different strain of Butteridges. For some years, in spite of a loud voice, a large presence, an aggressive swagger, and an implacable manner, he had been an undistinguished member of most of the existing aeronautical associations. Then one day he wrote to all the London papers to announce that he had made arrangements for an ascent from the Crystal Palace of a machine that would demonstrate satisfactorily that the outstanding difficulties in the way of flying were finally solved. Few of the papers printed his letter, still fewer were the people who believed in his claim. No one was excited even when a fracas on the steps of a leading hotel in Piccadilly, in which he tried to horsewhip a prominent German musician upon some personal account, delayed his promised ascent. The quarrel was inadequately reported, and his name spelt variously Betteridge and Betridge. Until his flight indeed, he did not and could not contrive to exist in the public mind. There were scarcely thirty people on the lookout for him, in spite of all his clamour, when about six o'clock one summer morning the doors of the big shed in which he had been putting together his apparatus opened – it was near the big model of a megatherium[37] in the Crystal Palace grounds – and his giant insect came droning out into a negligent and incredulous world.

But before he had made his second circuit of the Crystal Palace towers, Fame was lifting her trumpet, she drew a deep breath as the startled tramps who sleep on the seats of Trafalgar Square were roused by his buzz and awoke to discover him circling the Nelson column, and by the time he had got to Birmingham, which place he crossed about half past ten, her deafening blast was echoing throughout the country. The despaired-of thing was done. A man was flying securely and well.

Scotland was agape for his coming. Glasgow he reached by one o'clock, and it is related that scarcely a shipyard or factory in that busy hive of industry resumed work before half past two. The public mind was just sufficiently educated in the impossibility of flying to appreciate Mr Butteridge at his proper value. He circled the University buildings, and dropped to within shouting distance of the crowds in West End Park and on the slope of Gilmour Hill. The thing flew quite steadily at a pace of about three miles an hour, in a wide circle, making a deep hum that would have drowned his full, rich voice completely had he not provided himself with a megaphone. He avoided churches, buildings and monorail cables with consummate ease as he conversed.

'Me name's Butteridge,' he shouted; 'B-U-T-T-E-R-I-D-G-E. Got it? Me mother was Scotch.'

And having assured himself that he had been understood, he rose amidst cheers and shouting and patriotic cries, and then flew up very swiftly and easily into the south-eastern sky, rising and falling with long, easy undulations in an extraordinarily wasp-like manner.

His return to London – he visited and hovered over Manchester and Liverpool and Oxford on his way, and spelt his name out to each place – was an occasion of unparalleled excitement. Everyone was staring heavenward. More people were run over in the streets upon that one day than in the previous three months, and a County Council steamboat, the *Izaac Walton*, collided with a pier of Westminster Bridge, and narrowly escaped disaster by running ashore – it was low water – on the mud on the south side. He returned to the Crystal Palace grounds, that classic starting-point of aeronautical adventure, about sunset, re-entered his shed without disaster, and had the doors locked immediately upon the photographers and journalists who had been waiting his return.

'Look here, you chaps,' he said, as his assistant did so, 'I'm tired to death, and saddle sore. I can't give you a word of talk.

I'm too – done. My name's Butteridge. B-U-T-T-E-R-I-D-G-E. Get that right. I'm an Imperial Englishman. I'll talk to you all tomorrow.'

Foggy snapshots still survive to record that incident. His assistant struggles in a sea of aggressive young men carrying notebooks or upholding cameras and wearing bowler hats and enterprising tics. He himself towers up in the doorway, a big figure with a mouth – an eloquent cavity beneath a vast black moustache – distorted by his shout to those relentless agents of publicity. He towers there, the most famous man in the country. Almost symbolically he holds and gesticulates with a megaphone in his left hand.

§ 6

Tom and Bert Smallways both saw that return. They watched from the crest of Bun Hill, from which they had so often surveyed the pyrotechnics of the Crystal Palace. Bert was excited, Tom kept calm and lumpish, but neither of them realized how their own lives were to be invaded by the fruits of that beginning. 'P'raps old Grubb'll mind the shop a bit now,' he said, 'and put his blessed model in the fire. Not that that can save us, if we don't tide over with Steinhart's account.'[38]

Bert knew enough of things and the problem of aeronautics to realize that this gigantic imitation of a bee would, to use his own idiom, 'give the newspapers fits'. The next day it was clear the fits had been given even as he said, their magazine pages were black with hasty photographs, their prose was convulsive, they foamed at the headline. The next day they were worse. Before the week was out they were not so much published as carried screaming into the street.

The dominant fact in the uproar was the exceptional personality of Mr Butteridge, and the extraordinary terms he demanded for the secret of his machine.

For it was a secret, and he kept it secret in the most elaborate fashion. He built his apparatus himself, in the safe privacy of the great Crystal Palace sheds, with the assistance of inattentive workmen, and the day next following his flight he took it to pieces single-handed, packed certain portions, and then secured unintelligent assistance in packing and dispersing the rest. Sealed packing-cases went north and east and west to various pantechnicons, and the engines were boxed with peculiar care. It became evident these precautions were not inadvisable, in view of the violent demand for any sort of photograph or impressions of his machine. But Mr Butteridge, having once made his demonstration, intended to keep his secret safe from any further risk of leakage. He faced the British public now with the question whether they wanted his secret or not; he was, he said perpetually, an 'Imperial Englishman', and his first wish and his last was to see his invention the privilege and monopoly of the Empire. Only—

It was there the difficulty began.

Mr Butteridge, it became evident, was a man singularly free from any false modesty – indeed, from any modesty of any kind – singularly willing to see interviewers, answer questions upon any topic except aeronautics, volunteer opinions, criticisms and autobiography, supply portraits and photographs of himself, and generally spread his personality across the terrestrial sky. The published portraits insisted primarily upon an immense black moustache, and secondarily upon a fierceness behind the moustache. The general impression upon the public was that Butteridge was a small man. No one big, it was felt, could have so virulently aggressive an expression, though, as a matter of fact, Butteridge had a height of six feet two inches, and a weight altogether proportionate to that. Moreover, he had a love affair of large and unusual dimensions and irregular circumstances, and the still largely decorous British public learnt with reluctance and alarm that a sympathetic treatment of this story was inseparable from the exclusive acquisition by the British Empire of the priceless secret of aerial stability. The exact particulars of the irregularity never came to light, but apparently the lady had, in a fit of high-minded inadvertence, gone through the ceremony of marriage with – one quotes the unpublished discourse of Mr Butteridge – 'a white-livered skunk', and this zoological aberration did in some legal and vexatious manner mar her social happiness. Mr Butteridge wanted to talk about the business, to show the splendour of her nature in the light of its complications. It was really most embarrassing to a press that has always possessed a considerable turn for reticence, that wanted things personal indeed in the modern fashion, but not too personal. It was embarrassing, I say, to be inexorably confronted with Mr Butteridge's great heart, to see it laid open in relentless self-vivisection, and its pulsating dissepiments[39] adorned with emphatic flag labels.

Confronted they were, and there was no getting away from it. He would make this appalling viscus[40] beat and throb before the shrinking journalists – he was as insistent as an uncle with a big watch and a little baby; whatever evasion they attempted he set aside. He 'gloried in his love', he said, and compelled them to write it down.

'That's of course a private affair, Mr Butteridge,' they would object.

'The injustice, sorr, is public. I do not care whether I am up against institutions or individuals. I do not care if I am up against the Universal All. I am pleading the cause of a woman, a woman I lurve, sorr – a noble woman – misunderstood. I intend to vindicate her, sorr, to the four winds of heaven!

'I lurve England,' he used to say – 'I lurve England, but Puritanism, sorr, I abhor. It fills me with loathing. It raises my gorge. Take my own case. . . .'

He insisted relentlessly upon his heart, and upon seeing proofs of the interview. If they had not done justice to his erotic bellowings and gesticulations, he stuck in, in a large inky scrawl, all and more than they had omitted.

It was a strangely embarrassing thing for British journalism. Never was there a more obvious or uninteresting affair; never had the world heard the story of erratic affection with less appetite or sympathy. On the other hand, it was extremely curious about Mr Butteridge's invention. But when Mr Butteridge could be deflected for a moment from the cause of the lady he championed, then he talked chiefly, and usually with tears of tenderness in his voice, about his mother and his childhood – his mother who crowned a complete encyclopaedia of maternal virtue by being 'largely Scotch'. She was not quite neat, but nearly so. 'I owe everything in me to me mother,' he asserted – 'everything. Eh!' and – 'ask any man who's done anything. You'll hear the same story. All we have we owe to women. They are the species, sorr. Man is but a dream. He comes and goes. The woman's soul leadeth us upward and on!' He was always going on like that.

What in particular he wanted from the Government for his secret did not appear, nor what beyond a money payment could be expected from a modern state in such an affair. The general effect upon judicious observers, indeed, was not that he was treating for anything, but that he was using an unexampled opportunity to bellow and show off to an attentive world. Rumours of his real identity spread abroad. It was said that he had been the landlord of an ambiguous hotel in Cape Town, and had there given shelter to and witnessed the experiments, and finally stolen the papers and plans of an extremely shy and friendless young inventor named Palliser, who had come to South Africa from England in an advanced stage of consumption, and died there. This, at any rate, was the allegation of the more outspoken American press. But the proof or disproof of that never reached the public.

Mr Butteridge also involved himself passionately in a tangle of disputes for the possession of a great number of valuable money prizes. Some of these had been offered so long ago as 1906 for successful mechanical flight. By the time of Mr Butteridge's success a really very considerable number of newspapers, tempted by the impunity of the pioneers in this direction, had pledged themselves to pay in some cases quite overwhelming sums to the first person to fly from Manchester to Glasgow, from London to Manchester, one hundred miles, two hundred miles in England and the like. Most had hedged a little with ambiguous conditions, and now offered resistance; one or two paid at once, and vehemently called attention to the fact; and Mr Butteridge plunged into litigation with the more recalcitrant, while at the same time sustaining a vigorous agitation and canvass to induce the Government to purchase his invention.

One fact, however, remained permanent throughout all the

developments of this affair behind Butteridge's preposterous love interest, his politics and personality and all his shouting and boasting, and that was that so far as the mass of people knew he was in sole possession of the secret of the practicable aeroplane in which, for all one could tell to the contrary, the key of the future empire of the world resided. And presently, to the great consternation of innumerable people, including among others Mr Bert Smallways, it became apparent that whatever negotiations were in progress for the acquisition of this precious secret by the British Government were in danger of falling through. The London *Daily Requiem*[41] first voiced the universal alarm, and published an interview under the terrific caption of 'Mr Butteridge Speaks his Mind'.

Therein the inventor – if he was an inventor – poured out his heart.

'I came from the end of the earth,' he said, which rather seemed to confirm the Cape Town story, 'bringing me Motherland the secret that would give her the empire of the world. And what do I get?' He paused. 'I am sniffed at by elderly mandarins! . . . And the woman I love is treated like a leper!

'I am an Imperial Englishman,' he went on in a splendid outburst, subsequently written into the interview by his own hand; 'but there are limits to the human heart! There are younger nations – living nations! Nations that do not snore and gurgle helplessly in paroxysms of plethora upon beds of formality and red tape! There are nations that will not fling away the empire of earth in order to slight an unknown man and insult a noble woman whose boots they are not fitted to unlatch. There are nations not blinded to science, not given over hand and foot to effete snobocracies and Degenerate Decadents. In short, mark my words – *there are other nations*!' . . .

This speech it was that particularly impressed Bert Smallways. 'If them Germans or them Americans get hold of this,' he said impressively to his brother, 'the British Empire's done. It's U.P. The Union Jack, so to speak, won't be worth the paper it's written on, Tom.'

'I suppose you couldn't lend us a hand this morning,' said Jessica, in his impressive pause. 'Everybody in Bun Hill seems wanting early potatoes at once. Tom can't carry half of them.'

'We're living on a volcano,' said Bert, disregarding the suggestion. 'At any moment war may come – such a war!'

He shook his head portentously.

'You'd better take this lot first, Tom,' said Jessica. She turned briskly on Bert. 'Can you spare us a morning?' she asked.

'I dessay I can,' said Bert. 'The shop's very quiet s'morning. Though all this danger to the Empire worries me something frightful.'

'Work'll take it off your mind,' said Jessica.

And presently he too was going out into a world of change and wonder, bowed beneath a load of potatoes and patriotic insecurity, that merged at last into a very definite irritation at the weight and want of style of the potatoes and a very clear conception of the entire detestableness of Jessica.

2

HOW BERT SMALLWAYS
GOT INTO DIFFICULTIES

§ 1

It did not occur to either Tom or Bert Smallways that this remarkable aerial performance of Mr Butteridge was likely to
affect either of their lives in any special manner, that it would
in any way single them out from the millions about them; and
when they had witnessed it from the crest of Bun Hill, and seen
the fly-like mechanism, its rotating planes a golden haze in the
sunset, sink humming to the harbour of its shed again, they
turned back towards the sunken greengrocery beneath the
great iron standard of the London to Brighton monorail, and
their minds reverted to the discussion that had engaged them
before Mr Butteridge's triumph had come in sight out of the
London haze.

It was a difficult and unsuccessful discussion. They had to
carry it on in shouts because of the moaning and roaring of the
gyroscopic motor-cars that traversed the High Street, and in its
nature it was contentious and private. The Grubb business was
in difficulties, and Grubb in a moment of financial eloquence
had given a half-share in it to Bert, whose relations with his
employer had been for some time unsalaried and pallish and
informal.

Bert was trying to impress Tom with the idea that the reconstructed Grubb and Smallways offered unprecedented and
unparalleled opportunities to the judicious small investor. It
was coming home to Bert, as though it were an altogether new
fact, that Tom was entirely impervious to ideas. In the end he
put the financial issues on one side, and, making the thing

purely a matter of fraternal affection, succeeded in borrowing a sovereign on the security of his word of honour.

The firm of Grubb and Smallways, formerly Grubb, had indeed been persistently unlucky in the last year or so. For many years the business had struggled along with a flavour of romantic insecurity in a small, dissolute-looking shop in the High Street, adorned with brilliantly coloured advertisements of cycles, a display of bells, trouser clips, oilcans, pump clips, frame cases, wallets and other accessories, and the announcement of 'Bicycles on Hire', 'Repairs', 'Free Inflation', 'Petrol' and similar attractions. They were agents for several obscure makes of bicycle, two samples constituted the stock and occasionally they effected a sale, they also repaired punctures and did their best – though luck was not always on their side – with any other repairing that was brought to them. They handled a line of cheap gramophones, and did a little with musical boxes. The staple of their business was, however, the letting of bicycles on hire. It was a singular trade, obeying no known commercial or economic principles – indeed, no principles. There was a stock of ladies' and gentlemen's bicycles in a state of disrepair that passes description, the hiring stock, and these were let to unexacting and reckless people, inexpert in the things of this world, at a nominal rate of one shilling for the first hour and sixpence per hour afterwards. But really there were no fixed prices, and insistent boys could get bicycles and the thrill of danger for an hour for so low a sum as threepence, provided they could convince Grubb that that was all they had. The saddle and handlebar were then sketchily adjusted by Grubb, a deposit exacted, except in the case of familiar boys, the machine lubricated, and the adventurer started upon his career. Usually he or she came back, but at times, when the accident was serious, Bert or Grubb had to go out and fetch the machine home. Hire was always charged up to the hour of return to the shop and deducted from the deposit. It was rare that a bicycle started out from their hands in a state of pedantic efficiency. Romantic possibilities of accident lurked in the worn thread of the screw that adjusted the saddle, in the precarious pedals, in the loose-knit chain, in the handlebars, above all in the brakes and tyres. Tappings and clankings and strange rhythmic creakings awoke as the intrepid hirer pedalled out into the country. Then perhaps the bell would jam or a brake fail to act on a hill; or the seat pillar would get loose, and the saddle drop three or four inches with a disconcerting bump; or the loose and rattling chain would jump the cogs of the chain-wheel as the machine ran downhill, and so bring the mechanism to an abrupt and disastrous stop without at the same time arresting the forward momentum of the rider; or a tyre would bang, or sigh quietly, and give up the struggle and scrabble in the dust.

When the hirer returned, a heated pedestrian, Grubb would ignore all verbal complaints, and examine the machine gravely.

'This ain't 'ad fair usage,' he used to begin.

He became a mild embodiment of the spirit of reason. 'You can't expect a bicycle to take you up in its arms and carry you,' he used to say. 'You got to show intelligence. After all – it's machinery.'

Sometimes the process of liquidating the consequent claims bordered on violence. It was always a very rhetorical and often a trying affair, but in these progressive times you have to make a noise to get a living. It was often hard work, but nevertheless this hiring was a fairly steady source of profit, until one day all the panes in the window and door were broken and the stock on sale in the window greatly damaged and disordered by two overcritical hirers with no sense of rhetorical irrelevance. They were big, coarse stokers from Gravesend[1] – one was annoyed because his left pedal had come off, and the other because his tyre had become deflated, small and indeed negligible accidents by Bun Hill standards, due entirely to the ungentle handling of the delicate machines entrusted to them, and they failed to see clearly how they put themselves in the wrong by this method of argument. It is a poor way of convincing a man that he has let you a defective machine to throw his foot-pump about his shop, and take his stock of gongs outside in order to return them through the window-panes. It carried no real conviction to the minds of either Grubb or Bert; it only irritated and vexed them. One quarrel makes many, and this unpleasantness led to a violent dispute between Grubb and the landlord upon the moral aspects of and legal responsibility for the consequent reglazing. Matters came to a climax upon the even of the Whitsuntide[2] Holidays.

In the end Grubb and Smallways were put to the expense of a strategic nocturnal removal to another position.

It was a position they had long considered. It was a small, shed-like shop with a big window and one room behind, just at the sharp bend in the road at the bottom of Bun Hill, and here they struggled along bravely in spite of persistent annoyance from their former landlord, hoping for certain eventualities the peculiar situation of the shop seemed to promise. Here, too, they were doomed to disappointment.

The High Road from London to Brighton[3] that ran through Bun Hill was like the British Empire or the British Constitution – a thing that had grown to its present importance. Unlike any other roads in Europe, the British high roads have never been subjected to any organized attempts to grade or straighten them out, and to that no doubt their peculiar picturesqueness is to be ascribed. The old Bun Hill High Street drops at its end for perhaps eighty or a hundred feet of descent at an angle of one in five, turns at right angles to the left, runs in a curve for about thirty yards to a brick bridge over the dry ditch that had once been the Otterbourne, and then bends sharply to the right again round a dense clump of trees and goes on, a simple, straightforward, peaceful high road. There had been one or two horse and van and bicycle accidents in the place before the shop Bert and Grubb took was built, and, to be frank, it was the probability of others that attracted them to it.

Its possibilities had come to them first with a humorous flavour.

'Here's one of the places where a chap might get a living by keeping hens,' said Grubb.

'You can't get a living by keeping hens,' said Bert.

'You'd keep the hen and have it spatchcocked,'[4] said Grubb. 'The motor chaps would pay for it.'

When they really came to take the place they remembered this conversation. Hens, however, were out of the question;

there was no place for a run unless they had it in the shop. It would have been obviously out of place there. The shop was much more modern than their former one, and had a plate-glass front. 'Sooner or later,' said Bert, 'we shall get a motor-car through this.'

'That's all right,' said Grubb. 'Compensation. I don't mind *when* that motor-car comes along. I don't mind even if it gives me a shock to the system.'

'And meanwhile,' said Bert, with great artfulness, '*I'm* going to buy myself a dog.'

He did. He bought three in succession. He surprised the people at the Dog's Home in Battersea by demanding a deaf retriever, and rejecting every candidate that pricked up its ears. 'I want a good, deaf, slow-moving dog,' he said. 'A dog that doesn't put himself out for things.'

They displayed inconvenient curiosity; they declared a great scarcity of deaf dogs.

'You see,' they said, 'dogs aren't deaf.'

'Mine's got to be,' said Bert. 'I've *had* dogs that aren't deaf. All I want. It's like this, you see – I sell gramophones. Naturally I got to make 'em talk and tootle a bit to show 'em orf. Well, a dog that isn't deaf doesn't like it – gets excited, smells round, barks, growls. That upsets the customer. See? Then a dog that has his hearing fancies things. Makes burglars out of passing tramps. Wants to fight every motor that makes a whizz. All very well if you want livening up, but our place is lively enough. I don't want a dog of that sort. I want a quiet dog.'

In the end he got three in succession, but none of them turned out well. The first strayed off into the infinite, heeding no appeals; the second was killed in the night by a fruit motor-wagon which fled before Grubb could get down; the third got itself entangled in the front wheel of a passing cyclist, who came through the plate glass, and proved to be an actor out of work and an undischarged bankrupt. He demanded compensation for some fancied injury, would hear nothing of the valuable dog he had killed or the window he had broken, obliged Grubb by sheer physical obduracy to straighten his buckled front wheel, and pestered the struggling firm with a series of

inhumanly worded solicitor's letters. Grubb answered them –
stingingly, and put himself, Bert thought, in the wrong.

Affairs got more and more exasperating and strained under
these pressures. The window was boarded up, and an unpleasant altercation about their delay in repairing it with the
new landlord, a Bun Hill butcher – and a loud, bellowing,
unreasonable person at that – served to remind them of their
unsettled troubles with the old. Things were at this pitch when
Bert bethought himself of creating a sort of debenture capital in
the business for the benefit of Tom. But as I have said, Tom had
no enterprise in his composition. His idea of investment was the
stocking; he bribed his brother not to keep the offer open.

And then ill-luck made its last lunge at their crumbling
business and brought it to the ground.

§ 2

It is a poor heart that never rejoices, and Whitsuntide had an air
of coming as an agreeable break in the business complications of
Grubb and Smallways. Encouraged by the practical outcome of
Bert's negotiations with his brother, and by the fact that half the
hiring stock was out from Saturday to Monday, they decided to
ignore the residuum of hiring-trade on Sunday and devote that
day to much-needed relaxation and refreshment – to have, in
fact, an unstinted good time, a beano⁵ on Whit Sunday, and
return invigorated to grapple with their difficulties and the
Bank Holiday repairs on the Monday. No good thing was ever
done by exhausted and dispirited men. It happened that they
had made the acquaintance of two young ladies in employment
in Clapham, Miss Flossie Bright and Miss Edna Bunthorne, and
it was resolved therefore to make a cheerful little cyclist party
of four into the heart of Kent, and to picnic and spend an
indolent afternoon and evening among the trees and bracken
between Ashford and Maidstone.

Miss Bright could ride a bicycle, and a machine was found
for her, not among the hiring stock, but specially, in the sample
held for sale. Miss Bunthorne, whom Bert particularly affected,
could not ride, and so with some difficulty he hired a basket-

work trailer from the big business of Wray's in the Clapham Road. To see our young men, brightly dressed and cigarettes alight, wheeling off to the rendezvous, Grubb guiding the lady's machine beside him with one skilful hand, and Bert teuf-teuffing steadily, was to realize how pluck may triumph even over insolvency. Their landlord, the butcher, said 'Gurr!' as they passed, and shouted, 'Go it!' in a loud, savage tone to their receding backs.

Much they cared!

The weather was fine, and though they were on their way southward before nine o'clock, there was already a great multitude of holiday people abroad upon the roads. There were quantities of young men and women on bicycles and motor-bicycles, and a majority of gyroscopic motor-cars running bicycle-fashion on two wheels, mingled with old-fashioned four-wheeled traffic. Bank Holiday times always bring out old stored-away vehicles and odd people; one saw tricars and electric broughams and dilapidated old racing motors with huge pneumatic tyres. Once our holidaymakers saw a horse and cart, and once a youth riding a black horse amidst the badinage of the passers-by. And there were several navigable gas airships, not to mention balloons, in the sky. It was all immensely interesting and refreshing after the dark anxieties of the shop. Edna wore a brown straw hat with poppies that suited her admirably, and sat in the trailer like a queen, and the eight-year-old motor-bicycle ran like a thing of yesterday.

Little it seemed to matter to Mr Bert Smallways that a newspaper placard proclaimed:

GERMANY DENOUNCES THE MONROE DOCTRINE.[6]
AMBIGUOUS ATTITUDE OF JAPAN.
WHAT WILL BRITAIN DO?
IS IT WAR?

This sort of thing was always going on, and on holidays one disregarded it as a matter of course. Weekdays, in the slack

time after the midday meal, then perhaps one might worry
about the Empire and international politics; but not on a sunny
Sunday, with a pretty girl trailing behind one, and envious
cyclists trying to race you. Nor did our young people attach
any great importance to the flitting suggestions of military
activity they glimpsed ever and again. Near Maidstone they
came on a string of eleven motor-guns of peculiar construction
halted by the roadside, with a number of businesslike engineers
grouped about them watching through field-glasses some sort
of entrenchment that was going on near the crest of the downs.
It signified nothing to Bert.

'What's up?' said Edna.

'Oh! – manoeuvres,' said Bert.

'Oh! I thought they did them at Easter,' said Edna, and
troubled no more.

The last great British war, the Boer War,[7] was over and
forgotten, and the public had lost the fashion of expert military
criticism.

Our four young people picnicked cheerfully, and were happy
in the manner of a happiness that was an ancient mode in
Nineveh.[8] Eyes were bright, Grubb was funny and almost
witty, and Bert achieved epigrams; the hedges were full of
honeysuckle and dog-roses; in the woods the distant toot-toot-
toot of the traffic on the dust-hazy high road might have been
no more than the horns of elf-land. They laughed and gossiped
and picked flowers and made love and talked, and the girls
smoked cigarettes. Also they scuffled playfully. Among other
things they talked aeronautics, and how they would come for
a picnic together in Bert's flying machine before ten years were
out. The world seemed full of amusing possibilities that afternoon. They wondered what their great-grandparents would
have thought of aeronautics. In the evening, about seven, the
party turned homeward, expecting no disaster, and it was only
on the crest of the downs, between Wrotham and Kingsdown,
that disaster came.

They had come up the hill in the twilight, Bert was anxious
to get as far as possible before he lit – or attempted to light, for
the issue was a doubtful one – his lamps,[9] and they had scorched

past a number of cyclists, and by a four-wheeled motor-car of the old style lamed by a deflated tyre. Some dust had penetrated Bert's horn, and the result was a curious, amusing, wheezing sound had got into his 'honk, honk'. For the sake of merriment and glory he was making this sound as much as possible, and Edna was in fits of laughter in the trailer. They made a sort of rushing cheerfulness along the road that affected their fellow travellers variously, according to their temperaments. She did notice a good lot of bluish, evil-smelling smoke coming from about the bearings between his feet, but she thought this was one of the natural concomitants of motor-traction, and troubled no more about it, until abruptly it burst into a little yellow-tipped flame.

'Bert!' she screamed.

But Bert had put on the brakes with such suddenness that she found herself involved with his leg as he dismounted. She got to the side of the road and hastily readjusted her hat, which had suffered.

'Gaw!' said Bert.

He stood for some fatal seconds watching the petrol drip and catch; and the flame, which was now beginning to smell of enamel as well as oil, spread and grew. His chief idea was the sorrowful one that he had not sold the machine secondhand a year ago, and that he ought to have done so – a good idea in its way, but not immediately helpful. He turned upon Edna sharply. 'Get a lot of wet sand,' he said. Then he wheeled the machine a little towards the side of the roadway and laid it down and looked about for a supply of wet sand. The flames received this as a helpful attention, and made the most of it. They seemed to brighten and the twilight to deepen about them. The road was a flinty road in the chalk country, and ill-provided with sand.

Edna accosted a short, fat cyclist. 'We want wet sand,' she said, and added, 'our motor's on fire.' The short, fat cyclist stared blankly for a moment, then with a helpful cry began to scrabble in the road-grit. Whereupon Bert and Edna also scrabbled in the road-grit. Other cyclists arrived, dismounted and stood about, and their flame-lit faces expressed satisfaction, interest, curiosity. 'Wet sand,' said the short, fat man scrabbling terribly – 'wet sand.' One joined him. They threw hard-earned handfuls of road-grit upon the flames, which accepted them with enthusiasm.

Grubb arrived, riding hard. He was shouting something. He sprang off and threw his bicycle into the hedge. 'Don't throw water on it!' he said – 'don't throw water on it!' He displayed commanding presence of mind. He became captain of the occasion. Others were glad to repeat the things he said and imitate his actions. 'Don't throw water on it!' they cried. Also there was no water.

'Beat it out, you fools!' he said.

He seized a rug from the trailer (it was an Austrian blanket,[10] and Bert's winter coverlet) and began to beat at the burning petrol. For a wonderful minute he seemed to succeed. But he scattered burning pools of petrol on the road, and others, fired by his enthusiasm, imitated his action. Bert caught up a trailer-cushion and began to beat; there was another cushion and a tablecloth, and these also were seized. A young hero pulled off his jacket and joined the beating. For a moment there was less talking than hard breathing, and a tremendous flapping. Flossie, arriving on the outskirts of the crowd, cried, 'Oh, my God!' and burst loudly into tears. 'Help!' she said, and 'Fire!'

The lame motor-car arrived, and stopped in consternation. A tall, goggled, grey-haired man who was driving inquired with an Oxford intonation[11] and a clear, careful enunciation, 'Can *we* help at all?'

It became manifest that the rug, the tablecloth, the cushions, the jacket, were getting smeared with petrol and burning. The soul seemed to go out of the cushion Bert was swaying, and the air was full of feathers, like a snowstorm in the still twilight.

Bert had got very dusty and sweaty and strenuous. It seemed to him his weapon had been wrested from him at the moment of victory. The fire lay like a dying thing, close to the ground and wicked; it gave a leap of anguish at every whack of the beaters. But now Grubb had gone off to stamp out the burning blanket; the others were slacking just at the moment of victory. One was running to the motor-car. ''*Ere!*' cried Bert; 'keep on!'

He flung the deflated burning rags of cushion aside, whipped off his jacket and sprang at the flames with a shout. He stamped into the ruin until flames ran up his boots. Edna saw him, a red-lit hero, and thought it was good to be a man.

A bystander was hit by a hot halfpenny flying out of the air. Then Bert thought of the papers in his pockets, and staggered back, trying to extinguish his burning jacket – checked, repulsed, dismayed.

Edna was struck by the benevolent appearance of an elderly spectator in a silk hat and Sabbatical garments. 'Oh!' she cried to him. 'Help this young man! How can you stand and see it?'

A cry of 'The tarpaulin!'[12] arose.

An earnest-looking man in a very light-grey cycling suit had suddenly appeared at the side of the lame motor-car and addressed the owner. 'Have you a tarpaulin?' he said.

'Yes,' said the gentlemanly man. 'Yes. We've got a tarpaulin.'

'That's it,' said the earnest-looking man, suddenly shouting. 'Let's have it, quick!'

The gentlemanly man, with feeble and deprecatory gestures, and in the manner of a hypnotized person, produced an excellent large tarpaulin.

'Here!' cried the earnest-looking man to Grubb. 'Ketch holt!'

Then everybody realized that a new method was to be tried. A number of willing hands seized upon the Oxford gentleman's tarpaulin. The others stood away with approving noises. The tarpaulin was held over the burning bicycle like a canopy, and then smothered down upon it.

'We ought to have done this before,' panted Grubb.

There was a moment of triumph. The flames vanished. Everyone who could contrive to do so touched the edge of the tarpaulin. Bert held down a corner with two hands and a foot. The tarpaulin, bulged up in the centre, seemed to be suppressing triumphant exultation. Then its self-approval became too much for it; it burst into a bright-red smile in the centre. It was exactly like the opening of a mouth. It laughed with a gust of flames. They were reflected redly in the observant goggles of the gentleman who owned the tarpaulin. Everybody recoiled.

'Save the trailer!' cried someone, and that was the last round in the battle. But the trailer could not be detached; its wicker-work had caught, and it was the last thing to burn. A sort of hush fell upon the gathering. The petrol burnt low, the wickerwork trailer banged and crackled. The crowd divided itself into an outer circle of critics, advisers and secondary characters, who had played undistinguished parts or no parts at all in the affair, and a central group of heated and distressed principals. A young man with an inquiring mind and a con-siderable knowledge of motor-bicycles fixed on to Grubb and wanted to argue that the thing could not have happened. Grubb was short and inattentive with him, and the young man with-drew to the back of the crowd, and there told the benevolent old gentleman in the silk hat that people who went out with machines they didn't understand had only themselves to blame if things went wrong.

The old gentleman let him talk for some time, and then remarked in a tone of rapturous enjoyment: 'Stone deaf,' and added, 'Nasty things.'

A rosy-faced man in a straw hat claimed attention. 'I *did* save the front wheel,' he said, 'you'd have had that tyre catch too, if I hadn't kept turning it round.' It became manifest that this was so. The front wheel had retained its tyre, was intact, was still rotating slowly among the blackened and twisted ruins of the rest of the machine. It had something of the air of conscious virtue, of unimpeachable respectability, that distinguishes a rent collector in a low neighbourhood. 'That wheel's worth a pound,' said the rosy-faced man, making a song of it. 'I kep' turning it round.'

Newcomers kept arriving from the south with the question, 'What's up?' until it got on Grubb's nerves. Londonward the crowd was constantly losing people; they would mount their various wheels with the satisfied manner of spectators who have had the best. Their voices would recede into the twilight; one would hear a laugh at the memory of this particularly salient incident or that.

'I'm afraid,' said the gentleman of the motor-car, 'my tarpaulin's a bit done for.'

Grubb admitted that the owner was the best judge of that.

'Nothing else I can do for you?' said the gentleman of the motor-car, it may be, with a suspicion of irony.

Bert was roused to action. 'Look here,' he said. 'There's my young lady. If she ain't 'ome by ten they lock her out. See? Well, all my money was in my jacket pocket, and it's all mixed up with the burnt stuff, and that's too 'ot to touch. *Is* Clapham out of your way?'

'All in the day's work,' said the gentleman with the motor-car, and turned to Edna. 'Very pleased indeed,' he said, 'if you'll come with us. We're late for dinner as it is, so it won't make much difference for us to go home by way of Clapham.[13] We've got to get to Surbiton, anyhow. I'm afraid you'll find us a little slow.'

'But what's Bert going to do?' said Edna.

'I don't know that we can accommodate Bert,' said the motor-car gentleman, 'though we're tremendously anxious to oblige.'

'You couldn't take the whole lot?' said Bert, waving his hand at the deboshed and blackened ruins on the ground.

'I'm awfully afraid I can't,' said the Oxford man. 'Awfully sorry, you know.'

'Then I'll have to stick 'ere for a bit,' said Bert. 'I got to see the thing through. You go on, Edna.'

'Don't like leavin' you, Bert.'

'You can't 'elp it, Edna.' . . .

The last Edna saw of Bert was his figure, in charred and blackened shirt-sleeves, standing in the dusk. He was musing deeply by the mixed ironwork and ashes of his vanished motor-bicycle, a melancholy figure. His retinue of spectators had shrunk now to half a dozen figures. Flossie and Grubb were preparing to follow her desertion.

'Cheer up, old Bert,' cried Edna with artificial cheerfulness. 'So long.'

'So long, Edna,' said Bert.

'See you to-morrer.'

'See you to-morrer,' said Bert, though he was destined, as a matter of fact, to see much of the habitable globe before he saw her again.

Bert began to light matches from a borrowed boxful, and

search for a half-crown that still eluded him among the charred remains. His face was grave and melancholy.

'I *wish* that 'adn't 'appened,' said Flossie, riding on with Grubb. . . .

And at last Bert was left almost alone, a sad, blackened Promethean figure,[14] cursed by the gift of fire. He had entertained vague ideas of hiring a cart, of achieving miraculous repairs, of still snatching some residual value from his one chief possession. Now, in the darkening night, he perceived the vanity of such intentions. Truth came to him bleakly, and laid her chill conviction upon him. He took hold of the handlebar, stood the thing up, tried to push it forward. The tyreless hind wheel was jammed hopelessly, even as he feared. For a minute or so he stood upholding his machine, a motionless despair. Then with a great effort he thrust the ruins from him into the ditch, kicked at it once, regarded it for a moment, and turned his face resolutely Londonward.

He did not once look back.

'That's the end of *that* game,' said Bert. 'No more teuf-teuf-teuf for Bert Smallways for a year or two. Good-bye, 'Olidays! . . . Oh! I ought to 'ave sold the blasted thing when I had a chance three years ago.'

§ 3

The next morning found the firm of Grubb and Smallways in a state of profound despondency. It seemed a small matter to them that the newspaper and cigarette shop opposite displayed such placards as this:

REPORTED AMERICAN ULTIMATUM.
BRITAIN MUST FIGHT.
OUR INFATUATED WAR OFFICE STILL
REFUSES TO LISTEN TO MR BUTTERIDGE.
GREAT MONORAIL DISASTER AT
TIMBUCTOO.

or this:

> WAR A QUESTION OF HOURS.
> NEW YORK CALM.
> EXCITEMENT IN BERLIN.

or again:

> WASHINGTON STILL SILENT.
> WHAT WILL PARIS DO?
> THE PANIC ON THE BOURSE.
> THE KING'S GARDEN-PARTY TO THE
> MASKED TWAREGS.[15]
> MR BUTTERIDGE MAKES AN OFFER.
> LATEST BETTING FROM TEHERAN.

or this:

> WILL AMERICA FIGHT?
> ANTI-GERMAN RIOT IN BAGDAD.
> THE MUNICIPAL SCANDALS AT DAMASCUS.
> MR BUTTERIDGE'S INVENTION FOR
> AMERICA.

Bert stared at these over the card of pump clips in the pane in the door with unseeing eyes. He wore a blackened flannel shirt, and the jacketless ruins of the holiday suit of yesterday. The boarded-up shop was dark and depressing beyond words, the few scandalous hiring machines had never looked so hopelessly disreputable. He thought of their fellows who were 'out', and of the approaching disputations of the afternoon. He thought of their new landlord and of their old landlord, and of bills and claims. Life presented itself for the first time as a hopeless fight against fate. . . .

'Grubb, o' man,' he said, distilling the quintessence, 'I'm fair sick of this shop.'

'So'm I,' said Grubb.

'I'm out of conceit with it. I don't seem to care ever to speak to a customer again.'

'There's that trailer,' said Grubb, after a pause.

'Blow the trailer!' said Bert. 'Anyhow, I didn't leave a deposit on it. I didn't do that. Still—'

He turned round on his friend. 'Look 'ere,' he said, 'we aren't gettin' on here. We been losing money hand over fist. We got things tied up in fifty knots.'

'What can we do?' said Grubb.

'Clear out. Sell what we can for what it will fetch, and quit. See? It's no good 'anging on to a losing concern. No sort of good. Jest foolishness.'

'That's all right,' said Grubb – 'that's all right; but it ain't your capital been sunk in it.'

'No need for us to sink after our capital,' said Bert, ignoring the point.

'I'm not going to be held responsible for that trailer, anyhow. That ain't my affair.'

'Nobody arst you to make it your affair. If you like to stick on here, well and good. I'm quitting. I'll see Bank Holiday through, and then I'm O.R.P.H.[16] See?'

'Leavin' me?'

'Leavin' you. If you must be left.'

Grubb looked round the shop. It certainly had become distasteful. Once upon a time it had been bright with hope and new beginnings and stock and the prospect of credit. Now – now it was failure and dust. Very likely the landlord would be round presently to go on with the row about the window. . . . 'Where d'you think of going, Bert?' Grubb asked.

Bert turned round and regarded him. 'I thought it out as I was walking 'ome, and in bed. I couldn't sleep a wink.'

'What did you think out?'

'Plans.'

'What plans?'

'Oh! You're for sticking here.'

'Not if anything better was to offer.'

'It's only an ideer,' said Bert.

'Let's 'ear it.'

'You made the girls laugh yestiday, that song you sang.'

'Seems a long time ago now,' said Grubb.

'And old Edna nearly cried – over that bit of mine.'

'She got a fly in her eye,' said Grubb; 'I saw it. But what's this got to do with your plan?'

'No end,' said Bert.

' ''Ow?'

'Don't you see?'

'Not singing in the streets?'

'Streets! No fear! But 'ow about the Tour of the Waterin'-Places of England, Grubb? Singing! Young men of family doing it for a lark? You ain't got a bad voice, you know, and mine's all right. I never see a chap singing on the beach yet that I couldn't 'ave sung into a cocked hat.[17] And we both know how to put on the toff a bit. Eh? Well, that's my ideer. Me and you, Grubb, with a refined song and a breakdown.[18] Like we was doing for foolery yestiday. That was what put it into my 'ead. Easy make up a programme – easy. Six choice items, and one or two for encores and patter. I'm all right for the patter – anyhow.'

Grubb remained regarding his darkened and disheartening shop; he thought of his former landlord and his present landlord, and of the general disgustingness of business in an age which re-echoes to The Bitter Cry of the Middle Class;[19] and then it seemed to him that afar off he heard the twankle, twankle of a banjo, and the voice of a stranded siren singing. He had a sense of hot sunshine upon sand, of the children of at least transiently opulent holidaymakers in a circle round about him, of the whisper, 'They are really gentlemen,' and then dollop, dollop came the coppers in the hat. Sometimes even silver. It was all income; no outgoings, no bills. 'I'm on, Bert,' he said.

'Right O!' said Bert, and, 'Now we shan't be long.'

'We needn't start without capital neither,' said Grubb. 'If we take the best of these machines up to the Bicycle Mart in Finsbury we'd raise six or seven pounds on 'em. We could easy do that tomorrow before anybody much was about. . . .'

'Nice to think of old Suet-and-Bones coming round to make his usual row with us, and finding a card up "Closed for Repairs".'

'We'll do that,' said Grubb with zest – 'we'll do that. And we'll put up another notice, and jest arst all inquirers to go round to 'im and inquire. See? Then they'll know all about us.'

Before the day was out the whole enterprise was planned. They decided at first that they would call themselves the Naval Mr O's, a plagiarism, and not perhaps a very good one, from the title of the well-known troupe of 'Scarlet Mr E's', and Bert rather clung to the idea of a uniform of bright blue serge, with a lot of gold lace and cord and ornamentation, rather like a naval officer's, but more so. But that had to be abandoned as impracticable, it would have taken too much time and money to prepare. They perceived they must wear some cheaper and more readily prepared costume, and Grubb fell back on white dominoes.[20] They entertained the notion for a time of selecting the two worst machines from the hiring stock, painting them over with crimson enamel paint, replacing the bells by the loudest sort of motor-horn, and doing a ride about to begin and end the entertainment. They doubted the advisability of this step.

'There's people in the world,' said Bert, 'who wouldn't recognize us, who'd know them bicycles again like a shot, and we don't want to go on with no old stories. We want a fresh start.'

'*I* do,' said Grubb, 'badly.'

'We want to forget things – and cut all these rotten old worries. They ain't doin' us good.'

Nevertheless, they decided to take the risk of these bicycles, and they decided their costumes should be brown stockings and sandals, and cheap unbleached sheets with a hole cut in the middle, and wigs and beards of tow. The rest their normal selves! 'The Desert Dervishes', they would call themselves, and their chief songs would be those popular ditties,[21] 'In my Trailer', and 'What Price Hairpins Now?'

They decided to begin with small seaside places, and gradually, as they gained confidence, attack larger centres. To begin with they selected Littlestone in Kent,[22] chiefly because of its unassuming name.

So they planned, and it seemed a small and unimportant thing to them that as they chattered the governments of half the world and more were drifting into war. About midday they became aware of the first of the evening-paper placards shouting to them across the street:

> THE WAR-CLOUD DARKENS.

Nothing else but that.

'Always rottin' about war now,' said Bert. 'They'll get it in the neck in real earnest one of these days, if they ain't precious careful.'

§ 4

So you will understand the sudden apparition that surprised rather than delighted the quiet informality of Dymchurch sands. Dymchurch was one of the last places on the coast of England to be reached by the monorail, and so its spacious sands were still, at the time of this story, the secret and delight of a limited number of people. They went there to flee vulgarity and extravagance, and to bathe and sit and talk and play with their children in peace, and the Desert Dervishes did not please them at all.

The two white figures on scarlet wheels came upon them out of the infinite along the sands from Littlestone, grew nearer and larger and more audible, honk-honking and emitting weird cries, and generally threatening liveliness of the most aggressive type. 'Good heavens!' said Dymchurch, 'what's this?'

Then our young men, according to a preconcerted plan, wheeled round from file to line, dismounted and stood at attention. 'Ladies and gentlemen,' they said, 'we beg to present ourselves – the Desert Dervishes.' They bowed profoundly.

The few scattered groups upon the beach regarded them with horror for the most part, but some of the children and young people were interested and drew nearer. 'There ain't a bob on the beach,' said Grubb in an undertone, and the Desert Dervishes piled their bicycles with comic 'business', that got a laugh from one very unsophisticated little boy. Then they took a deep breath and struck into the cheerful strain of 'What Price Hairpins Now?' Grubb sang the song, Bert did his best to make the chorus a rousing one, and at the end of each verse they danced certain steps, skirts in hand, that they had carefully rehearsed.

> Ting-a-ling-a-ting-a-ling-a-ting-a-ling-a-tang.
> What Price Hairpins Now?

So they chanted and danced their steps in the sunshine on Dymchurch beach, and the children drew near these foolish young men, marvelling that they should behave in this way, and the older people looked cold and unfriendly.

All round the coasts of Europe that morning banjos were ringing, voices were bawling and singing, children were playing in the sun, pleasure-boats went to and fro; the common abundant life of the time, unsuspicious of the dangers that gathered darkly against it, flowed on its cheerful aimless way. In the cities men fussed about their businesses and engagements. The newspaper placards that had cried 'wolf!' so often, cried 'wolf!' now in vain.

§ 5

Now as Bert and Grubb bawled their chorus for the third time, they became aware of a very big, golden-brown balloon low in the sky to the north-west, and coming rapidly towards them. 'Jest as we're gettin' hold of 'em,' muttered Grubb, 'up comes a counter-attraction. Go it, Bert!'

> Ting-a-ling-a-ting-a-ling-a-ting-a-ling-a-tang.
> What Price Hairpins Now?

The balloon rose and fell, went out of sight – 'landed, thank goodness,' said Grubb – reappeared with a leap. '*Eng!*'[23] said Grubb. 'Step it, Bert, or they'll see it!'

They finished their dance, and then stood frankly staring.

'There's something wrong with that balloon,' said Bert.

Everybody now was looking at the balloon drawing rapidly nearer before a brisk north-westerly breeze. The song and dance were a 'dead frost'. Nobody thought any more about it. Even Bert and Grubb forgot it, and ignored the next item on their programme altogether. The balloon was bumping as though its occupants were trying to land; it would approach, sinking slowly, touch the ground and instantly jump fifty feet or so in the air and immediately begin to fall again. Its car touched a clump of trees, and the black figure that had been struggling in the ropes fell back, or jumped back, into the car. In another moment it was quite close. It seemed a huge affair, as big as a house, and it floated down swiftly towards the sands; a long rope trailed behind it, and enormous shouts came from the man in the car. He seemed to be taking off his clothes, then his head came over the side of the car. 'Catch hold of the rope!' they heard, quite plain.

'Salvage, Bert!' cried Grubb, and started to head off the rope.

Bert followed him, and collided, without upsetting, with a fisherman bent upon a similar errand. A woman carrying a baby in her arms, two small boys with toy spades and a stout gentleman in flannels all got to the trailing rope at about the same time, and began to dance over it in their attempts to secure it. Bert came up to this wriggling, elusive serpent and got his foot on it, went down on all fours and achieved a grip. In half a dozen seconds the whole diffused population of the beach had, as it were, crystallized on the rope, and was pulling against the balloon under the vehement and stimulating directions of the man in the car. 'Pull, I tell you,' said the man in the car – 'Pull!'

For a second or so the balloon obeyed its momentum and the wind and tugged its human anchor seaward. It dropped, touched the water and made a flat, silvery splash, and recoiled as one's finger recoils when one touches anything hot. 'Pull her in,' said the man in the car. 'She's *fainted!*'

He occupied himself with some unseen object while the people on the rope pulled him in. Bert was nearest the balloon, and much excited and interested. He kept stumbling over the tail of the Dervish costume in his zeal. He had never imagined before what a big, light, wallowing thing a balloon was. The car was of brown coarse wickerwork, and comparatively small. The rope he tugged at was fastened to a stout-looking ring, four or five feet above the car. At each tug he drew in a yard or so of rope, and the waggling wickerwork was drawn so much nearer. Out of the car came wrathful bellowings: 'Fainted, she has!' and then: 'It's her heart – broken with all she's had to go through.'

The balloon ceased to struggle, and sank downward. Bert dropped the rope, and ran forward to catch it in a new place. In another moment he had his hand on the car. 'Lay hold of it,' said the man in the car, and his face appeared close to Bert's – a strangely familiar face, fierce eyebrows, a flattish nose, a huge black moustache. He had discarded coat and waistcoat – perhaps with some idea of presently having to swim for his life – and his black hair was extraordinarily disordered. 'Will all you people get hold round the car,' he said. 'There's a lady here fainted – or got failure of the heart. Heaven alone knows which! My name is Butteridge. Butteridge, my name is – in a balloon. Now please, all on to the edge. This is the last time I trust myself to one of these palaeolithic contrivances. The ripping-cord failed, and the valve wouldn't act. If ever I meet the scoundrel who ought to have seen—'

He stuck his head out between the ropes abruptly, and said, in a note of earnest expostulation: 'Get some brandy! – some neat brandy!' Someone went up the beach for it.

In the car, sprawling upon a sort of bed-bench, in an attitude of elaborate self-abandonment, was a large, blonde lady, wearing a fur coat and a big floriferous hat. Her head lolled back against the padded corner of the car, and her eyes were shut and her mouth open. 'Me dear!' said Mr Butteridge, in a common loud voice, 'we're safe!'

She gave no sign.

'Me dear!' said Mr Butteridge, in a greatly intensified loud voice, 'we're safe!'

She was still quite impassive.

Then Mr Butteridge showed the fiery core of his soul. 'If she is dead,' he said, slowly lifting a fist towards the balloon above him and speaking in an immense tremulous bellow, 'if she is dead, I will r-r-rend the heavens like a garment! I must get her out,' he cried, his nostrils dilated with emotion; 'I must get her out. I cannot have her die in a wickerwork basket nine feet square – she who was made for kings' palaces! Keep holt of this car! Is there a strong man among ye to take her if I hand her out?'

He swept the lady together by a powerful movement of his arms, and lifted her. 'Keep the car from jumping,' he said to those who clustered about him. 'Keep your weight on it. She is no light woman, and when she is out of it – it will be relieved.'

Bert leapt lightly into a sitting position on the edge of the car. The others took a firmer grip upon the ropes and ring.

'Are you ready?' said Mr Butteridge.

He stood upon the bed-bench and lifted the lady carefully. Then he sat down on the wicker edge opposite to Bert, and put one leg over to dangle outside. A rope or so seemed to incommode him. 'Will someone assist me?' he said. 'If they would take this lady?'

It was just at this moment, with Mr Butteridge and the lady balanced finely on the basket brim, that she came to. She came to suddenly and violently with a loud, heartrending cry of 'Alfred! Save me!' And she waved her arms searchingly, and then clasped Mr Butteridge about.

It seemed to Bert that the car swayed for a moment and then buck-jumped and kicked him. Also he saw the boots of the lady and the right leg of the gentleman describing arcs through the air, preparatory to vanishing over the side of the car. His impressions were complex, but they also comprehended the fact that he had lost his balance, and was going to stand on his head inside this creaking basket. He spread out clutching arms. He did stand on his head, more or less, his tow beard[24] came off and got in his mouth, and his cheek slid along against padding. His nose buried itself in a bag of sand. The car gave a violent lurch, and became still.

'Confound it!' he said.

He had an impression he must be stunned, because of a surging in his ears, and because all the voices of the people about him had become small and remote. They were shouting like elves inside a hill.

He found it difficult to get on his feet. His limbs were mixed up with the garments Mr Butteridge had discarded when that gentleman had thought he must needs plunge into the sea. Bert bawled out, half angry, half rueful, 'You might have said you were going to tip the basket.' Then he stood up and clutched the ropes of the car convulsively.

Below him, far below him, shining blue, were the waters of the English Channel. Far off, minute in the sunshine, and rushing down as if someone was bending it hollow, was the beach and the irregular cluster of houses that constituted Dymchurch. He could see the little crowd of people he had so abruptly left. Grubb, in the white wrapper of a Desert Dervish, was running along the edge of the sea. Mr Butteridge was knee-deep in the water, bawling immensely. The lady was sitting up with her floriferous hat in her lap, shockingly neglected. The beach, east and west, was dotted with people – they seemed all heads and feet – looking up. And the balloon, released from the twenty-five stone or so of Mr Butteridge and his lady, was rushing up into the sky at the pace of a racing motor-car. 'My crikey!' said Bert; 'here's a go!'

He looked down with a pinched face at the receding beach, and reflected that he wasn't giddy; then he made a superficial survey of the cords and ropes about him with a vague idea of 'doing something'. 'I'm not going to mess about with the thing,' he said at last, and sat down upon the mattress. 'I'm not going to touch it. . . . I wonder what one ought to do?'

Soon he got up again and stared for a long time at the sinking world below, at white cliffs to the east and flattening marsh to the left, at a minute wide prospect of weald and downland, at dim towns and harbours, and rivers, and ribbon-like roads, at ships and ships, decks and foreshortened funnels upon the ever-widening sea, and at the great monorail bridge that straddled the Channel from Folkestone to Boulogne, until at length, first cobwebby wisps and then a veil of filmy cloud hid the prospect from his eyes. He wasn't at all giddy nor very much frightened, only in a state of enormous consternation.

3

THE BALLOON

Bert Smallways was a vulgar little creature, the sort of pert, limited soul that the old civilization of the early twentieth century produced by the million in every country of the world. He had lived all his life in narrow streets, and between mean houses he could not look over, and in a narrow circle of ideas from which there was no escape. He thought the whole duty of man was to be smarter than his fellows, get his hands, as he put it, 'on the dibs',[1] and have a good time. He was, in fact, the sort of man who had made England and America what they were. The luck had been against him so far, but that was by the way. He was a mere aggressive and acquisitive individual with no sense of the State, no habitual loyalty, no devotion, no code of honour, no code even of courage. Now by a curious accident he found himself lifted out of his marvellous modern world for a time, out of all the rush and confused appeals of it, and floating like a thing dead and disembodied between sea and sky. It was as if Heaven was experimenting with him, had picked him out as a sample from the English millions to look at him more nearly and to see what was happening to the soul of man. But what Heaven made of him in that case I cannot profess to imagine, for I have long since abandoned all theories about the ideals and satisfactions of Heaven.

To be alone in a balloon at a height of fourteen or fifteen thousand feet – and to that height Bert Smallways presently rose – is like nothing else in human experience. It is one of the supreme things possible to man. No flying machine can ever better it. It is to pass extraordinarily out of human things. It is to be still and alone to an unprecedented degree. It is solitude without the suggestion of intervention; it is calm without a single irrelevant murmur. It is to see the sky.

No sound reaches one of all the roar and jar of humanity, the air is clear and sweet beyond the thought of defilement. No bird, no insect comes so high. No wind blows ever in a balloon, no breeze rustles, for it moves with the wind and is itself a part of the atmosphere. Once started it does not rock nor sway; you cannot feel whether it rises or falls. Bert felt acutely cold, but he wasn't mountain-sick; he put on the coat and overcoat and gloves Butteridge had discarded – put them over the 'Desert Dervish' sheet that covered his cheap best suit – and sat very still for a long time, overawed by the new-found quiet of the world. Above him was the light, translucent, billowing globe of shining brown oiled silk and the blazing sunlight and the great deep-blue dome of the sky. Below, far below, was a torn floor of sunlit cloud, slashed by enormous rents, through which he saw the sea.

If you had been watching him from below you would have seen his head, a motionless little black knob, sticking out from the car first of all for a long time on one side, and then vanishing to reappear after a time at some other point.

He wasn't in the least degree uncomfortable nor afraid. He did think that as this uncontrollable thing had thus rushed up the sky with him it might presently rush down again, but this consideration did not trouble him very much. Essentially his state was wonder. There is no fear nor trouble in balloons – until they descend.

'Gollys!' he said at last, feeling a need for talking; 'it's better than a motor-bike.'

'It's all right!'

'I suppose they're telegraphing about, about me.' . . .

The second hour found him examining the equipment of the car with great particularity. Above him was the throat of the balloon, bunched and tied together, but with an open lumen through which Bert could peer up into a vast, empty, quiet interior, and out of which descended two fine cords of unknown import, one white, one crimson, to pockets below the ring. The netting about the balloon ended in cords attached to the ring, a big steel-bound hoop to which the car was slung by ropes. From it depended the trail-rope and grapnel, and over the sides of the car were a number of canvas bags that Bert decided must be ballast to 'chuck down' if the balloon fell. ('Not much falling just yet,' said Bert.)

There were an aneroid[2] and another box-shaped instrument hanging from the ring. The latter had an ivory plate bearing 'statoscope' and other words in French, and a little indicator quivered and waggled between *Montée* and *Descente*. 'That's all right,' said Bert. 'That tells if you're going up or down.' On the crimson padded seat of the balloon there lay a couple of rugs and a Kodak,[3] and in opposite corners of the bottom of the car were an empty champagne bottle and a glass. 'Refreshments,' said Bert meditatively, tilting the empty bottle. Then he had a brilliant idea. The two padded bed-like seats, each with blankets and mattress, he perceived, were boxes, and within he found Mr Butteridge's conception of an adequate equipment for a balloon ascent: a hamper which included a game pie, a Roman pie,[4] a cold fowl, tomatoes, lettuce, ham sandwiches, shrimp sandwiches, a large cake, knives and forks and paper plates, self-heating tins of coffee and cocoa, bread, butter and marmalade, several carefully packed bottles of champagne, bottles of Perrier water and a big jar of water for washing, a portfolio, maps and a compass, a rucksack containing a number of conveniences, including curling-tongs and hairpins, a cap with ear-flaps and so forth.

'A 'ome from 'ome,' said Bert, surveying this provision as he tied the ear-flaps under his chin.

He looked over the side of the car. Far below were the shining clouds. They had thickened so that the whole world was hidden. Southward they were piled in great snowy masses; he was half disposed to think them mountains; northward and eastward they were in wavelike levels, and blindingly sunlit.

'Wonder how long a balloon keeps up,' he said.

He imagined he was not moving, so insensibly did the monster drift with the air about it. 'No good coming down till we shift a bit,' he said.

He consulted the statoscope.

'Still Monty,' he said.

'Wonder what would happen if you pulled a cord?

'No,' he decided. 'I ain't going to mess it about.'

Afterwards he did pull both the ripping and the valve cords, but, as Mr Butteridge had already discovered, they had fouled a fold of silk in the throat. Nothing happened. But for that little hitch the ripping cord would have torn the balloon open as though it had been slashed by a sword, and hurled Mr Smallways to eternity at the rate of some thousand feet a second. 'No go!' he said, giving it a final tug. Then he lunched.

He opened a bottle of champagne, which, as soon as he cut the wire, blew its cork out with incredible violence, and for the most part followed it into space. Bert, however, got about a tumblerful. 'Atmospheric pressure,' said Bert, finding an application at last for the elementary physiography of his seventh-standard days. 'I'll have to be more careful next time. No good wastin' drink.'

Then he routed about for matches to utilize Mr Butteridge's cigars; but here again luck was on his side, and he couldn't find any wherewith to set light to the gas above him. Or else he would have dropped in a flare, a splendid but transitory pyrotechnic display. 'Eng old Grubb!' said Bert, slapping unproductive pockets. ''E didn't ought to 'ave kep' my box. 'E's always sneaking matches.'

He reposed for a time. Then he got up, paddled about, rearranged the ballast bags on the floor, watched the clouds for a time, and turned over the maps on the locker. Bert liked maps, and he spent some time in trying to find one of France or the Channel; but they were all British ordnance maps[5] of English counties. That set him thinking about languages and trying to recall his seventh-standard French. 'Je suis Anglais. C'est une méprise. Je suis arrivé par accident ici,'[6] he decided upon as convenient phrases. Then it occurred to him that he would entertain himself by reading Mr Butteridge's letters and examining his pocketbook, and in this manner he whiled away the afternoon.

§ 2

He sat upon the padded locker wrapped about very carefully; for the air, though calm, was exhilaratingly cold and clear. He was wearing first a modest suit of blue serge and all the unpretending underwear of a suburban young man of fashion, with sandal-like cycling-shoes and brown stockings drawn over his trouser ends; then the perforated sheet proper to a Desert Dervish; then the coat and waistcoat and big fur-trimmed overcoat of Mr Butteridge; then a lady's large fur cloak, and round his knees a blanket. Over his head was a tow wig, surmounted by a large cap of Mr Butteridge's with the flaps down over his ears. And some fur sleeping-boots of Mr Butteridge's warmed his feet. The car of the balloon was small and neat, some bags of ballast the untidiest of its contents, and he had found a light folding table and put it at his elbow, and on that was a glass with champagne. And about him, above and below, was space – such a clear emptiness and silence of space as only the aeronaut can experience.

He did not know where he might be drifting, or what might happen next. He accepted this state of affairs with a serenity creditable to the Smallways' courage, which one might reasonably have expected to be of a more degenerate and contemptible quality altogether. His impression was that he was bound to come down somewhere, and that then, if he wasn't smashed, someone, some 'society' perhaps, would probably pack him and the balloon back to England. If not, he would ask very firmly for the British consul. 'Le consuelo Britannique,' he decided this would be. 'Apportez moi à le consuelo Britannique s'il vous plaît,'[7] he would say, for he was by no means ignorant of French. In the meanwhile he found the intimate aspects of Mr Butteridge an interesting study.

There were letters of an entirely private character addressed to Mr Butteridge, and among others several love letters of a devouring sort in a large feminine hand. These are no business of ours, and one remarks with regret that Bert read them.

When he had read them he remarked, 'Gollys!' in an awestricken tone, and then, after a long interval, 'I wonder if that was her?

'Lord!'

He mused for a time.

He resumed his exploration of the Butteridge interior. It included a number of press-cuttings of interviews and also several letters in German, then some in the same German handwriting, but in English. 'Hul-*lo*!' said Bert.

One of the latter, the first he took, began with an apology to Butteridge for not writing to him in English before, and for the inconvenience and delay that had been caused him by that, and went on to matter that Bert found exciting in the highest degree. 'We can understand entirely the difficulties of your position, and that you shall possibly be watched at the present juncture. But, sir, we do not believe that any serious obstacles will be put in your way if you wished to endeavour to leave the country and come to us with your plans by the customary routes – either via Dover, Ostend, Boulogne, or Dieppe. We find it difficult to think you are right in supposing yourself to be in danger of murder for your invaluable invention.'

'Funny!' said Bert, and meditated.

Then he went through the other letters.

'They seem to want him to come,' said Bert; 'but they don't seem hurting themselves to get 'im. Or else they're shamming don't care to get his prices down.

'They don't quite seem to be the gov'ment,' he reflected, after an interval. 'It's more like some firm's paper. All this printed stuff at the top. *Drachenflieger.*[8] *Drachenballons. Ballonstoffe. Kugelballons.* Greek to me.

'But he was trying to sell his blessed secret abroad. That's all right. No Greek about that! Gollys! Here *is* the secret!'

He tumbled off the seat, opened the locker and had the portfolio open before him on the folding table. It was full of drawings done in the peculiar flat style and conventional colours engineers adopt. And, in addition, there were some rather underexposed photographs, obviously done by an amateur at close quarters, of the actual machine Butteridge had made, in its shed near the Crystal Palace. Bert found he was trembling. 'Lord!' he said, 'here am I and the whole blessed secret of flying – lost up here on the roof of everywhere.

'Let's see!' He fell studying the drawings and comparing them with the photographs. They puzzled him. Half of them seemed to be missing. He tried to imagine how they fitted together, and found the effort too great for his mind.

'It's tryin',' said Bert. 'I wish I'd been brought up to the engineering. If I could only make it out!'

He went to the side of the car and remained for a time staring with unseeing eyes at a huge cluster of great clouds – a cluster of slowly dissolving Monte Rosas,[9] sunlit below. His attention was arrested by a strange black spot that moved over them. It alarmed him. It was a black spot moving slowly with him far below, following him down there, indefatigably over the cloud mountains. Why should such a thing follow him? What could it be? . . .

He had an inspiration. 'Uv course!' he said. It was the shadow of the balloon. But he still watched it dubiously for a time.

He returned to the plans on the table.

He spent a long afternoon between his struggles to understand them and fits of meditation. He evolved a remarkable new sentence in French. 'Voici Mossoo! – Je suis un inventeur Anglais. Mon nom est Butteridge. Beh. oo. teh. teh. eh. arr. e. deh. ghe. eh. J'avais ici pour vendre le secret de le *flying machine*. Comprenez? Vendre pour l'argent tout suite, l'argent en main. Comprenez? C'est le machine à jouer dans l'air. Comprenez? C'est le machine à faire l'oiseau. Comprenez? Balancer? Oui exactement! Battir l'oiseau, en fait, à son propre jeu. Je désire de vendre ceci à votre government national. Voulez vous me directer là?[10]

'Bit rummy, I expect, from the point of view of grammar,' said Bert, 'but they ought to get the hang of it all right.

'But then, if they arst me to explain the blessed thing?'

He returned in a worried way to the plans. 'I don't believe it's all here!' he said. . . .

He got more and more perplexed up there among the clouds as to what he should do with this wonderful find of his. At any moment, so far as he could tell, he might descend amidst he knew not what foreign people.

'It's the chance of my life!' he said.

It became more and more manifest to him that it wasn't. 'Directly I come down they'll telegraph – put it in the papers. Butteridge'll know of it and come along – on my track.'

Butteridge would be a terrible person to be on anyone's track. Bert thought of the great black moustaches, the triangular nose, the searching bellow and the glare. His afternoon's dream of a marvellous seizure and sale of the great Butteridge secret crumpled up in his mind, dissolved and vanished. He awoke to sanity again.

'Wouldn't do. What's the good of thinking of it?' He proceeded slowly and reluctantly to replace the Butteridge papers in pockets and portfolio as he had found them. He became aware of a splendid golden light upon the balloon above him, and of a new warmth in the blue dome of the sky. He stood up and beheld the sun, a great ball of blinding gold, setting upon a tumbled sea of gold-edged crimson and purple clouds, strange and wonderful beyond imagining. Eastward cloudland stretched for ever, darkling blue, and it seemed to Bert the whole round hemisphere of the world was under his eyes.

Then far away over the blue he caught sight of three long, dark shapes like hurrying fish that drove one after the other, as porpoises follow one another in the water. They were very fishlike indeed – with tails. It was an unconvincing impression in that light. He blinked his eyes, stared again, and they had vanished. For a long time he scrutinized those remote blue levels and saw no more. . . .

'Wonder if I ever saw anything,' he said, and then: 'There ain't such things. . . .'

Down went the sun and down, not diving steeply but passing northward as it sank, and then suddenly daylight and the expansive warmth of daylight had gone altogether, and the index of the statoscope quivered over to *Descente*.

§ 3

'*Now* what's going to 'appen?' said Bert.

He found the cold, grey cloud wilderness rising towards him with a wide, slow steadiness. As he sank down among them the clouds ceased to seem the snow-clad mountain slopes they had resembled heretofore, became unsubstantial, confessed an immense silent drift and eddy in their substance. For a moment, when he was nearly among their twilight masses, his descent was checked. Then abruptly the sky was hidden, the last vestiges of daylight gone, and he was falling rapidly in an evening twilight through a whirl of fine snowflakes that streamed past him towards the zenith, that drifted in upon the things about him and melted, that touched his face with ghostly fingers. He shivered. His breath came smoking from his lips, and everything was instantly bedewed and wet.

He had an impression of a snowstorm pouring with un-exampled and increasing fury *upward*; then he realized that he was falling faster and faster.

Imperceptibly a sound grew upon his ears. The great silence of the world was at an end.

What was this confused sound?

He craned his head over the side, concerned, perplexed.

First he seemed to see, and then not to see. Then he saw clearly little edges of foam pursuing each other, and a wide waste of weltering waters below him. Far away was a pilot-boat with a big sail bearing dim black letters, and a little pinkish-yellow light, and it was rolling and pitching – rolling and pitching in a gale, while he could feel no wind at all. Soon the sound of waters was loud and near. He was dropping, dropping – into the sea!

He became convulsively active.

'Ballast!' he cried, and seized a little sack from the floor, and heaved it overboard. He did not wait for the effect of that, but sent another after it. He looked over in time to see a minute white splash in the dim waters below him, and then he was back in the snow and clouds again.

He sent out quite needlessly a third sack of ballast and a

fourth, and presently had the immense satisfaction of soaring up out of the damp and chill into the clear, cold, upper air in which the day still lingered. 'Thang-God!' he said, with all his heart.

A few stars now had pierced the blue, and in the east there shone brightly a prolate moon.[11]

§ 4

That first downward plunge filled Bert with a haunting sense of boundless waters below. It was a summer's night, but it seemed to him, nevertheless, extraordinarily long. He had a feeling of insecurity that he fancied quite irrationally the sunrise would dispel. Also he was hungry. He felt in the dark in the locker, put his fingers in the Roman pie, and got some sandwiches, and he also opened rather successfully a half-bottle of champagne. That warmed and restored him, he grumbled at Grubb about the matches, wrapped himself up warmly on the locker, and dozed for a time. He got up once or twice to make sure that he was still securely high above the sea. The first time the moonlit clouds were white and dense, and the shadow of the balloon ran athwart them like a dog that followed; afterwards they seemed thinner. As he lay still, staring up at the huge dark balloon above, he made a discovery. His – or rather Mr Butteridge's – waistcoat rustled as he breathed. It was lined with papers. But Bert could not see to get them out or examine them, much as he wished to do so. . . .

He was awakened by the crowing of cocks, the barking of dogs and a clamour of birds. He was driving slowly at a low level over a broad land lit golden by sunrise under a clear sky. He stared out upon hedgeless, well-cultivated fields intersected by roads, each lined with cable-bearing red poles. He had just passed over a compact, whitewashed village with a straight church tower and steep red-tiled roofs. A number of peasants, men and women, in shiny blouses and lumpish footwear, stood regarding him, arrested on their way to work. He was so low that the end of his rope was trailing.

He stared out at these people. 'I wonder how you land,' he thought.

'S'pose I *ought* to land?'

He found himself drifting down towards a monorail line, and hastily flung out two or three handsful of ballast to clear it.

'Lemme see! One might say just "Prenez"! Wish I knew the French for take hold of the rope! . . . I suppose they are French?'

He surveyed the country again. 'Might be Holland. Or Luxembourg. Or Lorraine's far as *I* know. Wonder what those big affairs over there are. Some sort of kiln? Prosperous-looking country. . . .'

The respectability of the country's appearance awakened answering chords in his nature.

'Make myself a bit shipshape first,' he said.

He resolved to rise a little and get rid of his wig (which now felt hot on his head) and so forth. He threw out a bag of ballast, and was astonished to find himself careering up through the air very rapidly.

'Blow!' said Mr Smallways. 'I've overdone the ballast trick. . . . Wonder when I shall get down again? . . . Brekfus' on board, anyhow.'

He removed his cap and wig, for the air was warm, and an improvident impulse made him cast the latter object overboard. The statoscope responded with a vigorous swing to '*Montée*'.

'The blessed thing goes up if you only *look* overboard,' he remarked, and assailed the locker. He found among other items several tins of liquid cocoa containing explicit directions for opening that he followed with minute care. He pierced the bottom with the key provided in the holes indicated, and forthwith the can grew from cold to hotter and hotter, until at last he could scarcely touch it, and then he opened the can at the other end, and there was his cocoa smoking, without the use of match or flame of any sort. It was an old invention,[12] but new to Bert. There was also ham and marmalade and bread, so that he had a really very tolerable breakfast indeed.

Then he took off his overcoat, for the sunshine was now inclined to be hot, and that reminded him of the rustling he had heard in the night. He took off the waistcoat and examined it. 'Old Butteridge won't like me unpicking this.' He hesitated, and finally proceeded to unpick it. He found the missing drawings of the lateral rotating planes, on which the whole stability of the flying machine depended.

An observant angel would have seen Bert sitting for a long time after this discovery in a state of intense meditation. Then at last he rose with an air of inspiration, took Mr Butteridge's ripped, demolished and ransacked waistcoat, and hurled it from the balloon – whence it fluttered down slowly and eddyingly until at last it came to rest with a contented flop upon the face of a German tourist sleeping peacefully beside the Höhenweg,[13] near Wildbad. Also this sent the balloon higher, and so into a position still more convenient for observation by our imaginary angel, who would next have seen Mr Smallways tear open his own jacket and waistcoat, remove his collar, open his shirt, thrust his hand into his bosom, and tear his heart out – or at least, if not his heart, some large bright scarlet object. If the observer, overcoming a thrill of celestial horror, had scrutinized this scarlet object more narrowly, one of Bert's most cherished secrets, one of his essential weaknesses, would have been laid bare. It was a red-flannel chest-protector, one of those large quasi-hygienic objects that with pills and medicines take the place of beneficial relics and images among the Protestant peoples of Christendom. Always Bert wore this thing; it was his cherished delusion, based on the advice of a shilling fortune-teller at Margate, that he was weak in the lungs.

He now proceeded to unbutton his fetish, to attack it with a penknife, and to thrust the newfound plans between the two layers of imitation Saxony flannel of which it was made. Then with the help of Mr Butteridge's small shaving-mirror and his folding canvas basin he readjusted his costume with the gravity of a man who has taken an irrevocable step in life, buttoned up his jacket, cast the white sheet of the Desert Dervish on one side, washed temperately, shaved, resumed the big cap and the fur overcoat, and, much refreshed by these exercises, surveyed the country below him.

It was indeed a spectacle of incredible magnificence. If perhaps it was not so strange and magnificent as the sunlit cloudland of the previous day, it was at any rate infinitely more interesting. The air was at its utmost clearness, and, except to the south and south-west, there was not a cloud in the sky. The country was hilly, with occasional fir plantations and bleak upland spaces, but also with numerous farms, and the hills were deeply intersected by the gorges of several winding rivers interrupted at intervals by the banked-up ponds and weirs of electric generating wheels. It was dotted with bright-looking, steep-roofed villages, and each showed a distinctive and interesting church beside its wireless telegraph steeple; here and there were large châteaux and parks and white roads, and paths lined with red and white cable posts were extremely conspicuous in the landscape. There were walled enclosures like gardens, and rickyards, and great roofs of barns and many electric dairy centres. The uplands were populous with cattle. At places he would see the track of one of the old railroads (converted now to monorails) dodging through tunnels and crossing embankments, and a rushing hum would mark the passing of a train. Everything was extraordinarily clear as well as minute. Once or twice he saw guns and soldiers, and was reminded of the stir of military preparations he had witnessed on the Bank Holiday in England; but there was nothing to tell him that these military preparations were abnormal, or to explain an occasional faint irregular firing of guns that drifted up to him.

'Wish I knew how to get down,' said Bert, ten thousand feet or so above it all, and gave himself to much futile tugging at the red and white cords. Afterwards he made a sort of inventory of the provisions. Life in the high air was giving him an appalling appetite, and it seemed to him discreet at this stage to portion out his supply into rations. So far as he could see he might pass a week in the air.

At first all the vast panorama below had been as silent as a painted picture. But as the day wore on and the gas diffused slowly from the balloon, it sank earthward again, details increased, men became more visible, and he began to hear the whistle and moan of trains and cars, sounds of cattle, bugles and kettledrums, and presently even men's voices. And at last his guide-rope was trailing again, and he found it possible to attempt a landing. Once or twice, as the rope dragged over cables, he found his hair erect with electricity, and once he had a slight shock, and sparks snapped about the car. He took these things among the chances of the voyage. He had one idea now very clear in his mind, and that was to drop the iron grapnel that hung from the ring.

From the first this attempt was unfortunate, perhaps because the place for descent was ill-chosen. A balloon should come in an empty open space, and he chose a crowd. He made his decision suddenly, and without proper reflection. As he trailed, Bert saw ahead of him one of the most attractive little towns in the world – a cluster of steep gables surmounted by a high church-tower and diversified with trees, walled, and with a fine, large gateway opening out upon a tree-lined high road. All the wires and cables of the countryside converged upon it like guests to entertainment. It had a most homelike and comfortable quality, and it was made gayer by abundant flags. Along the road a quantity of peasant folk, in big pair-wheeled carts and afoot, were coming and going, beside an occasional monorail car; and at the car junction, under the trees outside the town, was a busy little fair of booths. It seemed a warm, human, well-rooted and altogether delightful place to Bert. He came low over the tree-tops, with his grapnel ready to throw, and so anchor him – a curious, interested and interesting guest, so his imagination figured it, in the very middle of it all.

He thought of himself performing feats with the sign language and chance linguistics amidst a circle of admiring rustics. . . .

And then the chapter of adverse accidents began.

The rope made itself unpopular long before the crowd had fully realized his advent over the trees. An elderly and apparently intoxicated peasant in a shiny black hat, and carrying a large crimson umbrella, caught sight of it first as it trailed past him, and was seized with a discreditable ambition to kill it. He pursued it briskly with unpleasant cries. It crossed the road obliquely, splashed into a pan of milk upon a stall and slapped its milky tail athwart a motor-car load of factory girls halted outside the town gates. They screamed loudly. People looked up and saw Bert making what he meant to be genial salutations, but what they considered, in view of the feminine outcry, to be insulting gestures. Then the car hit the roof of the gate-house smartly, snapped a flagstaff, played a tune upon some telegraph wires, and sent a broken wire like a whiplash to do its share in accumulating unpopularity. Bert, by clutching convulsively, just escaped being pitched headlong. Two young soldiers and several peasants shouted things up to him and shook fists at him, and began to run in pursuit as he disappeared over the wall into the town. Admiring rustics, indeed!

The balloon leapt at once, in the manner of balloons when part of their weight is released by touching down, with a sort of flippancy, and in another moment Bert was over a street crowded with peasants and soldiers, that opened into a busy market square. The wave of unfriendliness pursued him.

'Grapnel,' said Bert, and then with an afterthought shouted, '*Têtes*[14] there, you! I say! I say! *Têtes*. Eng it!'

The grapnel clattered down a steeply sloping roof, followed by an avalanche of broken tiles, jumped the street amidst shrieks and cries, and smashed into a plate-glass window with an immense and sickening impact. The balloon rolled nauseatingly, and the car pitched. But the grapnel had not held. It emerged at once bearing on one fluke, with a ridiculous air of fastidious selection, a small child's chair, and pursued by a maddened shopman. It lifted its catch, swung about with an appearance of painful indecision amidst a roar of wrath, and dropped it at last neatly, and as if by inspiration, over the head of a peasant woman in charge of an assortment of cabbages in the marketplace.

Everybody now was aware of the balloon. Everybody was either trying to dodge the grapnel or catch the trail-rope. With a pendulum-like swoop through the crowd that sent people flying right and left, the grapnel came to earth again, tried for and missed a stout gentleman in a blue suit and a straw hat, smacked away a trestle from under a stall of haberdashery, made a cyclist soldier in knickerbockers leap like a chamois, and secured itself uncertainly among the hind legs of a sheep – which made convulsive, ungracious efforts to free itself, and was dragged into a position of rest against a stone cross in the middle of the place. The balloon pulled up with a jerk. In another moment a score of willing hands were tugging it earthward. At the same instant Bert became aware for the first time of a fresh breeze blowing about him.

For some seconds he stood staggering in the car, which now swayed sickeningly, surveying the exasperated crowd below him and trying to collect his mind. He was extraordinarily astonished at this run of mishaps. Were these people really so annoyed? Everybody seemed angry with him. No one seemed interested or amused by his arrival. A disproportionate amount of the outcry had the quality of imprecation – had, indeed, a strong flavour of riot. Several greatly uniformed officials in cocked hats struggled in vain to control the crowd. Fists and sticks were shaken. And when Bert saw a man on the outskirts of the crowd run to a haycart and get a brightly pronged pitchfork, and a blue-clad soldier unbuckle his belt, his doubt whether this little town was after all such a good place for a landing became a certainty.

He had clung to the fancy that they would make something of a hero of him. Now he knew that he was mistaken.

He was perhaps ten feet above the people when he made his decision. His paralysis ceased. He leapt up on the seat, and, at imminent risk of falling headlong, disengaged the grapnel-rope from the toggle that held it, sprang on to the trail-rope and released that also. A hoarse shout of disgust greeted the descent of the grapnel-rope and the swift leap of the balloon, and something – he fancied afterwards it was a turnip – whizzed by his head. The trail-rope followed its fellow. The crowd seemed to jump away from him. With an immense and horrifying rustle the balloon brushed against a telephone pole, and for a tense instant he anticipated either an electric explosion or a bursting of the oiled silk, or both. But fortune was with him.

In another second he was cowering in the bottom of the car, and, released from the weight of the grapnel and the two ropes, rushing up once more through the air. For a time he remained crouching, and when at last he looked out again, the little town was very small and travelling with the rest of lower Germany in a circular orbit round and round the car – or at least it appeared to be doing that.

When he got used to it he found this rotation of the balloon rather convenient; it saved moving about in the car.

§ 5

Late in the afternoon of a pleasant summer day in the year 191–, if one may borrow a mode of phrasing that once found favour with the readers of the late G. P. R. James,[15] a solitary balloonist – replacing the solitary horseman of the classic romances – might have been observed wending his way across Franconia[16] in a north-easterly direction, at a height of about eleven thousand feet above the sea and still spinning slowly. His head was craned over the side of the car, and he surveyed the country below with an expression of profound perplexity; ever and again his lips shaped inaudible words. 'Shootin' at a chap,' for example, and 'I'll come down right enough soon as I find out 'ow.' Over the side of the basket the robe of the Desert Dervish was hanging, an appeal for consideration, an ineffectual white flag.

He was now very distinctly aware that the world below him, so far from being the naïve countryside of his earlier imaginings that day, sleepily unconscious of him and capable of being amazed and nearly reverential at his descent, was acutely irritated by his career, and extremely impatient with the course he was taking. But indeed it was not he who took that course, but his masters, the winds of heaven. Mysterious voices spoke to him in his ear, jerking the words up to him by means of megaphones, in a weird and startling manner, in a great variety of languages. Official-looking persons had signalled to him by means of flag-flapping and arm-waving. On the whole a guttural variant of English prevailed in the sentences that alighted upon the balloon; chiefly he was told to 'gome down or you will be shot'.

'All very well,' said Bert, 'but 'OW?'

Then they shot a little wide of the car. Latterly he had been shot at six or seven times, and once the bullet had gone by with a sound so persuasively like the tearing of silk that he had resigned himself to the prospect of a headlong fall. But either they were aiming near him or they had missed, and as yet nothing was torn but the air about him – and his anxious soul.

He was now enjoying a respite from these attentions, but he felt it was at best an interlude, and he was doing what he could to appreciate his position. Incidentally he was having some hot coffee and pie in an untidy inadvertent manner with an eye fluttering nervously over the side of the car. At first he had ascribed the growing interest in his career to his ill-conceived attempt to land in the bright little upland town, but now he was beginning to realize that the military rather than the civil arm was concerned about him.

He was quite involuntarily playing that weird mysterious part – the part of an International Spy. He was seeing secret things. He had, in fact, crossed the designs of no less a power than the German Empire, he had blundered into the hot focus of Welt-Politik, he was drifting helplessly towards the great Imperial secret, the immense aeronautic park that had been established at a headlong pace in Franconia to develop silently, swiftly and on a colossal scale the great discoveries of Hunstedt and Stossel, and so to give Germany before all other nations a fleet of airships, the air power and the Empire of the world.

Later, just before they shot him down altogether, Bert saw that great area of passionate work, warm lit in the evening light, a great area of upland on which the airships lay like a herd of grazing monsters at their feed. It was a vast busy space stretching away northward as far as he could see, methodically cut up into numbered sheds, gasometers, squad encampments, storage areas, interlaced with the omnipresent monorail lines, and altogether free from overhead wires or cables. Everywhere was the white, black and yellow of Imperial Germany, every-where the black eagles spread their wings. Even without these indications, the large vigorous neatness of everything would have marked it German. Vast multitudes of men went to and fro, many in white and drab fatigue uniforms busy about the balloons, others drilling in sensible drab. Here and there a full uniform glittered.

The airships chiefly engaged his attention, and he knew at once it was three of these he had seen on the previous night, taking advantage of the cloud welkin to manoeuvre unobserved. They were altogether fishlike. For the great airships with which Germany attacked New York in her last gigantic effort for world supremacy – before humanity realized that world supremacy was a dream – were the lineal descendants of the Zeppelin airship[17] that flew over Lake Constance in 1906, and of the Lebaudy[18] navigables that made their memorable excursions over Paris in 1907 and 1908.

These German airships were held together by riblike skeletons of steel and aluminium and a stout inelastic canvas outer skin, within which was an impervious rubber gas-bag, cut up by transverse dissepiments into from fifty to a hundred compartments. These were all absolutely gas tight and filled with hydrogen,[19] and the entire aerostat[20] was kept at any level by means of a long internal ballonette of oiled and toughened silk canvas, into which air could be forced and from which it could be pumped. So the airship could be made either heavier or lighter than air, and losses of weight through the consumption of fuel, the casting of bombs and so forth, could also be compensated by admitting air to sections of the general gas-bag. Ultimately that made a highly explosive mixture; but in all these matters risks must be taken and guarded against. There was a steel axis to the whole affair, a central backbone which terminated in the engine and propeller, and the men and magazines were forward in a series of cabins under the expanded headlike fore part. The engine, which was of the extraordinarily powerful Pforzheim type,[21] that supreme triumph of German invention, was worked by electric controls from this fore part, which was indeed the only really habitable part of the ship. If anything went wrong, the engineers went aft along a rope ladder beneath the frame or along a passage through the gas-chambers. The tendency of the whole affair to roll was partly corrected by a horizontal lateral fin on either side, and steering was chiefly effected by two vertical fins, which normally lay back like gill-flaps on either side of the head. It was indeed a most complete adaptation of the fish form to aerial conditions, the position of swimming bladder, eyes and brain being, however, below instead of above. A striking and unfishlike feature was the apparatus for wireless telegraphy that dangled from the forward cabin – that is to say, under the chin of the fish.

These monsters were capable of ninety miles an hour in a calm, so that they could face and make headway against nearly everything except the fiercest tornado. They varied in length from eight hundred to two thousand feet, and they had a carry- ing power of from seventy to two hundred tons. How many Germany possessed history does not record, but Bert counted nearly eighty great bulks receding in perspective during his brief inspection. Such were the instruments on which she relied to sustain her in her repudiation of the Monroe Doctrine and her bold bid for a share in the empire of the New World. But not altogether did she rely on these; she had also a one-man bomb-throwing *Drachenflieger* of unknown value among her resources.

But the *Drachenflieger* were away in the second great aero- nautic park east of Hamburg, and Bert Smallways saw nothing of them in the bird's-eye view he took of the Franconian establishment before they shot him down. For they shot him down very neatly. They used the new bullets with steel trailers that Wolffe of Engelberg had invented for aerial warfare. The bullet tore past him and made a sort of pop as its trailer rent his balloon – a pop that was followed by a rustling sigh and a steady downward movement. And when in the confusion of the moment he dropped a bag of ballast, the Germans very politely but firmly overcame his scruples by shooting his balloon again twice.

4

THE GERMAN AIR-FLEET

Of all the productions of the human imagination that make the world in which Mr Bert Smallways lived confusingly wonderful, there was none quite so strange, so headlong and disturbing, so noisy and persuasive and dangerous, as the modernizations of patriotism produced by imperial and international politics. In the soul of all men is a liking for kind, a pride in one's own atmosphere, a tenderness for one's mother speech and one's familiar land. Before the coming of the Scientific Age this group of gentle and noble emotions had been a fine factor in the equipment of every worthy human being, a fine factor that had its less amiable aspect in a usually harmless hostility to strange people, and a usually harmless detraction of strange lands. But with the wild rush of change in the pace, scope, materials, scale and possibilities of human life that then occurred, the old boundaries, the old seclusions and separations were violently broken down. All the old settled mental habits and traditions of men found themselves not simply confronted by new conditions, but by constantly renewed and changing new conditions. They had no chance of adapting themselves. They were annihilated or perverted or inflamed beyond recognition.

Bert Smallways' grandfather, in the days when Bun Hill was a village under the sway of Sir Peter Bone's parent, had 'known his place' to the uttermost farthing, touched his hat to his betters, despised and condescended to his inferiors, and hadn't changed an idea from the cradle to the grave. He was Kentish and English, and that meant hops, beer, dog-roses, and the sort of sunshine that was best in the world. Newspapers and politics and visits to 'Lunnon' weren't for the likes of him. Then came the change. These earlier chapters have given an idea of what happened to Bun Hill, and how the flood of novel things had poured over its devoted rusticity. Bert Smallways was only one of countless millions in Europe and America and Asia who, instead of being born rooted in the soil, were born struggling in a torrent they never clearly understood. All the faiths of their fathers had been taken by surprise, and startled into the strangest forms and reactions. Particularly did the fine old tradition of patriotism get perverted and distorted in the rush of the new times. Instead of the sturdy establishment in prejudice of Bert's grandfather, to whom the word 'Frenchified' was the ultimate term of contempt, there flowed through Bert's brain a squittering succession of thinly violent ideas about German competition, about the Yellow Peril,[1] about the Black Menace, about the White Man's Burthen[2] – that is to say Bert's preposterous right to muddle further the naturally very muddled politics of the entirely similar little cads to himself (except for a smear of brown) who smoked cigarettes and rode bicycles in Buluwayo,[3] Kingston (Jamaica), or Bombay. These were Bert's 'Subject Races', and he was ready to die – by proxy in the person of anyone who cared to enlist – to maintain his hold upon that right. It kept him awake at nights to think that he might lose it.

The essential fact of the politics of the age in which Bert Smallways lived – the age that blundered at last into the catastrophe of the War in the Air – was a very simple one, if only people had had the intelligence to be simple about it. The development of Science had altered the scale of human affairs. By means of rapid mechanical traction it had brought men nearer together, so much nearer socially, economically, physically, that the old separations into nations and kingdoms were no longer possible, a newer, wider synthesis was not only needed but imperatively demanded. Just as the once independent dukedoms of France had to fuse into a nation, so now the nations had to adapt themselves to a wider coalescence, they had to keep what was precious and practicable, and concede

what was obsolete and dangerous. A saner world would have
perceived this patent need for a reasonable synthesis, would
have discussed it temperately, achieved and gone on to organize
the great civilization that was manifestly possible to mankind.
The world of Bert Smallways did nothing of the sort. Its national
governments, its national interests, would not hear of anything
so obvious; they were too suspicious of each other, too wanting
in generous imagination. They began to behave like ill-bred
people in a crowded public car, to squeeze against one another,
elbow, thrust, dispute and quarrel. Vain to point out to them
that they had only to rearrange themselves to be comfortable.
Everywhere, all over the world, the historian of the early twentieth century finds the same thing, the flow and rearrangement
of human affairs inextricably entangled by the old areas, the
old prejudices and a sort of heated irascible stupidity; and
everywhere congested nations in inconvenient areas, slopping
population and produce into each other, annoying each other
with tariffs and every possible commercial vexation, and threatening each other with navies and armies that grew every year
more portentous.

It is impossible now to estimate how much of the intellectual
and physical energy of the world was wasted in military preparation and equipment, but it was an enormous proportion.
Great Britain spent upon army and navy money and capacity
that, directed into the channels of physical culture and education, would have made the British the aristocracy of the
world. Her rulers could have kept the whole population learn-
ing and exercising up to the age of eighteen, and made a broad-
chested and intelligent man of every Bert Smallways in the
islands, had they given the resources they spent in war material
to the making of men. Instead of which they waggled flags at
him until he was fourteen, incited him to cheer, and then turned
him out of school to begin that career of private enterprise we
have compactly recorded. France achieved similar imbecilities;
Germany was, if possible, worse; Russia under the waste and
stresses of militarism festered towards bankruptcy and decay.
All Europe was producing big guns and countless swarms of
little Smallways. The Asiatic peoples had been forced in self-

defence into a like diversion of the new powers science had brought them. On the eve of the outbreak of the war there were six great powers in the world and a cluster of smaller ones, each armed to the teeth and straining every nerve to get ahead of the others in deadliness of equipment and military efficiency. The great powers were first the United States, a nation addicted to commerce, but roused to military necessities by the efforts of Germany to expand into South America, and by the natural consequences of her own unwary annexations of land in the very teeth of Japan. She maintained two immense fleets east and west, and internally she was in violent conflict between Federal and state governments upon the question of universal service in a defensive militia. Next came the great alliance of Eastern Asia, a close-knit coalescence of China and Japan, advancing with rapid strides year by year to predominance in the world's affairs. Then the German alliance still struggled to achieve its dream of imperial expansion, and its imposition of the German language upon a forcibly united Europe. These were the three most spirited and aggressive powers in the world. Far more pacific was the British Empire, perilously scattered over the globe, and distracted now by insurrectionary movements in Ireland and among all its Subject Races. It had given these Subject Races cigarettes, boots, bowler hats, cricket, race meetings, cheap revolvers, petroleum, the factory system of industry, halfpenny newspapers in both English and the vernacular, inexpensive university degrees, motor-bicycles and electric trams; it had produced a considerable literature expressing contempt for the Subject Races and rendered it freely accessible to them, and it had been content to believe that nothing would result from these stimulants because somebody once wrote 'the immemorial east'; and also, in the inspired words of Kipling –

East is east and west is west,
And never the twain shall meet.[4]

Instead of which, Egypt, India and the subject countries generally had produced new generations in a state of passionate indignation and the utmost energy, activity and modernity. The governing class in Great Britain was slowly adapting itself to a new conception of the Subject Races as waking peoples, and finding its efforts to keep the Empire together under these strains and changing ideas greatly impeded by the entirely sporting spirit with which Bert Smallways at home (by the million) cast his vote, and by the tendency of his more highly coloured equivalents to be disrespectful to irascible officials. Their impertinence was excessive; it was no mere stone-throwing and shouting. They would quote Burns at them and Mill and Darwin,[5] and confute them in arguments.

Even more pacific than the British Empire were France and its allies, the Latin powers, heavily armed states indeed but reluctant warriors, and in many ways socially and politically leading western civilization. Russia was a pacific power perforce, divided within itself, torn between revolutionaries and reactionaries who were equally incapable of social reconstruction, and so sinking towards a tragic disorder of chronic political vendetta. Wedged in among these portentous larger bulks, swayed and threatened by them, the smaller states of the world maintained a precarious independence, each keeping itself armed as dangerously as its utmost ability could contrive.

So it came about that in every country a great and growing proportion of its energetic and inventive men was busied, either for offensive or defensive ends, in elaborating the apparatus of war, until the accumulating tensions should reach the breaking-point. Each power sought to keep its preparations secret, to hold new weapons in reserve, to anticipate and learn the preparations of its rivals. The feeling of danger from fresh discoveries affected the patriotic imagination of every people in the world. Now it was rumoured the British had an overwhelming gun, now the French an invincible rifle, now the Japanese a new explosive, now the Americans a submarine that would drive every ironclad from the seas. Each time there would be a war panic.

The strength and heart of the nations was given to the thought of war, and yet the mass of their citizens was a teeming democracy as heedless of and unfitted for fighting, mentally, morally, physically, as any population has ever been – or, one ventures to add, could ever be. That was the paradox of the time. It was a period altogether unique in the world's history. The apparatus of warfare, the art and method of fighting, changed absolutely every dozen years in a stupendous progress towards perfection, and people grew less and less warlike, and there was no war.

And then at last it came. It came as a surprise to all the world because its real causes were hidden. Relations were strained between Germany and the United States because of the intense exasperation of a tariff conflict and the ambiguous attitude of the former power towards the Monroe Doctrine, and they were strained between the United States and Japan because of the perennial citizenship question. But in both cases these were standing causes of offence. The real deciding cause, it is now known, was the perfecting of the Pforzheim engine by Germany and the consequent possibility of a rapid and entirely practicable airship. At that time Germany was by far the most efficient power in the world, better organized for swift and secret action, better equipped with the resources of modern science, and with her official and administrative classes at a higher level of education and training. These things she knew, and she exaggerated that knowledge to the pitch of contempt for the secret counsels of her neighbours. It may be that with the habit of self-confidence her spying upon them had grown less thorough. Moreover, she had a tradition of unsentimental and unscrupulous action that vitiated her international outlook profoundly. With the coming of these new weapons her collective intelligence thrilled with the sense that now her moment had come. Once again in the history of progress it seemed she held the decisive weapon. Now she might strike and conquer – before the others had anything but experiments in the air.

Particularly she must strike America swiftly, because there, if anywhere, lay the chance of an aerial rival. It was known that America possessed a flying machine of considerable practical value, developed out of the Wright model; but it was not supposed that the Washington War Office had made any wholesale attempts to create an aerial navy. It was necessary to strike before they could do so. France had a fleet of slow navigables, several dating from 1908, that could make no possible headway against the new type. They had been built solely for reconnoitring purposes on the eastern frontier, they were mostly too small to carry more than a couple of dozen men without arms or provisions, and not one could do forty miles an hour. Great Britain, it seemed, in an access of meanness, temporized and wrangled with the imperial-spirited Butteridge and his extraordinary invention. That also was not in play – and could not be for some months at the earliest. From Asia there came no sign. The Germans explained this by saying the yellow peoples were without invention. No other competitor was worth considering. 'Now or never,' said the Germans – 'now or never we may seize the air – as once the British seized the seas! While all the other powers are still experimenting.'

Swift and systematic and secret were their preparations, and their plan most excellent. So far as their knowledge went, America was the only dangerous possibility; America, which was also now the leading trade rival of Germany and one of the chief barriers to her Imperial expansion. So at once they would strike at America. They would fling a great force across the Atlantic heavens and bear America down unwarned and unprepared.

Altogether it was a well-imagined and most hopeful and spirited enterprise, having regard to the information in the possession of the German Government. The chances of it being a successful surprise were very great. The airship and the flying machine were very different things from ironclads, which take a couple of years to build. Given hands, given plant, they could be made innumerably in a few weeks. Once the needful parks and foundries were organized, airships and *Drachenflieger* could be poured into the sky. Indeed, when the time came, they did pour into the sky like, as a bitter French writer put it, flies roused from filth.

The attack upon America was to be the first move in this tremendous game. But no sooner had it started than instantly the aeronautic parks were to proceed to put together and inflate the second fleet which was to dominate Europe and manoeuvre significantly over London, Paris, Rome, St Petersburg, or wherever else its moral effect was required. A World Surprise it was to be – no less, a World Conquest; and it is wonderful how near the calmly adventurous minds that planned it came to succeeding in their colossal design.

Von Sternberg was the Moltke[6] of this War in the Air, but it was the curious hard romanticism of Prince Karl Albert[7] that won over the hesitating Emperor to the scheme. Prince Karl Albert was indeed the central figure of the world drama. He was the darling of the Imperialist spirit in Germany, and the ideal of the new aristocratic feeling – the new Chivalry, as it was called – that followed the overthrow of Socialism through its internal divisions and lack of discipline, and the concentration of wealth in the hands of a few great families. He was compared by obsequious flatterers to the Black Prince,[8] to Alcibiades,[9] to the young Caesar. To many he seemed Nietzsche's Over-man[10] revealed. He was big and blond and virile, and splendidly non-moral. The first great feat that startled Europe, and almost brought about a new Trojan war, was his abduction of the Princess Helena of Norway and his blank refusal to marry her. Then followed his marriage with Gretchen Krass, a Swiss girl of peerless beauty. Then came the gallant rescue, which almost cost him his life, of three drowning tailors whose boat had upset in the sea near Heligoland.[11] For that and his victory over the American yacht *Defender*, C.C.I.,[12] the Emperor forgave him and placed him in control of the new aeronautic arm of the German forces. This he developed with marvellous energy and ability, being resolved, as he said, to give to Germany land and sea and sky. The national passion for aggression found in him its supreme exponent, and achieved through him its realization in this astounding war. But his fascination was more than national; all over the world his ruthless strength dominated minds as the Napoleonic legend had dominated minds. Englishmen turned in disgust from the slow, complex, civilized methods of their national politics to this uncompromising forceful figure. Frenchmen believed in him. Poems were written to him in American.

He made the war.

Quite equally with the rest of the world, the general German population was taken by surprise by the swift vigour of the Imperial government. A considerable literature of military forecasts beginning as early as 1906 with Rudolf Martin,[13] the author not merely of a brilliant book of anticipations but of a proverb, 'The future of Germany lies in the air', had, however, partially prepared the German imagination for some such enterprise.

§ 2

Of all these world forces and gigantic designs Bert Smallways knew nothing until he found himself in the very focus of it all and gaped down amazed on the spectacle of that giant herd of airships. Each one seemed as long as the Strand,[14] and as big about as Trafalgar Square. Some must have been a third of a mile in length. He had never before seen anything so vast and disciplined as this tremendous park. For the first time in his life he really had an intimation of the extraordinary and quite important things of which a contemporary may go in ignorance. He had always clung to the illusion that Germans were fat, absurd men who smoked china pipes, and were addicted to knowledge and horseflesh and sauerkraut and indigestible things generally.

His bird's-eye view was quite transitory. He ducked at the first shot; and directly his balloon began to drop, his mind ran confusedly upon how he might explain himself, and whether he should pretend to be Butteridge or not. 'O, Lord!' he groaned, in an agony of indecision. Then his eye caught his sandals, and he felt a spasm of self-disgust. 'They'll think I'm a bloomin' idiot,' he said, and then it was he rose up desperately and threw over the sandbag and provoked the second and third shots.

It flashed into his head, as he cowered in the bottom of the car, that he might avoid all sorts of disagreeable and complicated explanations by pretending to be mad.

That was his last idea before the airships seemed to rush up about him as if to look at him, and his car hit the ground and bounded and pitched him out on his head. . . .

He awoke to find himself famous, and to hear a voice crying, 'Booteraidge! Ja! Ja! Herr Booteraidge! Selbst!'[15]

He was lying on a little patch of grass beside one of the main avenues of the aeronautic park. The airships receded down a great vista, an immense perspective, and the blunt prow of each was adorned with a black eagle of a hundred feet or so spread. Down the other side of the avenue ran a series of gas generators, and big hosepipes trailed everywhere across the intervening space. Close at hand was his now nearly deflated balloon and the car on its side looking minutely small, a mere broken toy, a shrivelled bubble, in contrast with the gigantic bulk of the nearer airship. This he saw almost end-on, rising like a cliff and sloping forward towards its fellow on the other side so as to overshadow the alley between them. There was a crowd of excited people about him, mostly big men in tight uniforms. Everybody was talking, and several were shouting, in German; he knew that, because they splashed and aspirated sounds like startled kittens. Only one phrase, repeated again and again, could he recognize – the name of 'Herr Booteraidge'.

'Gollys!' said Bert. 'They've spotted it.'

'Besser,'[16] said someone, and some rapid German followed.

He perceived that close at hand was a field-telephone, and that a tall officer in blue was talking thereat about him. Another stood close beside him with the portfolio of drawings and photographs in his hand. They looked round at him.

'Do you spik Cherman, Herr Booteraidge?'

Bert decided that he had better be dazed. He did his best to seem thoroughly dazed. 'Where *am* I?' he asked.

Volubility prevailed. 'Der Prinz' was mentioned. A bugle sounded far away, and its call was taken up by one nearer, and then by one close at hand. This seemed to increase the excitement greatly. A monorail car bumbled past. The telephone bell rang passionately, and the tall officer seemed to engage in a heated altercation. Then he approached the group about Bert, calling out something about 'mitbringen'.[17]

An earnest-faced, emaciated man with a white moustache appealed to Bert. 'Herr Booteraidge, sir, we are chust to start!'

'Where am I?' Bert repeated.

Someone shook him by the other shoulder. 'Are you Herr Booteraidge?' he asked.

'Herr Booteraidge, we are chust to start!' repeated the white moustache, and then helplessly, 'What is de goot? What can we do?'

The officer from the telephone repeated his sentence about 'Der Prinz' and 'mitbringen'. The man with the moustache stared for a moment, grasped an idea and became violently energetic, stood up and bawled directions at unseen people. Questions were asked, and the doctor at Bert's side answered, 'Ja! Ja!' several times, also something about 'Kopf'.[18] With a certain urgency he got Bert rather unwillingly to his feet. Two huge soldiers in grey advanced upon Bert and seized hold of him. ''Ullo!' said Bert, startled. 'What's up?'

'It is all right,' the doctor explained; 'they are to carry you.'

'Where?' asked Bert, unanswered.

'Put your arms roundt their – hals[19] – round them!'

'Yes! but where?'

'Hold tight!'

Before Bert could decide to say anything more he was whisked up by the two soldiers. They joined hands to seat him, and his arms were put about their necks. 'Vorwärts!'[20] Someone ran before him with the portfolio, and he was borne rapidly along the broad avenue between the gas generators and the airships, rapidly and on the whole smoothly except that once or twice his bearers stumbled over hosepipes and nearly let him down.

He was wearing Mr Butteridge's Alpine cap, and his little shoulders were in Mr Butteridge's fur-lined overcoat, and he had responded to Mr Butteridge's name. The sandals dangled helplessly. Gaw! Everybody seemed in a devil of a hurry. Why? He was carried joggling and gaping through the twilight, marvelling beyond measure.

The systematic arrangement of wide convenient spaces, the quantities of businesslike soldiers everywhere, the occasional neat piles of material, the ubiquitous monorail lines, and the towering shiplike hulls about him, reminded him a little of impressions he had got as a boy on a visit to Woolwich

Dockyard.[21] The whole camp reflected the colossal power of modern science that had created it. A peculiar strangeness was produced by the lowness of the electric light, which lay upon the ground, casting all shadows upwards, and making a grotesque shadow figure of himself and his bearers on the airship sides, fusing all three of them into a monstrous animal with attenuated legs and an immense fan-like humped body. The lights were on the ground because as far as possible all poles and standards had been dispensed with to prevent complications when the airships rose.

It was deep twilight now, a tranquil blue-skyed evening; everything rose out from the splashes of light upon the ground into dim translucent tall masses; within the cavities of the airships small inspection lamps glowed like cloud-veiled stars, and made them seem marvellously unsubstantial. Each airship had its name in black letters on white on either flank, and forward the Imperial eagle sprawled, an overwhelming bird in the dimness. Bugles sounded, monorail cars of quiet soldiers slithered burbling by. The cabins under the heads of the airships were being lit up; doors opened in them, and revealed padded passages. Now and then a voice gave directions to workers indistinctly seen.

There was a matter of sentinels, gangways and a long narrow passage, a scramble over a disorder of baggage, and then Bert found himself lowered to the ground and standing in the door-way of a spacious cabin – it was perhaps ten feet square and eight high, furnished with crimson padding and aluminium. A tall, bird-like young man with a small head, a long nose and very pale hair, with his hands full of things like shaving-strops,[22] boot-trees, hairbrushes and toilet tidies, was saying things about Gott and thunder and Dummer[23] Booteraidge as Bert entered. He was apparently an evicted occupant. Then he vanished, and Bert was lying back on a locker in the corner with a pillow under his head and the door of the cabin shut upon him. He was alone. Everybody had hurried out again astonishingly.

'Gollys!' said Bert. 'What next?'

He stared about him at the room.

'Butteridge! Shall I try to keep it up, or shan't I?'

The room he was in puzzled him. ' 'Tisn't a prison and 'tisn't a norfis?'²⁴ Then the old trouble came uppermost. 'I wish to 'eaven I 'adn't these silly sandals on,' he cried querulously to the universe. 'They give the whole blessed show away.'

§ 3

His door was flung open, and a compact young man in uniform appeared, carrying Mr Butteridge's portfolio, rucksack and shaving-glass. 'I say!' he said, in faultless English, as he entered. He had a beaming face, and a sort of pinkish blond hair. 'Fancy you being Butteridge!'

He slapped Bert's meagre luggage down.

'We'd have started,' he said, 'in another half-hour! You didn't give yourself much time!'

He surveyed Bert curiously. His gaze rested for a fraction of a moment on the sandals. 'You ought to have come on your flying machine, Mr Butteridge.'

He didn't wait for an answer. 'The Prince says I've got to look after you. Naturally he can't see you now, but he thinks your coming's providential. Last grace of Heaven. Like a sign. Hullo!'

He stood still and listened.

Outside there was a going to and fro of feet, a sound of distant bugles suddenly taken up and echoed close at hand, men called out in loud tones short, sharp, seemingly vital things, and were answered distantly. A bell jangled, and feet went down the corridor. Then came a stillness more distracting than sound, and then a great gurgling and rushing and splashing of water. The young man's eyebrows lifted. He hesitated, and dashed out of the room. Presently came a stupendous bang to vary the noises without, then a distant cheering. The young-man reappeared.

'They're running the water out of the ballonette already.'

'What water?' asked Bert.

'The water that anchored us. Artful dodge. Eh?' Bert tried to take it in.

'Of course!' said the compact young man. 'You don't understand.'

A gentle quivering crept upon Bert's senses. 'That's the engine,' said the compact young man approvingly. 'Now we shan't be long.'

Another long listening interval.

The cabin swayed. 'By Jove! we're starting already,' he cried. 'We're starting!'

'Starting!' cried Bert, sitting up. 'Where?'

But the young man was out of the room again. There were noises of German in the passage, and other nerve-shaking sounds.

The swaying increased. The young man reappeared. 'We're off, right enough!'

'I say!' said Bert, 'where are we starting? I wish you'd explain. What's this place? I don't understand.'

'What!' cried the young man, 'you don't understand?'

'No. I'm all dazed-like from that crack on the nob[25] I got. Where *are* we? *Where* are we starting?'

'Don't you know where you are – what this is?'

'Not a bit of it! What's all the swaying and the row?'

'What a lark!' cried the young man. 'I say! What a thundering lark! Don't you know? We're off to America, and you haven't realized. You've just caught us by a neck. You're on the blessed old flagship with the Prince. You won't miss anything. Whatever's on, you bet the *Vaterland*[26] will be there.'

'Us! – off to America?'

'Ra-ther!'[27]

'In an airship?'

'What do *you* think?'

'Me! going to America on an airship! After that balloon! 'Ere! I say – I don't want to go! I want to walk about on my legs. Let me get out! I didn't understand.'

He made a dive for the door.

The young man arrested Bert with a gesture, took hold of a strap, lifted up a panel in the padded wall, and a window appeared. 'Look!' he said. Side by side they looked out.

'Gaw!' said Bert. 'We're going up!'

'We are!' said the young man, cheerfully; 'fast!'

They were rising in the air smoothly and quietly, and moving

slowly to the throb of the engine athwart the aeronautic park.
Down below it stretched, dimly geometrical in the darkness,
picked out at regular intervals by glow-worm spangles of light.
One black gap in the long line of grey, round-backed airships
marked the position from which the *Vaterland* had come.
Beside it a second monster now rose softly, released from its
bonds and cables, into the air. Then, taking a beautifully exact
distance, a third ascended, and then a fourth.

'Too late, Mr Butteridge!' the young man remarked. 'We're
off! I dare say it *is* a bit of a shock to you, but there you are!
The Prince said you'd have to come.'

'Look 'ere,' said Bert. 'I really *am* dazed. What's this thing?
Where are we going?'

'This, Mr Butteridge,' said the young man, taking pains to
be explicit, 'is an airship. It's the flagship of Prince Karl Albert.
This is the German air-fleet, and it is going over to America, to
give that spirited people "what for". The only thing we were
at all uneasy about was your invention. And here you are!'

'But! – you a German?' asked Bert.

'Lieutenant Kurt. Luft-lieutenant Kurt, at your service.'

'But you speak English!'

'Mother was English – went to school in England. Afterwards, Rhodes scholar.[28] German none the less for that.
Detailed for the present, Mr Butteridge, to look after you.
You're shaken by your fall. It's all right, really. They're going
to buy your machine and everything. You sit down, and take it
quite calmly. You'll soon get the hang of the position.'

§ 4

Bert sat down on the locker collecting his mind, and the young
man talked to him about the airship.

He was really a very tactful young man indeed, in a natural
sort of way. 'Dare say all this is new to you,' he said; 'not your
sort of machine. These cabins aren't half bad.'

He got up and walked round the little apartment, showing
its points.

'Here is the bed,' he said, whipping down a couch from the

wall and throwing it back again with a click. 'Here are toilet things,' and he opened a neatly arranged cupboard. 'Not much washing. No water we've got; no water at all except for drinking. No baths or anything until we get to America and land. Rub over with loofah. One pint of hot for shaving. That's all. In the locker below you are rugs and blankets; you will need them presently. They say it gets cold. I don't know. Never been up before. Except a little work with gliders – which is mostly going down. Three-quarters of the chaps in the fleet haven't. Here's a folding chair and table behind the door. Compact, eh?'

He took the chair and balanced it on his little finger. 'Pretty light, eh? Aluminium and magnesium alloy and a vacuum inside. All these cushions stuffed with hydrogen. Foxy! The whole ship's like that. And not a man in the fleet, except the Prince and one or two others, over eleven stone. Couldn't sweat the Prince, you know. We'll go all over the thing tomorrow. I'm frightfully keen on it.'

He beamed at Bert. 'You *do* look young,' he remarked. 'I always thought you'd be an old man with a beard – a sort of philosopher. I don't know why one should expect clever people always to be old. I do.'

Bert parried that compliment a little awkwardly, and then the lieutenant was struck with the riddle why Herr Butteridge had not come in his own flying machine.

'It's a long story,' said Bert. 'Look here!' he said abruptly, 'I wish you'd lend me a pair of slippers, or something. I'm regular sick of these sandals. They're rotten things. I've been trying them for a friend.'

'Right O!'

The ex-Rhodes scholar whisked out of the room and reappeared with a considerable choice of footwear, pumps, cloth bath-slippers, and a purple pair adorned with golden sunflowers.

But these he repented of at the last moment. 'I don't even wear them myself,' he said. 'Only brought 'em in the zeal of the moment.' He laughed confidentially. 'Had 'em worked for me – in Oxford. By a friend. Take 'em everywhere.'

So Bert chose the pumps.

The lieutenant broke into a cheerful snigger. 'Here we are trying on slippers,' he said, 'and the world going by like a panorama below. Rather a lark, eh? Look!'

Bert peeped with him out of the window, looking from the bright pettiness of the red-and-silver cabin into a dark immensity. The land below, except for a lake, was black and featureless, and the other airships were hidden. 'See more outside,' said the lieutenant. 'Let's go! There's a sort of little gallery.'

He led the way into the long passage, which was lit by one small electric light, past some notices in German to an open balcony and a light ladder and gallery of metal lattice overhanging empty space. Bert followed his leader down to the gallery slowly and cautiously. From it he was able to watch the wonderful spectacle of the first air-fleet flying through the night. They flew in a wedge-shaped formation, the *Vaterland* highest and leading, the tail receding into the corners of the sky. They flew in long, regular undulations, great dark fish-like shapes, showing hardly any light at all, the engines making a throb-throb-throbbing sound that was very audible out on the gallery. They were going at a level of five or six thousand feet, and rising steadily. Below the country lay silent, a clear darkness dotted and lined out with clusters of furnaces, and the lit streets of a group of big towns. The world seemed to lie in a bowl; the overhanging bulk of the airship above hid all but the lowest levels of the sky.

They watched the landscape for a space.

'Jolly it must be to invent things,' said the lieutenant suddenly. 'How did you come to think of your machine first?'

'Worked it out,' said Bert, after a pause. 'Jest ground away at it.'

'Our people are frightfully keen on you. They thought the British had got you. Weren't the British keen?'

'In a way,' said Bert. 'Still – it's a long story.'

'I think it's an immense thing – to invent. I couldn't invent a thing to save my life.'

They both fell silent, watching the darkened world and following their thoughts until a bugle summoned them to a belated dinner. Bert was suddenly alarmed. 'Don't you 'ave to dress and things?' he said. 'I've always been too hard at Science and things to go into Society and all that.'

'No fear,' said Kurt. 'Nobody's got more than the clothes they wear. We're travelling light. You might perhaps take your overcoat off. They've an electric radiator each end of the room.'

And so presently Bert found himself sitting to eat in the presence of the 'German Alexander'[29] – that great and puissant Prince, Prince Karl Albert, the War Lord, the hero of two hemispheres. He was a handsome blond man, with deep-set eyes, a snub nose, upturned moustache, and long white hands. He sat higher than the others, under a black eagle with wide-spread wings and the German Imperial flags; he was, as it were, enthroned, and it struck Bert greatly that as he ate he did not look at people, but over their heads like one who sees visions. Twenty officers of various ranks stood about the table – and Bert. They all seemed extremely curious to see the famous Butteridge, and their astonishment at his appearance was ill-controlled. The Prince gave him a dignified salutation, to which, by an inspiration, he bowed. Standing next the Prince was a brown-faced, wrinkled man with silver spectacles and fluffy, dingy-grey side-whiskers, who regarded Bert with a peculiar and disconcerting attention. The company sat after ceremonies Bert could not understand. At the other end of the table was the bird-faced officer Bert had dispossessed, still looking hostile and whispering about Bert to his neighbour. Two soldiers waited. The dinner was a plain one – a soup, some fresh mutton and cheese – and there was very little talk.

A curious solemnity indeed brooded over everyone. Partly this was reaction after the intense toil and restrained excitement of starting; partly it was the overwhelming sense of strange new experiences, of portentous adventure. The Prince was lost in thought. He roused himself to drink to the Emperor in champagne, and the company cried 'Hoch!'[30] like men repeating responses in church.

No smoking was permitted, but some of the officers went down to the little open gallery to chew tobacco. No lights whatever were safe amidst that bundle of inflammable things.

Bert suddenly fell yawning and shivering. He was overwhelmed by a sense of his own insignificance amidst these great rushing monsters of the air. He felt life was too big for him – too much for him altogether.

He said something to Kurt about his head, went up the steep ladder from the swaying little gallery into the airship again, and so, as if it were a refuge, to bed.

§ 5

Bert slept for a time, and then his sleep was broken by dreams. Mostly he was fleeing from formless terrors down an interminable passage in an airship – a passage paved at first with ravenous trapdoors, and then with openwork canvas of the most careless description.

'Gaw!' said Bert, turning over after his seventh fall through infinite space that night.

He sat up in the darkness and nursed his knees. The progress of the airship was not nearly so smooth as a balloon; he could feel a regular swaying up, up, up and then down, down, down, and the throbbing and tremulous quiver of the engines.

His mind began to teem with memories – more memories and more.

Through them, like a struggling swimmer in broken water, came the perplexing question, what am I to do tomorrow? Tomorrow, Kurt had told him, the Prince's secretary, the Graf von Winterfeld, would come to him and discuss his flying machine, and then he would see the Prince. He would have to stick it out now that he was Butteridge, and sell his invention. And then, if they found him out! He had a vision of infuriated Butteridges. . . . Suppose after all he owned up? Pretended it was their misunderstanding? He began to scheme devices for selling the secret and circumventing Butteridge.

What should he ask for the thing? Somehow twenty thousand pounds struck him as about the sum indicated.

He fell into that despondency that lies in wait in the small hours. He had got too big a job on – too big a job. . . .

Memories swamped his scheming.

'Where was I this time last night?'

He recapitulated his evenings tediously and lengthily. Last night he had been up above the clouds in Butteridge's balloon. He thought of the moment when he dropped through them and saw the cold twilight sea close below. He still remembered that disagreeable incident with a nightmare vividness. And the night before he and Grubb had been looking for cheap lodgings at Littlestone in Kent. How remote that seemed now. It might be years ago. For the first time he thought of his fellow Desert Dervish, left with the two red-painted bicycles on Dymchurch sands. ''E won't make much of a show of it, not without me. Any'ow 'e did 'ave the treasury – such as it was – in his pocket!' ... The night before that was Bank Holiday night, and they had sat discussing their minstrel enterprise, drawing up a programme and rehearsing steps. And the night before was Whit Sunday.

'Lord!' cried Bert, 'what a doing that motor-bicycle give me!' He recalled the empty flapping of the eviscerated cushion, the feeling of impotence as the flames rose again.

From among the confused memories of that tragic flare one little figure emerged very bright and poignantly sweet, Edna, crying back reluctantly from the departing motor-car, 'See you to-morrer, Bert?'

Other memories of Edna clustered round that impression. They led Bert's mind step by step to an agreeable state that found expression in, 'I'll marry 'er if she don't look out.' And then in a flash it followed in his mind that if he sold the Butteridge secret he could! Suppose after all he did get twenty thousand pounds; such sums have been paid! With that he could buy house and garden, buy new clothes beyond dreaming, buy a motor, travel, have every delight of the civilized life as he knew it, for himself and Edna. Of course, risks were involved. 'I'll 'ave old Butteridge on my track, I expect!'

He meditated upon that. He declined again to despondency. As yet he was only in the beginning of the adventure. He had still to deliver the goods and draw the cash. And before that— Just now he was by no means on his way home. He was flying off to America to fight there. 'Not much fighting,' he considered;

'all our own way.' Still, if a shell did happen to hit the *Vaterland* on the underside! . . .

'S'pose I ought to make my will.'

He lay back for some time composing wills – chiefly in favour of Edna. He had settled now it was to be twenty thousand pounds. He left a number of minor legacies. The wills became more and more meandering and extravagant. . . .

He woke from the eighth repetition of his nightmare fall through space. 'This flying gets on one's nerves,' he said.

He could feel the airship diving down, down, down, then slowly swinging to up, up, up. Throb, throb, throb, throb, quivered the engine.

He got up presently and wrapped himself about with Mr Butteridge's overcoat and all the blankets, for the air was very keen. Then he peeped out of the window to see a grey dawn breaking over clouds, then turned up his light and bolted his door, sat down to the table and produced his chest-protector.

He smoothed the crumpled plans with his hand, and contemplated them. Then he referred to the other drawings in the portfolio. Twenty thousand pounds. If he worked it right! It was worth trying, anyhow.

Presently he opened the drawer in which Kurt had put paper and writing materials.

Bert Smallways was by no means a stupid person, and up to a certain limit he had not been badly educated. His board-school had taught him to draw up to certain limits, taught him to calculate and understand a specification. If at that point his country had tired of its efforts, and handed him over unfinished to scramble for a living in an atmosphere of advertisements and individual enterprise, that was really not his fault. He was as his State had made him, and the reader must not imagine because he was a little Cockney[31] cad, that he was absolutely incapable of grasping the idea of the Butteridge flying machine. But he found it stiff and perplexing. His motor-bicycle and Grubb's experiments and the 'mechanical drawing' he had done in standard seven all helped him out; and, moreover, the maker of these drawings, whoever he was, had been anxious to make his intentions plain. Bert copied sketches, he made notes, he made a quite tolerable and intelligent copy of the essential drawings and sketches of the others. Then he fell into a meditation upon them.

At last he rose with a sigh, folded up the originals that had formerly been in his chest-protector and put them into the breast-pocket of his jacket, and then very carefully deposited the copies he had made in the place of the originals. He had no very clear plan in his mind in doing this, except that he hated the idea of altogether parting with the secret. For a long time he meditated profoundly – nodding. Then he turned out his light and went to bed again and schemed himself to sleep.

§ 6

The hochgeborene[32] Graf von Winterfeld was also a light sleeper that night, but then he was one of those people who sleep little and play chess problems in their heads to while away the time – and that night he had a particularly difficult problem to solve.

He came in upon Bert while he was still in bed in the glow of the sunlight reflected from the North Sea below, consuming the rolls and coffee a soldier had brought him. He had a portfolio under his arm, and in the clear, early morning light his dingy grey hair and heavy, silver-rimmed spectacles made him look almost benevolent. He spoke English fluently, but with a strong German flavour. He was particularly bad with his 'b's', and his 'th's' softened towards weak 'zd's'. He called Bert explosively, 'Pooterage'. He began with some indistinct civilities, bowed, took a folding table and chair from behind the door, put the former between himself and Bert, sat down on the latter, coughed drily and opened his portfolio. Then he put his elbows on the table, pinched his lower lip with his two forefingers and regarded Bert disconcertingly with magnified eyes. 'You came to us, Herr Pooterage, against your will,' he said at last.

''Ow d'you make that out?' asked Bert, after a pause of astonishment.

'I chuge by ze maps in your car. Zey were all English. And your provisions. Zey were all picnic. Also your cords were

entangled. You haf been tugging – but no good. You could not
manage ze balloon, and anuzzer power than yours prought you
to us. Is it not so?'

Bert thought.

'Also – where is ze laty?'

' 'Ere! – what lady?'

'You started with a laty. That is evident. You shtarted for an
afternoon excursion – a picnic. A man of your temperament –
he would take a laty. She was not wiz you in your balloon when
you came down at Dornhof. No! Only her chacket! It is your
affair. Still I am curious.'

Bert reflected. ' 'Ow d'you know that?'

'I chuge by ze nature of your farious provisions. I cannot
account, Mr Pooterage, for ze laty, what you haf done with
her. Nor can I tell why you should wear nature-sandals, nor
why you should wear such cheap plue clothes. Zese are outside my instructions. Trifles, perhaps. Officially they are to be
ignored. Laties come and go – I am a man of ze worldt. I haf
known wise men wear sandals and efen practise vegetarian
habits. I haf known men – or at any rate I haf known chemists
– who did not schmoke. You haf, no doubt, put ze laty down
somewhere. Well. Let us get to business. A higher power' – his
voice changed its emotional quality, his magnified eyes seemed
to dilate – 'has prought you and your secret straight to us. So!'
– he bowed his head – 'so pe it. It is ze Destiny of Chermany
and my Prince. I can undershtandt you always carry zat secret.
You are afraidt of roppers and spies. So it comes wiz you – to
us. Mr Pooterage, Chermany will puy it.'

'Will she?'

'She will,' said the secretary, looking hard at Bert's abandoned sandals in the corner of the locker. He roused himself,
consulted a paper of notes for a moment, and Bert eyed
his brown and wrinkled face with expectation and terror. 'Chermany, I am instructed to say,' said the secretary, with his eyes
on the table and his notes spread out, 'has always been willing
to puy your secret. We haf indeed peen eager to acquire it –
fery eager; and it was only ze fear zat you might be, on patriotic
groundts, acting in collusion with your Pritish War Office zat

has made us discreet in offering for your marvellous invention through intermediaries. We haf no hesitation whatefer now, I am instructed, in agreeing to your proposal of a hundert tousand poundts.'

'Crikey!' said Bert, overwhelmed.

'I peg your pardon?'

'Jest a twinge,' said Bert, raising his hand to his bandaged head.

'Ah! Also I am instructed to say zat as for zat noble, unrightly accused laty you haf championed so brafely against Pritish hypocrisy and coldness, all ze chivalry of Chermany is on her site.'

'Lady?' said Bert faintly, and then recalled the great Butteridge love story. Had the old chap also read the letters? He must think him a scorcher if he had. 'Oh! that's aw-right,' he said, 'about 'er. I 'adn't any doubts about that. I—'

He stopped. The secretary certainly had a most appalling stare. It seemed ages before he looked down again. 'Well, ze laty as you please. She is your affair. I haf performt my instructions. And ze title of Paron, zat also can pe done. It can all pe done, Herr Pooterage.' He drummed on the table for a second or so, and resumed. 'I haf to tell you, sir, zat you come to us at a crisis in – Welt-Politik. Zere can be no harm now for me to tell our plans to you. Pefore you leafe this ship again zey will be manifest to all ze worldt. War is perhaps already declared. We go – to America. Our fleet will descend out of ze air upon ze United States – it is a country quite unprepared for war eferywhere – eferywhere. Zey have always relied on ze Atlantic. And zair navy. We have selected a certain point – it is at present ze secret of our commanders – which we shall seize, and zen we shall establish a depot – a sort of inland Gibraltar. It will be – what will it be? – an eagle's nest.[33] Zere our airships will gazzer and repair, and zence zey will fly to and fro ofer ze United States, terrorizing cities, dominating Washington, levying what is necessary, until ze terms we dictate are accepted. You follow me?'

'Go on!' said Bert.

'We could haf done all zis wiz such *Luftschiffe*[34] and *Drachenflieger* as we possess, but ze accession of your machine renders our project complete. It not only gifs us a better *Drachenflieger*, but it remofes our last uneasiness as to Great Pritain. Wizout you, sir, Great Pritain, ze land you lofed so well and zat has requited you so ill, zat land of Pharisees and reptiles, can do nozzing! – nozzing! You see, I am perfectly frank wiz you. Well, I am instructed that Chermany recognizes all this. We want you to blace yourself at our disposal. We want you to become our Chief Head Flight Engineer. We want you to manufacture, we want to equib a swarm of hornets unter your direction. We want you to direct zis force. And it is at our depot in America we want you. So we offer you simply, and wizout haggling, ze full terms you demanded weeks ago – one hundert tousand poundts in cash, a salary of dree tousand poundts a year, a pension of one tousand poundts a year, and ze title of Paron as you desired. Zese are my instructions.'

He resumed his scrutiny of Bert's face.

'That's all right, of course,' said Bert, a little short of breath, but otherwise resolute and calm; and it seemed to him that now was the time to bring his nocturnal scheming to the issue.

The secretary contemplated Bert's collar with sustained attention. Only for one moment did his gaze move to the sandals and back.

'Jes' lemme think a bit,' said Bert, finding the stare debilitating. 'Look 'ere!' he said at last, with an air of great explicitness, 'I *got* the secret.'

'Yes.'

'But I don't want the name of Butteridge to appear – see? I been thinking that over.'

'A little delicacy?'

'Exactly. You buy the secret – leastways, I give it you – from Bearer – see?'

His voice failed him a little, and the stare continued. 'I want to do the thing Enonymously. See?'

Still staring. Bert drifted on like a swimmer caught by a current. 'Fact is, I'm going to edop' the name of Smallways. I don't want no title of Baron; I've altered my mind. And I want the money quiet-like. I want the hundred thousand pounds paid into benks – thirty thousand into the London and

County Benk Branch at Bun Hill in Kent directly I 'and over the plans; twenty thousand into the Benk of England; 'arf the rest into a good French bank, the other 'arf the German National Bank, see? I want it put there, right away. I don't want it put in the name of Butteridge. I want it put in the name of Albert Peter Smallways; that's the name I'm going to edop'. That's condition one.'

'Go on!' said the secretary.

'The nex' condition,' said Bert, 'is that you don't make any inquiries as to title. I mean what English gentlemen do when they sell or let you land. You don't arst 'ow I got it. See? 'Ere I am – I deliver you the goods; that's all right. Some people 'ave the cheek to say this isn't my invention, see? It is, you know – *that's* all right; but I don't want that gone into. I want a fair and square agreement saying that's all right. See?'

His 'See?' faded into a profound silence.

The secretary sighed at last, leant back in his chair and produced a toothpick, and used it to assist his meditation on Bert's case. 'What was that name?' he asked at last, putting away the toothpick; 'I must write it down.'

'Albert Peter Smallways,' said Bert, in a mild tone.

The secretary wrote it down, after a little difficulty about the spelling because of the different names of the letters of the alphabet in the two languages.

'And now, Mr Schmallvays,' he said at last, leaning back and resuming the stare, 'tell me: how did you ket hold of Mister Pooterage's balloon?'

§ 7

When at last the Graf von Winterfeld left Bert Smallways, he left him in an extremely deflated condition, with all his little story told.

He had, as people say, made a clean breast of it. He had been pursued into details. He had had to explain the blue suit, the sandals, the Desert Dervishes – everything. For a time scientific zeal consumed the secretary, and the question of the plans remained in suspense. He even went into speculation about the previous occupants of the balloon. 'I suppose,' he said, 'the laty *was* the laty. Bot that is not our affair.

'It is fery curious and amusing, yes: but I am afraid the Prince may be annoyt. He acted wiz his usual decision – always he acts wiz wonterful decision. Like Napoleon. Directly he was tolt of your descent into ze camp at Dornhof, he said, "Pring him! – pring him! It is my schtar!" His schtar of Destiny! You see? He will be dthwarted. He directed you to come as Herr Pooterage, and you haf not done so. You haf triet, of course; but it has peen a poor try. His chugments of men are fery just and right, and it is better for men to act up to them – gompletely. Especially now. Barticularly now.'

He resumed that attitude of his, with his under lip pinched between his forefingers. He spoke almost confidentially. 'It will be awkward. I triet to suggest some doubt, but I was overruled. The Prince does not listen. He is impatient in the high air. Perhaps he will think his schtar has been making a fool of him. Perhaps he will think *I* haf been making a fool of him.' He wrinkled his forehead, and drew in the corners of his mouth.

'I got the plans,' said Bert.

'Yes. Zere is zat! Yes. But you see the Prince was interested in Herr Pooterage because of his romantic seit. Herr Pooterage was so much more – ah! – in the picture. I am afraid you are not equal to controlling ze flying-machine department of our aerial park as he wished you to do. He hadt promised himself zat. . . .

'And der was also ze prestige – ze worldt prestige of Pooterage wiz us. . . . Well, we must see what we can do.' He held out his hand. 'Gif me ze plans.'

A terrible chill ran through the being of Mr Smallways. To the end of his life he was never clear in his mind whether he wept or no, but certainly there was weeping in his voice. ' 'Ere I say!' he protested. 'Ain't I to 'ave – nothin' for 'em?'

The secretary regarded him with benevolent eyes. 'You do not deserve anyzing!' he said.

'I might 'ave tore 'em up.'

'Zey are not yours!'

'They weren't his, very likely.'

'No need to pay anyzing.'

Bert's being seemed to tighten towards desperate deeds. 'Gaw!' he said, clutching his coat, '*ain't* there?'

'Pe galm,' said the secretary. 'Listen! You shall haf five hundert poundts. You shall haf it on my promise. I will do zat for you, and zat is all I can do. Take it from me. Gif me ze name of zat bank. Write it down. So! I tell you ze Prince – is no choke. I do not think he approffed of your appearance last night. No! I can't answer for him. He wanted Pooterage, and you haf spoilt it. Ze Prince – I do not understandt quite, he is in a strange state. It is the excitement of the starting and this great soaring in the air. I cannot account for what he does. But if all goes well I will see to it – you shall haf five hundert poundts. Will that do? Then gif me the plans.'

'Old beggar!' said Bert, as the door clicked. 'Gaw! – what an ole beggar! – *Sharp!*'

He sat down in the folding chair, and whistled noiselessly for a time.

'Nice old swindle for 'im if I tore 'em up! I could 'ave.'

He rubbed the bridge of his nose thoughtfully. 'I gave the whole blessed show away. If I'd jes' kep' quiet about being Enonymous.... Gaw! ... Too soon, Bert my boy – too soon and too rushy. I'd like to kick my silly self.'

'I couldn't 'ave kep' it up.'

'After all, it ain't so very bad,' he said.

'After all, five 'undred pounds.... It isn't *my* secret, anyhow. It's jes' a pick-up on the road. Five 'undred.

'Wonder what the fare is from America back 'ome?'

§ 8

And later in the day an extremely shattered and disorganized Bert Smallways stood in the presence of the Prince Karl Albert. The proceedings were in German. The Prince was in his own cabin, the end room of the airship, a charming apartment furnished in wickerwork with a long window across its entire breadth, looking forward. He was sitting at a folding table of green baize, with Von Winterfeld and two officers sitting beside

him, and littered before them were American maps and Mr
Butteridge's letters and his portfolio and a number of loose
papers. Bert was not asked to sit down, and remained standing
throughout the interview. Von Winterfeld told his story, and
every now and then the words balloon and Pooterage struck
on Bert's ears. The Prince's face remained stern and ominous,
and the two officers watched it cautiously or glanced at Bert.
There was something a little strange in their scrutiny of the
Prince – a curiosity, an apprehension. Then presently he was
struck by an idea, and they fell discussing the plans. The Prince
asked Bert abruptly in English: 'Did you ever see this thing
go op?'

Bert jumped. 'Saw it from Bun 'Ill, your Royal Highness.'

Von Winterfeld made some explanation.

'How fast did it go?'

'Couldn't say, your Royal Highness. The papers, leastways
The Daily Courier,[35] said eighty miles an hour.'

They talked German over that for a time.

'Couldt it standt still? Op in the air? That is what I want
to know.'

'It could 'ovver, your Royal Highness, like a wasp,' said Bert.

'*Viel besser, nicht wahr?*'[36] said the Prince to Von Winterfeld,
and then went on in German for a time.

Presently they came to an end, and the two officers looked
at Bert. One rang a bell, and the portfolio was handed to an
attendant, who took it away.

Then they reverted to the case of Bert, and it was evident
the Prince was inclined to be hard with him. Von Winterfeld
protested. Apparently theological considerations came in, for
there were several mentions of 'Gott!' Some conclusions emerged, and it was apparent that Von Winterfeld was instructed to
convey them to Bert.

'Mr Schmallvays, you haf obtained a footing in zis airship,'
he said, 'by disgraceful and systematic lying.'

' 'Ardly systematic,' said Bert. 'I—'

The Prince silenced him by a gesture.

'And it is within ze power of his Highness to dispose of you
as a spy.'

'Ere! – I came to sell—'

'Ssh!' said one of the officers.

'However, in consideration of ze happy chance zat mate you ze instrument unter Gott of zis Pooterage flying machine reaching his Highness's hand, you haf been spared. Yes – you were ze pearer of goot tidings. You will be allowed to remain on zis ship until it is convenient to dispose of you. Do you understandt?'

'We will bring him,' said the Prince, and added terribly with a terrible glare, 'als Ballast.'[37]

'You are to come wiz us,' said Winterfeld, 'as – pallast. Do you understandt?'

Bert opened his mouth to ask about the five hundred pounds, and then a saving gleam of wisdom silenced him. He met Von Winterfeld's eye, and it seemed to him the secretary nodded slightly. 'Go!' said the Prince, with a sweep of the great arm and hand towards the door. Bert went out like a leaf before a gale.

§ 9

But in between the time when the Graf von Winterfeld had talked to him and this alarming conference with the Prince, Bert had explored the *Vaterland* from end to end. He had found it interesting in spite of grave preoccupations. Kurt, like the greater number of the men upon the German air-fleet, had known hardly anything of aeronautics before his appointment to the new flagship. But he was extremely keen upon this wonderful new weapon Germany had assumed so suddenly and dramatically. He showed things to Bert with a boyish eagerness and appreciation. It was as if he showed them over again to himself, like a child showing a new toy. 'Let's go all over the ship,' he said with zest. He pointed out particularly the lightness of everything, the use of exhausted aluminium tubing, of springy cushions inflated with compressed hydrogen; the partitions were hydrogen bags covered with light imitation leather, the very crockery was a light biscuit glazed in a vacuum, and weighed next to nothing. Where strength was needed there was the new Charlottenburg alloy, German steel as it was called, the toughest and most resistent metal in the world.

There was no lack of space. Space did not matter, so long as load did not grow. The habitable part of the ship was two hundred and fifty feet long, and the rooms in two tiers; above these one could go up into remarkable little white-metal turrets with big windows and air-tight double doors that enabled one to inspect the vast cavity of the gas-chambers. This inside view impressed Bert very much. He had never realized before that an airship was not one simple continuous gas-bag containing nothing but gas. Now he saw far above him the backbone of the apparatus and its big ribs, 'like the neural and haemal canals,'[38] said Kurt, who had dabbled in biology.

'Rather!' said Bert appreciatively, though he had not the ghost of an idea what these phrases meant.

Little electric lights could be switched on up there if anything went wrong in the night. There were even ladders across the space. 'But you can't go into the gas,' protested Bert. 'You can't breve it.'

The lieutenant opened a cupboard door and displayed a diver's suit, only that it was made of oiled silk, and both its compressed-air knapsack and its helmet were of an alloy of aluminium and some light metal. 'We can go all over the inside netting and stick up bullet-holes or leaks,' he explained. 'There's netting inside and out. The whole outer case is rope ladder, so to speak.'

Aft of the habitable part of the airship was the magazine of explosives, coming near the middle of its length. They were all bombs of various types – mostly in glass – none of the German airships carried any guns at all except one small pom-pom (to use the old English nickname dating from the Boer War), which was forward in the gallery upon the shield at the heart of the eagle. From the magazine amidships a covered canvas gallery with aluminium treads on its floor and a hand-rope ran back underneath the gas-chamber to the engine-room at the tail; but along this Bert did not go, and from first to last he never saw the engines. But he went up a ladder against a gale of ventilation – a ladder that was encased in a kind of gas-tight fire-escape and ran right athwart the great forward air-chamber to the little lookout gallery with a telephone, that gallery that bore the light pom-pom of German steel and its locker of shells. This gallery was all of aluminium-magnesium alloy, the tight front of the airship swelled cliff-like above and below and the black eagle sprawled overwhelmingly gigantic, its extremities hidden by the bulge of the gas-bag.

And far down, under the soaring eagles, was England, four thousand feet below perhaps, and looking very small and defenceless indeed in the morning sunlight.

The realization that there was England gave Bert sudden and unexpected qualms of patriotic compunction. He was struck by a quite novel idea. After all, he might have torn up those plans and thrown them away. These people could not have done so very much to him. And even if they did, ought not an Englishman to die for his country? It was an idea that had hitherto been rather smothered up by the cares of a competitive civilization. He became violently depressed. He ought, he perceived, to have seen it in that light before. Why hadn't he seen it in that light before?

Indeed, wasn't he a sort of traitor? . . .

He wondered how the aerial fleet must look from down there. Tremendous, no doubt, and dwarfing all the buildings.

He was passing between Manchester and Liverpool, Kurt told him; a gleaming band across the prospect was the Ship Canal,[39] and a weltering ditch of shipping far away ahead, the Mersey estuary. Bert was a southerner; he had never been north of the Midland counties, and the multitude of factories and chimneys – the latter for the most part obsolete and smokeless now, superseded by huge electric generating stations that consumed their own reek – old railway viaducts, monorail networks and goods yards, and the vast areas of dingy homes and narrow streets, spreading aimlessly, struck him as though Camberwell and Rotherhithe[40] had run to seed. Here and there, as if caught in a net, were fields and agricultural fragments. It was a sprawl of undistinguished population. There were, no doubt, museums and town halls, and even cathedrals of a sort to mark theoretical centres of municipal and religious organization in this confusion; but Bert could not see them, they did not stand out at all in that wide disorderly vision of congested workers' houses and places to work, and shops and meanly conceived chapels and churches. And across this landscape of an industrial civilization swept the shadows of the German airships like a hurrying shoal of fishes. . . .

Kurt and he fell talking of aerial tactics, and presently went down to the under-gallery in order that Bert might see the *Drachenflieger* that the airships of the right wing had picked up overnight and were towing behind them; each airship towing three or four. They looked like big box-kites of an exaggerated form, soaring at the ends of invisible cords. They had long, square heads and flattened tails, with lateral propellers.

'Much skill is required for those! – much skill!'

'Rather!'

Pause.

'Your machine is different from that, Mr Butteridge?'

'Quite different,' said Bert. 'More like an insect, and less like a bird. And it buzzes, and don't drive about so. What can those things do?'

Kurt was not very clear upon that himself, and was still explaining when Bert was called to the conference we have recorded with the Prince. . . .

And after that was over, the last traces of Butteridge fell from Bert like a garment, and he became Smallways to all on board. The soldiers ceased to salute him, and the officers ceased to seem aware of his existence, except Lieutenant Kurt. He was turned out of his nice cabin, and packed in with his belongings to share that of Lieutenant Kurt, whose luck it was to be junior, and the bird-headed officer, still swearing slightly and carrying strops and aluminium boot-trees and weightless hairbrushes and hand-mirrors and pomade in his hands, resumed possession. Bert was put in with Kurt because in that close-packed vessel there was nowhere else for him to lay his bandaged head. He was to mess, he was told, with the men.

Kurt came and stood with his legs wide apart, and surveyed him for a moment as he sat despondent in his new quarters.

'What's your real name, then?' said Kurt, who was only imperfectly informed of the new state of affairs.

'Smallways.'

'I thought you were a bit of a fraud – even when I thought you were Butteridge. You're jolly lucky the Prince took it calmly. He's a pretty tidy blazer when he's roused. He wouldn't stick a moment at pitching a chap of your sort overboard if he thought fit. No! . . . They've shoved you on to me, but it's my cabin, you know.'

'I won't forget,' said Bert.

Kurt left him, and when he came to look about him the first thing he saw pasted on the padded wall was a reproduction of the great picture by Siegfried Schmalz[41] of the War God, that terrible, trampling figure with the Viking helmet and the scarlet cloak, wading through destruction, sword in hand, which had so strong a resemblance to Karl Albert, the prince it was painted to please.

5

THE BATTLE OF THE
NORTH ATLANTIC

§ 1

The Prince Karl Albert had made a profound impression upon Bert. He was quite the most terrifying person Bert had ever encountered. He filled the Smallways soul with passionate dread and antipathy. For a long time Bert sat alone in Kurt's cabin, doing nothing and not venturing even to open the door lest he should be by so much nearer that appalling presence.

So it came about that he was probably the last person on board to hear the news that wireless telegraphy was bringing to the airship in throbs and fragments of a great naval battle in progress in mid-Atlantic.

He learnt it at last from Kurt.

Kurt came in with a general air of ignoring Bert, but muttering to himself in English nevertheless. 'Stupendous!' Bert heard him say. 'Here!' he said, 'get off this locker.' And he proceeded to rout out two books and a case of maps. He spread them on the folding table, and stood regarding them. For a time his Germanic discipline struggled with his English informality and his natural kindliness and talkativeness, and at last lost.

'They're at it, Smallways,' he said.

'At what, sir?' said Bert, broken and respectful.

'Fighting! The American North Atlantic Squadron and pretty nearly the whole of our fleet. Our *Eiserne Kreuz*[1] has had a gruelling and is sinking, and their *Miles Standish*[2] – she's one of their biggest – has sunk with all hands. Torpedoes, I suppose. She was a bigger ship than the *Karl der Grosse*,[3] but five or six years older. . . . Gods! I wish we could see it, Smallways; a square fight in blue water, guns or nothing, and all of 'em steaming ahead!'

He spread his maps, he had to talk, and so he delivered a lecture on the naval situation to Bert.

'Here it is,' he said, 'latitude 30° 50' N., longitude 30° 50' W. It's a good day off us anyhow, and they're all going southwest by south full pelt as hard as they can go. We shan't see a bit of it, worse luck! Not a sniff we shan't get!'

§ 2

The naval situation in the North Atlantic at that time was a peculiar one. The United States was by far the stronger of the two powers upon the sea, but the bulk of the American fleet was still in the Pacific. It was in the direction of Asia that war had been most feared, for the situation between Asiatic and white had become unusually violent and dangerous, and the Japanese Government had shown itself quite unprecedentedly difficult. The German attack found half the American strength at Manila, and what was called the Second Fleet strung out across the Pacific in wireless contact between the Asiatic station and San Francisco. The North Atlantic Squadron was the sole American force on her eastern shore; it was returning from a friendly visit to France and Spain, and was pumping oil fuel from tenders in mid-Atlantic – for most of its ships were steamships – when the international situation became acute. It was made up of four battleships and five armoured cruisers, ranking almost with battleships, not one of which was of a later date than 1913. The Americans had indeed grown so accustomed to the idea that Great Britain could be trusted to keep the peace of the Atlantic that a naval attack on the eastern seaboard found them unprepared even in their imaginations. But long before the declaration of war – indeed, on Whit Monday – the whole German fleet of eighteen battleships, with a flotilla of fuel tenders and converted liners containing stores, to be used in support of the air-fleet, had passed through the Straits of Dover and headed boldly for New York. Not only did these

German battleships outnumber the Americans two to one, but they were more heavily armed and more modern in construction – at least seven of them having high-explosive engines built of Charlottenburg steel, and all carrying Charlottenburg steel guns.

The fleets came into contact on Wednesday before any actual declaration of war. The Americans had strung out in the modern fashion at distances of thirty miles or so, and were steaming to keep themselves between the Germans and either the eastern states or Panama; because, vital as it was to defend the seaboard cities, and particularly New York, it was still more vital to save the canal from any attack that might prevent the return of the main fleet from the Pacific. No doubt, said Kurt, this was now making records across that ocean, 'unless the Japanese have had the same idea as the Germans'. It was obviously beyond human possibility that the American North Atlantic fleet could hope to meet and defeat the German; but, on the other hand, with luck it might fight a delaying action and inflict such damage as to weaken greatly the attack upon the coast defences. Its duty, indeed, was not victory but devotion, the severest task in the world. Meanwhile the submarine defences of New York, Panama, and the other more vital points could be put in some sort of order.

This was the naval situation, and until Wednesday in Whit week it was the only situation the American people had realized. It was then they heard for the first time of the real scale of the Dornhof aeronautic park, and the possibility of an attack coming upon them not only by sea, but by the air. But it is curious that so discredited were the newspapers of that period, that a large majority of New Yorkers, for example, did not believe the most copious and circumstantial accounts of the German air-fleet until it was actually in sight of New York.

Kurt's talk was half soliloquy. He stood with a map on Mercator's projection before him, swaying to the swaying of the ship and talking of guns and tonnage, of ships and their build and powers and speed, of strategic points and bases of operation. A certain shyness that reduced him to the status of a listener at the officers' table no longer silenced him.

Bert stood by, saying very little, but watching Kurt's finger on the map. 'They've been saying things like this in the papers for a long time,' he remarked. 'Fancy it coming real!'

Kurt had a detailed knowledge of the *Miles Standish*. 'She used to be a crack ship for gunnery – held the record. I wonder if we beat her shooting or how? I wish I was in it. I wonder which of our ships beat her. Maybe she got a shell in her engines. It's a running fight! I wonder what the *Barbarossa*[4] is doing,' he went on. 'She's my old ship. Not a first-rater, but good stuff. I bet she's got a shot or two home by now if old Schneider's up to form. Just think of it! There they are whacking away at each other, great guns going, shells exploding, magazines bursting, ironwork flying about like straw in a gale, all we've been dreaming of for years! I suppose we shall fly right away to New York – just as though it wasn't anything at all. I suppose we shall reckon we aren't wanted down there. It's no more than a covering fight on our side. All those tenders and storeships of ours are going on south-west by west to New York to make a floating depot for us. See?' He dabbed his forefinger on the map. 'Here we are. Our train of stores goes there, our battleships elbow the Americans out of our way there.' . . .

When Bert went down to the men's mess-room to get his evening ration, hardly anyone took notice of him, except just to point him out for an instant. Everyone was talking of the battle, suggesting, contradicting – at times, until the petty officers hushed them, it rose to a great uproar. There was a new bulletin, but what it said he did not gather, except that it concerned the *Barbarossa*. Some of the men stared at him, and he heard the name of 'Booteraidge' several times; but no one molested him, and there was no difficulty about his soup and bread when his turn at the end of the queue came. He had feared there might be no ration for him, and if so he did not know what he would have done.

Afterwards he ventured out upon the little hanging gallery with the solitary sentinel. The weather was still fine, but the wind was rising and the rolling swing of the airship increasing. He clutched the rail tightly and felt rather giddy. They were now out of sight of land, and over blue water rising and falling in great masses. A dingy old brigantine under the British flag rose and plunged amid the broad blue waves – the only ship in sight.

§ 3

In the evening it began to blow and the airship to roll like a porpoise as it swung through the air. Kurt said that several of the men were seasick, but the motion did not inconvenience Bert, whose luck it was to be of that mysterious gastric disposition which constitutes a good sailor. He slept well, but in the small hours the light awoke him, and he found Kurt staggering about in search of something. He found it at last in the locker, and held it in his hand unsteadily – a compass. Then he compared his map.

'We've changed our direction,' he said, 'and come into the wind. I can't make it out. We've turned away from New York to the south. Almost as if we were going to take a hand—'

He continued talking to himself for some time.

Day came, wet and windy. The window was bedewed externally, and they could see nothing through it. It was also very cold, and Bert decided to keep rolled up in his blankets on the locker until the bugle summoned him to his morning ration. That consumed, he went out on the little gallery; but he could see nothing but eddying clouds driving headlong by, and the dim outlines of the nearer airships. Only at rare intervals could he get a glimpse of grey sea through the pouring cloud-drift.

Later in the morning the *Vaterland* changed altitude, and soared up suddenly into a high, clear sky, going, Kurt said, to a height of nearly thirteen thousand feet.

Bert was in his cabin, and chanced to see the dew vanish from the window and caught the gleam of sunlight outside. He looked out, and saw once more that sunlit cloud floor he had seen first from the balloon, and the ships of the German air-fleet rising one by one from the white, as fish might rise and become visible from deep water. He stared for a moment and then ran out to the little gallery to see this wonder better. Below was cloudland and storm, a great drift of tumbled weather going hard away to the north-east, and the air about him was clear and cold and serene save for the faintest chill breeze and a rare drifting snowflake. Throb, throb, throb, throb went the engines in the stillness. That huge herd of airships rising one after another had an effect of strange, portentous monsters breaking into an altogether unfamiliar world. . . .

Either there was no news of the naval battle that morning, or the Prince kept to himself whatever came until past midday. Then the bulletins came with a rush, bulletins that made the lieutenant wild with excitement.

'*Barbarossa* disabled and sinking!' he cried. 'Gott im Himmel! Der alte *Barbarossa*! Aber welch ein braver Krieger!'[5]

He walked about the swinging cabin, and for a time he was wholly German.

Then he became English again. 'Think of it, Smallways! The old ship we kept so clean and tidy! All smashed about, and the iron flying about in fragments, and the chaps one knew – Gott! – flying about too! Scalding water squirting, fire, and the smash, smash of the guns! They smash when you're near! Like everything bursting to pieces! Wool won't stop it – nothing! And me up here – so near and so far! Der alte *Barbarossa*!'

'Any other ships?' asked Smallways presently.

'Gott! Yes! We've lost the *Karl der Grosse*, our best and biggest. Run down in the night by a British liner that blundered into the fighting – in trying to blunder out. They're fighting in a gale. The liner's afloat with her nose broken, sagging about! There never was such a battle! – never before! Good ships and good men on both sides – and a storm and the night and the dawn and all in the open ocean full steam ahead! No stabbing! No submarines! Guns and shooting! Half our ships we don't hear of any more, because their masts are shot away. Latitude, 30° 38' N. – longitude, 40° 31' W. – where's that?'

He routed out his map again, and stared at it with eyes that did not see.

'Der alte *Barbarossa*! I can't get it out of my head – with shells in her engine-room, and the fires flying out of her furnaces, and the stokers and engineers scalded and dead. Men I've messed

with, Smallways – men I've talked to close! And they've had
their day at last! And it wasn't all luck for them!

'Disabled and sinking! I suppose everybody can't have all
the luck in a battle. Poor old Schneider! I bet he gave 'em
something back!'

So it was the news of the battle came filtering through to
them all that afternoon. The Americans had lost a second ship,
name unknown; the *Hermann* had been damaged in covering
the *Barbarossa*. . . . Kurt fretted like an imprisoned animal
about the airship, now going up to the forward gallery under
the eagle, now down into the swinging gallery, now poring over
his maps. He infected Smallways with a sense of the immediacy
of this battle that was going on just over the curve of the earth.
But when Bert went down to the gallery the world was empty
and still, a clear inky-blue sky above and a rippled veil of still,
thin sunlit cirrus below, through which one saw a racing drift
of rain-cloud, and never a glimpse of sea. Throb, throb, throb,
throb went the engines, and the long, undulating wedge of
airships hurried after the flagship like a flight of swans after
their leader. Save for the quiver of the engines it was as noiseless
as a dream. And down there, somewhere in the wind and rain,
guns roared, shells crashed home, and, after the old manner of
warfare, men toiled and died.

§ 4

As the afternoon wore on the lower weather abated, and the
sea became intermittently visible again. The air-fleet dropped
slowly to the middle air, and towards sunset they had a glimpse
of the disabled *Barbarossa* far away to the east. Smallways
heard men hurrying along the passage, and was drawn out to
the gallery, where he found nearly a dozen officers collected
and scrutinizing the helpless ruins of the battleship through
field-glasses. Two other vessels stood by her, one an exhausted
petrol tank, very high out of the water, and the other a converted liner. Kurt was at the end of the gallery, a little apart
from the others.

'Gott!' he said at last, lowering his binocular, 'it is like seeing an old friend with his nose cut off – waiting to be finished. Der *Barbarossa*!'

With a sudden impulse he handed his glass to Bert, who had peered beneath his hands, ignored by everyone, seeing the three ships merely as three brown-black lines upon the sea.

Never had Bert seen the like of that magnified slightly hazy image before. It was not simply a battered ironclad that wallowed helpless, it was a mangled ironclad. It seemed wonderful she still floated. Her powerful engines had been her ruin. In the long chase of the night she had got out of line with her consorts, and nipped in between the *Susquehanna*[6] and the *Kansas City*. They discovered her proximity, dropped back until she was nearly broadside on to the former battleship, and signalled up the *Theodore Roosevelt* and the little *Monitor*. As dawn broke she had found herself hostess of a circle. The fight had not lasted five minutes before the appearance of the *Hermann* to the east, and immediately after the *Fürst Bismarck* in the west, forced the Americans to leave her, but in that time they had smashed her iron to rags. They had vented the accumulated tensions of their hard day's retreat upon her. As Bert saw her, she seemed a mere metal-worker's fantasy of frozen metal writhings. He could not tell part from part of her, except by its position.

'Gott!' murmured Kurt, taking the glasses Bert restored to him – 'Gott! Da waren Albrecht – der gute Albrecht und der alte Zimmermann – und von Rosen!' . . .[7]

Long after the *Barbarossa* had been swallowed up in the twilight and distance he remained on the gallery peering through his glasses, and when he came back into his cabin he was unusually silent and thoughtful.

'This is a rough game, Smallways,' he said at last – 'this war is a rough game. Somehow one sees it different after a thing like that. Many men there were worked to make that *Barbarossa*, and there were men in it – one does not meet the like of them every day. Albrecht – there was a man named Albrecht – played the zither and improvised; I keep on wondering what has happened to him. He and I – we were very close friends, after the German fashion.'

§ 5

Smallways woke the next night to discover the cabin in darkness, a draught blowing through it, and Kurt talking to himself in German. He could see him dimly by the window, which he had unscrewed and opened, peering down. That cold, clear, attenuated light which is not so much light as a going of darkness, which casts inky shadows and so often heralds the dawn in the high air, was on his face.

'What's the row?' said Bert.

'Shut up!' said the lieutenant. 'Can't you hear?'

Into the stillness came the repeated heavy thud of guns, one, two, a pause, then three in quick succession.

'Gaw!' said Bert – 'guns!' and was instantly at the lieutenant's side. The airship was still very high and the sea below was masked by a thin veil of clouds. The wind had fallen, and Bert, following Kurt's pointing finger, saw dimly through the colourless veil first a red glow, then a quick red flash and then at a little distance from it another. They were, it seemed for a while, silent flashes, and seconds after, when one had ceased to expect them, came the belated thuds – thud, thud. Kurt spoke in German, very quickly.

A bugle call rang through the airship.

Kurt sprang to his feet, saying something in an excited tone, still using German, and went to the door.

'I say! What's up?' cried Bert. 'What's that?'

The lieutenant stopped for an instant in the doorway, dark against the light passage. 'You stay where you are, Smallways. You keep there and do nothing. We're going into action,' he explained, and vanished.

Bert's heart began to beat rapidly. He felt himself poised over the fighting vessels far below. In a moment, were they to drop like a hawk striking a bird? 'Gaw!' he whispered at last, in awestricken tones.

Thud! . . . thud! He discovered far away a second ruddy flare flashing back at the first. He perceived some difference on the *Vaterland* for which he could not account, and then he realized that the engines had slowed to an almost inaudible beat. He stuck his head out of the window and saw in the bleak air the other airships slowed down to a scarcely perceptible motion.

A second bugle sounded, was taken up faintly from ship to ship. Out went the lights; the fleet became dim, dark bulks against an intense blue sky that still retained an occasional star. For a long time they hung, for an interminable time it seemed to him, and then began the sound of air being pumped into the ballonette, and slowly, slowly the *Vaterland* sank down towards the clouds.

He craned his neck, but he could not see if the rest of the fleet was following them; the overhang of the gas-chambers intervened. There was something that stirred his imagination deeply in that stealthy, noiseless descent.

The obscurity deepened for a time, the last fading star on the horizon vanished, and he felt the cold presence of cloud. Then suddenly the glow beneath assumed distinct outlines, became flames, and the *Vaterland* ceased to descend and hung observant, and it would seem unobserved just beneath a drifting stratum of cloud a thousand feet, perhaps, over the battle below.

In the night the straggling naval battle and retreat had entered upon a new phase. The Americans had drawn together the ends of the flying line skilfully and dexterously, until at last it was a column and well to the south of the lax sweeping pursuit of the Germans. Then in the darkness before the dawn they had come about and steamed northward in close order with the idea of passing through the German battle line and falling upon the flotilla that was making for New York in support of the German air-fleet. Much had altered since the first contact of the fleets. By this time the American admiral, O'Connor, was fully informed of the existence of the airships, and he was no longer vitally concerned for Panama, since the submarine flotilla was reported arrived there from Key West, and the *Delaware* and *Abraham Lincoln*, two powerful and entirely modern ships, were already at Rio Grande, on the Pacific side of the canal. His manoeuvre was, however, delayed by a boiler explosion on board the *Susquehanna*, and dawn found this ship in sight of and indeed so close to the *Bremen* and *Weimar* that they instantly engaged. There was no alternative to her abandonment but a fleet engagement. O'Connor chose the latter course. It was by no means a hopeless fight. The Germans, though much more numerous and powerful than the Americans, were in a dispersed line measuring nearly forty-five miles from end to end, and there were many chances that before they could gather in for the fight the column of seven Americans would have ripped them from end to end.

The day broke dim and overcast, and neither the *Bremen* nor the *Weimar* realized they had to deal with more than the *Susquehanna* until the whole column drew out from behind her at a distance of a mile or less and bore down on them. This was the position of affairs when the *Vaterland* appeared in the sky. The red glow Bert had seen through the column of clouds came from the luckless *Susquehanna*; she lay almost immediately below, burning fore and aft, but still fighting two of her guns and steaming slowly southward. The *Bremen* and the *Weimar*, both hit in several places, were going west by south and away from her. The American fleet, headed by the *Theodore Roosevelt*, was crossing behind them, pounding them in succession, steaming in between them and the big modern *Fürst Bismarck*, which was coming up from the west. To Bert, however, the names of all these ships were unknown, and for a considerable time, indeed, misled by the direction in which the combatants were moving, he imagined the Germans to be Americans and the Americans Germans. He saw what appeared to him to be a column of six battleships pursuing three others, who were supported by a newcomer, until the fact that the *Bremen* and *Weimar* were firing into the *Susquehanna* upset his calculations. Then for a time he was hopelessly at a loss. The noise of the guns, too, confused him, they no longer seemed to boom; they went whack, whack, whack, whack, and each faint flash made his heart jump in anticipation of the instant impact. He saw these ironclads, too, not in profile, as he was accustomed to see ironclads in pictures, but in plan and curiously foreshortened. For the most part they presented empty decks, but here and there little knots of men sheltered behind steel bulwarks. The long agitated noses of their big guns jetting thin transparent flashes and the broadside activity of the quick-firers were the chief facts in this bird's-eye view. The Americans, being steam-turbine ships, had from two to four blast-funnels each; the Germans lay lower in the water, having explosive engines which now for some reason made an unwonted muttering roar. Because of their steam propulsion, the American ships were larger and with a more graceful outline. He saw all these fore-shortened ships rolling considerably and fighting their guns over a sea of huge low waves and under the cold, explicit light of dawn. The whole spectacle waved slowly with the long rhythmic rising and beat of the airship.

At first only the *Vaterland* of all the flying fleet appeared upon the scene below. She hovered high over the *Theodore Roosevelt*, keeping pace with the full speed of that ship. From that ship she must have been intermittently visible through the drifting clouds. The rest of the German fleet remained above the cloud canopy at a height of six or seven thousand feet, communicating with the flagship by wireless telegraphy,[8] but risking no exposure to the artillery below.

It is doubtful at what particular time the unlucky Americans realized the presence of this new factor in the fight. No account now survives of their experience. We have to imagine as well as we can what it must have been to a battle-strained sailor suddenly glancing upwards to discover that huge long silent shape overhead, vaster than any battleship, and trailing now from its hinder quarter a big German flag. Presently, as the sky cleared, more of such ships appeared in the blue through the dissolving clouds, and more, all disdainfully free of guns or armour, all flying fast to keep pace with the running fight below.

From first to last no gun whatever was fired at the *Vaterland*, and only a few rifle-shots. It was a mere adverse stroke of chance that she had a man killed aboard her. Nor did she take any direct share in the fight until the end. She flew above the doomed American fleet while the Prince by wireless telegraphy directed the movements of her consorts. Meanwhile the *Vogel-stern* and *Preussen*, each with half a dozen *Drachenflieger* in tow, went full speed ahead and then dropped through the clouds, perhaps five miles ahead of the Americans. The

Theodore Roosevelt let fly at once with the big guns in her forward barbette,[9] but the shells burst far below the *Vogelstern*, and forthwith a dozen single-man *Drachenflieger* were swooping down to make their attack.

Bert, craning his neck through the cabin porthole, saw the whole of that incident, that first encounter of aeroplane and ironclad. He saw the queer German *Drachenflieger*, with their wide flat wings and square box-shaped heads, their wheeled bodies and their single-man riders, soar down the air like a flight of birds. 'Gaw!' he said. One to the right pitched extravagantly, shot steeply up into the air, burst with a loud report, and flamed down into the sea; another plunged nose forward into the water and seemed to fly to pieces as it hit the waves. He saw little men on the deck of the *Theodore Roosevelt* below, men foreshortened in plan into mere heads and feet, running out preparing to shoot at the others. Then the foremost flying machine was rushing between Bert and the American's deck, and then bang! came the thunder of its bomb flung neatly at the forward barbette, and a thin little crackling of rifle-shots in reply. Whack, whack, whack went the quick-firing guns of the American's battery and smash came an answering shell from the *Fürst Bismarck*. Then a second and third flying machine passed between Bert and the American ironclad, dropping bombs also, and a fourth, its rider hit by a bullet, reeled down and dashed itself to pieces and exploded between the shot-torn funnels, blowing them apart. Bert had a momentary glimpse of a little black creature jumping from the crumpling frame of the flying machine, hitting the funnel, and falling limply, to be instantly caught and driven to nothingness by the blaze and rush of the explosion.

Smash! came a vast explosion in the forward part of the flagship, and a huge piece of metalwork seemed to lift out of her and dump itself into the sea, dropping men and leaving a gap into which a prompt *Drachenflieger* planted a flaring bomb. And then for an instant Bert perceived only too clearly in the growing, pitiless light a number of minute, convulsively active animalculae scorched and struggling in the *Theodore Roosevelt*'s foaming wake. What were they? Not men – surely not men? Those drowning, mangled little creatures tore with their clutching fingers at Bert's soul. 'Oh, Gord!' he cried, 'Oh, Gord!' almost whimpering. He looked again and they had gone, and the black stem of the *Andrew Jackson*, disfigured by the sinking *Bremen*'s last shot, was parting the water that had swallowed them into two neatly symmetrical waves. For some moments sheer blank horror blinded Bert to the destruction below.

Then with an immense rushing sound, bearing as it were a straggling volley of crashing minor explosions on its back, the *Susquehanna*, three miles and more now to the east, blew up and vanished abruptly in a boiling, steaming welter. For a moment nothing was to be seen but tumbled water, and then there came belching up from below, with immense gulping noises, eructations of steam and air and petrol and fragments of canvas and woodwork and men.

That made a distinct pause in the fight. It seemed a long pause to Bert. He found himself looking for the *Drachenflieger*. The flattened ruin of one was floating abeam of the *Monitor*, the rest had passed, dropping bombs down the American column; several were in the water and apparently uninjured, and three or four were still in the air and coming round now in a wide circle to return to their mother airships. The American ironclads were no longer in column formation; the *Theodore Roosevelt*, badly damaged, had turned to the south-east, and the *Andrew Jackson*, greatly battered but uninjured in any fighting part, was passing between her and the still fresh and vigorous *Fürst Bismarck* to intercept and meet the latter's fire. Away to the west the *Hermann* and the *Germanicus* had appeared and were coming into action.

In the pause after the *Susquehanna*'s disaster Bert became aware of a trivial sound like the noise of an ill-greased, ill-hung door that falls ajar – the sound of the men in the *Fürst Bismarck* cheering.

And in that pause in the uproar, too, the sun rose, the dark waters became luminously blue and a torrent of golden light irradiated the world. It came like a sudden smile in a scene of hate and terror. The cloud veil had vanished as if by magic, and the whole immensity of the German air-fleet was revealed in the sky, the air-fleet stooping now upon its prey.

'Whack-bang, whack-bang,' the guns resumed, but ironclads were not built to fight the zenith, and the only hits the Americans scored were a few lucky chances in a generally ineffectual rifle-fire. Their column was now badly broken, the *Susquehanna* had gone, the *Theodore Roosevelt* had fallen astern out of the line, with her forward guns disabled, in a heap of wreckage, and the *Monitor* was in some grave trouble. These two had ceased fire altogether, and so had the *Bremen* and *Weimar*, all four ships lying within shot of each other in an involuntary truce and with their respective flags still displayed. Only four American ships now, with the *Andrew Jackson* leading, kept to the south-easterly course. And the *Fürst Bismarck*, the *Hermann* and the *Germanicus* steamed parallel to them and drew ahead of them, fighting heavily. The *Vaterland* rose slowly in the air in preparation for the concluding act of the drama.

Then falling into place one behind the other, a string of a dozen airships dropped with unhurrying swiftness down the air in pursuit of the American fleet. They kept at a height of two thousand feet or more until they were over and a little in advance of the rearmost ironclad, and then stooped swiftly down into a fountain of bullets, and going just a little faster than the ship below, pelted her thinly protected decks with bombs until they became sheets of detonating flame. So the airships passed one after the other along the American column as it sought to keep up its fight with the *Fürst Bismarck*, the *Hermann* and the *Germanicus*, and each airship added to the destruction and confusion its predecessor had made. The American gunfire ceased, except for a few heroic shots, but they still steamed on, obstinately unsubdued, bloody, battered and wrathfully resistant, spitting bullets at the airships and unmercifully pounded by the German ironclads. But now Bert had but intermittent glimpses of them between the nearer bulks of the airships that assailed them. . . .

It struck Bert suddenly that the whole battle was receding and growing small and less thunderously noisy. The *Vaterland* was rising in the air, steadily and silently, until the impact of the guns no longer smote upon the heart but came to the ear dulled by distance, until the four silenced ships to the eastward were little distant things: but were there four? Bert now could see only three of those floating, blackened and smoking rafts of ruin against the sun. But the *Bremen* had two boats out; the *Theodore Roosevelt* was also dropping boats to where the drift of minute objects struggled, rising and falling on the big, broad Atlantic waves. . . . The *Vaterland* was no longer following the fight. The whole of that hurrying tumult drove away to the south-eastward, growing smaller and less audible as it passed. One of the airships lay on the water burning, a remote monstrous fount of flames, and far in the south-west appeared first one and then three other German ironclads hurrying in support of their consorts. . . .

§ 6

Steadily the *Vaterland* soared, and the air-fleet soared with her and came round to head for New York, and the battle became a little thing far away, an incident before breakfast. It dwindled to a string of dark shapes and one smoking yellow flare that presently became a more indistinct smear upon the vast horizon and the bright new day, that was at last altogether lost to sight. . . .

So it was that Bert Smallways saw the first fight of the airship and the final fight of those strangest things in the whole history of war: the ironclad battleships, which began their career with the floating batteries of the Emperor Napoleon III in the Crimean war[10] and lasted, with an enormous expenditure of human energy and resources, for seventy years. In that space of time the world produced over twelve thousand five hundred of these strange monsters, in schools, in types, in series, each larger and heavier and more deadly than its predecessors. Each in its turn was hailed as the last birth of time, most in their turn were sold for old iron. Only about five per cent of them ever fought in a battle. Some foundered, some went ashore and broke up, several rammed one another by accident and sank. The lives of countless men were spent in their service, the splendid genius and patience of thousands of engineers and inventors, wealth and material beyond estimating; to their account we must put stunted and starved lives on land, millions of children sent to toil unduly, innumerable opportunities of fine living undeveloped and lost. Money had to be found for them at any cost – that was the law of a nation's existence during that strange time. Surely they were the weirdest, most destructive and wasteful megatheria in the whole history of mechanical invention.

And then cheap things of gas and basketwork made an end of them altogether, smiting out of the sky! . . .

Never before had Bert Smallways seen pure destruction, never had he realized the mischief and waste of war. His startled mind rose to the conception, this also is in life. Out of all this fierce torrent of sensation one impression rose and became cardinal – the impression of the men of the *Theodore Roosevelt* who had struggled in the water after the explosion of the first bomb. 'Gaw!' he said at the memory; 'It might 'ave been me and Grubb! . . . I suppose you kick about, and get the water in your mouf. I don't suppose it lasts long.'

He became anxious to see how Kurt was affected by these things. Also he perceived he was hungry. He hesitated towards the door of the cabin and peeped out into the passage. Down forward, near the gangway to the men's mess, stood a little group of air-sailors looking at something that was hidden from him in a recess. One of them was in the light diver's costume Bert had already seen in the gas-chamber turret, and he was moved to walk along and look at this person more closely and examine the helmet he carried under his arm. But he forgot about the helmet when he got to the recess, because there he found lying on the floor the dead body of the boy who had been killed by a bullet from the *Theodore Roosevelt*.

Bert had not observed that any bullets at all had reached the *Vaterland* or, indeed, imagined himself under fire. He could not understand for a time what had killed the lad and no one explained to him.

The boy lay just as he had fallen and died, with his jacket torn and scorched, his shoulder-blade smashed and burst away from his body and all the left side of his body ripped and rent. There was much blood. The sailors stood listening to the man with the helmet, who made explanations and pointed to the round bullet-hole in the floor and the smash in the panel of the passage upon which the still vicious missile had spent the residue of its energy. All the faces were grave and earnest; they were the faces of sober blond, blue-eyed men accustomed to obedience and an orderly life, to whom this waste, wet, painful thing that had been a comrade came almost as strangely as it did to Bert.

A peal of wild laughter sounded down the passage in the direction of the little gallery and something spoke – almost shouted – in German, in tones of exultation.

Other voices at a lower, more respectful pitch replied.

'*Der Prinz*,' said a voice, and all the men became stiffer and less natural. Down the passage appeared a group of figures, Lieutenant Kurt walking in front carrying a packet of papers.

He stopped pointblank when he saw the thing in the recess, and his ruddy face went white. 'So!' said he in surprise.

The Prince was following him, talking over his shoulder to Von Winterfeld and the Kapitän. 'Eh?' he said to Kurt, stopping in mid-sentence, and followed the gesture of Kurt's hand. He glared at the crumpled object in the recess and seemed to think for a moment.

He made a slight, careless gesture towards the boy's body and turned to the Kapitän.

'Dispose of that,' he said in German, and passed on, finishing his sentence to Von Winterfeld in the same cheerful tone in which it had begun.

§ 7

The deep impression of helplessly drowning men that Bert had brought from the actual fight in the Atlantic mixed itself up inextricably with that of the lordly figure of Prince Karl Albert gesturing aside the dead body of the *Vaterland* sailor. Hitherto he had rather liked the idea of war as being a jolly, smashing, exciting affair, something like a Bank Holiday rag[11] on a large scale, and on the whole agreeable and exhilarating. Now he knew it a little better.

The next day there was added to his growing disillusionment a third ugly impression, trivial indeed to describe, a mere necessary everyday incident of a state of war, but very distressing to his urbanized imagination. One writes 'urbanized' to express the distinctive gentleness of the period. It was quite peculiar to the crowded townsmen of that time, and different altogether from the normal experience of any preceding age, that they never saw anything killed, never encountered, save through the mitigating media of book or picture, the fact of lethal violence that underlies all life. Three times in his existence, and three times only, had Bert seen a dead human being, and he had never assisted at the killing of anything bigger than a new-born kitten.

The incident that gave him his third shock was the execution of one of the men on the *Adler* for carrying a box of matches. The case was a flagrant one. The man had forgotten he had it upon him when coming aboard. Ample notice had been given to everyone of the gravity of this offence, and notices appeared at numerous points all over the airships. The man's defence was that he had grown so used to the notices, and had been so preoccupied with his work, that he hadn't applied them to himself; he pleaded, in his defence, what is indeed in military affairs another serious crime, inadvertency. He was tried by his captain, and the sentence confirmed by wireless telegraphy by the Prince, and it was decided to make his death an example to the whole fleet. 'The Germans,' the Prince declared, 'hadn't crossed the Atlantic to go wool-gathering.' And in order that this lesson in discipline and obedience might be visible to everyone, it was determined not to electrocute or drown, but hang the offender.

Accordingly the air-fleet came clustering round the flagship like carp in a pond at feeding-time. The *Adler* hung at the zenith immediately alongside the flagship. The whole crew of the *Vaterland* assembled upon the hanging gallery; the crews of the other airships manned the air-chambers, that is to say, clambered up the outer netting to the upper sides. The officers appeared upon the machine-gun platforms. Bert thought it an altogether stupendous sight, looking down, as he was, upon the entire fleet. Far off below two steamers on the rippled blue water, one British, and the other flying the American flag, seemed the minutest objects, and marked the scale. They were immensely distant. Bert stood on the gallery, curious to see the execution, but uncomfortable because that terrible blond Prince was within a dozen feet of him, glaring terribly, with his arms folded, and his heels together in military fashion.

They hung the man from the *Adler*. They gave him sixty feet of rope, so that he should hang and dangle in the sight of all evil-doers who might be hiding matches or contemplating any kindred disobedience. Bert saw the man standing, a living, reluctant man, no doubt scared and rebellious enough in his heart, but outwardly erect and obedient, on the lower gallery of the *Adler* about a hundred yards away. Then they had thrust him overboard. . . .

Down he fell, hands and feet extending, until with a jerk he was at the end of the rope. Then he ought to have died and swung edifyingly, but instead a more terrible thing happened; his head came right off, and down the body went spinning to the sea, feeble, grotesque, fantastic, with the head racing it in its fall.

'Ugh!' said Bert, clutching the rail before him, and a sympathetic grunt came from several of the men beside him.

'So!' said the Prince, stiffer and sterner, glared for some seconds, then turned to the gangway up into the airship.

For a long time Bert remained clinging to the railing of the gallery. He was almost physically sick with the horror of this trifling incident. He found it far more dreadful than the battle. He was indeed a very degenerate, latter-day, civilized person.

Late that afternoon Kurt came into the cabin and found him curled up on his locker, and looking very white and miserable. Kurt had also lost something of his pristine freshness.

'Seasick?' he asked.

'No!'

'We ought to reach New York this evening. There's a good breeze coming up under our tails. Then we shall see things.'

Bert did not answer.

Kurt opened out folding chair and table, and rustled for a time with his maps. Then he fell thinking darkly. He roused himself presently, and looked at his companion. 'What's the matter?' he said.

'Nothing!'

Kurt stared threateningly. 'What's the matter?' he repeated.

'I saw them kill that chap. I saw that flying-machine man hit the funnels of the big ironclad. I saw that dead chap in the passage. I seen too much smashing and killing today. That's the matter. I don't like it. I didn't know war was this sort of thing. I'm a civilian. I don't like it.'

'*I* don't like it,' said Kurt. 'By Jove, no!'

'I've read about war, and all that, but when you see it it's different. And I'm gettin' giddy. I'm gettin' giddy. I didn't mind a bit being up in that balloon at first, but all this looking down and floating over things and smashing up people, it's getting on my nerves. See?'

'It'll have to get off again. . . .'

Kurt thought. 'You're not the only one. The men are all getting strung up. The flying – that's just flying. Naturally it makes one a little swimmy in the head at first. As for the killing, we've got to be blooded; that's all. We're tame, civilized men. And we've got to get blooded. I suppose there's not a dozen men on the ship who've really seen bloodshed. Nice, quiet, law-abiding Germans they've been so far. . . . Here they are – in for it. They're a bit squeamy now, but you wait till they've got their hands in.'

He reflected. 'Everybody's getting a bit strung up,' he said.

He turned again to his maps. Bert sat crumpled up in the corner, apparently heedless of him. For some time both kept silence.

'Whadid the Prince want to go and 'ang that chap for?' asked Bert suddenly.

'That was all right,' said Kurt, 'that was all right. *Quite* right. Here were the orders, plain as the nose on your face, and here was that fool going about with matches—'

'Gaw! I shan't forget that bit in a 'urry,' said Bert irrelevantly.

Kurt did not answer him. He was measuring their distance

from New York and speculating. 'Wonder what the American aeroplanes are like?' he said. 'Something like our *Drachenflieger*. . . . We shall know by this time tomorrow. . . . I wonder what we shall know? I wonder. Suppose, after all, they put up a fight. . . . Rum sort of fight!'

He whistled softly and mused. Presently he fretted out of the cabin, and later Bert found him in the twilight upon the swinging platform, staring ahead, and speculating about the things that might happen on the morrow. Clouds veiled the sea again, and the long straggling wedge of airships rising and falling as they flew seemed like a flock of strange new births in a Chaos that had neither earth nor water, but only mist and sky.

6

HOW WAR CAME TO
NEW YORK

§ 1

The City of New York was in the year of the German attack
the largest, richest, in many respects the most splendid and in
some the wickedest city the world had ever seen. She was the
supreme type of the City of the Scientific Commercial Age; she
displayed its greatness, its power, its ruthless anarchic enterprise, and its social disorganization most strikingly and completely. She had long ousted London from her pride of place as
the modern Babylon, she was the centre of the world's finance,
the world's trade and the world's pleasure; and men likened
her to the apocalyptic cities of the ancient prophets. She sat
drinking up the wealth of a continent, as Rome once drank the
wealth of the Mediterranean, and Babylon the wealth of the
east. In her streets one found the extremes of magnificence and
misery, of civilization and disorder. In one quarter, palaces of
marble, laced and crowned with light and flame and flowers,
towered up into her marvellous twilights beautiful beyond
description; in another, a black and sinister polyglot population[1] sweltered in indescribable congestion in warrens and
excavations beyond the power and knowledge of government.
Her vice, her crime, her law alike were inspired by a fierce and
terrible energy, and like the great cities of mediaeval Italy, her
ways were dark and adventurous with private war.

It was the peculiar shape of Manhattan Island, pressed in by
arms of the sea on either side, and incapable of comfortable
expansion except along a narrow northward belt, that first
gave the New York architects their bias for extreme vertical
dimensions. Every need was lavishly supplied them – money,

material, labour; only space was restricted. To begin with, therefore, they built high perforce. But to do so was to discover a whole new world of architectural beauty, of exquisite ascendant lines, and long after the central congestion had been relieved by tunnels under the sea, four colossal bridges over the East River, and a dozen monorail cables east and west, the upward growth went on. In many ways New York and her gorgeous plutocracy repeated Venice; in the magnificence of her architecture, painting, metalwork and sculpture, for example, in the grim intensity of her political method, in her maritime and commercial ascendancy. But she repeated no previous state at all in the lax disorder of her internal administration, a laxity that made vast sections of her area lawless beyond precedent, so that it was possible for whole districts to be impassable while civil war raged between street and street, and for Alsatias[2] to exist in her midst in which the official police never set foot. She was an ethnic whirlpool. The flags of all nations flew in her harbour, and at the climax, the yearly coming and going overseas numbered together upwards of two million human beings. To Europe she was America, to America she was the gateway of the earth. But to tell the story of New York would be to write a social history of the world; saints and martyrs, dreamers and scoundrels, the traditions of a thousand races and a thousand religions, went to her making and throbbed and jostled in her streets. And over all that torrential confusion of men and purposes fluttered that strange flag, the stars and stripes, that meant at once the noblest thing in life and the least noble, that is to say Liberty on the one hand and on the other the base jealousy the individual self-seeker feels towards the common purpose of the State.

For many generations New York had taken no heed of war, save as a thing that happened far away, that affected prices and supplied the newspapers with exciting headlines and pictures. The New Yorkers felt perhaps even more certainly than the English had done that war in their own land was an impossible thing. In that they shared the delusion of all North America. They felt as secure as spectators at a bullfight; they risked their money perhaps on the result, but that was all. And such ideas of war as the common Americans possessed were derived from the limited, picturesque, adventurous war of the past. They saw war as they saw history, through an iridescent mist, deodorized, scented indeed, with all its essential cruelties tactfully hidden away. They were inclined to regret it as something ennobling, to sigh that it could no longer come into their own private experience. They read with interest, if not with avidity, of their new guns, of their immense and still more immense ironclads, of their incredible and still more incredible explosives, but just what these tremendous engines of destruction might mean for their personal lives never entered their heads. They did not, so far as one can judge from their contemporary literature, think that they meant anything to their personal lives at all. They thought America was safe[3] amidst all this piling up of explosives. They cheered the flag by habit and tradition, they despised other nations, and whenever there was an international difficulty they were intensely patriotic, that is to say they were ardently against any native politician who did not threaten and do harsh and uncompromising things to the antagonist people. They were spirited to Asia, spirited to Germany, so spirited to Great Britain that the international attitude of the mother country to her great daughter was constantly compared in contemporary caricature to that between a henpecked husband and a vicious young wife. For the rest, they all went about their business and pleasure as if war had died out with the megatherium. . . .

And then suddenly, into a world peacefully busied for the most part upon armaments and the perfection of explosives, war came; came the shock of realizing that the guns were going off, that the masses of inflammable material all over the world were at last ablaze.

§ 2

The immediate effect upon New York of the sudden onset of war was merely to intensify her normal vehemence.

The newspapers and magazines that fed the American mind – for books upon this impatient continent had become simply

material for the energy of collectors – were instantly a corus-
cation of war pictures and of headlines that rose like rockets
and burst like shells. To the normal high-strung energy of New
York streets was added a touch of war-fever. Great crowds
assembled, more especially in the dinner-hour, in Madison
Square about the Farragut monument,[4] to listen to and cheer
patriotic speeches, and a veritable epidemic of little flags and
buttons swept through these great torrents of swiftly moving
young people, who poured into New York of a morning by car
and monorail and subway and train, to toil and ebb home again
between the hours of five and seven. It was dangerous not to
wear a war button. The splendid music halls of the time sank
every topic in patriotism and evolved scenes of wild enthusiasm,
strong men wept at the sight of the national banner sustained
by the whole strength of the ballet, and special searchlights
and illuminations amazed the watching angels. The churches
re-echoed the national enthusiasm in graver key and slower
measure, and the aerial and naval preparations on the East
River were greatly incommoded by the multitude of excursion
steamers which thronged, helpfully cheering, about them. The
trade in small arms was enormously stimulated, and many
overwrought citizens found an immediate relief for their emotions in letting off fireworks of a more or less heroic, dangerous
and national character in the public streets. Small children's
air-balloons of the latest model attached to string became a
serious check to the pedestrian in Central Park. And amidst
scenes of indescribable emotion the Albany legislature[5] in permanent session, with a generous suspension of rules and precedents, passed through both Houses the long-disputed bill for
universal military service in New York State.

Critics of the American character are disposed to consider
that up to the actual impact of the German attack the people
of New York dealt altogether too much with the war as if it
was a political demonstration. Little or no damage, they urge,
was done to either the German or Japanese forces by the wearing of buttons, the waving of small flags, the fireworks, or the
songs. They forgot that under the conditions of warfare a century of science had brought about, the non-military section of

the population could do no serious damage in any form to their enemies, and that there was no reason, therefore, why they should not do as they did. The balance of military efficiency was shifting back from the many to the few, from the common to the specialized. The days when the emotional infantryman decided battles had passed by for ever. War had become a matter of apparatus, of special training and skill of the most intricate kind. It had become undemocratic. And whatever the value of the popular excitement, there can be no denying that the small regular establishment of the United States Government, confronted by this totally unexpected emergency of an armed invasion from Europe, acted with vigour, science and imagination. They were taken by surprise so far as the diplomatic situation was concerned, and their equipment for building either navigables or aeroplanes was contemptible in comparison with the huge German parks. Still they set to work at once to prove to the world that the spirit that had created the *Monitor* and the Southern submarines of 1864[6] was not dead. The chief of the aeronautic establishment near West Point was Cabot Sinclair,[7] and he allowed himself but one single moment of the posturing that was so universal in that democratic time. 'We have chosen our epitaphs,' he said to a reporter, 'and we are going to have, "They did all they could." Now run away!'

The curious thing is that they did do all they could; there is no exception known. Their only defect indeed was a defect of style.

One of the most striking facts historically about this war, and the one that makes the complete separation that had arisen between the methods of warfare and the necessity of democratic support, is the effectual secrecy of the Washington authorities about their airships. They did not bother to confide a single fact of their preparations to the public. They did not even condescend to talk to Congress. They burked and suppressed every inquiry. The war was fought by the President and the secretaries of state in an entirely autocratic manner. Such publicity as they sought was merely to anticipate and prevent inconvenient agitation to defend particular points. They realized that the chief danger in aerial warfare from an excitable and intelligent public would be a clamour for local airships and aeroplanes to defend local interests. This, with such resources as they possessed, might lead to a fatal division and distribution of the national forces. Particularly they feared that they might be forced into a premature action to defend New York. They realized with prophetic insight that this would be the particular advantage the Germans would seek. So they took great pains to direct the popular mind towards defensive artillery, and to divert it from any thought of aerial battle. Their real preparations they masked beneath ostensible ones. There was at Washington a large reserve of naval guns, and these were distributed rapidly, conspicuously, and with much press attention, among the Eastern cities. They were mounted for the most part upon hills and prominent crests round the threatened centres of population. They were mounted upon rough adaptations of the Doan swivel,[8] which at that time gave the maximum vertical range to a heavy gun. Much of this artillery was still unmounted, and nearly all of it was unprotected when the German air-fleet reached New York. And down in the crowded streets when that occurred, the readers of the New York papers were regaling themselves with wonderful and wonderfully illustrated accounts of such matters as:

THE SECRET OF THE THUNDERBOLT.

AGED SCIENTIST PERFECTS ELECTRIC GUN
TO ELECTROCUTE AIRSHIP CREWS
BY UPWARD LIGHTNING.

WASHINGTON ORDERS FIVE HUNDRED.

WAR SECRETARY LODGE DELIGHTED.

SAYS THEY WILL SUIT THE GERMANS DOWN
TO THE GROUND.

PRESIDENT PUBLICLY APPLAUDS
THIS MERRY QUIP.

---

§ 3

The German fleet reached New York in advance of the news of the American naval disaster. It reached New York in the late afternoon and was first seen by watchers at Ocean Grove[9] and Long Branch coming swiftly out of the southward sea and going away to the north-west. The flagship passed almost vertically over the Sandy Hook observation station, rising rapidly as it did so, and in a few minutes all New York was vibrating to the Staten Island guns.

Several of these guns, and especially that at Giffords and the one on Beacon Hill above Matawan,[10] were remarkably well handled. The former, at a distance of five miles, and with an elevation of six thousand feet, sent a shell to burst so close to the *Vaterland* that a pane of the Prince's forward window was smashed by a fragment. This sudden explosion made Bert tuck in his head with the celerity of a startled tortoise. The whole air-fleet immediately went up steeply to a height of about twelve thousand feet, and at that level passed unscathed over the ineffectual guns. The airships lined out as they moved forward into the form of a flattened V, with its apex towards the city, and with the flagship going highest at the apex. The two ends of the V passed over Plumfield and Jamaica Bay, respectively, and the Prince directed his course a little to the east of the Narrows, soared over the Upper Bay, and came to rest above Jersey City in a position that dominated lower New York. There the monsters hung, large and wonderful in the evening light, serenely regardless of the occasional rocket explosions and flashing shell-bursts in the lower air.

It was a pause of mutual inspection. For a time naïve humanity swamped the conventions of warfare altogether; the interest of the millions below and of the thousands above alike was spectacular. The evening was unexpectedly fine – only a few thin level bands of clouds at seven or eight thousand feet broke its luminous clarity. The wind had dropped; it was an evening infinitely peaceful and still. The heavy concussions of the distant guns and those incidental harmless pyrotechnics at the level of the clouds seemed to have as little to do with killing and force, terror and submission, as a salute at a naval review. Below, every point of vantage bristled with spectators, the roofs of the towering buildings, the public squares, the active ferry-boats, and every favourable street intersection had its crowds: all the river piers were dense with people, the Battery Park was solid black with East-Side population, and every position of advantage in Central Park and along Riverside Drive had its peculiar and characteristic assembly from the adjacent streets. The footways of the great bridges over the East River were also closely packed and blocked. Everywhere shopkeepers had left their shops, men their work, and women and children their homes, to come out and see the marvel.

'It beat,' they declared, 'the newspapers.'

And from above, many of the occupants of the airships stared with an equal curiosity. No city in the world was ever so finely placed as New York, so magnificently cut up by sea and bluff and river, so admirably disposed to display the tall effects of buildings, the complex immensities of bridges and monorailways and feats of engineering. London, Paris, Berlin were shapeless, low agglomerations beside it. Its port reached to its heart like Venice, and like Venice it was obvious, dramatic and proud. Seen from above it was alive with crawling trains and cars, and at a thousand points it was already breaking into quivering light. New York was altogether at its best that evening, its splendid best.

'Gaw! *What* a place!' said Bert.

It was so great, and in its collective effect so pacifically magnificent, that to make war upon it seemed incongruous beyond measure, like laying siege to the National Gallery or attacking respectable people in an hotel dining-room with battleaxe and mail. It was in its entirety so large, so complex, so delicately immense, that to bring it to the issue of warfare was like driving a crowbar into the mechanism of a clock. And the fishlike shoal of great airships hovering light and sunlit above, filling the sky, seemed equally remote from the ugly forcefulness of war. To Kurt, to Smallways, to I know not how many more of the people in the air-fleet came the distinctest apprehension of these incompatibilities. But in the head of the Prince Karl Albert were the vapours of romance: he was a conqueror, and this was the enemy's city. The greater the city, the greater the triumph. No doubt he had a time of tremendous exultation and sensed beyond all precedent the joys of power that night.

There came an end at last to that pause. Some wireless communications had failed of a satisfactory ending and fleet and city remembered they were hostile powers. 'Look!' cried the multitude. 'Look!'

'What are they doing?'

'What?' . . . Down through the twilight sank five attacking airships, one to the Navy-Yard on East River, one to City Hall, two over the great business buildings of Wall Street and lower Broadway, one to the Brooklyn Bridge, dropping from among their fellows through the danger zone from the distant guns smoothly and rapidly to a safe proximity to the city masses. At that descent all the cars in the streets stopped with dramatic suddenness, and all the lights that had been coming on in the streets and houses went out again. For the City Hall had awakened and was conferring by telephone with the Federal command and taking measures for defence. The City Hall was asking for airships, refusing to surrender as Washington advised, and developing into a centre of intense emotion, of hectic activity. Everywhere and hastily the police began to clear the assembled crowds. 'Go to your homes,' they said; and the word was passed from mouth to mouth: 'There's going to be trouble.' A chill of apprehension ran through the city, and men hurrying in the unwonted darkness across City Hall Park and Union Square came upon the dim forms of soldiers and guns, and were challenged and sent back. In half an hour New York had passed from serene sunset and gaping admiration to a troubled and threatening twilight.

The first loss of life occurred in the panic rush from Brooklyn Bridge as the airship approached it.

With the cessation of the traffic an unusual stillness came upon New York, and the disturbing concussions of the futile defending guns on the hills about grew more and more audible. At last these ceased also. A pause of further negotiation followed. People sat in darkness, sought counsel from telephones that were dumb. Then into the expectant hush came a great crash and uproar, the breaking down of the Brooklyn Bridge, the rifle fire from the Navy-Yard, and the bursting of bombs in Wall Street and the City Hall. New York as a whole could do nothing, could understand nothing. New York in the darkness peered and listened to these distant sounds until presently they died away as suddenly as they had begun. 'What could be happening?' They asked it in vain.

A long vague period intervened, and people looking out of the windows of upper rooms discovered the dark hulls of German airships, gliding slowly and noiselessly, quite close at hand. Then quietly the electric lights came on again, and an uproar of nocturnal newsvendors began in the streets.

The units of that vast and varied population bought and learnt what had happened; there had been a fight and New York had hoisted the white flag. . . .

§ 4

The lamentable incidents that followed the surrender of New York seem now in the retrospect to be but the necessary and inevitable consequence of the clash of modern appliances and social conditions produced by the scientific century on the one hand, and the tradition of a crude, romantic patriotism on the other. At first people received the fact with an irresponsible detachment, much as they would have received the slowing down of the train in which they were travelling or the erection of a public monument by the city to which they belonged. 'We have surrendered. Dear me! *have* we?' was rather the manner in which the first news was met. They took it in the same spectacular spirit they had displayed at the first apparition of the air-fleet. Only slowly was this realization of a capitulation suffused with the flush of patriotic passion, only with reflection did they make any personal application. '*We* have surrendered!' came later; 'in us America is defeated.' Then they began to burn and tingle.

The newspapers which were issued about one in the morning contained no particulars of the terms upon which New York had yielded – nor did they give any intimation of the quality of the brief conflict that had preceded the capitulation. The later issues remedied these deficiencies. There came the explicit statement of the agreement to victual the German airships, to supply the complement of explosives to replace those employed in the fight and in the destruction of the North Atlantic fleet, to pay the enormous ransom of forty million dollars, and to surrender the flotilla in the East River. There came, too, longer and longer descriptions of the smashing up of the City Hall[11] and the Navy-Yard, and people began to realize faintly what those brief minutes of uproar had meant. They read the tale of men blown to bits, of futile soldiers in that localized battle fighting against hope amidst an indescribable wreckage, of flags hauled down by weeping men. And these strange nocturnal editions contained also the first brief cables from Europe of the fleet disaster, the North Atlantic fleet for which New York had always felt an especial pride and solicitude. Slowly, hour by hour, the collective consciousness woke up, the tide of patriotic astonishment and humiliation came flowing in. America had come upon disaster; suddenly New York discovered herself, with amazement giving place to wrath unspeakable, a conquered city under the hand of her conqueror.

As that fact shaped itself in the public mind, there sprang up, as flames spring up, an angry repudiation. 'No!' cried New York waking in the dawn. 'No! I am not defeated. This is a dream.'

Before day broke the swift American anger was running through all the city, through every soul in those contagious millions. Before it took action, before it took shape, the men in the airships could feel the gigantic insurgence of emotion, as cattle and natural creatures feel, it is said, the coming of an earthquake. The newspapers of the Knype group[12] first gave the thing words and a formula. 'We do not agree,' they said simply. 'We have been betrayed!' Men took that up everywhere, it passed from mouth to mouth, at every street corner under the paling lights of dawn orators stood unchecked, calling upon the spirit of America to arise, making the shame a personal reality to everyone who heard. To Bert, listening five hundred feet above, it seemed that the city, which had at first produced only confused noises, was now humming like a hive of bees – of very angry bees.

After the smashing of the City Hall and Post Office, the white flag had been hoisted from a tower of the old Park Row Building, and thither had gone Mayor O'Hagen,[13] urged thither indeed by the terror-stricken property-owners of lower New York, to negotiate the capitulation with Von Winterfeld. The *Vaterland* having dropped the secretary by a rope ladder, remained hovering, circling very slowly above the great buildings, old and new, that clustered round City Hall Park, while the *Helmholz*, which had done the fighting there, rose overhead to a height of perhaps two thousand feet. So Bert had a near view of all that occurred in that central place. The City Hall and Court-House, the Post Office, and a mass of buildings on the west side of Broadway, had been badly damaged, and the three former were a heap of blackened ruins. In the case of the first two the loss of life had not been considerable, but a great multitude of workers, including many girls and women, had been caught in the destruction of the Post Office, and a little army of volunteers with white badges entered behind the firemen, bringing out the often still living bodies, for the most part frightfully charred, and carrying them into the big Monson Building[14] close at hand. Everywhere the busy firemen were directing their bright streams of water upon the smouldering masses: their hose lay about the square, and long cordons of police held back the gathering hordes of people, chiefly from the East Side.

In violent and extraordinary contrast with this scene of destruction, close at hand were the huge newspaper establishments of Park Row. They were all alight and working; they had not been abandoned even while the actual bomb-throwing was going on, and now staff and presses were vehemently active, getting out the story, the immense and dreadful story of the night, developing comment and, in most cases, spreading the idea of resistance under the very noses of the airships. For a

long time Bert could not imagine what these callously active
offices could be, then he detected the noise of the presses and
emitted his 'Gaw!'

Beyond these newspaper buildings again, and partially
hidden by the arches of the old Elevated Railway of New York
(long since converted into a monorail), there was another
cordon of police and a sort of encampment of ambulances and
doctors, busy with the dead and wounded who had been killed
earlier that night in the panic upon Brooklyn Bridge. All this
he saw in the perspectives of a bird's-eye view, as things happening in a big, irregular-shaped pit below him, between cliffs of
high buildings. Northward he looked along the steep canyon
of Broadway, down whose length at intervals crowds were
assembling about excited speakers; and when he lifted his eyes
he saw the chimneys and cable-stacks and roof spaces of New
York, and everywhere now over these the watching, debating
people clustered, except where the fires raged and the jets of
water flew. Everywhere, too, were flagstaffs devoid of flags; one
white sheet drooped and flapped and drooped again over the
Park Row buildings. And upon the lurid lights, the festering
movement and intense shadows of this strange scene there was
breaking now the cold, impartial dawn.

For Bert Smallways all this was framed in the frame of the
open porthole. It was a pale, dim world outside that dark and
tangible rim. All night he had clutched at that rim, jumped and
quivered at explosions, and watched phantom events. Now
he had been high and now low; now almost beyond hearing,
now flying close to crashings and shouts and outcries. He had
seen airships flying low and swift over darkened and groaning
streets; watched great buildings, suddenly red-lit amidst the
shadows, crumple at the smashing impact of bombs; witnessed
for the first time in his life the grotesque, swift onset of insatiable
conflagrations. From it all he felt detached, disembodied. The
Vaterland did not even fling a bomb; she watched and ruled.
Then down they had come at last to hover over City Hall Park,
and it had crept in upon his mind, chillingly, terrifyingly, that
these illuminated black masses were great offices afire, and that
the going to and fro of minute dim spectres of lantern-lit grey

and white was a harvesting of the wounded and the dead. As the light grew clearer he began to understand more and more what these crumpled black things signified. . . .

He had watched hour after hour since first New York had risen out of the blue indistinctness of the landfall. With the daylight he experienced an intolerable fatigue.

He lifted weary eyes to the pink flush in the sky, yawned immensely, and crawled back whispering to himself across the cabin to the locker. He did not so much lie down upon that as fall upon it and instantly become asleep.

There, hours after, sprawling undignified and sleeping profoundly, Kurt found him, a very image of the democratic mind confronted with the problems of a time too complex for its apprehension. His face was pale and indifferent, his mouth wide open, and he snored. He snored disagreeably.

Kurt regarded him for a moment with a mild distaste. Then he kicked his ankle.

'Wake up!' he said to Smallways' stare, 'and lie down decent.'

Bert sat up and rubbed his eyes.

'Any more fightin' yet?' he asked.

'No,' said Kurt, and sat down, a tired man.

'Gott!' he cried presently, rubbing his hands over his face, 'but I'd like a cold bath! I've been looking for stray bullet-holes in the air-chambers all night until now.' He yawned. 'I must sleep. You'd better clear out, Smallways. I can't stand you here this morning. You're so infernally ugly and useless. Have you had your rations? No! Well, go in and get 'em, and don't come back. Stick in the gallery.' . . .

§ 5

So Bert, slightly refreshed by coffee and sleep, resumed his helpless co-operation in the War in the Air. He went down into the little gallery as the lieutenant had directed, and clung to the rail at the extreme end beyond the lookout man, trying to seem as inconspicuous and harmless a fragment of life as possible.

A wind was rising rather strongly from the south-east. It obliged the *Vaterland* to come about in that direction, and

made her roll a great deal as she went to and fro over Manhattan
Island. Away in the north-west clouds gathered. The throb-
throb of her slow screw working against the breeze was much
more perceptible than when she was going full speed ahead; and
the friction of the wind against the underside of the gas-chamber
drove a series of shallow ripples along it and made a faint
flapping sound like, but fainter than, the beating of ripples
under the stem of a boat. She was stationed over the temporary
City Hall in the Park Row building, and every now and then
she would descend to resume communication with the mayor
and with Washington. But the restlessness of the Prince would
not suffer him to remain for long in any one place. Now he
would circle over the Hudson and East Rivers; now he would
go up high, as if to peer away into the blue distances; once he
ascended so swiftly and so far that mountain-sickness overtook
him and the crew and forced him down again; and Bert shared
the dizziness and nausea.

The swaying view varied with these changes of altitude. Now
they would be low and close, and he would distinguish in
that steep, unusual perspective, windows, doors, street and sky
signs, people and the minutest details, and watch the enigmatical behaviour of crowds and clusters upon the roofs and in the
streets; then as they soared the details would shrink, the sides
of streets draw together, the view widen, the people cease to
be significant. At the highest the effect was that of a concave
relief map; Bert saw the dark and crowded land everywhere
intersected by shining waters, saw the Hudson River like a
spear of silver, and Long Island Sound like a shield. Even to
Bert's unphilosophical mind the contrast of city below and fleet
above pointed an opposition, the opposition of the adventurous
American's tradition and character with German order and
discipline. Below, the immense buildings, tremendous and fine
as they were, seemed like the giant trees of a jungle fighting
for life; their picturesque magnificence was as planless as the
chances of crag and gorge, their casualness enhanced by the
smoke and confusion of still unsubdued and spreading conflagrations. In the sky soared the German airships like beings in a
different, entirely more orderly, world, all oriented to the same

angle of the horizon, uniform in build and appearance, moving accurately with one purpose as a pack of wolves will move, distributed with the most precise and effectual co-operation.

It dawned upon Bert that hardly a third of the fleet was visible. The others had gone upon errands he could not imagine, beyond the compass of that great circle of earth and sky. He wondered, but there was no one to ask. As the day wore on, about a dozen reappeared in the east with their stores replenished from the flotilla and towing a number of *Drachenflieger*. Towards afternoon the weather thickened, driving clouds appeared in the south-west and ran together and seemed to engender more clouds, and the wind came round into that quarter and blew stronger. Towards the evening the wind became a gale into which the now tossing airships had to beat.

All that day the Prince was negotiating with Washington, while his detached scouts sought far and wide over the Eastern States for anything resembling an aeronautic park. A squadron of twenty airships detached overnight had dropped out of the air upon Niagara and was holding the town and power works.

Meanwhile the insurrectionary movement in the giant city grew uncontrollable. In spite of five great fires already involving many acres, and spreading steadily, New York was still not satisfied that she was beaten.

At first the rebellious spirit below found vent only in isolated shouts, street-crowd speeches, and newspaper suggestions; then it found much more definite expression in the appearance in the morning sunlight of American flags at point after point above the architectural cliffs of the city. It is quite possible that in many cases this spirited display of bunting by a city already surrendered was the outcome of the innocent informality of the American mind, but it is also undeniable that in many it was a deliberate indication that the people 'felt wicked'.

The German sense of correctitude was deeply shocked by this outbreak. The Graf von Winterfeld immediately communicated with the mayor, and pointed out the irregularity, and the fire lookout stations were instructed in the matter. The New York police was speedily hard at work, and a foolish contest in full swing between impassioned citizens resolved to keep the flag flying, and irritated and worried officers instructed to pull it down.

The trouble became acute at last in the streets above Columbia University. The captain of the airship watching this quarter seems to have stooped to lasso and drag from its staff a flag hoisted upon Morgan Hall. As he did so a volley of rifle and revolver shots was fired from the upper windows of the huge apartment building that stands between the university and Riverside Drive.

Most of these were ineffectual, but two or three perforated gas-chambers, and one smashed the hand and arm of a man upon the forward platform. The sentinel on the lower gallery immediately replied, and the machine-gun on the shield of the eagle let fly and promptly stopped any further shots. The airship rose and signalled the flagship and City Hall, police and militiamen were directed at once to the spot, and this particular incident closed.

But hard upon that came the desperate attempt of a party of young clubmen from New York who, inspired by patriotic and adventurous imaginations, slipped off in half a dozen motor-cars to Beacon Hill, and set to work with remarkable vigour to improvise a fort about the Doan swivel gun that had been placed there. They found it still in the hands of the disgusted gunners, who had been ordered to cease fire at the capitulation, and it was easy to infect these men with their own spirit. They declared their gun hadn't had half a chance, and were burning to show what it could do. Directed by the newcomers, they made a trench and bank about the mounting of the piece, and constructed flimsy shelter-pits of corrugated iron.

They were actually loading the gun when they were observed by the airship *Preussen*, and the shell they succeeded in firing before the bombs of the latter smashed them and their crude defences to fragments, burst over the middle gas-chambers of the *Bingen*, and brought her to earth, disabled, upon Staten Island. She was badly deflated, and dropped among trees, over which her empty central gas-bags spread in canopies and festoons. Nothing, however, had caught fire, and her men were speedily at work upon her repair. They behaved with a confidence that verged upon indiscretion. While most of them commenced patching the tears of the membrane, half a dozen of them started off for the nearest road in search of a gas main, and presently found themselves prisoners in the hands of a hostile crowd. Close at hand were a number of villa residences, whose occupants speedily developed from an unfriendly curiosity to aggression. At that time the police control of the large polyglot population of Staten Island had become very lax, and scarcely a household but had its rifle or pistols and ammunition. These were presently produced, and after two or three misses one of the men at work was hit in the foot. Thereupon the Germans left their sewing and mending, took cover among the trees, and replied.

The crackling of shots speedily brought the *Preussen* and *Kiel* on the scene, and with a few hand grenades they made short work of every villa within a mile. A number of non-combatant American men, women and children were killed and the actual assailants driven off. For a time the repairs went on in peace under the immediate protection of these two airships. Then when they returned to their quarters an intermittent sniping and fighting round the stranded *Bingen* was resumed, and went on all the afternoon, and merged at last in the general combat of the evening. . . .

About eight the *Bingen* was rushed by an armed mob, and all its defenders killed after a fierce, disorderly struggle.

The difficulty of the Germans in both these cases came from the impossibility of landing any efficient force or, indeed, any force at all from the air-fleet. The airships were quite unequal to the transport of any adequate landing parties; their complement of men was just sufficient to manoeuvre and fight them in the air. From above they could inflict immense damage; they could reduce any organized government to a capitulation in the briefest space, but they could not disarm, much less could they occupy, the surrendered areas below. They had to trust to the pressure upon the authorities below of a threat to renew the bombardment. It was their sole resource. No doubt, with a highly organized and undamaged government and a homogeneous and well-disciplined people that would have sufficed to

keep the peace. But this was not the American case. Not only
was the New York government a weak one and insufficiently
provided with police, but the destruction of the City Hall and
Post Office and other central ganglia[15] had hopelessly disorganized the co-operation of part with part. The streetcars and
railways had ceased; the telephone service was out of gear and
worked only intermittently. The Germans had struck at the
head, and the head was conquered and stunned – only to release
the body from its rule. New York had become a headless monster, no longer capable of collective submission. Everywhere it
lifted itself rebelliously; everywhere authorities and officials,
left to their own initiative, were joining in the arming and
flag-hoisting and excitement of that afternoon.

§ 6

The disintegrating truce gave place to a definite general breach
with the assassination of the *Wetterhorn* – for that is the only
possible word for the act – above Union Square,[16] and not a
mile away from the exemplary ruins of City Hall. This occurred
late in the afternoon, between five and six. By that time the
weather had changed very much for the worse, and the operations of the airships were embarrassed by the necessity they
were under of keeping head on to the gusts. A series of squalls,
with hail and thunder, followed one another from the south by
south-east, and in order to avoid these as much as possible, the
air-fleet came low over the houses, diminishing its range of
observation and exposing itself to a rifle attack.

Overnight there had been a gun placed in Union Square. It
had never been mounted, much less fired, and in the darkness
after the surrender it was taken with its supplies and put out of
the way under the arches of the great Dexter building.[17] Here
late in the morning it was remarked by a number of patriotic
spirits. They set to work to hoist and mount it inside the upper
floors of the place. They made, in fact, a masked battery behind
the decorous office blinds, and there lay in wait as simply
excited as children, until at last the stem of the luckless *Wetterhorn* appeared, beating and rolling at quarter speed over the

recently reconstructed pinnacles of Tiffany's.[18] Promptly that one-gun battery unmasked. The airship's lookout man must have seen the whole of the tenth storey of the Dexter building crumble out and smash in the street below, to discover the black muzzle looking out from the shadows behind. Then perhaps the shell hit him.

The gun fired two shells before the frame of the Dexter building collapsed, and each shell raked the *Wetterhorn* from stem to stern. They smashed her exhaustively. She crumpled up like a can that has been kicked by a heavy boot, her forepart came down in the square, and the rest of her length, with a great snapping and twisting of shafts and stays, descended, collapsing athwart Tammany Hall[19] and the streets towards Second Avenue. Her gas escaped to mix with air, and the air of her rent ballonette poured into her deflating gas-chambers. Then with an immense impact she exploded. . . .

The *Vaterland* at that time was beating up to the south of City Hall from over the ruins of the Brooklyn Bridge, and the reports of the gun, followed by the first crashes of the collapsing Dexter building, brought Kurt and Smallways to the cabin porthole. They were in time to see the flash of the exploding gun, and then they were first flattened against the window and then rolled head over heels across the floor of the cabin by the airwave of the explosion. The *Vaterland* bounded like a football someone has kicked, and when they looked out again Union Square was small and remote and shattered, as though some cosmically vast giant had rolled over it. The buildings to the east of it were ablaze at a dozen points, under the flaming tatters and warping skeleton of the airship, and all the roofs and walls were ridiculously askew and crumbling as one looked. 'Gaw!' said Bert. 'What's happened? Look at the people!'

But before Kurt could produce an explanation, the shrill bells of the airship were ringing to quarters, and he had to go. Bert hesitated and stepped thoughtfully into the passage, looking back at the window as he did so. He was knocked off his feet at once by the Prince, who was rushing headlong from his cabin to the central magazine.

Bert had a momentary impression of the great figure of the

Prince, white with rage, bristling with gigantic anger, his huge fist swinging. 'Blut und Eisen!' cried the Prince, as one who swears. 'Ach! Blut und Eisen!'[20]

Someone fell over Bert – something in the manner of falling suggested Von Winterfeld – and someone else paused and kicked him spitefully and hard. Then he was sitting up in the passage, rubbing a freshly bruised cheek and readjusting the bandage he still wore on his head. 'Dem that Prince,' said Bert, indignant beyond measure. ''E 'asn't the menners of a 'og!'

He stood up, collected his wits for a minute, and then went slowly towards the gangway of the little gallery. As he did so he heard noises suggestive of the return of the Prince. The lot of them were coming back again. He shot into his cabin like a rabbit into its burrow, just in time to escape that shouting terror.

He shut the door, waited until the passage was still, then went across to the window and looked out. A drift of cloud made the prospect of the streets and squares hazy, and the rolling of the airship swung the picture up and down. A few people were running to and fro, but for the most part the aspect of the district was desertion. The streets seemed to broaden out, they became clearer, and the little dots that were people larger as the *Vaterland* came down again. Presently she was swaying along above the lower end of Broadway. The dots below, Bert saw, were not running now, but standing and looking up. Then suddenly they were all running again.

Something had dropped from the aeroplane, something that looked small and flimsy. It hit the pavement near a big archway just underneath Bert. A little man was sprinting along the sidewalk within half a dozen yards, and two or three others and one woman were bolting across the roadway. They were odd little figures, so very small were they about the heads, so very active about the elbows and legs. It was really funny to see their legs going. Foreshortened humanity has no dignity. The little man on the pavement jumped comically – no doubt with terror – as the bomb fell beside him.

Then blinding flames squirted out in all directions from the point of impact, and the little man who had jumped became, for an instant, a flash of fire and vanished – vanished absolutely. The people running out into the road took preposterous clumsy leaps, then flopped down and lay still, with their torn clothes smouldering into flame. Then pieces of the archway began to drop, and the lower masonry of the building to fall in with the rumbling sound of coals being shot into a cellar. A faint screaming reached Bert, and then a crowd of people ran out into the street, one man limping and gesticulating awkwardly. He halted, and went back towards the building. A falling mass of brickwork hit him and sent him sprawling to lie still and crumpled where he fell. Dust and black smoke came pouring into the street, and were presently shot with red flame. . . .

In this manner the massacre of New York began. She was the first of the great cities of the Scientific Age to suffer by the enormous powers and grotesque limitations of aerial warfare. She was wrecked as in the previous century endless barbaric cities had been bombarded, because she was at once too strong to be occupied, and too undisciplined and proud to surrender in order to escape destruction. Given the circumstances, the thing had to be done. It was impossible for the Prince to desist and own himself defeated, and it was impossible to subdue the city except by largely destroying it. The catastrophe was the logical outcome of the situation created by the application of science to warfare. It was unavoidable that great cities should be destroyed. In spite of his intense exasperation with his dilemma, the Prince sought to be moderate even in massacre. He tried to give a memorable lesson with the minimum waste of life and the minimum expenditure of explosives. For that night he proposed only the wrecking of Broadway. He directed the air-fleet to move in column over the route of this thoroughfare, dropping bombs, the *Vaterland* leading. And so our Bert Smallways became a participant in one of the most cold-blooded slaughters in the world's history, in which men who were neither excited nor, except for the remotest chance of a bullet, in any danger, poured death and destruction upon homes and crowds below.

He clung to the frame of the porthole as the airship tossed and swayed, and stared down through the light rain that now drove before the wind, into the twilit streets, watching people running out of the houses, watching buildings collapse and fires begin. As the airships sailed along they smashed up the city as a child will shatter its cities of brick and card. Below, they left ruins and blazing conflagrations and heaped and scattered dead; men, women and children mixed together as though they had been no more than Moors, or Zulus, or Chinese. Lower New York was soon a furnace of crimson flames, from which there was no escape. Cars, railways, ferries, all had ceased, and never a light led the way of the distracted fugitives in that dusky confusion but the light of burning. He had glimpses of what it must mean to be down there – glimpses. And it came to him suddenly as an incredible discovery, that such disasters were not only possible now in this strange, gigantic, foreign New York, but also in London – in Bun Hill! that the little island in the silver seas was at the end of its immunity, that nowhere in the world any more was there a place left where a Smallways might lift his head proudly and vote for war and a spirited foreign policy, and go secure from such horrible things.

7

THE *VATERLAND* IS
DISABLED

§ 1

And then above the flames of Manhattan Island came a battle,
the first battle in the air. The Americans had realized the price
their waiting game must cost, and struck with all the strength
they had, if haply they might still save New York from this mad
Prince of Blood and Iron, and from fire and death.

They came down upon the Germans on the wings of a great
gale in the twilight, amidst thunder and rain. They came from
the yards of Washington and Philadelphia, full tilt in two squadrons, and but for one sentinel airship hard by Trenton, the
surprise would have been complete.

The Germans, sick and weary with destruction, and half
empty of ammunition, were facing up into the weather when
the news of this onset reached them. New York they had left
behind to the south-eastward, a darkened city with one hideous
red scar of flames. All the airships rolled and staggered, bursts
of hail-storm bore them down and forced them to fight their
way up again; the air had become bitterly cold. The Prince was
on the point of issuing orders to drop earthward and trail
copper lightning-chains when the news of the aeroplane attack
came to him. He faced his fleet in line abreast south, had
the *Drachenflieger* manned and held ready to cast loose, and
ordered a general ascent into the freezing clearness above the
wet and darkness.

The news of what was imminent came slowly to Bert's percep-
tions. He was standing in the mess-room at the time, and the
evening rations were being served out. He had resumed
Butteridge's coat and gloves, and, in addition, he had wrapped

his blanket about him. He was dipping his bread into his soup and biting off big mouthfuls. His legs were wide apart, and he leant against the partition in order to steady himself amidst the pitching and oscillation of the airship. The men about him looked tired and depressed; a few talked, but most were sullen and thoughtful, and one or two were air-sick. They all seemed to share the peculiarly outcast feeling that had followed the murders of the evening, a sense of a land beneath them and an outraged humanity grown more hostile than the sea.

Then the news hit them. A red-faced sturdy man, a man with light eyelashes and a scar, appeared in the doorway and shouted something in German that manifestly startled everyone. Bert felt the shock of the altered tone though he could not understand a word that was said. The announcement was followed by a pause, and then a great outcry of questions and suggestions. Even the air-sick men flushed and spoke. For some minutes the mess-room was Bedlam, and then, as if it were a confirmation of the news, came the shrill bugles that called the men to their posts.

Bert, with pantomime suddenness, found himself alone.

'What's up?' he said, though he partly guessed.

He stayed only to gulp down the remainder of his soup and then ran along the swaying passage and, clutching tightly, down the ladder to the little gallery. The weather hit him like cold water squirted from a hose. The airship engaged in some new feat of atmospheric jiu-jitsu[1]. He drew his blanket closer about him, clutching with one straining hand. He found himself tossing in a wet twilight, with nothing to be seen but mist pouring past him. Above him the airship was warm with lights and busy with the movements of men going to their quarters. Then abruptly the lights went out, and the *Vaterland* with bounds and twists and strange writhings was fighting her way up the air.

He had a glimpse, as the *Vaterland* rolled over, of some large buildings burning close below them, a quivering acanthus of flames, and then he saw indistinctly through the driving weather another airship wallowing along like a porpoise, and also working up. Presently the clouds swallowed her again for a time, and then she came back to sight as a dark and whalelike monster, amidst streaming weather. The air was full of flappings and pipings, of void, gusty shouts and noises; it buffeted him and confused him; ever and again his attention became rigid – a blind and deaf balancing and clutching.

'Wow!'

Something fell past him out of the vast darknesses above and vanished into the tumults below, going obliquely downward. It was a German *Drachenflieger*. The thing was going so fast he had but an instant apprehension of the dark figure of the aeronaut crouched together clutching at his wheel. It might be a manoeuvre, but it looked like a catastrophe.

'Gaw!' said Bert.

'Pup-pup-pup,' went a gun somewhere in the mirk ahead, and suddenly and quite horribly the *Vaterland* lurched, and Bert and the sentinel were clinging to the rail for dear life. 'Bang!' came a vast impact out of the zenith, followed by another huge roll, and all about him the tumbled clouds flashed red and lurid in response to flashes unseen, revealing immense gulfs. The rail went right overhead, and he was hanging loose in the air holding on to it.

For a time Bert's whole mind and being was given to clutching. 'I'm going into the cabin,' he said, as the airship righted again and brought back the gallery floor to his feet. He began to make his way cautiously towards the ladder. 'Whee-wow!' he cried as the whole gallery reared itself up forward and then plunged down like a desperate horse.

Crack! Bang! Bang! Bang! And then hard upon this little rattle of shots and bombs came, all about him, enveloping him, engulfing him, immense and overwhelming, a quivering white blaze of lightning and a thunderclap that was like the bursting of a world.

Just for the instant before that explosion, the universe seemed to be standing still in a shadowless glare.

It was then he saw the American aeroplane. He saw it in the light of the flash as a thing altogether motionless. Even its screw appeared still, and its men were rigid dolls. (For it was so near he could see the men upon it quite distinctly.) Its stern was

tilting down and the whole machine was heeling over. It was of
the Colt-Coburn-Langley[2] pattern, with double uptilted wings
and the screw ahead, and the men were in a boat-like body
netted over. From this very light long body, magazine guns
projected on either side. One thing that was strikingly odd and
wonderful in that moment of revelation was that the left upper
wing was burning *downward* with a reddish, smoky flame. But
this was not the most wonderful thing about this apparition.
The most wonderful thing was that it and a German airship
five hundred yards below were threaded as it were on the
lightning flash, which turned out of its path as if to take them,
and that out from the corners and projecting points of its huge
wings everywhere, little branching thorn trees of lightning were
streaming.

Like a picture Bert saw these things, a picture a little blurred
by a thin veil of wind-torn mist.

The crash of the thunderclap followed the flash and seemed
a part of it, so that it is hard to say whether Bert was the rather
deafened or blinded in that instant.

And then darkness, utter darkness, and a heavy report and a
thin small sound of voices that went wailing downward into
the abyss below.

§ 2

There followed upon these things a long, deep swaying of
the airship, and then Bert began a struggle to get back to his
cabin. He was drenched and cold and terrified beyond measure,
and now more than a little air-sick. It seemed to him that
the strength had gone out of his knees and hands, and that his
feet had become icily slippery over the metal they trod upon.
But that was because a thin film of ice had frozen upon the
gallery.

He never knew how long his ascent of the ladder back into
the airship took him, but in his dreams afterwards, when he
recalled it, that experience seemed to last for hours. Below,
above, around him were gulfs, monstrous gulfs of howling wind
and eddies of dark, whirling snowflakes, and he was protected

from it all by a little metal grating and a rail, a grating and rail that seemed madly infuriated with him, passionately eager to wrench him off and toss him into the tumult of space.

Once he had a fancy that a bullet tore by his ear, and that the clouds and snowflakes were lit by a flash, but he never even turned his head to see what new assailant whirled past them in the void. He wanted to get into the passage! He wanted to get into the passage! He wanted to get into the passage! Would the arm by which he was clinging hold out, or would it give way and snap? A handful of hail smacked him in the face, so that for a time he was breathless and nearly insensible. Hold tight, Bert! He renewed his efforts.

He found himself, with an enormous sense of relief and warmth, in the passage. The passage was behaving like a dice-box, its disposition was evidently to rattle him about and then throw him out again. He hung on with the convulsive clutch of instinct until the passage lurched down ahead. Then he would make a short run cabinward, and clutch again as the fore end rose.

Behold! He was in the cabin!

He snapped to the door, and for a time he was not a human being, he was a case of air-sickness. He wanted to get somewhere that would fix him, that he needn't clutch. He opened the locker and got inside among the loose articles, and sprawled there helplessly, with his head sometimes bumping one side and sometimes the other. The lid shut upon him with a click. He did not care then what was happening any more. He did not care who fought who, or what bullets were fired or explosions occurred. He did not care if presently he was shot or smashed to pieces. He was full of feeble, inarticulate rage and despair. 'Foolery!' he said, his one exhaustive comment on human enterprise, adventure, war and the chapter of accidents that had entangled him. 'Foolery! Ugh!' He included the order of the universe in that comprehensive condemnation. He wished he was dead.

He saw nothing of the stars as presently the *Vaterland* cleared the rush and confusion of the lower weather, nor of the duel she fought with two circling aeroplanes, how they shot her rearmost chambers through, and how she fought them off with explosive bullets and turned to run as she did so.

The rush and swoop of these wonderful night-birds was all lost upon him; their heroic dash and self-sacrifice. The *Vater-land* was rammed, and for some moments she hung on the verge of destruction, and sinking swiftly, with the American aero-plane entangled with her smashed propeller, and the Americans trying to scramble aboard. It signified nothing to Bert. To him it conveyed itself simply as vehement swaying. Foolery! When the American airship dropped off at last, with most of its crew shot or fallen, Bert in his locker appreciated nothing but that the *Vaterland* had taken a hideous upward leap.

But then came infinite relief, incredibly blissful relief. The rolling, the pitching, the struggle ceased, ceased instantly and absolutely. The *Vaterland* was no longer fighting the gale; her smashed and exploded engines throbbed no more; she was disabled and driving before the wind as smoothly as a balloon, a huge, wind-spread, tattered cloud of aerial wreckage.

To Bert it was no more than the end of a series of disagreeable sensations. He was not curious to know what had happened to the airship, nor what had happened to the battle. For a long time he lay waiting apprehensively for the pitching and tossing and his qualms to return, and so lying, boxed up in the locker, he presently fell asleep.

§ 3

He awoke tranquil but very stuffy, and at the same time very cold, and quite unable to recollect where he could be. His head ached, and he felt suffocated. He had been dreaming confusedly of Edna and Desert Dervishes, and of riding bicycles in an extremely perilous manner through the upper air amidst a pyro-technic display of crackers and Bengal lights[3] – to the great annoyance of a sort of composite person made up of the Prince and Mr Butteridge. Then for some reason Edna and he had begun to cry pitifully for each other, and he woke up with wet eyelashes into this ill-ventilated darkness of the locker. He would never see Edna any more, never see Edna any more.

He thought he must be back in the bedroom behind the cycle shop at the bottom of Bun Hill, and he was sure the vision he had had of the destruction of a magnificent city, a city quite incredibly great and splendid, by means of bombs, was no more than a particularly vivid dream.

'Grubb!' he called, anxious to tell him.

The answering silence, and the dull resonance of the locker to his voice, supplementing the stifling quality of the air, set going a new train of ideas. He lifted up his hands and feet, and met an inflexible resistance. He was in a coffin, he thought! He had been buried alive! He gave way at once to wild panic. ''Elp!' he screamed. ''Elp!' and drummed with his feet, and kicked and struggled. 'Let me out! Let me out!'

For some seconds he struggled with this intolerable horror, and then the side of his imagined coffin gave way, and he was flying out into daylight. Then he was rolling about on what seemed to be a padded floor with Kurt, and being punched and sworn at lustily.

He sat up. His head bandage had become loose and got over one eye, and he whipped the whole thing off. Kurt was also sitting up, a yard away from him, pink as ever, wrapped in blankets, and with an aluminium diver's helmet over his knee, staring at him with a severe expression, and rubbing his downy unshaven chin. They were both on a slanting floor of crimson padding, and above them was an opening like a long low cellar flap that Bert by an effort perceived to be the cabin door in a half-inverted condition. The whole cabin had in fact turned on its side.

'What the deuce do you mean by it, Smallways?' said Kurt, 'jumping out of that locker when I was certain you had gone overboard with the rest of them? Where have you been?'

'What's up?' asked Bert.

'This end of the airship is up. Most other things are down.'

'Was there a battle?'

'There was.'

'Who won?'

'I haven't seen the papers, Smallways. We left before the finish. We got disabled and unmanageable, and our colleagues

– consorts, I mean – were too busy most of them to trouble about us, and the wind blew us – Heaven knows where the wind *is* blowing us. It blew us right out of action at the rate of eighty miles an hour or so. Gott! what a wind that was! What a fight! And here we are!'

'Where?'

'In the air, Smallways – in the air! When we get down on the earth again we shan't know what to do with our legs.'

'But what's below us?'

'Canada, to the best of my knowledge – and a jolly bleak, empty, inhospitable country it looks.'

'But why ain't we right ways up?'

Kurt made no answer for a space.

'Last I remember was seeing a sort of flying machine in a lightning flash,' said Bert. 'Gaw! that was 'orrible. Guns going off! Things explodin'! Clouds and 'ail. Pitching and tossing. I got so scared and desperate – and sick. . . . You don't know how the fight came off?'

'Not a bit of it. I was up with my squad in those divers' dresses, inside the gas-chambers, with sheets of silk for caulking. We couldn't see a thing outside except the lightning flashes. I never saw one of those American aeroplanes. Just saw the shots flicker through the chambers and sent off men for the tears. We caught fire a bit – not much, you know. We were too wet, so the fires spluttered out before we banged. And then one of their infernal things dropped out of the air on us and rammed. Didn't you feel it?'

'I felt everything,' said Bert. 'I didn't notice any particular smash —'

'They must have been pretty desperate if they meant it. They slashed down on us like a knife; simply ripped the after gas-chambers like gutting herrings, crumpled up the engines and screw. Most of the engines dropped out as they fell off us, or we'd have grounded – but the rest is sort of dangling. We just turned up our nose to the heavens and stayed there. Eleven men rolled off us from various points, and poor old Winterfeld fell through the door of the Prince's cabin into the chart-room and broke his ankle. Also we got our electric gear shot or carried away – no one knows how. That's the position, Smallways. We're driving through the air like a common aerostat, at the mercy of the elements, almost due north – probably to the North Pole. We don't know what aeroplanes the Americans have, or anything at all about it. Very likely we have finished 'em up. One fouled us, one was struck by lightning, some of the men saw a third upset, apparently just for fun. They were going cheap anyhow. Also we've lost most of our *Drachen-flieger*. They just skated off into the night. No stability in 'em. That's all. We don't know if we've won or lost. We don't know if we're at war with the British Empire yet or at peace. Consequently we daren't get down. We don't know what we are up to or what we are going to do. Our Napoleon is alone, forward, and I suppose he's rearranging his plans. Whether New York was our Moscow[4] or not remains to be seen. We've had a high old time and murdered no end of people! War! Noble war! I'm sick of it this morning. I like sitting in rooms right way up and not on slippery partitions. I'm a civilized man. I keep thinking of old Albrecht and the *Barbarossa*. . . . I feel I want a wash and kind words and a quiet home. When I look at you, I *know* I want a wash. Gott!' – he stifled a vehement yawn – 'What a Cockney tadpole of a ruffian you look!'

'Can we get any grub?' asked Bert.

'Heaven knows!' said Kurt.

He meditated upon Bert for a time. 'So far as I can judge, Smallways,' he said, 'the Prince will probably want to throw you overboard – next time he thinks of you. He certainly will if he sees you. . . . After all, you know, you came *als Ballast*. . . . And we shall have to lighten ship extensively pretty soon. Unless I'm mistaken, the Prince will wake up presently and start doing things with tremendous vigour. . . . I've taken a fancy to you. It's the English strain in me. You're a rum little chap. I shan't like seeing you whizz down the air. . . . You'd better make yourself useful, Smallways. I think I shall requisition you for my squad. You'll have to work, you know, and be infernally intelligent, and all that. And you'll have to hang about upside down a bit. Still, it's the best chance you have. We shan't carry passengers much farther this trip, I fancy. Ballast goes overboard – if we don't want to ground precious soon and be taken prisoners of war. The Prince won't do that anyhow. He'll be game to the last.'

§ 4

By means of a folding chair, which was still in its place behind the door, they got to the window and looked out in turn and contemplated a sparsely wooded country below, with no railways nor roads, and only occasional signs of habitation. Then a bugle sounded, and Kurt interpreted it as a summons to food. They got through the door and clambered with some difficulty up the nearly vertical passage, holding on desperately with toes and finger-tips to the ventilating perforations in its floor. The mess stewards had found their fireless heating arrangements intact, and there was hot cocoa for the officers and hot soup for the men.

Bert's sense of the queerness of this experience was so keen that it blotted out any fear he might have felt. Indeed, he was far more interested now than afraid. He seemed to have touched down to the bottom of fear and abandonment overnight. He was growing accustomed to the idea that he would probably be killed presently, that this strange voyage in the air was in all probability his death journey. No human being can keep permanently afraid: fear goes at last to the back of one's mind, accepted, and shelved, and done with. He consumed all his soup, sopping it up with his bread, and contemplated his comrades. They were all rather yellow and dirty with four-day beards, and they grouped themselves in the tired, unpremeditated manner of men on a wreck. They talked little. The situation perplexed them beyond any suggestion of ideas. Three had been hurt in the pitching up of the ship during the fight, and one had a bandaged bullet wound. It was incredible that this small band of men had committed murder and massacre on a scale beyond precedent. None of those who squatted on the sloping gas-padded partition, soup mug in hand, seemed really guilty of anything of the sort, seemed scarcely capable of hurting a dog wantonly. They were all so manifestly built for homely chalets on the solid earth and carefully tilled fields and blonde wives and cheery merrymaking. The red-faced sturdy man with light eyelashes who had brought the first news of the air battle to the men's mess had finished his soup, and with an expression of maternal solicitude was readjusting the bandages of a youngster whose arm had been sprained.

Bert was crumbling the last of his bread into the last of his soup, eking it out as long as possible, when suddenly he became aware that everyone was looking at a pair of feet that were dangling across the down-turned open doorway. Kurt appeared and adjusted himself across the hinge. In some mysterious way he had shaved his face and smoothed down his light golden hair. He looked extraordinarily cherubic. 'Der Prinz,' he said.

A second pair of boots followed, making wide and magnificent gestures in their attempts to feel the door frame. Kurt guided them to a foothold, and the Prince, shaved and brushed and beeswaxcd and clean and big and terrible, slid down into position astride of the door. All the men and Bert also stood up and saluted.

The Prince surveyed them with the gesture of a man who sits a steed. The head of the Kapitän appeared beside him.

Then Bert had a terrible moment. The blue blaze of the Prince's eye fell upon him, the great finger pointed, a question was asked. Kurt intervened with explanations.

'So,' said the Prince, and Bert was disposed of.

Then the Prince addressed the men in short, heroic sentences, steadying himself on the hinge with one hand and waving the other in a fine variety of gesture. What he said Bert could not tell, but he perceived that their demeanour changed, their backs stiffened. They began to punctuate the Prince's discourse with cries of approval. At the end their leader burst into song and all the men with him. 'Ein feste Burg ist unser Gott,'[5] they chanted in deep, strong tones, with an immense moral uplifting. It was glaringly inappropriate in a damaged, half-overturned and sinking airship, which had been disabled and blown out of action after inflicting the cruellest bombardment in the world's history; but it was immensely stirring nevertheless. Bert was deeply moved. He could not sing any of the words of Luther's great hymn, but he opened his mouth and emitted loud, deep and partially harmonious notes. . . .

Far below, this deep chanting struck on the ears of a little camp of Christianized half-breeds who were lumbering. They were breakfasting, but they rushed out cheerfully, quite prepared for the Second Advent. They stared at the shattered and twisted *Vaterland*, driving before the gale, amazed beyond words. In so many respects it was like their idea of the Second Advent, and then again in so many respects it wasn't. They stared at its passage, awestricken and perplexed. The hymn ceased. Then after a long interval a voice came out of heaven. 'Vat id diss blace here galled itself; vat?'

They made no answer. Indeed, they did not understand, though the question was repeated.

And at last the monster drove away northward over a crest of pine woods and was no more seen. They fell into a hot and long disputation. . . .

The hymn ended. The Prince's legs dangled up the passage again, and everyone was briskly prepared for heroic exertion and triumphant acts. 'Smallways!' cried Kurt, 'come here!'

§ 5

Then Bert, under Kurt's direction, had his first experience of the work of an air-sailor.

The immediate task before the captain of the *Vaterland* was a very simple one. He had to keep afloat. The wind, though it had fallen from its earlier violence, was still blowing strongly enough to render the grounding of so clumsy a mass extremely dangerous, even if it had been desirable for the Prince to land in inhabited country, and so risk capture. It was necessary to keep the airship up until the wind fell and then, if possible, to descend in some lonely district of the Territory where there would be a chance of repair or rescue by some searching consort. In order to do this weight had to be dropped, and Kurt was detailed with a dozen men to climb down among the wreckage of the deflated air-chambers, and cut the stuff clear, portion by portion, as the airship sank. So Bert, armed with a sharp cutlass, found himself clambering about upon netting four thousand feet up in the air, trying to understand Kurt when he spoke in English and to divine him when he used German.

It was giddy work, but not nearly so giddy as a rather over-nourished reader sitting in a warm room might imagine. Bert found it quite possible to look down and contemplate the wild subarctic landscape below, now devoid of any sign of habitation, a land of rocky cliffs and cascades and broad swirling desolate rivers, and of trees and thickets that grew more stunted and scrubby as the day wore on. Here and there on the hills were patches and pockets of snow. And over all this he worked, hacking away at the tough and slippery oiled silk and clinging stoutly to the netting. Presently they cleared and dropped a tangle of bent steel rods and wires from the frame, and a big chunk of silk bladder. That was trying. The airship flew up at once as this loose hamper parted. It seemed almost as though they were dropping all Canada. The stuff spread out in the air and floated down and hit and twisted up in a nasty fashion on the lip of a gorge. Bert clung like a frozen monkey to his ropes, and did not move a muscle for five minutes.

But there was something very exhilarating, he found, in this dangerous work, and above everything else, there was the sense of fellowship. He was no longer an isolated and distrustful stranger among these others, he had now a common object with them, he worked with a friendly rivalry to get through with his share before them. And he developed a great respect and affection for Kurt, which had hitherto been only latent in him. Kurt with a job to direct was altogether admirable: he was resourceful, helpful, considerate, swift. He seemed to be everywhere. One forgot his pinkness, his light cheerfulness of manner. Directly one had trouble he was at hand with sound and confident advice. He was like an elder brother to his men.

Altogether they cleared three considerable chunks of wreckage, and then Bert was glad to clamber up into the cabins again and give place to a second squad. He and his companions were given hot coffee, and, indeed, even gloved as they were, the job had been a cold one. They sat drinking it and regarding each other with satisfaction. One man spoke to Bert amiably in German, and Bert nodded and smiled. Through Kurt, Bert, whose ankles were almost frozen, succeeded in getting a pair of top-boots from one of the disabled men.

In the afternoon the wind abated greatly, and small, infrequent snowflakes came drifting by. Snow also spread more abundantly below, and the only trees were clumps of pine and spruce in the lower valleys. Kurt went with three men into the still intact gas-chambers, let out a certain quantity of gas from them, and prepared a series of ripping panels for the descent. Also the residue of the bombs and explosives in the magazine were thrown overboard and fell, detonating loudly in the wilderness below. And about four o'clock in the afternoon, upon a wide and rocky plain within sight of snow-crested cliffs, the *Vaterland* ripped and grounded.

It was necessarily a difficult and violent affair, for the *Vaterland* had not been planned for the necessities of a balloon. The captain got one panel ripped too soon and the others not soon enough. She dropped heavily, bounced clumsily, and smashed the hanging gallery into the fore-part, mortally injuring Von Winterfeld, and then came down in a collapsing heap after dragging for some moments. The forward shield and its machine-gun tumbled in upon the things below. Two men were hurt badly – one got a broken leg and one was internally injured – by flying rods and wires, and Bert was pinned for a time under the side. When at last he got clear and could take a view of the situation, the great black eagle that had started so splendidly from Franconia six evenings ago, sprawled deflated over the cabins of the airship and the frost-bitten rocks of this desolate place and looked a most unfortunate bird – as though someone had caught it and wrung its neck and cast it aside. Several of the crew of the airship were standing about in silence, contemplating the wreckage and the empty wilderness into which they had fallen. Others were busy under the impromptu tent made by the empty gas-chambers. The Prince had gone a little way off and was scrutinizing the distant heights through his field-glass. They had the appearance of old sea-cliffs; here and there were small clumps of conifers, and in two places tall cascades.

The nearer ground was strewn with glaciated boulders and supported nothing but a stunted Alpine vegetation of compact clustering stems and stalkless flowers. No river was visible, but the air was full of the rush and babble of a torrent close at hand. A bleak and biting wind was blowing. Ever and again a snowflake drifted past. The springless frozen earth under Bert's feet felt strangely dead and heavy after the buoyant airship.

§ 6

So it came about that that great and powerful Prince Karl Albert was for a time thrust out of the stupendous conflict he chiefly had been instrumental in provoking. The chances of battle and the weather conspired to maroon him in Labrador,[6] and there he raged for six long days, while war and wonder swept the world. Nation rose against nation and air-fleet grappled air-fleet, cities blazed and men died in multitudes; but in Labrador one might have dreamt that, except for a little noise of hammering, the world was at peace.

There the encampment lay; from a distance the cabins, covered over with the silk of the balloon part, looked like a gipsy's tent on a rather exceptional scale, and all the available hands were busy in building out of the steel of the framework a mast from which the *Vaterland*'s electricians might hang the long conductors of the apparatus for wireless telegraphy that was to link the Prince to the world again. There were times when it seemed they would never rig that mast. From the onset the party suffered hardship. They were not too abundantly provisioned, and they were put on short rations, and for all the thick garments they had, they were but ill-equipped against the piercing wind and inhospitable violence of this wilderness. The first night was spent in darkness and without fires. The engines that had supplied power were smashed and dropped far away to the south, and there was never a match among the company. It had been death to carry matches. All the explosives had been thrown out of the magazine, and it was only towards morning that the bird-faced man whose cabin Bert had taken in the beginning confessed to a brace of duelling-pistols and cartridges, with which a fire could be started. Afterwards the lockers of the machine-gun were found to contain a supply of unused ammunition.

The night was a distressing one and seemed almost interminable. Hardly anyone slept. There were seven wounded men aboard, and Von Winterfeld's head had been injured and he was shivering and in delirium, struggling with his attendant and shouting strange things about the burning of New York. The men crept together in the mess-room in the darkling, wrapped in what they could find, and drank cocoa from the fireless heaters and listened to his cries. In the morning the Prince made them a speech about Destiny, and the God of his Fathers, and the pleasure and glory of giving one's life for his dynasty, and a number of similar considerations that might otherwise have been neglected in that bleak wilderness. The men cheered without enthusiasm, and far away a wolf howled.

Then they set to work, and for a week they toiled to put up a mast of steel, and hang from it a gridiron of copper wires two hundred feet by twelve. The theme of all that time was work, work continually, straining and toilsome work, and all the rest was grim hardship and evil chances, save for a certain wild splendour in the sunset and sunrise, in the torrents and drifting weather, in the wilderness about them. They built and tended a ring of perpetual fires, gangs roamed for brushwood and met with wolves, and the wounded men and their beds were brought out from the airship cabins, and put in shelters about the fires. There old Von Winterfeld raved and became quiet and presently died, and three of the other wounded sickened for want of good food, while their fellows mended. These things happened, as it were, in the wings; the central facts before Bert's consciousness were always, firstly, the perpetual toil, the holding and lifting, and lugging at heavy and clumsy masses, the tedious filing and winding of wires; and secondly, the Prince, urgent and threatening whenever a man relaxed. He would stand over them and point over their heads, southward into the empty sky. 'The world there,' he said in German, 'is waiting for us! Fifty centuries come to their Consummation.' Bert did not understand the words, but he read the gesture. Several times the

Prince grew angry; once with a man who was working slowly, once with a man who stole a comrade's ration. The first he scolded and set to a more tedious task; the second he struck in the face and ill-used. He did no work himself. There was a clear space near the fires, in which he would walk up and down, sometimes for hours together, with arms folded, muttering to himself of Patience and his destiny. At times these mutterings broke out into rhetoric, into shouts and gestures that would arrest the workers; they would stare at him until they perceived that his blue eyes glared and his waving hand addressed itself always to the southward hills. On Sunday the work ceased for half an hour, and the Prince preached on faith and God's friendship for David, and afterwards they all sang: 'Ein feste Burg ist unser Gott.'

In an improvised hovel lay Von Winterfeld, and all one morning he raved of the greatness of Germany. 'Blut und Eisen!' he shouted, and then, as if in derision, 'Welt-Politik – ha, ha!' Then he would explain complicated questions of polity to imaginary hearers, in low, wily tones. The other sick men kept still, listening to him. Bert's distracted attention would be recalled by Kurt. 'Smallways, take that end. So!'

Slowly, tediously, the great mast was rigged, and hoisted foot by foot into place. The electricians had contrived a catchment pool and a wheel in the torrent close at hand – for the little Mülhausen dynamo with its turbinal volute used by the telegraphists was quite adaptable to water driving, and on the sixth day in the evening the apparatus was in working order and the Prince was calling – weakly, indeed, but calling – to his air-fleet across the empty spaces of the world. For a time he called unheeded.

The effect of that evening was to linger long in Bert's memory. A red fire spluttered and blazed close by the electricians at their work, and red gleams ran up the vertical steel mast and threads of copper wire towards the zenith. The Prince sat on a rock close by, with his chin on his hand, waiting. Beyond and to the northward was the cairn that covered Von Winterfeld, surmounted by a cross of steel, and from among the tumbled rocks in the distance the eyes of a wolf gleamed redly. On the other

hand was the wreckage of the great airship and the men bivou-
acked about a second ruddy flare. They were all keeping very
still, as if waiting to hear what news might presently be given
them. Far away, across many hundreds of miles of desolation,
other wireless masts would be clicking and snapping, and
waking into responsive vibration. Perhaps they were not. Perhaps these throbs upon the ether wasted themselves upon a
regardless world. When the men spoke, they spoke in low
tones. Now and then a bird shrieked remotely, and once a
wolf howled. All these things were set in the immense cold
spaciousness of the wild.

§ 7

Bert got the news last, and chiefly in broken English, from a
linguist among his mates. It was only far on in the night that
the weary telegraphist got an answer to his calls, but then the
messages came clear and strong. And such news it was!

'I say,' said Bert at his breakfast, amidst a great clamour, 'tell
us a bit.'

'All de vorlt is at vor!' said the linguist, waving his cocoa in
an illustrative manner, 'all de vorlt is at vor!'

Bert stared southward into the dawn. It did not seem so.

'All de vorlt is at vor! They haf burn' Berlin; they haf burn'
London; they haf burn' Hamburg and Paris. Chapan hass burn'
San Francisco. We haf mate a camp at Niagara. Dat is whad
they are telling us. China has cot *Drachenflieger* and *Luftschiffe*
beyont counting. All de vorlt is at vor!'

'Gaw!' said Bert.

'Yess,' said the linguist, drinking his cocoa.

'Burnt up London, 'ave they? Like we did New York?'

'It wass a bombardment.'

'They don't say anything about a place called Clapham, or
Bun Hill, do they?'

'I haf heard noding,' said the linguist.

That was all Bert could get for a time. But the excitement of
the men about him was contagious, and presently he saw Kurt
standing alone, hands behind him, and looking at one of the

distant waterfalls very steadfastly. He went up and saluted, soldier-fashion. 'Beg pardon, lieutenant,' he said.

Kurt turned his face. It was unusually grave that morning. 'I was just thinking I would like to see that waterfall closer,' he said. 'It reminds me – what do you want?'

'I can't make 'ead or tail of what they're saying, sir. Would you mind telling me the news?'

'Damn the news,' said Kurt. 'You'll get news enough before the day's out. It's the end of the world. They're sending the *Graf Zeppelin* for us. She'll be here by the morning, and we ought to be at Niagara – or eternal smash – within eight-and-forty hours. . . . I want to look at that waterfall. You'd better come with me. Have you had your rations?'

'Yessir.'

'Very well. Come.'

And musing profoundly, Kurt led the way across the rocks towards the distant waterfall. For a time Bert walked behind him in the character of an escort; then as they passed out of the atmosphere of the encampment, Kurt lagged for him to come alongside.

'We shall be back in it all in two days' time,' he said. 'And it's a devil of a war to go back to. That's the news. The world's gone mad. Our fleet beat the Americans the night we got disabled, that's clear. We lost eleven – eleven airships certain, and all their aeroplanes got smashed. God knows how much we smashed or how many we killed. But that was only the beginning. Our start's been like firing a magazine. Every country was hiding flying machines. They're fighting in the air all over Europe – all over the world. The Japanese and Chinese have joined in. That's the great fact. That's the supreme fact. They've pounced into our little quarrels. . . . The Yellow Peril was a peril after all! They've got thousands of airships. They're all over the world. We bombarded London and Paris, and the French and English have smashed up Berlin. And now Asia is at us all, and on the top of us all. . . . It's mania. China on the top. And they don't know where to stop. It's limitless. It's the last confusion. They're bombarding capitals, smashing up dockyards and factories, mines and fleets.'

'Did they do much to London, sir?' asked Bert.

'Heaven knows. . . .'

He said no more for a time.

'This Labrador seems a quiet place,' he resumed at last. 'I'm half a mind to stay here. Can't do that. No! I've got to see it through. I've got to see it through. You've got to, too. Everyone. . . . But why? . . . I tell you – our world's gone to pieces. There's no way out of it, no way back. Here we are! We're like mice caught in a house on fire, we're like cattle overtaken by a flood. Presently we shall be picked up, and back we shall go into the fighting. We shall kill and smash again – perhaps. It's a Chino-Japanese air-fleet this time, and the odds are against us. Our turn will come. What will happen to you I don't know, but for myself, I know quite well; I shall be killed.'

'You'll be all right,' said Bert, after a queer pause.

'No!' said Kurt, 'I'm going to be killed. I didn't know it before, but this morning at dawn I knew it – as though I'd been told.'

''Ow?'

'I tell you I know.'

'But 'ow *could* you know?'

'I know.'

'Like being told?'

'Like being certain.

'I know,' he repeated, and for a time they walked in silence towards the waterfall.

Kurt, wrapped in his thoughts, walked heedlessly, and at last broke out again. 'I've always felt young before, Smallways, but this morning I feel old – old. So old! Nearer to death than old men feel. And I've always thought life was a lark. It isn't. . . . This sort of thing has always been happening, I suppose – these things, wars and earthquakes, that sweep across all the decency of life. It's just as though I had woke up to it all for the first time. Every night since we were at New York I've dreamt of it. . . . And it's always been so – it's the way of life. People are torn away from the people they care for; homes are smashed, creatures full of life and memories and little peculiar gifts are scalded and smashed and torn to pieces, and starved and spoilt.

London! Berlin! San Francisco! Think of all the human histories we ended in New York! ... And the others go on again as though such things weren't possible. As I went on! Like animals! Just like animals.'

He said nothing for a long time, and then he dropped out, 'The Prince is a lunatic!'

They came to a place where they had to climb, and then to a long peat level beside a rivulet. There a quantity of delicate little pink flowers caught Bert's eye. 'Gaw!' he said, and stooped to pick one. 'In a place like this.'

Kurt stopped and half turned. His face winced.

'I never see such a flower,' said Bert. 'It's so delicate.'

'Pick some more if you want to,' said Kurt.

Bert did so, while Kurt stood and watched him. 'Funny 'ow one always wants to pick flowers,' said Bert.

Kurt had nothing to add to that.

They went on again, without talking, for a long time.

At last they came to a rocky hummock, from which the view of the waterfall opened out. There Kurt stopped and seated himself on a rock. 'That's as much as I wanted to see,' he explained. 'It isn't very like, but it's like enough.'

'Like what?'

'Another waterfall I knew.'

He asked a question abruptly. 'Got a girl, Smallways?'

'Funny thing,' said Bert, 'those flowers, I suppose— I was jes' thinking of 'er.'

'So was I.'

'*What?* Edna?'

'No. I was thinking of *my* Edna. We've all got Ednas, I suppose, for our imaginations to play about. This was a girl. But all that's past for ever. It's hard to think I can't see her just for a minute – just let her know I'm thinking of her.'

'Very likely,' said Bert, 'you'll see 'er all right.'

'No,' said Kurt with decision, 'I *know*.

'I met her,' he went on, 'in a place like this – in the Alps – Engstlen Alp. There's a waterfall rather like this one – a broad waterfall down towards Innertkirchen.[7] That's why I came here this morning. We slipped away and had half a day together beside it. And we picked flowers. Just such flowers as you picked. The same, for all I know. And gentian.'

'I know,' said Bert; 'me and Edna – we done things like that. Flowers. And all that. Seems years off now.'

'She was beautiful and daring and shy. Mein Gott! . . . I can hardly hold myself for the desire to see her and hear her voice again before I die. Where is she? . . . Look here, Smallways, I shall write a sort of letter— And there's her portrait.' He touched his breast pocket.

'You'll see 'er again all right,' said Bert.

'No! I shall never see her again. . . . I don't understand why people should meet just to be torn apart. But I know she and I will never meet again. That I know as surely as that the sun will rise, and that cascade come shining over the rocks after I am dead and done. . . . Oh! It's all foolishness and haste and violence and cruel folly, stupidity and blundering hate and selfish ambition – all the things that men have done – all the things they will ever do. Gott! Smallways, what a muddle and confusion life has always been – the battles and massacres and disasters, the hates and harsh acts, the murders and sweatings, the lynchings and cheatings. This morning I am tired of it all, as though I'd just found it out for the first time. I *have* found it out. When a man is tired of life I suppose it is time for him to die. I've lost heart, and death is over me. Death is close to me, and I know I have got to end. But think of all the hopes I had only a little time ago, the sense of fine beginnings! . . . It was all a sham. There were no beginnings. . . . We're just ants in anthill cities, in a world that doesn't matter; that goes on and rambles into nothingness. New York – New York doesn't even strike me as horrible. New York was nothing but an anthill kicked to pieces by a fool!

'Think of it, Smallways; there's war everywhere! They're smashing up their civilization before they have made it. The sort of thing the English did at Alexandria, the Japanese at Port Arthur, the French at Casablanca,[8] is going on everywhere. Everywhere! Down in South America even they are fighting among themselves! No place is safe – no place is at peace. There is no place where a woman and her daughter can hide and be at peace. The war comes through the air, bombs drop in the night. Quiet people go out in the morning, and see air-fleets passing overhead – dripping death – dripping death!'

8

A WORLD AT WAR

§ 1

It was only very slowly that Bert got hold of this idea that the whole world was at war, that he formed any image at all of the crowded countries south of these Arctic solitudes stricken with terror and dismay as these new-born aerial navies swept across their skies. He was used to thinking of the world not as a whole, but as a limitless hinterland of happenings beyond the range of his immediate vision. War in his imagination was something, a source of news and emotion, that happened in a restricted area called the Seat of War. But now the whole atmosphere was the Seat of War, and every land a cockpit. So closely had the nations raced along the path of research and invention, so secret and yet so parallel had been their plans and acquisitions, that it was within a few hours of the launching of the first fleet in Franconia that an Asiatic Armada beat its westward way across, high above, the marvelling millions in the plain of the Ganges. But the preparations of the Confederation of Eastern Asia had been on an altogether more colossal scale than the German. 'With this step,' said Tan Ting-siang,[1] 'we overtake and pass the West. We recover the peace of the world that these barbarians have destroyed.'

Their secrecy and swiftness and inventions had far surpassed those of the Germans, and where the Germans had had a hundred men at work the Asiatics had ten thousand. There came to their great aeronautic parks at Chinsi-fu and Tsingyen, by the monorails that now laced the whole surface of China, a limitless supply of skilled and able workmen, workmen far above the average European in industrial efficiency. The news of the German World Surprise simply quickened their efforts. At the time of the bombardment of New York it is doubtful if the Germans had three hundred airships altogether in the world; the score of Asiatic fleets flying east and west and south must have numbered several thousand. Moreover, the Asiatics had a real fighting flying machine, the *Niaio* as it was called, a light but quite efficient weapon, infinitely superior to the German *Drachenflieger*. Like that, it was a one-man machine; but it was built very lightly of steel and cane and chemical silk, with a transverse engine and a flapping side-wing. The aeronaut carried a gun firing explosive bullets loaded with oxygen, and in addition, and true to the best tradition of Japan, a sword. The riders were Japanese, and it is characteristic that from the first it was contemplated that the aeronaut should be a swordsman. The wings of these fliers had bat-like hooks forward, by which they were to cling to their antagonist's gas-chambers while boarding him. These light flying machines were carried with the fleets, and also sent overland or by sea to the front with the men. They were capable of flights of from two to five hundred miles, according to the wind.

So, hard upon the uprush of the first German air-fleet, these Asiatic swarms took to the atmosphere. Instantly every organized government in the world was frantically and vehemently building airships and whatever approach to a flying machine its inventors had discovered. There was no time for diplomacy. Warnings and ultimatums were telegraphed to and fro, and in a few hours all the panic-fierce world was openly at war, and at war in the most complicated way. For Britain and France and Italy had declared war upon Germany and outraged Swiss neutrality; India, at the sight of Asiatic airships, had broken into a Hindoo insurrection in Bengal and a Mahometan revolt hostile to this in the North-west Provinces – the latter spreading like wildfire from Gobi to the Gold Coast – and the Confederation of Eastern Asia had seized the oil wells of Burmah and was impartially attacking America and Germany. In a week they were building airships in Damascus and Cairo and Johannesburg; Australia and New Zealand were frantically equipping themselves. One unique and terrifying aspect of this development was the swiftness with which these monsters could be produced. To build an ironclad took from two to four years; an airship could be put together in as many weeks. Moreover, compared with even a torpedo boat the airship was remarkably simple to construct: given the air-chamber material, the engines, the gas plant and the design, it was really not more complicated and far easier than an ordinary wooden boat had been a hundred years before. And now from Cape Horn to Nova Zembla,[2] and from Canton round to Canton again, there were factories and workshops and industrial resources.

And the German airships were barely in sight of the Atlantic waters, the first Asiatic fleet was scarcely reported from Upper Burmah, before the fantastic fabric of credit and finance that had held the world together economically for a hundred years strained and snapped. A tornado of realization swept through every stock exchange in the world; banks stopped payment, business shrank and ceased, factories ran on for a day or so by a sort of inertia, completing the orders of bankrupt and extinguished customers, then stopped. The New York Bert Smallways saw, for all its glare of light and traffic, was in the pit of an economic and financial collapse unparalleled in history. The flow of the food supply was already a little checked. And before the World War had lasted two weeks – by the time that mast was rigged in Labrador – there was not a city or town in the world outside China, however far from the actual centres of destruction, where police and government were not adopting special emergency methods to deal with a want of food and a glut of unemployed people.

The special peculiarities of aerial warfare were of such a nature as to trend, once it had begun, almost inevitably towards social disorganization. The first of these peculiarities was brought home to the Germans in their attack upon New York; the immense power of destruction an airship has over the thing below, and its relative inability to occupy or police or guard or garrison a surrendered position. Necessarily, in the face of urban populations in a state of economic disorganization and infuriated and starving, this led to violent and destructive collisions, and even where the air-fleet floated inactive above, there would be civil conflict and passionate disorder below. Nothing comparable to this state of affairs had been known in the previous history of warfare, unless we take such a case as that of a nineteenth-century warship attacking some large savage or barbaric settlement, or one of those naval bombardments that disfigure the history of Great Britain in the late eighteenth century. Then, indeed, there had been cruelties and destruction that faintly foreshadowed the horrors of the aerial war. Moreover, before the twentieth century the world had had but one experience, and that a comparatively light one, in the Communist insurrection[3] of Paris, 1871, of the possibilities of a modern urban population under warlike stresses.

A second peculiarity of airship war as it first came to the world that also made for social collapse was the ineffectiveness of the early airships against each other. Upon anything below they could rain explosives in the most deadly fashion, forts and ships and cities lay at their mercy, but unless they were prepared for a suicidal grapple they could do remarkably little mischief to each other. The armament of the huge German airships, big as the biggest mammoth liners afloat, was one machine-gun that could easily have been packed up on a couple of mules. In addition, when it became evident that the air must be fought for, the air-sailors were provided with rifles with explosive bullets of oxygen or inflammable substance, but no airship at any time ever carried as much in the way of guns and armour as the smallest gunboat on the navy list had been accustomed to do. Consequently, when these monsters met in battle they manoeuvred for the upper place, or grappled and fought like junks, throwing grenades, fighting hand to hand in an entirely mediaeval fashion. The risks of a collapse and fall on either side came near to balancing in every case the chances of victory. As a consequence, and after their first experiences of battle, one finds a growing tendency on the part of the air-fleet admirals to evade joining battle and to seek rather the moral advantage of a destructive counter-attack.

And if the airships were too ineffective, the early *Drachen-flieger* were either too unstable, like the German, or too light, like the Japanese, to produce immediately decisive results.

Later, it is true, the Brazilians launched a flying machine of a type and scale that was capable of dealing with an airship, but they built only three or four, they operated only in South America and they vanished from history untraceably in the time when world bankruptcy put a stop to all further engineering production on any considerable scale.

The third peculiarity of aerial warfare was that it was at once enormously destructive and entirely indecisive. It had this unique feature, that both sides lay open to punitive attack. In all previous forms of war, both by land and sea, the losing side was speedily unable to raid its antagonist's territory and communications. One fought on a 'front', and behind that front the winner's supplies and resources, his towns and factories and capital, the peace of his country, were secure. If the war was a naval one, you destroyed your enemy's battle fleet and then blockaded his ports, secured his coaling stations, and hunted down any stray cruisers that threatened your ports of commerce. But to blockade and watch a coastline is one thing, to blockade and watch the whole surface of a country is another, and cruisers and privateers are things that take long to make, that cannot be packed up and hidden and carried unostentatiously from point to point. In aerial war the stronger side, even supposing it destroyed the main battle fleet of the weaker, had then either to patrol and watch or destroy every possible point at which he might produce another and perhaps novel and more deadly form of flier. It meant darkening his air with airships. It meant building them by the thousand and making aeronauts by the hundred thousand. A small uninflated airship could be hidden in a railway shed, in a village street, in a wood; a flying machine is even less conspicuous.

And in the air are no streets, no channels, no point where one can say of an antagonist, 'If he wants to reach my capital he must come by here.' In the air all directions lead everywhere.

Consequently it was impossible to end a war by any of the established methods. A having outnumbered and overwhelmed B, hovers, a thousand airships strong, over his capital, threatening to bombard it unless B submits. B replies by wireless telegraphy that he is now in the act of bombarding the chief manufacturing city of A by means of three raider airships. A denounces B's raiders as pirates and so forth, bombards B's capital and sets off to hunt down B's airships, while B, in a state of passionate emotion and heroic unconquerableness, sets to work amidst his ruins, making fresh airships and explosives for the benefit of A. The war became perforce a universal guerilla war, a war inextricably involving civilians and homes and all the apparatus of social life.

These aspects of aerial fighting took the world by surprise. There had been no foresight to deduce these consequences. If there had been, the world would have arranged for a Universal Peace Conference[4] in 1900. But mechanical invention had gone faster than intellectual and social organization, and the world, with its silly old flags, its silly unmeaning tradition of nationality, its cheap newspapers and cheaper passions and imperialisms, its base commercial motives and habitual insincerities and vulgarities, its race lies and conflicts, was taken by surprise. Once the war began there was no stopping it. The flimsy fabric of credit that had grown with no man foreseeing, and that had held those hundreds of millions in an economic interdependence that no man clearly understood, dissolved in panic. Everywhere went the airships dropping bombs, destroying any hope of a rally, and everywhere below were economic catastrophe, starving workless people, rioting, and social disorder. Whatever constructive guiding intelligence there had been among the nations vanished in the passionate stresses of the time. Such newspapers and documents and histories as survive from this period all tell one universal story of towns and cities with the food supply interrupted and their streets congested with starving unemployed; of crises in administration and states of siege, of provisional Governments and Councils of Defence, and in the cases of India and Egypt, insurrectionary committees taking charge, of the rearming of the population, of the making of batteries and gun-pits, of the vehement manufacture of airships and flying machines.

One sees these things in glimpses, in illuminated moments, as if through a driving reek of clouds, going on all over the world. It was the dissolution of an age; it was the collapse of the civilization that had trusted to machinery, and the instruments of its destruction were machines. But while the collapse of the previous great civilization, that of Rome, had been a matter of centuries, had been a thing of phase and phase like the ageing and dying of a man, this, like his killing by railway or motor-car, was one swift, conclusive smashing and an end.

§ 2

The early battles of the aerial war were no doubt determined by attempts to realize the old naval maxim, to ascertain the position of the enemy's fleet and to destroy it. There was first the battle of the Bernese Oberland, in which the Italian and French navigables in their flank raid upon the Franconian Park were assailed by the Swiss experimental squadron, supported as the day wore on by German airships; and then the encounter of the British Winterhouse-Dunne[5] aeroplanes with three unfortunate Germans.

Then came the battle of North India, in which the entire Anglo-Indian aeronautic settlement establishment fought for three days against overwhelming odds, and was dispersed and destroyed in detail.

And simultaneously with the beginning of that commenced the momentous struggle of the Germans and Asiatics that is usually known as the Battle of Niagara because of the objective of the Asiatic attack. But it passed gradually into a sporadic conflict over half a continent. Such German airships as escaped destruction in battle descended and surrendered to the Americans, and were remanned; and in the end it became a series of pitiless and heroic encounters between the Americans, savagely resolved to exterminate their enemies, and a continually reinforced army of invasion from Asia quartered upon the Pacific slope and supported by an immense fleet. From the first the war in America was fought with implacable bitterness; no quarter was asked, no prisoners were taken. With ferocious and magnificent energy the Americans constructed and launched ship after ship to battle and perish against the Asiatic multitudes. All other affairs were subordinate to this war, the whole population was presently living or dying for it. Presently, as I shall tell, the white men found in the Butteridge machine a weapon that could meet and fight the flying machines of the Asiatic swordsmen.

The Asiatic invasion of America completely effaced the German-American conflict. It vanishes from history. At first it had seemed to promise quite sufficient tragedy in itself – beginning as it did in unforgettable massacre. After the destruction of central New York all America had risen like one man, resolved to die a thousand deaths rather than submit to Germany. The Germans grimly resolved upon beating the Americans into submission and, following out the plans developed by the Prince, had seized Niagara – in order to avail themselves of its enormous power works, expelled all its inhabitants and made a desert of its environs as far as Buffalo. They had also, directly Great Britain and France declared war, wrecked the country upon the Canadian side for nearly ten miles inland. They began to bring up men and material from the fleet off the east coast, stringing out to and fro like bees getting honey. It was then that the Asiatic forces appeared, and it was in their attack upon this German base at Niagara that the air-fleets of East and West first met and the greater issue became clear.

One conspicuous peculiarity of the early aerial fighting arose from the profound secrecy with which the airships had been prepared. Each power had had but the dimmest inkling of the schemes of its rivals, and even experiments with its own devices were limited by the needs of secrecy. None of the designers of airships and aeroplanes had known clearly what their inventions might have to fight; many had not imagined they would have to fight anything whatever in the air, and had planned them only for the dropping of explosives. Such had been the German idea. The only weapon for fighting another airship with which the Franconian fleet had been provided was the machine-gun forward. Only after the fight over New York were the men given short rifles with detonating bullets. Theoretically, the *Drachenflieger* were to have been the fighting weapon. They were declared to be aerial torpedo boats, and the aeronaut was supposed to swoop close to his antagonist and cast his bombs as he whirled past. But indeed these contrivances were hopelessly unstable; not one-third in any engagement succeeded in getting back to the mother airship. The rest were either smashed up or grounded.

The allied Chino-Japanese fleet made the same distinction as the Germans between airships and fighting machines heavier than air, but the type in both cases was entirely different from the Occidental models, and – it is eloquent of the vigour with which these great peoples took up and bettered the European methods of scientific research – in almost every particular the invention of Asiatic engineers. Chief among these, it is worth remarking, was Mohini K. Chatterjee,[6] a political exile who had formerly served in the British-Indian aeronautic park at Lahore.

The German airship was fish-shaped, with a blunted head; the Asiatic airship was also fish-shaped, but not so much on the lines of a cod or goby as of a ray or sole. It had a wide flat underside, unbroken by windows or any opening except along the middle line. Its cabins occupied its axis, with a sort of bridge deck above, and the gas-chambers gave the whole affair the shape of a gipsy's hooped tent, except that it was much flatter. The German airship was essentially a navigable balloon very much lighter than air; the Asiatic airship was very little lighter than air and skimmed through it with much greater velocity if with considerably less stability. They carried fore and aft guns, the latter much the larger, throwing inflammatory shells, and in addition they had nests for riflemen on both the upper and the underside. Light as this armament was in comparison with the smallest gunboat that ever sailed, it was sufficient for them to outfight as well as outfly the German monster airships. In action they flew to get behind or over the Germans: they even dashed underneath, avoiding only passing immediately beneath the magazine, and then as soon as they had crossed let fly with their rear gun, and sent flares or oxygen shells into the antagonist's gas-chambers.

It was not in their airships but, as I have said, in their flying-machines proper that the strength of the Asiatics lay. Next only to the Butteridge machine these were certainly the most efficient heavier-than-air fliers that had ever appeared. They were the invention of a Japanese artist, and they differed in type extremely from the box-kite quality of the German *Drachenflieger*. They had curiously curved, flexible side wings, more like *bent* butterfly's wings than anything else, and made of a substance like celluloid and of brightly painted silk, and they had a long humming-bird tail. At the forward corner of the wings were hooks, rather like the claws of a bat, by which the machine could catch and hang and tear at the walls of an airship's gas-chamber. The solitary rider sat between the wings above a transverse explosive engine, an explosive engine that differed in no essential particular from those in use in the light motor-bicycles of the period. Below was a single large wheel. The rider sat astride a saddle, as in the Butteridge machine, and he carried a large double-edged two-handed sword, in addition to his explosive-bullet firing rifle.

§ 3

One sets down these particulars and compares the points of the American and German pattern of aeroplane and navigable, but none of these facts were clearly known to any of those who fought in this monstrously confused battle above the American great lakes.

Each side went into action against it knew not what, under novel conditions and with apparatus that even without hostile attacks was capable of producing the most disconcerting surprises. Schemes of action, attempts at collective manoeuvring necessarily went to pieces directly the fight began, just as they did in almost all the early ironclad battles of the previous century. Each captain then had to fall back upon individual action and his own devices; one would see triumph in what another read as a cue for flight and despair. It is as true of the Battle of Niagara as of the Battle of Lissa[7] that it was not a battle but a bundle of 'battlettes'!

To such a spectator as Bert it presented itself as a series of incidents, some immense, some trivial, but collectively incoherent. He never had a sense of any plain issue joined, of any point struggled for and won or lost. He saw tremendous things happen, and in the end his world darkened to disaster and ruin.

He saw the battle from the ground, from Prospect Park[8] and from Goat Island,[9] whither he fled.

But the manner in which he came to be on the ground needs explaining.

The Prince had resumed command of his fleet through wireless telegraphy long before the *Zeppelin* had located his encampment in Labrador. By his direction the German air-fleet, whose advance scouts had been in contact with the Japanese over the Rocky Mountains, had concentrated upon Niagara and awaited his arrival. He had rejoined his command early in the morning of the 12th, and Bert had his first prospect of the Gorge of Niagara while he was doing net drill outside the middle gas-chamber at sunrise. The *Zeppelin* was flying very high at the time, and far below he saw the water in the gorge marbled with froth, and then away to the west the great crescent of the Canadian Fall shining, flickering and foaming in the level sunlight, and sending up a deep, incessant thudding rumble to the sky. The air-fleet was keeping station in an enormous crescent, with its horns pointing south-westward, a long array of shining monsters with tails rotating slowly, and German ensigns now trailing from their bellies aft of their Marconi pendants.

Niagara city was still largely standing then, albeit its streets were empty of all life. Its bridges were intact, its hotels and restaurants still flying flags and inviting sky signs, its power stations running. But about it the country on both sides of the gorge might have been swept by a colossal broom. Everything that could possibly give cover to an attack upon the German position at Niagara had been levelled as ruthlessly as machinery and explosives could contrive; houses blown up and burnt, woods burnt, fences and crops destroyed. The monorails had been torn up, and the roads in particular cleared of all possibility of concealment or shelter. Seen from above the effect of this wreckage was grotesque. Young woods had been destroyed wholesale by dragging wires, and the spoilt saplings, smashed or uprooted, lay in swathes like corn after the sickle. Houses had an appearance of being flattened down by the pressure of a gigantic finger. Much burning was still going on, and large areas had been reduced to patches of smouldering and sometimes still glowing blackness. Here and there lay the débris of belated fugitives, carts and dead bodies of horses and men; and where houses had had water supplies there were pools of water and running springs from the ruptured pipes. In unscorched fields horses and cattle still fed peacefully. Beyond this desolated area the countryside was still standing, but almost all the people had fled. Buffalo was on fire to an enormous extent, and there were no signs of any efforts to grapple with the flames.

Niagara city itself was being rapidly converted to the needs of a military depot. A large number of skilled engineers had already been brought from the fleet, and were busily at work adapting the exterior industrial apparatus of the place to the purposes of an aeronautic park. They had made a gas recharging station at the corner of the American Fall above the funicular railway, and they were opening up a much larger area to the south for the same purpose. Over the power houses and hotels and suchlike prominent or important points, the German flag was flying.

The *Zeppelin* circled slowly over this scene twice while the Prince surveyed it from the swinging gallery; it then rose towards the centre of the crescent and transferred the Prince and his suit, Kurt included, to the *Hohenzollern*, which had been chosen as the flagship during the impending battle. They were swung up on a small cable from the forward gallery, and the men of the *Zeppelin* manned the outer netting as the Prince and his staff left them. The *Zeppelin* then came about, circled down and grounded in Prospect Park, in order to land the wounded and take aboard explosives; for she had come to Labrador with her magazines empty, it being uncertain what weight she might need to carry. She also replenished the hydrogen in one of her forward chambers which had leaked.

Bert was detailed as a bearer and helped carry the wounded one by one into the nearest of the large hotels that faced the Canadian shore. The hotel was quite empty except that there were two trained American nurses and a Negro porter, and three or four Germans awaiting them. Bert went with the

Zeppelin's doctor into the main street of the place, and they broke into a drug-shop and obtained various things of which they stood in need. As they returned they found an officer and two men making a rough inventory of the available material in the various stores. Except for them the wide, main street of the town was quite deserted, the people had been given three hours to clear out, and everybody, it seemed, had done so. At one corner a dead man lay against the wall – shot. Two or three dogs were visible up the empty vista, but towards its river end the passage of a string of monorail cars broke the stillness and the silence. They were loaded with hose, and were passing to the trainful of workers who were converting Prospect Park into an airship dock.

Bert pushed a case of medicine balanced on a bicycle taken from an adjacent shop, to the hotel, and then he was sent to load bombs into the *Zeppelin* magazine, a duty that called for elaborate care. From this job he was presently called off by the captain of the *Zeppelin*, who sent him with a note to the officer in charge of the Anglo-American Power Company, for the field telephone had still to be adjusted. Bert received his instructions in German, whose meaning he guessed, and saluted and took the note, not caring to betray his ignorance of the language. He started off with a bright air of knowing his way and turned a corner or so and was only beginning to suspect that he did not know where he was going when his attention was recalled to the sky by the report of a gun from the *Hohenzollern* and celestial cheering.

He looked up and found the view obstructed by the houses on either side of the street. He hesitated, and then curiosity took him back towards the bank of the river. Here his view was inconvenienced by trees, and it was with a start that he discovered the *Zeppelin*, which he knew had still a quarter of her magazines to fill, was rising over Goat Island. She had not waited for her complement of ammunition. It occurred to him that he was left behind. He ducked back among the trees and bushes until he felt secure from any afterthought on the part of the *Zeppelin*'s captain. Then his curiosity to see what the German air-fleet faced overcame him, and drew him at last halfway across the bridge to Goat Island. From that point he had nearly a hemisphere of sky and got his first glimpse of the Asiatic airships low in the sky above the glittering tumults of the Upper Rapids.

They were far less impressive than the German ships. He could not judge the distance, and they flew edgeways to him, so as to conceal the broader aspect of their bulk.

Bert stood there in the middle of the bridge, in a place that most people who knew it remembered as a place populous with sightseers and excursionists, and he was the only human being in sight there. Above him, very high in the heavens, the contending air-fleets manoeuvred; below him the river seethed like a sluice towards the American Fall. He was curiously dressed. His cheap blue serge trousers were thrust into German airship rubber boots, and on his head he wore an aeronaut's white cap that was a trifle too large for him. He thrust that back to reveal his staring little Cockney face, still scarred upon the brow. 'Gaw!' he whispered.

He stared. He gesticulated. Once or twice he shouted and applauded.

Then at a certain point terror seized him and he took to his heels in the direction of Goat Island.

§ 4

For a time after they were in sight of each other, neither fleet attempted to engage. The Germans numbered sixty-seven great airships and they maintained the crescent formation at a height of nearly four thousand feet. They kept a distance of about one and a half lengths, so that the horns of the crescent were nearly thirty miles apart. Closely in tow of the airships of the extreme squadrons on either wing were about thirty *Drachenflieger* ready manned, but these were too small and distant for Bert to distinguish.

At first, only what was called the Southern fleet of the Asiatics was visible to him. It consisted of forty airships, carrying altogether nearly four hundred one-man flying machines upon their flanks, and for some time it flew slowly and at a minimum distance of perhaps a dozen miles from the Germans, eastward across their front. At first Bert could distinguish only the greater bulks, then he perceived the one-man machines as a multitude of very small objects drifting like motes in the sunshine about and beneath the larger shapes.

He saw nothing then of the second fleet of the Asiatics, though that was probably coming into sight of the Germans at the time, in the north-west.

The air was very still, the sky almost without a cloud, and the German fleet had risen to an immense height, so that the airships seemed no longer of any considerable size. Both ends of their crescent showed plainly. As they beat southward they passed slowly between Bert and the sunlight, and became black outlines of themselves. The *Drachenflieger* appeared as little flecks of black on either wing of this aerial Armada.

The two fleets seemed in no hurry to engage. The Asiatics went far away into the east, quickening their pace and rising as they did so, and then tailed out into a long column and came flying back, rising towards the German left. The squadrons of the latter came about, facing this oblique advance, and suddenly little flickerings and a faint crepitating sound told that they had opened fire. For a time no effect was visible to the watcher on the bridge. Then, like a handful of snowflakes, the *Drachenflieger* swooped to the attack, and a multitude of red specks whirled up to meet them. It was to Bert's sense not only enormously remote but singularly inhuman. Not four hours since he had been on one of those very airships, and yet they seemed to him now not gas-bags carrying men, but strange sentient creatures that moved about and did things with a purpose of their own. The flight of the Asiatic and German flying machines joined and dropped earthward, became like a handful of white and red rose petals flung from a distant window, grew larger until Bert could see the overturned ones spinning through the air, and were hidden by great volumes of dark smoke that were rising in the direction of Buffalo. For a time they all were hidden; then two or three white and a number of red ones rose again into the sky like a swarm of big butterflies, and circled fighting and drove away out of sight again towards the east.

A heavy report recalled Bert's eyes to the zenith, and behold the great crescent had lost its dressing and burst into a disorderly long cloud of airships! One had dropped halfway down the sky. It was flaming fore and aft, and even as Bert looked it turned over and fell, spinning over and over itself, and vanished into the smoke of Buffalo.

Bert's mouth opened and shut, and he clutched tighter on the rail of the bridge. For some moments – they seemed long moments – the two fleets remained without any further change, flying obliquely towards each other, and making what came to Bert's ears as a midget uproar. Then suddenly from either side airships began dropping out of alignment, smitten by missiles he could neither see nor trace. The string of Asiatic ships swung round and either charged into or over (it was difficult to say from below) the shattered line of the Germans, who seemed to open out to give way to them. Some sort of manoeuvring began, but Bert could not grasp its import. The left of the battle became a confused dance of airships. For some minutes up there the two crossing lines of ships looked so close it seemed like a hand-to-hand scuffle in the sky. Then they broke up into groups and duels. The descent of German airships towards the lower sky increased. One of them flared down and vanished far away in the north; two dropped with something twisted and crippled in their movements; then a group of antagonists came down from the zenith in an eddying conflict, two Asiatics against one German, and were presently joined by another, and drove away eastward all together with others dropping out of the German line to join them. One Asiatic either rammed or collided with a still more gigantic German, and the two went spinning to destruction together. The northern squadron of Asiatics came into the battle unnoted by Bert, except that the multitude of ships above seemed presently increased. In a little while the fight was utter confusion, drifting on the whole to the southwest against the wind. It became more and more a series of group encounters. Here a huge German airship flamed earthward with a dozen flat Asiatic craft about her, crushing her every attempt to recover. Here another hung with its crew fighting off the swordsmen from a swarm of flying machines.

Here, again, an Asiatic aflame at either end swooped out of the
battle. His attention went from incident to incident in the vast
clearness overhead; these conspicuous cases of destruction
caught and held his mind; it was only very slowly that any sort
of scheme manifested itself between those nearer, more striking
episodes.

The mass of the airships that eddied remotely above was,
however, neither destroying nor destroyed. The majority of
them seemed to be going at full speed and circling upward for
position, exchanging ineffectual shots as they did so. Very little
ramming was essayed after the first tragic downfall of rammer
and rammed, and whatever attempts at boarding were made
were invisible to Bert. There seemed, however, a steady endeavour to isolate antagonists, to cut them off from their fellows
and bear them down, causing a perpetual sailing back and
interlacing of these shoaling bulks. The greater numbers of the
Asiatics and their swifter heeling movements gave them the
effect of persistently attacking the Germans. Overhead, and
evidently endeavouring to keep itself in touch with the works
of Niagara, a body of German airships drew itself together into
a compact phalanx, and the Asiatics became more and more
intent upon breaking this up. He was grotesquely reminded of
fish in a fish-pond struggling for crumbs. He could see puny
puffs of smoke and the flash of bombs, but never a sound came
down to him. . . .

A flapping shadow passed for a moment between Bert and
the sun and was followed by another. A whirring of engines,
click, clock, clitter clock, smote upon his ears. Instantly he
forgot the zenith.

Perhaps a hundred yards above the water, out of the south,
riding like Valkyries swiftly through the air on the strange
steeds the engineering of Europe had begotten upon the artistic
inspiration of Japan, came a long string of Asiatic swordsmen.
The wings flapped jerkily, click, clock, clitter clock, and the
machines drove up; they spread and ceased, and the apparatus
came soaring through the air. So they rose and fell and rose
again. They passed so closely overhead that Bert could hear
their voices calling to one another. They swooped towards

Niagara city and landed one after another in a long line in a clear space before the hotel. But he did not stay to watch them land. One yellow face had craned over and looked at him, and for one enigmatical instant met his eyes. . . .

It was then the idea came to Bert that he was altogether too conspicuous in the middle of the bridge, and that he took to his heels towards Goat Island. Thence, dodging about among the trees, with perhaps an excessive self-consciousness, he watched the rest of the struggle.

§ 5

When Bert's sense of security was sufficiently restored for him to watch the battle again, he perceived that a brisk little fight was in progress between the Asiatic aeronauts and the German engineers for the possession of Niagara city. It was the first time in the whole course of the war that he had seen anything resembling fighting as he had studied it in the illustrated papers of his youth. It seemed to him almost as though things were coming right. He saw men carrying rifles and taking cover and running briskly from point to point in a loose attacking formation. The first batch of aeronauts had probably been under the impression that the city was deserted. They had grounded in the open near Prospect Park and approached the houses towards the power works before they were disillusioned by a sudden fire. They had scattered back to the cover of a bank near the water – it was too far for them to reach their machines again; they were lying and firing at the men in the hotels and frame-houses about the power works.

Then to their support came a second string of red flying-machines driving up from the east. They rose up out of the haze above the houses and came round in a long curve as if surveying the position below. The fire of the Germans rose to a roar, and one of those soaring shapes gave an abrupt jerk backwards and fell among the houses. The others swooped down exactly like great birds upon the roof of the powerhouse. They caught upon it, and from each sprang a nimble little figure and ran towards the parapet.

Other flapping bird-shapes came into this affair, but Bert had not seen their coming. A staccato of shots came over to him, reminding him of army manoeuvres, of newspaper descriptions of fights, of all that was entirely correct in his conception of warfare. He saw quite a number of Germans running from the outlying houses towards the powerhouse. Two fell. One lay still, but the other wriggled and made efforts for a time. The hotel that was used as a hospital, and to which he had helped carry the wounded men from the *Zeppelin* earlier in the day, suddenly ran up the Geneva flag. The town that had seemed so quiet had evidently been concealing a considerable number of Germans, and they were now concentrating to hold the central powerhouse. He wondered what ammunition they might have. More and more of the Asiatic flying machines came into the conflict. They had disposed of the unfortunate German *Drachenflieger* and were now aiming at the incipient aeronautic park, the electric gas generators and repair stations which formed the German base. Some landed, and their aeronauts took cover and became energetic infantry soldiers. Others hovered above the fight, their men ever and again firing shots down at some chance exposure below. The firing came in paroxysms; now there would be a watchful lull and now a rapid tattoo of shots, rising to a roar. Once or twice flying machines, as they circled warily, came right overhead, and for a time Bert gave himself body and soul to cowering.

Ever and again a larger thunder mingled with the rattle and reminded him of the grapple of airships far above, but the nearer fight held his attention.

Abruptly something dropped from the zenith; something like a barrel or a huge football.

CRASH! It smashed with an immense report. It had fallen among the grounded Asiatic aeroplanes that lay among the turf and flowerbeds near the river. They flew in scraps and fragments, turf, trees and gravel leapt and fell; the aeronauts still lying along the canal bank were thrown about like sacks, catspaws[10] flew across the foaming water. All the windows of the hotel hospital that had been shiningly reflecting blue sky

and airships the moment before became vast black stars. Bang!
– a second followed. Bert looked up and was filled with a sense
of a number of monstrous bodies swooping down, coming
down on the whole affair like a flight of bellying blankets,
like a string of vast dish-covers. The central tangle of the battle
above was circling down as if to come into touch with the
powerhouse fight. He got a new effect of airships altogether, as
vast things coming down upon him, growing swiftly larger and
larger and more overwhelming, until the houses over the way
seemed small, the American rapids narrow, the bridge flimsy,
the combatants infinitesimal. As they came down they became
audible as a complex of shoutings and vast creakings and groan
ings and beatings and throbbings and shouts and shots. The
foreshortened black eagles at the fore-ends of the Germans had
an effect of actual combat of flying feathers.

Some of these fighting airships came within five hundred feet
of the ground. Bert could see men on the lower galleries of the
Germans firing rifles; could see Asiatics clinging to the ropes;
saw one man in aluminium diver's gear fall flashing headlong
into the waters above Goat Island. For the first time he saw the
Asiatic airships closely. From this aspect they reminded him
more than anything else of colossal snowshoes; they had a
curious patterning in black and white, in forms that reminded
him of the engine-turned cover of a watch. They had no hanging
galleries, but from little openings on the middle line peeped out
men and the muzzles of guns. So, driving in long descending
and ascending curves, these monsters wrestled and fought. It
was like clouds fighting, like puddings trying to assassinate each
other. They whirled and circled about each other, and for a
time threw Goat Island and Niagara into a smoky twilight,
through which the sunlight smote in shafts and beams. They
spread and closed and spread and grappled and drove round
over the rapids, and two miles away or more into Canada, and
back over the Falls again. A German caught fire, and the whole
crowd broke away from her flare and rose about her dispersing,
leaving her to drop towards Canada and blow up as she
dropped. Then with renewed uproar the others closed again.

Once from the men in Niagara city came a sound like an anthill cheering. Another German burnt, and one badly deflated by the prow of an antagonist, flopped out of action southward. It became more and more evident that the Germans were getting the worst of the unequal fight. More and more obviously were they being persecuted. Less and less did they seem to fight with any object other than escape. The Asiatics swept by them and above them, ripped their bladders, set them alight, picked off their dimly seen men in diving clothes, who struggled against fire and tear with fire extinguishers and silk ribbons in the inner netting. They answered only with ineffectual shots. Thence the battle circled back over Niagara, and then suddenly the Germans, as if at a preconcerted signal, broke and dispersed, going east, west, north and south, in open and confused flight. The Asiatics, as they realized this, rose to fly above them and after them. Only one little knot of four German and perhaps a dozen Asiatics remained fighting about the *Hohenzollern* and the Prince as he circled in a last attempt to save Niagara.

Round they swooped once again over the Canadian Fall, over the waste of waters eastward, until they were distant and small, and then round and back, hurrying, bounding, swooping towards the one gaping spectator.

The whole struggling mass approached very swiftly, growing rapidly larger, and coming out black and featureless against the afternoon sun and above the blinding welter of the Upper Rapids. It grew like a storm cloud until once more it darkened the sky. The flat Asiatic airships kept high above the Germans and behind them, and fired unanswered bullets into their gas-chambers and upon their flanks; the one-man flying machines hovered and alighted like a swarm of attacking bees. Nearer they came and nearer, filling the lower heaven. Two of the Germans swooped and rose again, but the *Hohenzollern* had suffered too much for that. She lifted weakly, turned sharply as if to get out of the battle, burst into flames fore and aft, swept down to the water, splashed into it obliquely and rolled over and over and came downstream rolling and smashing and writhing like a thing alive, halting and then coming on again, with her torn and bent propeller still beating the air. The burst-

ing flames spluttered out again in clouds of steam. It was a
disaster gigantic in its dimensions. She lay across the rapids like
an island, like tall cliffs, tall cliffs that came rolling, smoking,
and crumpling and collapsing, advancing with a sort of fluctu-
ating rapidity upon Bert. One Asiatic airship – it looked to Bert
from below like three hundred yards of pavement – whirled
back and circled two or three times over that great overthrow,
and half a dozen crimson flying machines danced for a moment
like great midges in the sunlight before they swept on after
their fellows. The rest of the fight had already gone over the
island, a wild crescendo of shots and yells and smashing uproar.
It was hidden from Bert now by the trees of the island, and
forgotten by him in the nearer spectacle of the huge advance of
the defeated German airship. Something fell with a mighty
smashing and splintering of boughs unheeded behind him.

It seemed for a time that the *Hohenzollern* must needs break
her back upon the Parting of the Waters, and then for a time
her propeller flopped and frothed in the river and thrust the
mass of buckling, crumpled wreckage towards the American
shore. Then the sweep of the torrent that foamed down to the
American Fall caught her, and in another minute the immense
mass of deflating wreckage, with flames spurting out in three
new places, had crashed against the bridge that joined Goat
Island and Niagara city, and forced a long arm, as it were, in a
heaving tangle under the central span. Then the middle chambers blew up with a loud report, and in another moment the
bridge had given way and the main bulk of the airship, like
some grotesque cripple in rags, staggered, flapping and waving
flambeaux, to the crest of the fall and hesitated there and
vanished in a desperate suicidal leap.

Its detached fore-end remained jammed against that little
island, Green Island it used to be called, which forms the
stepping-stone between the mainland and Goat Island's patch
of trees.

Bert followed this disaster from the Parting of the Waters to
the bridgehead. Then, regardless of cover, regardless of the
Asiatic airship hovering like a huge house roof without walls
above the Suspension Bridge, he sprinted along towards the

north and came out for the first time upon that rocky point by
Luna Island that looks sheer down upon the American Fall.
There he stood breathless amidst that eternal rush of sound,
breathless and staring.

Far below, and travelling rapidly down the gorge, whirled
something like a huge empty sack. For him it meant – what did
it not mean? – the German air-fleet, Kurt, the Prince, Europe,
all things stable and familiar, the forces that had brought him,
the forces that had seemed indisputably victorious. And it went
down the rapids like an empty sack and left the visible world
to Asia, to yellow people beyond Christendom, to all that was
terrible and strange!

Remote over Canada receded the rest of that conflict and
vanished beyond the range of his vision. . . .

9
ON GOAT ISLAND

§ 1

The whack of a bullet on the rocks beside him reminded him that he was a visible object and wearing at least portions of a German uniform. It drove him into the trees again, and for a time he dodged and dropped and sought cover like a chick hiding among reeds from imaginary hawks. 'Beaten,' he whispered. 'Beaten and done for.... Chinese! Yellow chaps chasing 'em!'

At last he came to rest in a clump of bushes near a locked-up and deserted refreshment shed within view of the American side. They made a sort of hole and harbour for him; they met completely overhead. He looked across the rapids, but the firing had ceased now altogether and everything seemed quiet. The Asiatic aeroplane had moved from its former position above the Suspension Bridge, was motionless now above Niagara city, shadowing all that district about the powerhouse which had been the scene of the land fight. The monster had an air of quiet and assured predominance, and from its stern it trailed, serene and ornamental, a long streaming flag, the red, black and yellow of the great alliance, the Sunrise and the Dragon. Beyond to the east, and at a much higher level, hung a second; and Bert, presently gathering courage, wriggled out and craned his neck to find another still airship against the sunset in the south.

'Gaw!' he said. 'Beaten and chased! My Gawd!'

The fighting, it seemed at first, was quite over in Niagara city, though a German flag was still flying from one shattered house. A white sheet was hoisted above the powerhouse, and this remained flying all through the events that followed. But presently came a sound of shots and then German soldiers running. They disappeared among the houses, and then came two engineers in blue shirts and trousers hotly pursued by three Japanese swordsmen. The foremost of the two fugitives was a shapely man, and ran lightly and well; the second was a sturdy little man, and rather fat. He ran comically in leaps and bounds, with his plump arms bent up by his side and his head thrown back. The pursuers ran with uniforms and dark thin metal and leather headdresses. The little man stumbled, and Bert gasped, realizing a new horror in war.

The foremost swordsman won three strides on him and was near enough to slash at him and miss as he spurted.

A dozen yards they ran, and then the swordsman slashed again, and Bert could hear across the waters a faint sound like the moo of an elfin cow as the fat little man fell forward. Slash went the swordsman and slash at something on the ground that tried to save itself with ineffectual hands. 'Oh I carn't!' cried Bert, near blubbering and staring with starting eyes.

The swordsman slashed a fourth time and went on as his fellows came up after the better runner. The hindmost swordsman stopped and turned back. He had perceived some movement perhaps; but at any rate he stood, and ever and again slashed at the fallen body.

'Oo-oo!' groaned Bert at every slash, and shrank closer into the bushes and became very still. Presently came a sound of shots from the town, and then everything was quiet, everything, even the hospital.

He saw presently little figures sheathing swords come out from the houses and walk to the débris of the flying machines the bomb had destroyed. Others appeared wheeling undamaged aeroplanes upon their wheels as men might wheel bicycles, and sprang into the saddles and flapped into the air. A string of three airships appeared far away in the east and flew towards the zenith. The one that hung low above Niagara city came still lower and dropped a rope ladder to pick up men from the powerhouse.

For a long time he watched the further happenings in Niagara city as a rabbit might watch a meet. He saw men going from building to building to set fire to them, as he presently realized, and he heard a series of dull detonations from the wheel-pit of the powerhouse. Some similar business went on among the works on the Canadian side. Meanwhile more and more airships appeared, and many more flying machines, until at last it seemed to him nearly a third of the Asiatic fleet had reassembled. He watched them from his bush, cramped but immovable, watched them gather and range themselves and signal and pick up men, until at last they sailed away towards the glowing sunset, going to the great Asiatic rendezvous above the oil wells of Cleveland. They dwindled and passed away, leaving him alone, so far as he could tell, the only living man in a world of ruin and strange loneliness almost beyond describing. He watched them recede and vanish. He stood gaping after them.

'Gaw!' he said at last, like one who rouses himself from a trance.

It was far more than any personal desolation and extremity that flooded his soul. It seemed to him indeed that this must be the sunset of his race.

§ 2

He did not at first envisage his own plight in any definite and comprehensible terms. Things had happened to him so much of late, his own efforts had counted for so little, that he had become passive and planless. His last scheme had been to go round the coast of England as a Desert Dervish giving refined entertainment to his fellow creatures. Fate had quashed that. Fate had seen fit to direct him to other destinies, had hurried him from point to point, and dropped him at last upon this little wedge of rock between the cataracts. It did not instantly occur to him that now it was his turn to play. He had a singular feeling that all must end as a dream ends, that presently surely he would be back in the world of Grubb and Edna and Bun Hill, that this roar, this glittering presence of incessant water, would be drawn aside as a curtain is drawn aside after a holiday lantern-show, and old, familiar, customary things reassume their sway. It would be interesting to tell people how he had seen Niagara. And then Kurt's words came into his head: 'People torn away from the people they care for; homes smashed, creatures full of life and memories and peculiar little gifts – torn to pieces, starved and spoilt.' . . .

He wondered, half incredulous, if that was indeed true. It was so hard to realize it. Out beyond there was it possible that Tom and Jessica were also in some dire extremity? That the little greengrocer's shop was no longer standing open, with Jessica serving respectfully, warming Tom's ear in sharp asides, or punctually sending out the goods?

He tried to think what day of the week it was, and found he had lost his reckoning. Perhaps it was Sunday. If so were they going to church – or were they hiding perhaps in bushes? What had happened to the landlord, the butcher, and to Butteridge and all those people on Dymchurch beach? Something, he knew, had happened to London – a bombardment. But who had bombarded? Were Tom and Jessica too being chased by strange brown men with long bare swords and evil eyes? He thought of various possible aspects of affliction, but presently one phase ousted all the others. Were they getting much to eat? The question haunted him, obsessed him.

If one was very hungry would one eat rats?

It dawned upon him that a peculiar misery that oppressed him was not so much anxiety and patriotic sorrow as hunger. Of course he was hungry!

He reflected and turned his steps towards the refreshment shed that stood near the end of the ruined bridge. 'Ought to be somethin'—'

He strolled round it once or twice, and then attacked the shutters with his pocket-knife, reinforced presently by a wooden stake he found conveniently near. At last he got a shutter to give, and tore it back and stuck in his head.

'Grub,' he remarked, 'anyhow. Leastways—'

He got at the inside fastening of the shutter and had presently this establishment open for his exploration. He found several sealed bottles of sterilized milk, much mineral water, two tins of biscuits and a crock of very stale cakes, cigarettes in great quantities but very dry, some rather dry oranges, nuts, some tins of canned meat and fruit, and plates and knives and forks and glasses sufficient for several score of people. There was also a zinc locker, but he was unable to negotiate the padlock of this.

'Shan't starve,' said Bert, 'for a bit, anyhow.' He sat on the vendor's seat and regaled himself with biscuits and milk, and felt for a moment quite contented.

'Quite restful,' he muttered, munching and glancing about him restlessly, 'after what I been through.

'Crikey! *Wot* a day! Oh! *Wot* a day!'

Wonder took possession of him. 'Gaw!' he cried: 'What a fight it's been! Smashing up the poor fellers! 'Eadlong! The airships – the fliers and all. I wonder what happened to the *Zeppelin*? . . . And that chap Kurt – I wonder what happened to 'im? 'E was a good sort of chap was Kurt.'

Some phantom of imperial solicitude floated through his mind. 'Injia,' he said. . . .

A more practical interest arose.

'I wonder if there's anything to open one of these tins of corned beef?'

§ 3

After he had feasted, Bert lit a cigarette and sat meditative for a time. 'Wonder where Grubb is,' he said. 'I do wonder that! Wonder if any of 'em wonder about me?'

He reverted to his own circumstances. 'Dessay I shall 'ave to stop on this island for some time.'

He tried to feel at his ease and secure, but presently the indefinable restlessness of the social animal in solitude distressed him. He began to want to look over his shoulder, and, as a corrective, roused himself to explore the rest of the island.

It was only very slowly that he began to realize the peculiarities of his position, to perceive that the breaking down of the arch between Green Island and the mainland had cut him off completely from the world. Indeed it was only when he came back to where the fore-end of the *Hohenzollern* lay like a stranded ship, and was contemplating the shattered bridge, that this dawned upon him. Even then it came with no sort of shock to his mind, a fact among a number of other extraordinary and unmanageable facts. He stared at the shattered cabins of the *Hohenzollern* and its widow's garment of dishevelled silk for a time, but without any idea of its containing any living thing; it was all so twisted and smashed and entirely upside down. Then for a while he gazed at the evening sky. A cloud haze was now appearing and not an airship was in sight. A swallow flew by and snapped some invisible victim. 'Like a dream,' he repeated.

Then for a time the rapids held his mind. 'Roaring. It keeps on roaring and splashin' always and always. Keeps on. . . .'

At last his interests became personal. 'Wonder what I ought to do now?'

He reflected. 'Not an idee,' he said.

He was chiefly conscious that a fortnight ago he had been in Bun Hill with no idea of travel in his mind, and that now he was between the Falls of Niagara amidst the devastation and ruins of the greatest air fight in the world, and that in the interval he had been across France, Belgium, Germany, England, Ireland and a number of other countries. It was an interesting thought and suitable for conversation, but of no great practical utility. 'Wonder 'ow I can get orf this?' he said. 'Wonder if there is a way out? If not . . . rummy!'[1]

Further reflection decided, 'I believe I got myself in a bit of a 'ole coming over that bridge. . . .

'Any'ow – got me out of the way of them Japanesy chaps. Wouldn't 'ave taken 'em long to cut *my* froat. No. Still—'

He resolved to return to the point of Luna Island. For a long time he stood without stirring, scrutinizing the Canadian shore and the wreckage of hotels and houses and the fallen trees of the Victoria Park, pink now in the light of sundown. Not a human being was perceptible in that scene of headlong destruction. Then he came back to the American side of the island, crossed close to the crumpled aluminium wreckage of the *Hohenzollern* to Green Island, and scrutinized the hopeless breach in the further bridge and the water that boiled beneath it. Towards Buffalo there was still much smoke, and near the position of the Niagara railway station the houses were burning vigorously. Everything was deserted now, everything was still. One little abandoned thing lay on a transverse path between town and road, a crumpled heap of clothes with sprawling limbs. . . .

''Ave a look round,' said Bert, and taking a path that ran through the middle of the island he presently discovered the wreckage of the two Asiatic aeroplanes that had fallen out of the struggle that ended the *Hohenzollern.*

With the first he found the wreckage of an aeronaut, too.

The machine had evidently dropped vertically and was badly knocked about amidst a lot of smashed branches in a clump of trees. Its bent and broken wings and shattered stays sprawled amidst new splintered wood, and its forepeak stuck into the ground. The aeronaut dangled weirdly head downward among the leaves and branches some yards away, and Bert only discovered him as he turned from the aeroplane. In the dusky evening light and stillness – for the sun had gone now and the wind had altogether fallen – this inverted yellow face was anything but a tranquillizing object to discover suddenly a couple of yards away. A broken branch had run clean through the man's thorax, and he hung, so stabbed, looking limp and absurd. In his hand he still clutched, with the grip of death, a short light rifle.

For some time Bert stood very still, inspecting this thing.

Then he began to walk away from it, looking constantly back at it.

Presently in an open glade he came to a stop.

'Gaw!' he whispered, 'I don't like dead bodies some'ow! I'd almost rather that chap was alive.'

He would not go along the path athwart which the Chinaman hung. He felt he would rather not have trees round him any more, and that it would be more comfortable to be quite close to the sociable splash and uproar of the rapids.

He came upon the second aeroplane in a clear grassy space by the side of the streaming water, and it seemed scarcely damaged at all. It looked as though it had floated down into a position of rest. It lay on its side with one wing in the air. There was no aeronaut near it, dead or alive. There it lay abandoned, with the water lapping about its long tail.

Bert remained a little aloof from it for a long time, looking into the gathering shadows among the trees, in the expectation of another Chinaman alive or dead. Then very cautiously he approached the machine and stood regarding its widespread vans, its big steering wheel and empty saddle. He did not venture to touch it.

'I wish that other chap wasn't there,' he said. 'I do wish 'e wasn't there!'

He saw, a few yards away, something bobbing about in an eddy that spun within a projecting head of rock. As it went round it seemed to draw him unwillingly towards it. . . .

What could it be?

'Blow!' said Bert. 'It's another of 'em.'

It held him. He told himself that it was the other aeronaut that had been shot in the fight and fallen out of the saddle as he strove to land. He tried to go away, and then it occurred to him that he might get a branch or something and push this rotating object out into the stream. That would leave him with only one dead body to worry about. Perhaps he might get along with one. He hesitated, and then with a certain emotion forced himself to do this. He went towards the bushes and cut himself a wand and returned to the rocks and clambered out to a corner between the eddy and the stream. By that time the sunset was over and the bats were abroad, and he was wet with perspiration.

He prodded the floating blue-clad thing with his wand, failed, tried again successfully as it came round, and as it went out into the stream it turned over, the light gleamed on golden hair, and – it was Kurt!

It was Kurt, white and dead and very calm. There was no mistaking him. There was still plenty of light for that. The stream took him and he seemed to compose himself in its swift grip as one who stretches himself to rest. Whitefaced he was now, and all the colour gone out of him.

A feeling of infinite distress swept over Bert as the body swept out of sight towards the fall. 'Kurt!' he cried. 'Kurt! I didn't mean to! Kurt! don' leave me 'ere! Don' leave me!'

Loneliness and desolation overwhelmed him. He gave way. He stood on the rock in the evening light, weeping and wailing passionately like a child. It was as though some link that had held him to all these things had broken and gone. He was afraid like a child in a lonely room, shamelessly afraid.

The twilight was closing about him. The trees were full now of strange shadows. All the things about him became strange and unfamiliar with that subtle queerness one feels oftenest in dreams. 'O God! I carn't stand this,' he said, and crept back from the rocks to the grass and crouched down, and suddenly wild sorrow for the death of Kurt, Kurt the brave, Kurt the kindly, came to his help, and he broke from whimpering to weeping. He ceased to crouch; he sprawled upon the grass and clenched an impotent fist.

'This war,' he cried, 'this blarsted foolery of a war.

'O Kurt! Lieutenant Kurt!

'I done,' he said: 'I done. I've 'ad all I want, and more than I want. The world's all rot, and there ain't no sense in it. The night's coming. . . . If 'E comes after me— 'E can't come after me— 'E can't! . . .

'If 'E comes after me, I'll fro' myself into the water.' . . .

Presently he was talking again in a low undertone.

'There ain't nothing to be afraid of reely. It's jest imagination. Poor old Kurt – he thought it would happen. Prevision like. 'E never gave me that letter or tole me who the lady was. It's like what 'e said – people tore away from everything they belonged to – everywhere. Exactly like what 'e said. . . . 'Ere I am cast away – thousand of miles from Edna or Grubb or any of my lot – like a plant tore up by the roots. . . . And every war's been like this, only I 'adn't the sense to understand it. Always. All sorts of 'oles and corners chaps 'ave died in. And people 'adn't the sense to understand, 'adn't the sense to feel it and stop it. Thought war was fine. My Gawd! . . .

'Dear old Edna. She was a fair bit of all right – she was. That time we 'ad a boat at Kingston. . . .

'I bet – I'll see 'er again yet. Won't be my fault if I don't.' . . .

§ 4

Suddenly, on the very verge of this heroic resolution, Bert became rigid with terror. Something was creeping towards him through the grass. Something was creeping and halting and creeping again towards him through the dim, dark grass. The night was electrical with horror. For a time everything was still. Bert ceased to breathe. It could not be. No, it was too small!

It advanced suddenly upon him with a rush, with a little meawling cry and tail erect. It rubbed its head against him and purred. It was a tiny, skinny little kitten.

'Gaw, pussy! 'ow you frightened me!' said Bert, with drops of perspiration on his brow.

§ 5

He sat with his back to a tree stump all that night, holding the kitten in his arms. His mind was tired, and he talked or thought coherently no longer. Towards dawn he dozed.

When he awoke he was stiff but in better heart, and the kitten slept warmly and reassuringly inside his jacket. And fear, he found, had gone from amidst the trees.

He stroked the kitten, and the little creature woke up to excessive fondness and purring. 'You want some milk,' said Bert. 'That's what you want. And I could do with a bit of brekker too.'

He yawned and stood up, with the kitten on his shoulder, and started about him, recalling the circumstances of the previous day, the grey, immense happenings.

'Mus' do something,' he said.

He turned towards the trees, and was presently contemplating the dead aeronaut again. The kitten he held companionably against his neck. The body was horrible, but not nearly so horrible as it had been at twilight, and now the limbs were limper and the gun had slipped to the ground and lay half hidden in the grass.

'I suppose we ought to bury 'im, Kitty,' said Bert, and looked helplessly at the rocky soil about him. 'We got to stay on the island with 'im.'

It was some time before he could turn away and go on towards that provision shed. 'Brekker first,' he said, 'anyhow,' stroking the kitten on his shoulder. She rubbed his cheek affectionately with her furry little face and presently nibbled at his ear. 'Wan' some milk, eh?' he said, and turned his back on the dead man as though he mattered nothing.

He was puzzled to find the door of the shed open, though he had closed and latched it very carefully overnight, and he found also some dirty plates he had not noticed before on the bench. He discovered that the hinges of the tin locker were unscrewed and that it could be opened. He had not observed this overnight.

'Silly of me!' said Bert. ''Ere I was puzzlin' and whackin' away at the padlock, never noticing.' It had been used apparently as an ice-chest, but it contained nothing now but the remains of half a dozen boiled chickens, some ambiguous substance that might once have been butter, and a singularly unappetizing smell. He closed the lid again carefully.

He gave the kitten some milk in a dirty plate and sat watching its busy little tongue for a time. Then he was moved to make an inventory of the provisions. There were six bottles of milk unopened and one opened, sixty bottles of mineral water and a large stock of syrups, about two thousand cigarettes and upward of a hundred cigars, nine oranges, two unopened tins of corned beef and one opened, two tins of biscuits and eleven hard cakes, a hatful of nuts and five large tins of Californian peaches. He jotted it down on a piece of paper. ''Ain't much solid food,' he said. 'Still— A fortnight, say!

'Anything might happen in a fortnight.'

He gave the kitten a small second helping and a scrap of beef and then went down with the little creature running after him, tail erect and in high spirits, to look at the remains of the *Hohenzollern*. It had shifted in the night and seemed on the whole more firmly grounded on Green Island than before. From it his eye went to the shattered bridge and then across to the still desolation of Niagara city. Nothing moved over there but

a number of crows. They were busy with the engineer he had
seen cut down on the previous day. He saw no dogs, but he
heard one howling.

'We got to get out of this some'ow, Kitty,' he said. 'That milk
won't last for ever – not at the rate you lap it.'

He regarded the sluice-like flood before him. 'Plenty of
water,' he said. 'Won't be drink we shall want.'

He decided to make a careful exploration of the island. Presently he came to a locked gate labelled 'Biddle Stairs', and
clambered over to discover a steep old wooden staircase leading
down the face of the cliff amidst a vast and increasing uproar
of waters. He left the kitten above and descended these, and
discovered with a thrill of hope a path leading among the rocks
at the foot of the roaring downrush of the centre fall. Perhaps
this was a sort of way!

It led him only to the choking and deafening experience of
the Cave of the Winds, and after he had spent a quarter of an
hour in a partially stupefied condition flattened between solid
rock and nearly as solid waterfall, he decided that this was after
all no practicable route to Canada, and retraced his steps. As
he reascended the Biddle Stairs, he heard what he decided at
last must be a sort of echo, a sound of someone walking about
on the gravel paths above. When he got to the top the place
was as solitary as before.

Thence he made his way, with the kitten skirmishing along
beside him in the grass, to a staircase that led to a lump of
projecting rock that enfiladed the huge green majesty of the
Horseshoe Fall. He stood there for some time in silence.

'You wouldn't think,' he said at last, 'there was so much
water. . . . This roarin' and splashin', it gets on your nerves. . . .
Sounds like people talking. . . . Sounds like people going
about. . . . Sounds like anything you fancy.'

He retired up the staircase again. 'I s'pose I shall keep on
goin' round this blessed island,' he said drearily. 'Round and
round and round.'

He found himself presently beside the less damaged Asiatic
aeroplane again. He stared at it and the kitten smelt it. 'Broke!'
he said.

He looked up with a convulsive start.

Advancing slowly towards him out from among the trees were two tall, gaunt figures. They were blackened and tattered and bandaged; the hindmost one limped and had his head swathed in white, but the foremost one still carried himself as a Prince should do, for all that his left arm was in a sling and one side of his face scalded a livid crimson. He was the Prince Karl Albert, the War Lord, the 'German Alexander', and the man behind him was the bird-faced man whose cabin had once been taken from him and given to Bert.

§ 6

With that apparition began a new phase of Goat Island in Bert's experience. He ceased to be a solitary representative of humanity in a vast and violent and incomprehensible universe, and became once more a social creature, a man in a world of other men. For an instant these two were terrible, then they seemed sweet and desirable as brothers. They too were in this scrape with him, marooned and puzzled. He wanted extremely to hear exactly what had happened to them. What mattered it, if one was a Prince and both were foreign soldiers, if neither perhaps had adequate English? His native Cockney freedom flowed too generously for him to think of that, and surely the Asiatic fleets had purged all such trivial differences. ' 'Ul-*lo*!' he said; ' 'ow did you get 'ere?'

'It is the Englishman who brought us the Butteridge machine,' said the bird-faced officer in German, and then in a tone of horror as Bert advanced, 'Salute!' and again louder, '*Salute!*'

'Gaw!' said Bert, and stopped with a second comment under his breath. He started and saluted awkwardly and became at once a masked defensive thing with whom co-operation was impossible.

For a time these two perfected modern aristocrats stood regarding the difficult problem of the Anglo-Saxon citizen, that ambiguous citizen who, obeying some mysterious law in his blood, would neither drill nor be a democrat. Bert was by no means a beautiful object, but in some inexplicable way he looked resistant. He wore his cheap suit of serge, now showing many signs of wear, and its loose fit made him seem sturdier than he was; above his disengaging face was a white German cap that was altogether too big for him, and his trousers were crumpled up his legs and their ends tucked into the rubber highlows of a deceased German aeronaut. He looked an inferior, though by no means an easy inferior, and instinctively they hated him.

The Prince pointed to the flying-machine and said something in broken English that Bert took for German and failed to understand. He intimated as much.

'Dummer Kerl!'[2] said the bird-faced officer from among his bandages.

The Prince pointed again with his undamaged hand. 'You understan' dis *Drachenflieger*?'

Bert began to comprehend the situation. He regarded the Asiatic machine. The habits of Bun Hill returned to him. 'It's a foreign make,' he said ambiguously.

The two Germans consulted. 'You are – an expert?' said the Prince.

'We reckon to repair,' said Bert, in the exact manner of Grubb.

The Prince sought in his vocabulary. 'Is dat,' he said, 'goot to fly?'

Bert reflected, and scratched his chin slowly. 'I got to look at it,' he replied. . . . 'It's 'ad rough usage!'

He made a sound with his teeth he had also acquired from Grubb, put his hands in his trouser pockets and strolled back to the machine. Typically Grubb chewed something, but Bert could chew only imaginatively. 'Three days' work in this,' he said, teething. For the first time it dawned on him that there were possibilities in this machine. It was evident that the wing that lay on the ground was disabled. The three stays that held it rigid had snapped across a ridge of rock, and there was also a strong possibility of the engine being badly damaged. The wing hook on that side was also askew, but probably that would not affect the flight. Beyond that there probably wasn't much the matter. Bert scratched his cheek again, and contemplated the broad sunlit waste of the Upper Rapids. 'We might make a job of this. . . . You leave it to me.'

He surveyed it intently again, and the Prince and his officer watched him. In Bun Hill Bert and Grubb had developed to a very high pitch among the hiring stock a method of repair by substitution; they substituted bits of other machines. A machine that was too utterly and obviously done for even to proffer for hire had nevertheless still capital value. It became a sort of quarry for nuts and screws and wheels, bars and spokes, chain-links and the like; a mine of ill-fitting 'parts' to replace the defects of machines still current. And back among the trees was a second Asiatic aeroplane.

The kitten caressed Bert's airship boots unheeded.

'Mend dat *Drachenflieger*,' said the Prince.

'If I do mend it,' said Bert, struck by a new thought, 'none of us ain't to be trusted to fly it.'

'*I* vill fly it,' said the Prince.

'Very likely break your neck,' said Bert, after a pause.

The Prince did not understand him and disregarded what he said. He pointed his gloved finger to the machine and turned to the bird-faced officer with some remark in German. The officer answered and the Prince responded with a sweeping gesture towards the sky. Then he spoke – it seemed eloquently. Bert watched him and guessed his meaning. 'Much more likely to break your neck,' he said: ' 'Owever. 'Ere goes.'

He began to pry about the saddle and engine of the *Drachen-flieger* in a search for tools. Also he wanted some black oily stuff for his hands and face. For the first rule in the art of repairing as it was known to the firm of Grubb and Smallways was to get your hands and face thoroughly and conclusively blackened. Also he took off his jacket and waistcoat and put his cap carefully to the back of his head in order to facilitate scratching.

The Prince and the officer seemed disposed to watch him, but he succeeded in making it clear to them that this would inconvenience him and that he had to 'puzzle out a bit' before he could get to work. They thought him over, but his shop experience had given him something of the authoritative way of the expert with common men. And at last they went away. Thereupon he went straight to the second aeroplane, got the aeronaut's gun and ammunition and hid them in a clump of nettles close at hand. 'That's all right,' said Bert, and then proceeded to a careful inspection of the débris of the wings in the trees. Then he went back to the first aeroplane to compare the two. The Bun Hill method was quite possibly practicable if there was nothing hopeless or incomprehensible in the engine.

The Germans returned presently to find him already generously smutty and touching and testing knobs and screws and levers with an expression of profound sagacity. When the bird-faced officer addressed a remark to him he waved him aside with, 'Nong comprong. Shut it! It's no good.'

Then he had an idea. 'Dead chap back there wants burying,' he said, jerking a thumb over his shoulder.

§ 7

With the appearance of these two men Bert's whole universe had changed again. A curtain fell before the immense and terrible desolation that had overwhelmed him. He was in a world of three people, a minute human world that nevertheless filled his brain with eager speculations and schemes and cunning ideas. What were they thinking of? What did they think of him? What did they mean to do? A hundred busy threads interlaced in his mind as he pottered studiously over the Asiatic aeroplane. New ideas came up like bubbles in soda water.

'Gaw!' he said suddenly. He had just appreciated as a special aspect of this irrational injustice of fate that these two men were alive and that Kurt was dead. All the crew of the *Hohenzollern* were shot or burnt or smashed or drowned, and these two lurking in the padded forward cabin had escaped.

'I suppose 'e thinks it's 'is bloomin' Star,' he muttered, and found himself uncontrollably exasperated.

He stood up, facing round to the two men. They were standing side by side regarding him. 'It's no good,' he said, 'starin' at me. You only put me out.' And then seeing they did not understand, he advanced towards them, wrench in hand. It occurred to him as he did so that the Prince was really a very big and powerful and serene-looking person. But he said, nevertheless, pointing through the trees, 'Dead man!'

The bird-faced man intervened with a reply in German.

'Dead man!' said Bert to him. 'There.'

He had great difficulty in inducing them to inspect the dead Chinaman, and at last led them to him. Then they made it evident that they proposed that he, as a common person below the rank of officer, should have the sole and undivided privilege of disposing of the body by dragging it to the water's edge. There was some heated gesticulation, and at last the bird faced officer abased himself to help. Together they dragged the limp and now swollen Asiatic through the trees, and after a rest or so – for he trailed very heavily – dumped him into the westward rapid. Bert returned to his expert investigation of the flying machine at last with aching arms and in a state of gloomy rebellion. 'Brasted cheek!' he said. 'One'd think I was one of 'is beastly German slaves!

'Prancing beggar!'

And then he fell speculating what would happen when the flying machine was repaired – if it could be repaired.

The two Germans went away again, and after some reflection Bert removed several nuts, resumed his jacket and vest, pocketed those nuts and his tools and hid the set of tools from the second aeroplane in the fork of a tree. 'Right O,' he said, as he jumped down after the last of these precautions. The Prince and his companion reappeared as he returned to the machine by the water's edge. The Prince surveyed his progress for a time, and then went towards the Parting of the Waters and stood with folded arms gazing upstream in profound thought. The bird-faced officer came up to Bert, heavy with a sentence in English.

'Go,' he said with a helping gesture, 'und eat.'

When Bert got to the refreshment shed he found all the food had vanished except one measured ration of corned beef and three biscuits. He regarded this with open eyes and mouth. The kitten appeared from under the vendor's seat with an ingratiating purr. 'Of course!' said Bert. 'Why! Where's your milk?'

He accumulated wrath for a moment or so, then seized the plate in one hand, and the biscuits in another, and went in search of the Prince, breathing vile words anent[3] 'grub' and his intimate interior. He approached without saluting.

''Ere!' he said fiercely. 'Whad the devil's this?'

An entirely unsatisfactory altercation followed. Bert expounded the Bun Hill theory of the relations of grub to efficiency in English, the bird-faced man replied with points about nations and discipline in German. The Prince, having made an estimate of Bert's quality and physique, suddenly hectored. He gripped Bert by the shoulder and shook him, making his pockets rattle, shouted something to him, and flung him struggling back. He hit him as though he was a German private. Bert went back, white and scared, but resolved by all his Cockney standards upon one thing. He was bound in honour to 'go for' the Prince. 'Gaw!' he gasped, buttoning his coat.

'Now,' cried the Prince, 'vill you go!' and then, catching the heroic gleam in Bert's eyes, drew his sword.

The bird-faced officer intervened, saying something in German and pointing skyward.

Far away in the south-west appeared a Japanese airship coming fast towards them. Their conflict ended at that. The Prince was first to grasp the situation and lead the retreat. All three scuttled like rabbits for the trees, and ran to and fro for cover until they found a hollow in which the grass grew rank. There they all squatted within six yards of one another. They sat in this place for a long time, up to their necks in the grass and watching through the branches for the airship. Bert had dropped some of his corned beef, but he found the biscuits in his hand and ate them quietly. The monster came nearly overhead and then went away to Niagara and dropped beyond the power works. When it was near they all kept silence, and then presently they fell into an argument that was robbed perhaps of immediate explosive effect only by their failure to understand one another.

It was Bert began the talking, and he talked on, regardless of what they understood or failed to understand. But his voice must have conveyed his cantankerous intentions.

'You want that machine done,' he said first, 'you better keep your 'ands off me!'

They disregarded that and he repeated it.

Then he expanded his idea, and the spirit of speech took hold of him. 'You think you got 'old of a chap you can kick and 'it like you do your private soldiers – you're jolly well mistaken. See? I've 'ad about enough of you and your antics. I been thinking you over, you and your war and your Empire, and all the rot of it. Rot it is. It's you Germans made all the trouble in Europe first and last. And all for nothin'. Jest silly prancing! Jest because you've got the uniforms and flags! 'Ere I was – I didn't want to 'ave anything to do with you. I jest didn't care a 'eng at all about you. Then you get 'old of me – steal me practically – and 'ere I am, thousands of miles away from 'ome and everything, and all your silly fleet smashed up to rags. And you want to go on prancin' *now*! Not if I know it!

'Look at the mischief you done. Look at the way you smashed up New York – the people you killed, the stuff you wasted. Can't you learn?'

'Dummer Kerl!' said the bird-faced man suddenly, in a tone of concentrated malignity, glaring under his bandages. 'Esel!'

'That's German for silly ass! I know. But who's the silly ass – 'im or me? When I was a kid I used to read penny dreadfuls about 'aving adventures and being a great c'mander and all that rot. I stowed it. But what's 'e got in 'is 'ead? Rot about Napoleon, rot about Alexander, rot about 'is blessed family and 'im and Gawd and David and all that. Anyone who wasn't a dressed-up silly fool of a Prince could 'ave told all this was goin' to 'appen. There was us in Europe all at sixes and sevens with our silly flags and our silly newspapers raggin' us up against each other and keepin' us apart, and there was China as solid as a cheese, with millions and millions of men only wantin' a bit of science, and a bit of enterprise, to be as good as all of us. You thought they couldn't get at you. And then they got flying machines. And bif! – 'ere we are. Why, when they didn't go on making guns and armies in China we went

and poked 'em up until they did. They *'ad* to give us this lickin'
they've give us. We wouldn't be 'appy till they did. And, as
I say, 'ere we are!'

The bird-faced officer shouted to him to be quiet, and then
began a conversation with the Prince.

'British citizen,' said Bert. 'You ain't obliged to listen, but
I ain't obliged to shut up.' And for some time he continued
his dissertation upon Imperialism, militarism and international
politics. But their talking put him out, and for a time he was
merely repeating abusive terms, 'prancin' nincompoops' and
the like, old terms and new.

Then suddenly he remembered his essential grievance.
''Owever, look 'ere – 'ere! – the thing I started this talk about
is where's that food there was in that shed? That's what I want
to know. Where you put it?'

He paused. They went on talking in German. He repeated
his question. They disregarded him. He asked a third time in a
manner insupportably aggressive.

There fell a tense silence. For some seconds the three regarded
one another. The Prince eyed Bert steadfastly, and Bert quailed
under his eye. Slowly the Prince rose to his feet and the bird-
faced officer jerked up beside him. Bert remained squatting.

'Be quaiat,' said the Prince.

Bert perceived this was no moment for eloquence.

The two Germans regarded him as he crouched there. Death
for a moment seemed near.

Then the Prince turned away and the two of them went
towards the flying machine.

'Gaw!' whispered Bert, and then uttered under his breath one
single word of abuse. He sat crouched together for perhaps
three minutes, then he sprang to his feet and went off towards
the Chinese aeronaut's gun hidden among the weeds.

§ 8

There was no pretence after that moment that Bert was under
the orders of the Prince or that he was going on with the
repairing of the flying machine. The two Germans took pos-

session of that and set to work upon it. Bert, with his new weapon, went off to the neighbourhood of Terrapin Rock, and there sat down to examine it. It was a short rifle with a big cartridge and a nearly full magazine. He took out the cartridges carefully and then tried the trigger and fittings until he felt sure he had the use of it. He reloaded carefully. Then he remembered he was hungry and went off, gun under his arm, to hunt in and about the refreshment shed. He had the sense to perceive that he must not show himself with the gun to the Prince and his companion. So long as they thought him unarmed they would leave him alone, but there was no knowing what the Napoleonic person might do if he saw Bert's weapon. Also he did not go near them because he knew that within himself boiled a reservoir of rage and fear, that he wanted to shoot these two men. He wanted to shoot them, and he thought that to shoot them would be a quite horrible thing to do. The two sides of his inconsistent civilization warred within him.

Near the shed the kitten turned up again, obviously keen for milk. This greatly enhanced his own angry sense of hunger. He began to talk as he hunted about, and presently stood still shouting insults. He talked of war and pride and Imperialism. 'Any other Prince but you would have died with his men and his ship!' he cried.

The two Germans at the machine heard his voice going ever and again amidst the clamour of the waters. Their eyes met and they smiled slightly.

He was disposed for a time to sit in the refreshment shed waiting for them, but then it occurred to him that so he might get them both at close quarters. He strolled off presently to the point of Luna Island to think the situation out.

It had seemed a comparatively simple one at first, but as he turned it over in his mind its possibilities increased and multiplied. Both these men had swords – had either a revolver?

Also if he shot them both he might never find the food!

So far he had been going about with his gun under his arm and a sense of lordly security in his mind, but what if they saw the gun and decided to ambush him? Goat Island is nearly all cover, trees, rocks, thickets and irregularities.

Why not go and murder them both now?

'I carn't,' said Bert, dismissing that. 'I got to be worked up.'

But it was a mistake to get right away from them. That suddenly became clear. He ought to keep them under observation, ought to 'scout' them. Then he would be able to see what they were doing, whether either of them had a revolver, where they had hidden the food. He would be better able to determine what they meant to do to him. If he didn't 'scout' them, presently they would begin to 'scout' him. This seemed so eminently reasonable that he acted upon it forthwith. He thought over his costume and threw his collar and the telltale aeronaut's white cap into the water far below. He turned his coat collar up to hide any gleam of his dirty shirt. The tools and nuts in his pockets were disposed to clank, but he rearranged them and wrapped some letters and his pocket-handkerchief about them. He started off circumspectly and noiselessly, listening and peering at every step. As he drew near his antagonists, much grunting and creaking served to locate them. He discovered them engaged in what looked like a wrestling match with the Asiatic flying machine. Their coats were off, their swords laid aside, they were working magnificently. Apparently they were turning it round and were having a good deal of difficulty with the long tail among the trees. He dropped flat at the sight of them and wriggled into a little hollow, and so lay watching their exertions. Ever and again, to pass the time, he would cover one or other of them with his gun.

He found them quite interesting to watch, so interesting that at times he came near shouting advice to them. He perceived that when they had the machine turned round they would then be in immediate want of the nuts and tools he carried. Then they would come after him. They would certainly conclude he had them or had hidden them. Should he hide his gun and do a deal for food with these tools? He felt he would not be able to part with the gun again now he had once felt its reassuring company. The kitten turned up and made a great fuss with him and licked and bit his ear.

The sun clambered to midday, and once that morning he

saw, though the Germans did not, an Asiatic airship very far to the south, going swiftly eastward.

At last the flying machine was turned and stood poised on its wheels, with its hooks pointing up the rapids. The two Germans wiped their faces, resumed jackets and swords, spoke and bore themselves like men who congratulated themselves on a good laborious morning. Then they went off briskly towards the refreshment shed, the Prince leading. Bert became active in pursuit; but he found it impossible to stalk them quickly enough and silently enough to discover the hiding-place of the food. He found them, when he came into sight of them again, seated with their backs against the shed, plates on knee, and a tin of corned beef and a plateful of biscuits between them. They seemed in fairly good spirits, and once the Prince laughed. At this vision of eating Bert's plans gave way. Fierce hunger carried him. He appeared before them suddenly at a distance of perhaps twenty yards gun in hand. ''Ands up!' he said in a hard, ferocious voice.

The Prince hesitated, and then up went two pairs of hands. The gun had surprised them both completely.

'Stand up,' said Bert. . . . 'Drop that fork!'

They obeyed again.

'What nex'?' said Bert to himself. ''Orf stage I suppose. That way,' he said. 'Go!'

The Prince obeyed with remarkable alacrity. When he reached the head of the clearing he said something quickly to the bird-faced man and they both, with an entire lack of dignity, *ran*!

Bert was struck with an exasperating afterthought.

'Gord!' he cried with infinite vexation. 'Why! I ought to 'ave took their swords! 'Ere!'

But the Germans were already out of sight, and no doubt taking cover among the trees. Bert fell back upon imprecations, then he went up to the shed, cursorily examined the possibility of a flank attack, put his gun handy and set to work, with a convulsive listening pause before each mouthful, on the Prince's plate of corned beef. He had finished that up and handed its

gleanings to the kitten and he was falling-to on the second
plateful, when the plate broke in his hand! He stared, with the
fact slowly creeping upon him that an instant before he had
heard a crack among the thickets. Then he sprang to his feet,
snatched up his gun in one hand and the tin of corned beef in
the other, and fled round the shed to the other side of the
clearing. As he did so came a second crack from the thickets,
and something went *phwit!* by his ear.

He didn't stop running until he was in what seemed to him
a strongly defensible position near Luna Island. Then he took
cover, panting, and crouched expectant.

'They got a revolver after all!' he panted. . . . 'Wonder if they
got two? If they 'ave – Gord! – I'm done!

'Where's the kitten? Finishin' up that corned beef, I suppose.
Little beggar!'

§ 9

So it was that war began upon Goat Island. It lasted a day and
a night, the longest day and the longest night in Bert's life. He
had to lie close and listen and watch. Also he had to scheme
what he should do. It was clear now that he had to kill these
two men if he could, and that if they could they would kill him.
The prize was first food and then the flying machine, and the
doubtful privilege of trying to ride it. If one failed one would
certainly be killed, if one succeeded one would get away somewhere over there. For a time Bert tried to imagine what it was
like over there. His mind ran over possibilities, deserts, angry
Americans, Japanese, Chinese – perhaps Red Indians! (Were
there still Red Indians?)

'Got to take what comes,' said Bert. 'No way out of it that
I can see!'

Was that voices? He realized that his attention was wandering. For a time all his senses were alert. The uproar of the falls
was very confusing, and it mixed in all sorts of sounds, like feet
walking, like voices talking, like shouts and cries.

'Silly great catarac',' said Bert. 'There ain't no sense in it,
fallin' and fallin'.'

Never mind that now! What were the Germans doing?

Would they go back to the flying machine? They couldn't do anything with it, because he had those nuts and screws and the wrench and other tools. But suppose they found the second set of tools he had hidden in a tree! He had hidden the things well, of course, but they *might* find them. One wasn't sure, of course – one wasn't sure. He tried to remember just exactly how he had hidden those tools. He tried to persuade himself they were certainly and surely hidden, but his memory began to play antics. Had he really left the handle of the wrench sticking out, shining out at the fork of the branch?

Ssh! What was that? Someone stirring in those bushes? Up went an expectant muzzle. No! Where was the kitten? No! It was just imagination, not even the kitten.

The Germans would certainly miss and hunt about for the tools and nuts and screws he carried in his pockets; that was clear. Then they would decide he had them and come for him. He had only to remain still under cover, therefore, and he would get them. Was there any flaw in that? Would they take off more removable parts of the flying machine and then lie up for him? No, they wouldn't do that, because they were two to one; they would have no apprehension of his getting off in the flying machine, and no sound reason for supposing he would approach it, and so they would do nothing to damage or disable it. That, he decided, was clear. But suppose they lay up for him by the food. Well, that they wouldn't do, because they would know he had this corned beef; there was enough in this can to last, with moderation, several days. Of course they might try to tire him out instead of attacking him—

He roused himself with a start. He had just grasped the real weakness of his position. He might go to sleep!

It needed but ten minutes under the suggestion of that idea before he realized that he was going to sleep!

He rubbed his eyes and handled his gun. He had never before realized the intensely soporific effect of the American sun, of the American air, the drowsy, sleep-compelling uproar of Niagara. Hitherto these things had on the whole seemed stimulating. . . .

If he had not eaten so much and eaten it so fast, he would not be so heavy. Are vegetarians always bright? . . .

He roused himself with a jerk again.

If he didn't do something he would fall asleep, and if he fell asleep it was ten to one they would find him snoring, and finish him forthwith. If he sat motionless and noiseless he would inevitably sleep. It was better, he told himself, to take even the risks of attacking than that. This sleep trouble, he felt, was going to beat him, must beat him in the end. They were all right; one could sleep and the other could watch. That, come to think of it, was what they would always do; one would do anything they wanted done, the other would lie under cover near at hand, ready to shoot. They might even trap him like that. One might act as a decoy.

That set him thinking of decoys. What a fool he had been to throw his cap away. It would have been invaluable on a stick – especially at night.

He found himself wishing for a drink. He settled that for a time by putting a pebble in his mouth. And then the sleep craving returned.

It became clear to him he must attack.

Like many great generals before him, he found his baggage, that is to say his tin of corned beef, a serious impediment to mobility. At last he decided to put the beef loose in his pocket and abandon the tin. It was not perhaps an ideal arrangement, but one must make sacrifices when one is campaigning. He crawled perhaps ten yards, and then for a time the possibilities of the situation paralysed him.

The afternoon was still. The roar of the cataract simply threw up that immense stillness in relief. He was doing his best to contrive the deaths of two better men than himself. Also they were doing their best to contrive his. What, behind this silence, were they doing?

Suppose he came upon them suddenly and fired and missed?

§ 10

He crawled, and halted listening, and crawled again until night-fall, and no doubt the German Alexander and his lieutenant did the same. A large-scale map of Goat Island marked with red and blue lines to show these strategic movements would no doubt have displayed much interlacing, but as a matter of fact neither side saw anything of the other throughout that age-long day of tedious alertness. Bert never knew how near he got to them nor how far he kept from them. Night found him no longer sleepy, but athirst, and near the American Fall. He was inspired by the idea that his antagonists might be in the wreck-age of the *Hohenzollern* cabins that was jammed against Green Island. He became enterprising, broke from any attempt to conceal himself, and went across the little bridge at the double. He found nobody. It was his first visit to these huge fragments of airship, and for a time he explored them curiously in the dim light. He discovered the forward cabin was nearly intact, with its door slanting downward and a corner under water. He crept in, drank, and then was struck by the brilliant idea of shutting the door and sleeping on it.

But now he could not sleep at all.

He nodded towards morning and woke up to find it fully day. He breakfasted on corned beef and water, and sat for a long time appreciative of the security of his position. At last he became enterprising and bold. He would, he decided, settle this business forthwith, one way or the other. He was tired of all this crawling. He set out in the morning sunshine, gun in hand, scarcely troubling to walk softly. He went round the refresh-ment shed without finding anyone, and then through the trees towards the flying machine. He came upon the bird-faced man sitting on the ground with his back against a tree, bent up over his folded arms, sleeping, his bandage very much over one eye.

Bert stopped abruptly and stood perhaps fifteen yards away, gun in hand ready. Where was the Prince? Then, sticking out at the side of the tree beyond, he saw a shoulder. Bert took five deliberate paces to the left. The great man became visible, leaning up against the trunk, pistol in one hand and sword in the other, and yawning – yawning. You can't shoot a yawning man, Bert found. He advanced upon his antagonist with his gun levelled, some foolish fancy of 'hands up!' in his mind. The Prince became aware of him, the yawning mouth shut like a trap, and he stood stiffly up. Bert stopped, silent. For a moment the two regarded one another.

Had the Prince been a wise man he would, I suppose, have dodged behind the tree. Instead, he gave vent to a shout, and raised pistol and sword. At that, like an automaton, Bert pulled his trigger.

It was his first experience of an oxygen-containing bullet. A great flame spurted from the middle of the Prince, a blinding flare, and there came a thud like the firing of a gun. Something hot and wet struck Bert's face. Then through a whirl of blinding smoke and steam he saw limbs and a collapsing, burst body fling themselves to earth.

Bert was so astonished that he stood agape, and the bird-faced officer might have cut him to the earth without a struggle. But instead the bird-faced officer was running away through the undergrowth, dodging as he went. Bert roused himself to a brief ineffectual pursuit, but he had no stomach for further killing. He returned to the mangled, scattered thing that had so recently been the great Prince Karl Albert. He surveyed the scorched and splashed vegetation about it. He made some speculative identifications. He advanced gingerly and picked up the hot revolver, to find all its chambers strained and burst. He became aware of a cheerful and friendly presence. He was greatly shocked that one so young should see so frightful a scene.

''Ere, Kitty,' he said, 'this ain't no place for you.'

He made three strides across the devastated area, captured the kitten neatly, and went his way towards the shed, with her purring loudly on his shoulder.

'*You* don't seem to mind,' he said.

For a time he fussed about the shed, and at last discovered the rest of the provisions hidden in the roof. 'Seems 'ard,' he said, as he administered a saucerful of milk, 'when you get three men in a 'ole like this, they can't work together. But 'im and 'is princing was jest a bit too thick!

'Gaw!' he reflected, sitting on the counter and eating, 'what a thing life is! 'Ere am I; I seen 'is picture, 'eard 'is name since I was a kid in frocks.[4] Prince Karl Albert! And if anyone 'ad tole me I was going to blow 'im to smithereens – there! I shouldn't 'ave believed it, Kitty.

'That chap at Margit ought to 'ave tole me about it. All 'e tole me was that I got a weak chess.

'That other chap, 'e ain't going to do much. Wonder what I ought to do about 'im?'

He surveyed the trees with a keen blue eye and fingered the gun on his knee. 'I don't like this killing, Kitty,' he said. 'It's like Kurt said about being blooded. Seems to me you got to be blooded young. . . . If that Prince 'ad come up to me and said: "Shake 'ands!" I'd 'ave shook 'ands. . . . Now 'ere's that other chap, dodging about! 'E's got 'is 'ead 'urt already, and there's something wrong with his leg. And burns. Golly! it isn't three weeks ago I first set eyes on 'im, and then 'e was smart and set up – 'ands full of 'airbrushes and things, and swearin' at me. A regular gentleman! Now 'e's 'arf-way to a wild man. What am I to do with 'im? What the 'ell am I to do with 'im? I can't let 'im 'ave that flying machine; that's a bit *too* good, and if I don't kill 'im 'e'll jest hang about this island and starve. . . .

' 'E's got a sword, of course.' . . .

He resumed his philosophizing after he had lit a cigarette.

'War's a silly gaim, Kitty. It's a silly gaim! We common people – we were fools. We thought those big people knew what they were up to – and they didn't. Look at that chap! 'E 'ad all Germany be'ind 'im, and what 'as 'e made of it? Smeshin' and blunderin' and destroyin', and there 'e 'is! Jest a mess of blood and boots and things! Jest an 'orrid splash! Prince Karl Albert! And all the men 'e led and the ships 'e 'ad, the airships and the dragonfliers – all scattered like a paperchase between this 'ole and Germany. And fightin' going on and burnin' and killin' that 'e started, war without end all over the world!

'I suppose I shall 'ave to kill that other chap. I suppose I must. But it ain't at all the sort of job I fancy, Kitty!'

For a time he hunted about the island amidst the uproar of the waterfall looking for the wounded officer, and at last he started him out of some bushes near the head of Biddle Stairs. But as he saw the bent and bandaged figure in limping flight before him, he found his Cockney softness too much for him again; he could neither shoot nor pursue. 'I carn't,' he said, 'that's flat. I 'aven't the guts for it! 'E'll 'ave to go.'

He turned his steps towards the flying machine. . . .

He never saw the bird-faced officer again, nor any further evidence of his presence. Towards evening he grew fearful of ambushes and hunted vigorously for an hour or so but in vain. He slept in a good defensible position at the extremity of the rocky point that runs out to the Canadian Fall, and in the night he woke in panic terror and fired his gun. But it was nothing. He slept no more that night. In the morning he became curiously concerned for the vanished man, and hunted for him as one might for an erring brother. 'If I knew some German,' he said, 'I'd 'oller. It's jest not knowing German does it. You can't explain.'

He discovered, later, traces of an attempt to cross the gap in the broken bridge. A rope with a bolt attached had been flung across and had caught in a fenestration of a projecting fragment of railing. The end of the rope trailed in the seething water towards the fall.

But the bird-faced officer was already rubbing shoulders with certain inert matter that had once been Lieutenant Kurt and the Chinese aeronaut and a dead cow, and much other uncongenial company, in the huge circle of the Whirlpool two and a quarter miles away. Never had that great gathering-place, that incessant, aimless, unprogressive hurry of waste and battered things, been so crowded with strange and melancholy derelicts. Round they went and round, and every day brought its new contributions, luckless brutes, shattered fragments of boat and flying machine, endless citizens from the cities upon the shores of the great lakes above. Much came from Cleveland. It all gathered here, and whirled about indefinitely, and over it all gathered daily a greater abundance of birds.

THE WORLD UNDER
THE WAR

§ 1

Bert spent two more days upon Goat Island, and finished all
his provisions except the cigarettes and mineral water, before
he brought himself to try the Asiatic flying machine.

Even at last he did not so much go off upon it as get carried
off. It had taken only an hour or so to substitute wing stays
from the second flying machine and to replace the nuts he had
himself removed. The engine was in working order, and differed
only very simply and obviously from that of a contemporary
motor-bicycle. The rest of the time was taken up by a vast
musing and delaying and hesitation. Chiefly he saw himself
splashing into the rapids and whirling down them to the fall,
clutching and drowning, but also he had a vision of being
hopelessly in the air, going fast and unable to ground. His mind
was too concentrated upon the business of flying for him to
think very much of what might happen to an indefinite-spirited
Cockney without credentials who arrived on an Asiatic flying
machine amidst the war-infuriated population beyond.

He still had a lingering solicitude for the bird-faced officer.
He had a haunting fancy he might be lying disabled or badly
smashed in some nook or cranny of the island; and it was
only after a most exhaustive search that he abandoned that
distressing idea. 'If I found 'im,' he reasoned the while, 'what
could I do wiv 'im? You can't blow a chap's brains out when
'e's down. And I don' see 'ow else I can 'elp 'im.'

Then the kitten bothered his highly developed sense of social
responsibility. 'If I leave 'er she'll starve. . . . Ought to catch

mice for 'erself. . . . *Are* there mice? . . . Birds? . . . She's too young. . . . She's like me; she's a bit too civilized.'

Finally he stuck her in his side pocket, and she became greatly interested in the memories of corned beef she found there.

With her in his pocket, he seated himself in the saddle of the flying machine. Big, clumsy thing it was – and not a bit like a bicycle. Still the working of it was fairly plain. You set the engine going – *so*; kicked yourself up until the wheel was vertical, *so*; engaged the gyroscope, *so*, and then – then – you just pulled up this lever.

Rather stiff it was, but suddenly it came over—

The big curved wings on either side flapped disconcertingly,[1] flapped again, click, clock, click, clock, clitter-clock!

Stop! The thing was heading for the water; its wheel was in the water. Bert groaned from his heart and struggled to restore the lever to its first position. Click, clock, clitter-clock, he was rising! The machine was lifting its dripping wheel out of the eddies, and he was going up! There was no stopping now, no good in stopping now. In another moment Bert, clutching and convulsive and rigid, with staring eyes and a face pale as death, was flapping up above the rapids, jerking to every jerk of the wings, and rising, rising.

There was no comparison in dignity and comfort between a flying machine and a balloon. Except in its moments of descent, the balloon was a vehicle of faultless urbanity; this was a buck-jumping mule, a mule that jumped up and never came down again. Click, clock, click, clock; with each beat of the strangely shaped wings it jumped Bert upward and caught him neatly again half a second later on the saddle. And while in ballooning there is no wind, since the balloon is a part of the wind, flying is a wild perpetual creation of, and plunging into, wind. It was a wind that above all things sought to blind him, to force him to close his eyes. It occurred to him presently to twist his knees and legs inward and grip with them, or surely he would have been bumped into two clumsy halves. And he was going up, a hundred yards high, two hundred, three hundred, over the streaming, frothing wilderness of water below – up, up, up. That was all right, but how presently would one go horizontally? He tried to think if these things did go horizontally. No! They flapped up and then they soared down. For a time he would keep on flapping up. Tears streamed from his eyes. He wiped them with one temerariously disengaged hand.

Was it better to risk a fall over land or over water – such water?

He was flapping up above the upper rapids towards Buffalo. It was at any rate a comfort that the falls and the wild swirl of waters below them were behind him. He was flying up straight. That he could see. How did one turn?

He was presently almost cool, and his eyes got more used to the rush of air, but he was getting very high, very high. He tilted his head forwards and surveyed the country, blinking. He could see all over Buffalo, a place with three great blackened scars of ruin, and hills and stretches beyond. He wondered if he was half a mile high, or more. There were some people among some houses near a railway station between Niagara and Buffalo, and then more people. They went like ants busily in and out of the houses. He saw two motor-cars gliding along the road towards Niagara city. Then far away in the south he saw a great Asiatic airship going eastward. 'Oh, Gord!' he said, and became earnest in his ineffectual attempts to alter his direction. But that airship took no notice of him, and he continued to ascend convulsively. The world got more and more extensive and map-like. Click, clock, clitter-clock. Above him and very near to him now was a hazy stratum of cloud.

He determined to disengage the wing clutch. He did so. The lever resisted his strength for a time, then over it came, and instantly the tail of the machine cocked up and the wings became rigidly spread. Instantly everything was swift and smooth and silent. He was gliding rapidly down the air against a wild gale of wind, his eyes three-quarters shut. . . .

A little lever that had hitherto been obdurate now confessed itself mobile. He turned it over gently to the right, and whiroo! – the left wing had in some mysterious way given at its edge, and he was sweeping round and downward in an immense right-handed spiral. For some moments he experienced all the helpless sensations of catastrophe. He restored the lever to

its middle position with some difficulty, and the wings were
equalized again.

He turned it to the left and had a sensation of being spun
round backwards. 'Too much!' he gasped.

He discovered that he was rushing down at a headlong pace
towards a railway line and some factory buildings. They appeared to be tearing up to him to devour him. He must have
dropped all that height. For a moment he had the ineffectual
sensations of one whose bicycle bolts downhill. The ground
had almost taken him by surprise. ''Ere!' he cried; and then
with a violent effort of all his being he got the beating engine
at work again and set the wings flapping. He swooped down
and up and resumed his quivering and pulsating ascent of
the air.

He went high again, until he had a wide view of the pleasant
upland country of western New York State, and then made a
long coast down, and so up again, and then a coast. Then as
he came swooping a quarter of a mile above a village he saw
people running about, running away – evidently in relation to
his hawk-like passage. He got an idea that he had been shot at.

'Up!' he said, and attacked that lever again. It came over with
remarkable docility, and suddenly the wings seemed to give
way in the middle. But the engine was still! It had stopped. He
flung the lever back rather by instinct than design. What to do?

Much happened in a few seconds, but also his mind was
quick, he thought very quickly. He couldn't get up again, he
was gliding down the air; he would have to hit something.

He was travelling at the rate of perhaps thirty miles an hour,
down, down.

That plantation of larches looked the softest thing – mossy
almost!

Could he get it? He gave himself to the steering. Round to
the right – left!

Swirroo! Crackle! He was gliding over the tops of the trees,
ploughing through them, tumbling into a cloud of green sharp
leaves and black twigs. There was a sudden snapping, and he
fell off the saddle forward, a thud and a crashing of branches.
Some twigs hit him smartly in the face. . . .

He was between a tree stem and the saddle, with his leg over the steering lever and, so far as he could realize, not hurt. He tried to alter his position and free his leg, and found himself slipping and dropping through branches with everything giving way beneath him. He clutched, and found himself in the lower branches of a tree beneath the flying machine. The air was full of a pleasant resinous smell. He stared for a moment motionless, and then very carefully clambered down branch by branch to the soft needle-covered ground below.

'Good business,' he said, looking up at the bent and tilted kite-wings above.

'I dropped soft!'

He rubbed his chin with his hand and meditated. 'Blowed if I don't think I'm a rather lucky fellow!' he said, surveying the pleasant, sun-bespattered ground under the trees. Then he became aware of a violent tumult at his side. 'Lord!' he said, 'you must be 'arf smothered,' and extracted the kitten from his pocket-handkerchief and pocket. She was twisted and crumpled and extremely glad to see the light again. Her little tongue peeped between her teeth. He put her down, and she ran a dozen paces and shook herself and stretched and sat up and began to wash.

'Nex'?' he said, looking about him, and then with a gesture of vexation, 'Desh it! I ought to 'ave brought that gun!'

He had rested it against a tree when he had seated himself in the flying-machine saddle.

He was puzzled for a time by the immense peacefulness in the quality of the world, and then he perceived that the roar of the cataract was no longer in his ears.

§ 2

He had no very clear idea of what sort of people he might come upon in this country. It was, he knew, America. Americans he had always understood were the citizens of a great and powerful nation, dry and humorous in their manner, addicted to the use of the bowie-knife[2] and revolver, and in the habit of talking through the nose like Norfolk, and saying 'allow' and 'reckon' and 'calculate', after the manner of the people who live on the New Forest[3] side of Hampshire. Also they were very rich, had rocking-chairs, and put their feet at unusual altitudes, and they chewed tobacco, gum and other substances with untiring industry. Commingled with them were cowboys, Red Indians and comic, respectful niggers.[4] This he had learnt from the fiction in his public library. Beyond that he had learnt very little. He was not surprised therefore when he met armed men.

He decided to abandon the shattered flying machine. He wandered through the trees for some time, and then struck a road that seemed to his urban English eyes to be remarkably wide but not properly 'made'. Neither hedge nor ditch nor kerbed distinctive footpath separated it from the woods, and it went in that long easy curve which distinguishes the tracks of an open continent. Ahead he saw a man carrying a gun under his arm, a man in a soft black hat, a blue blouse and black trousers, and with a broad round fat face quite innocent of goatee.[5] This person regarded him askance and heard him speak with a start.

'Can you tell me whereabouts I am at all?' asked Bert.

The man regarded him, and more particularly his rubber boots, with sinister suspicion. Then he replied in a strange outlandish tongue that was, as a matter of fact, Czech. He ended suddenly at the sight of Bert's blank face with 'Don't spik English.'

'Oh!' said Bert. He reflected gravely for a moment, and then went his way.

'Thenks,' he said as an afterthought. The man regarded his back for a moment, was struck with an idea, began an abortive gesture, sighed, gave it up and went on also with a depressed countenance.

Presently Bert came to a big wooden house standing casually among the trees. It looked a bleak, bare box of a house to him, no creeper grew on it, no hedge nor wall nor fence parted it off from the woods about it. He stopped before the steps that led up to the door, perhaps thirty yards away. The place seemed deserted. He would have gone up to the door and rapped, but suddenly a big black dog appeared at the side and regarded him. It was a huge heavy-jawed dog of some unfamiliar breed, and it wore a spike-studded collar. It did not bark nor approach him, it just bristled quietly and emitted a single sound like a short, deep cough.

Bert hesitated and went on.

He stopped thirty paces away and stood peering about him among the trees. 'If I 'aven't been and lef' that kitten,' he said.

Acute sorrow wrenched him for a time. The black dog came through the trees to get a better look at him and coughed that well-bred cough again. Bert resumed the road.

'She'll do all right,' he said. . . . 'She'll catch things. . . .

'She'll do all right,' he said presently, without conviction. But if it had not been for the black dog he would have gone back.

When he was out of sight of the house and the black dog, he went into the woods on the other side of the way and emerged after an interval trimming a very tolerable cudgel with his pocket-knife. Presently he saw an attractive-looking rock by the track and picked it up and put it in his pocket. Then he came to three or four houses, wooden like the last, each with an ill-painted white veranda (that was his name for it) and all standing in the same casual way upon the ground. Behind, through the woods, he saw pigsties and a rooting black sow leading a brisk, adventurous family. A wild-looking woman with sloe-black eyes and dishevelled black hair sat upon the steps of one of the houses nursing a baby, but at the sight of Bert she got up and went inside, and he heard her bolting the door. Then a boy appeared among the pigsties, but he would not understand Bert's hail.

'I suppose it is America!'[6] said Bert.

The houses became more frequent down the road, and he passed two other extremely wild and dirty-looking men without addressing them. One carried a gun and the other a hatchet, and they scrutinized him and his cudgel scornfully. Then he struck a crossroad with a monorail at its side, and there was a noticeboard at the corner with 'Wait here for the cars'. 'That's all right any'ow,' said Bert. 'Wonder 'ow long I should 'ave to wait?' It occurred to him that in the present disturbed state of the country the service might be interrupted, and as there

seemed more houses to the right than the left he turned to
the right. He passed an old Negro. ''Ullo!' said Bert. 'Goo'
morning!'

'Good day, sah!' said the old Negro in a voice of almost
incredible richness.

'What's the name of this place?' asked Bert.

'Tanooda,[7] sah!' said the Negro.

'Thenks,' said Bert.

'Thank *you*, sah!' said the Negro overwhelmingly.

Bert came to houses of the same detached, unwalled, wooden
type, but adorned now with enamelled advertisements partly in
English and partly in Esperanto.[8] Then he came to what he
concluded was a grocer's shop. It was the first house that pro-
fessed the hospitality of an open door, and from within came
a strangely familiar sound. 'Gaw!' he said, searching in his
pockets. 'Why! I 'aven't wanted money for free weeks! I wonder
if I— Grubb 'ad most of it. Ah!' He produced a handful of
coins and regarded it; three pennies, sixpence and a shilling.
'That's all right,' he said, forgetting a very obvious consideration.

He approached the door, and as he did so a compactly built,
grey-faced man in shirt-sleeves appeared in it and scrutinized
him and his cudgel. 'Mornin',' said Bert. 'Can I get anything to
eat 'r drink in this shop?'

The man in the door replied, thank Heaven, in clear, good
American. 'This, sir, is not A shop, it is A store.'[9]

'Oh!' said Bert, and then, 'Well, can I get anything to eat?'

'You can,' said the American in a tone of confident encouragement, and led the way inside.

The shop seemed to him by his Bun Hill standards extremely
roomy, well lit and unencumbered. There was a long counter
to the left of him, with drawers and miscellaneous commodities
ranged behind it, a number of chairs, several tables and two
spittoons to the right, various barrels, cheeses and bacon up
the vista, and beyond, a large archway leading to more space.
A little group of men was assembled round one of the tables,
and a woman of perhaps five-and-thirty leant with her elbows
on the counter. All the men were armed with rifles, and the
barrel of a gun peeped above the counter. They were all listening

idly, inattentively, to a cheap, metallic-toned gramophone that occupied a table near at hand. From its brazen throat came words that gave Bert a qualm of homesickness, that brought back in his memory a sunlit beach, a group of children, red-painted bicycles, Grubb and an approaching balloon:

> Ting a-ling-a-ting-a-ling-a-ting-a-ling-a-tang
> What price hairpins now?

A heavy-necked man in a straw hat, who was chewing something, stopped the machine with a touch, and they all turned their eyes on Bert. And all their eyes were tired eyes.

'Can we give this gentleman anything to eat, mother, or can we not?' said the proprietor.

'He kin have what he likes,' said the woman at the counter, without moving, 'right up from a cracker to a square meal.' She struggled with a yawn, after the manner of one who has been up all night.

'I want a meal,' said Bert, 'but I 'aven't very much money. I don't want to give mor'n a shillin'.'

'Mor'n a *what*?' said the proprietor sharply.

'Mor'n a shillin',' said Bert, with a sudden disagreeable realization coming into his mind.

'Yes,' said the proprietor, startled for a moment from his courtly bearing, 'but what in hell *is* a shilling?'

'He means a quarter,' said a wise-looking, lank young man in riding gaiters.

Bert, trying to conceal his consternation, produced a coin. 'That's a shilling,' he said.

'He calls A store A shop,' said the proprietor, 'and he wants A meal for A shilling. May I ask you, sir, what part of America you hail from?'

Bert replaced the shilling in his pocket as he spoke. 'Niagara,' he said.

'And when did you leave Niagara?'

''Bout an hour ago.'

'Well,' said the proprietor, and turned with a puzzled smile to the others. 'Well!'

They asked various questions simultaneously.

Bert selected one or two for reply. 'You see,' he said, 'I been with the German air-fleet. I got caught up by them, sort of by accident, and brought over here.'

'From England?'

'Yes – from England. Way of Germany. I was in a great battle with them Asiatics, and I got lef' on a little island between the falls.'

'Goat Island?'

'I don't know what it was called. But any'ow I found a flying machine and made a sort of fly with it and got here.'

Two men stood up with incredulous eyes on him. 'Where's the flying machine?' they asked; 'outside?'

'It's back in the woods here – 'bout 'arf a mile away.'

'Is it good?' said a thick-lipped man with a scar.

'I come down rather a smash—'

Everybody got up and stood about him and talked confusingly. They wanted him to take them to the flying machine at once.

'Look 'ere,' said Bert, 'I'll show you – only I 'aven't 'ad anything to eat since yestiday – except mineral water.'

A gaunt, soldierly looking young man with long lean legs in riding gaiters and a bandolier, who had hitherto not spoken, intervened now on his behalf in a note of confident authority. 'That's aw right,' he said. 'Give him a feed, Mr Logan – from me. I want to hear more of that story of his. We'll see his machine afterwards. If you ask me, I should say it's a remarkably interesting accident had dropped this gentleman here. I guess we requisition that flying machine – if we find it – for local defence.'

§ 3

So Bert fell on his feet again, and sat eating cold meat and good bread and mustard and drinking very good beer, and telling in the roughest outline and with the omissions and inaccuracies of statement natural to his type of mind, the simple story of his adventures. He told how he and a 'gentleman friend' had been visiting the seaside for their health, how a 'chep' came along in a balloon and fell out as he fell in, how he had drifted to Franconia, how the Germans had seemed to mistake him for someone and had 'took him prisoner' and brought him to New York, how he had been to Labrador and back, how he had got to Goat Island and found himself there alone. He omitted the matter of the Prince and the Butteridge aspect of the affair, not out of any deep deceitfulness, but because he felt the inadequacy of his narrative powers. He wanted everything to seem easy and natural and correct, to present himself as a trustworthy and understandable Englishman in a sound mediocre position, to whom refreshment and accommodation might be given with freedom and confidence.

When his fragmentary story came to New York and the battle of Niagara they suddenly produced newspapers which had been lying about on the table, and began to check him and question him by these vehement accounts. It became evident to him that his descent had revived and roused to flames again a discussion, a topic, that had been burning continuously, that had smouldered only through sheer exhaustion of material during the temporary diversion of the gramophone, a discussion that had drawn these men together, rifle in hand, the one supreme topic of the whole world, the War and the methods of War. He found any question of his personality and his personal adventures falling into the background, found himself taken for granted, and no more than a source of information. The ordinary affairs of life, the buying and selling of everyday necessities, the cultivation of the ground, the tending of beasts, was going on as it were by force of routine, as the common duties of life go on in a house whose master lies under the knife of some supreme operation. The overruling interest was furnished by those great Asiatic airships that went upon incalculable missions across the sky, the crimson-clad swordsmen who might come fluttering down demanding petrol, or food, or news. These men were asking, all the continent was asking, 'What are we to do? What can we try? How can we get at them?' Bert fell into his place as an item, ceased even in his own thoughts to be a central and independent thing.

After he had eaten and drunken his fill and sighed and stretched and told them how good the food seemed to him, he lit a cigarette they gave him and led the way, with some doubts and trouble, to the flying machine amidst the larches. It became manifest that the gaunt young man, whose name, it seemed, was Laurier, was a leader both by position and natural aptitude. He knew the names and characters and capabilities of all the men who were with him, and he set them to work at once with vigour and effect to secure this precious instrument of war. They got the thing down to the ground deliberately and carefully, felling a couple of trees in the process, and they built a wide flat roof of timbers and tree boughs to guard their precious find against its chance discovery by any passing Asiatics. Long before evening they had an engineer from the next township at work upon it, and they were casting lots among the seventeen picked men who wanted to take it for its first flight. And Bert found his kitten and carried it back to Logan's store and handed it with earnest admonition to Mrs Logan. And it was reassuringly clear to him that in Mrs Logan both he and the kitten had found a congenial soul.

Laurier was not only a masterful person and a wealthy property-owner and employer – he was president, Bert learnt with awe, of the Tanooda Canning Corporation – but he was popular and skilful in the arts of popularity. In the evening quite a crowd of men gathered in the store and talked of the flying machine and of the war that was tearing the world to pieces. And presently came a man on a bicycle with an ill-printed newspaper of a single sheet which acted like fuel in a blazing furnace of talk. It was nearly all American news; the old-fashioned cables had fallen into disuse for some years, and the Marconi stations across the ocean and along the Atlantic coastline seemed to have furnished particularly tempting points of attack.

But such news it was.

Bert sat in the background – for by this time they had gauged his personal quality pretty completely – listening. Before his staggering mind passed strange vast images as they talked, of great issues at a crisis, of nations in tumultuous march, of continents overthrown, of famine and destruction beyond measure. Ever and again, in spite of his efforts to suppress them, certain personal impressions would scamper across the weltering confusion, the horrible mess of the exploded Prince, the Chinese aeronaut upside down, the limping and bandaged bird-faced officer blundering along in miserable and hopeless flight. . . .

They spoke of fire and massacre, of cruelties and counter-cruelties, of things that had been done to harmless Asiatics by race-mad men, of the wholesale burning and smashing up of towns, railway junctions, bridges, of whole populations in hiding and exodus. 'Every ship they've got is in the Pacific,' he heard one man exclaim. 'Since the fighting began they can't have landed on the Pacific slope less than a million men. They've come to stay in these States, and they will – living or dead.'

Slowly, broadly, invincibly, there grew upon Bert's mind realization of the immense tragedy of humanity into which his life was flowing; the appalling and universal nature of the epoch that had arrived; the conception of an end to security and order and habit. The whole world was at war and it could not get back to peace; it might never recover peace.

He had thought the things he had seen had been exceptional, conclusive things, that the besieging of New York and the battle of the Atlantic were epoch-making events between long years of security. And they had been but the first warning impacts of universal cataclysm. Each day destruction and hate and disaster grew, the fissures widened between man and man, new regions of the fabric of civilization crumbled and gave way. Below, the armies grew and the people perished; above, the airships and aeroplanes fought and fled, raining destruction.

It is difficult perhaps for the broad-minded and long-perspectived reader to understand how incredible the breaking down of the scientific civilization seemed to those who actually lived at this time, who in their own persons went down in that débâcle. Progress had marched as it seemed invincible about the earth, never now to rest again. For three hundred years and more the long, steadily accelerated diastole[10] of Europeanized civilization had been in progress: towns had been multiplying, populations increasing, values rising, new countries developing; thought, literature, knowledge unfolding and spreading. It seemed but a part of the process that every year the instruments of war were vaster and more powerful, and that armies and explosives outgrew all other growing things. . . .

Three hundred years of diastole, and then came the swift and unexpected systole, like the closing of a fist. They could not understand it was a systole. They could not think of it as anything but a jolt, a hitch, a mere oscillatory indication of the swiftness of their progress. Collapse, though it happened all about them, remained incredible. Presently some falling mass smote them down, or the ground opened beneath their feet. They died incredulous. . . .

These men in the store made a minute, remote group under this immense canopy of disaster. They turned from one little aspect to another. What chiefly concerned them was defence against Asiatic raiders swooping for petrol or to destroy weapons or communications. Everywhere levies were being formed at that time to defend the plant of the railroads day and night in the hope that communication would speedily be restored. The land war was still far away. A man with a flat voice distinguished himself by a display of knowledge and cunning. He told them all with confidence just what had been wrong with the German *Drachenflieger* and the American aeroplanes, just what advantage the Japanese fliers possessed. He launched out into a romantic description of the Butteridge machine and riveted Bert's attention. 'I *see* that,' said Bert, and was smitten silent by a thought. The man with the flat voice talked on, without heeding him, of the strange irony of Butteridge's death. At that Bert had a little twinge of relief – he would never meet Butteridge again. It appeared Butteridge had died suddenly, very suddenly.

'And his secret, sir, perished with him! When they came to look for the parts – none could find them. He had hidden them all too well.'

'But couldn't he tell?' asked the man in the straw hat. 'Did he die so suddenly as that?'

'Struck down, sir. Rage and apoplexy. At a place called Dymchurch in England.'

'That's right,' said Laurier. 'I remember a page about it in the Sunday *American*. At the time they said it was a German spy had stolen his balloon.'

'Well, sir,' said the flat-voiced man, 'that fit of apoplexy at Dymchurch was the worst thing – ab-so-lutely the worst thing that ever happened to the world. For if it had not been for the death of Mr Butteridge—'

'No one knows his secret?'

'Not a soul. It's gone. His balloon, it appears, was lost at sea, with all the plans. Down it went, and they went with it.'

Pause.

'With machines such as he made we could fight these Asiatic fliers on more than equal terms. We could outfly and beat down those scarlet humming-birds wherever they appeared. But it's gone, it's gone, and there's no time to reinvent it now. We got to fight with what we got – and the odds are against us. *That* won't stop us fightin'. No! but just think of it!'

Bert was trembling violently. He cleared his throat hoarsely. 'I say,' he said, 'look here, I—'

Nobody regarded him. The man with the flat voice was opening a new branch of the subject. 'I allow—' he began.

Bert became violently excited. He stood up. He made clawing motions with his hands. 'I say!' he exclaimed, 'Mr Laurier. Look 'ere – I want – about that Butteridge machine—'

Mr Laurier, sitting on an adjacent table, with a magnificent gesture arrested the discourse of the flat-voiced man. 'What's *he* saying?' said he.

Then the whole company realized that something was happening to Bert; either he was suffocating or going mad. He was spluttering, 'Look 'ere! I say! 'Old on a bit!' and trembling and eagerly unbuttoning himself.

He tore open his collar and opened vest and shirt. He plunged into his interior and for an instant it seemed he was plucking forth his liver. Then as he struggled with buttons on his shoulder they perceived this flattened horror was in fact a terribly dirty flannel chest-protector. In another moment Bert, in a state of irregular décolletage,[11] was standing over the table displaying a sheaf of papers.

'These!' he gasped. 'These are the plans! . . . You know! Mr Butteridge – his machine! What died! I was the chap that went off in that balloon!'

For some seconds everyone was silent. They stared from these papers to Bert's white face and blazing eyes, and back to the papers on the table. Nobody moved. Then the man with the flat voice spoke.

'Irony!' he said, with a note of satisfaction. 'Real right-down Irony! *When it's too late to think of making 'em any more!*'

§ 4

They would all no doubt have been eager to hear Bert's story over again, but it was at this point that Laurier showed his quality. 'No, *sir*,' he said, and slid from off his table.

He impounded the dispersing Butteridge plans with one comprehensive sweep of his arms, rescuing them even from the expository fingermarks of the man with the flat voice, and handed them to Bert. 'Put those back,' he said, 'where you had 'em. We have a journey before us.'

Bert took them.

'Whar?' said the man in the straw hat.

'Why, sir, we are going to find the President of these States and give these plans over to him. I decline to believe, sir, we are too late.'

'Where is the President?' asked Bert weakly in the pause that followed.

'Logan,' said Laurier, disregarding that feeble inquiry, 'you must help us in this.'

It seemed only a matter of a few minutes before Bert and Laurier and the storekeeper were examining a number of bicycles that were stowed in the hinder room of the store. Bert didn't like any of them very much. They had wood rims, and an experience of wood rims in the English climate had taught him to hate them. That, however, and one or two other objections to an immediate start were overruled by Laurier. 'But where *is* the President?' Bert repeated as they stood behind Logan while he pumped up a deflated tyre.

Laurier looked down on him. 'He is reported in the neighbourhood of Albany – out towards the Berkshire Hills.[12] He is moving from place to place and, as far as he can, organizing the defence by telegraph and telephone. The Asiatic air-fleet is trying to locate him. When they think they have located the seat of government they throw bombs. This inconveniences him, but so far they have not come within ten miles of him. The Asiatic air-fleet is at present scattered all over the Eastern States, seeking out and destroying gasworks and whatever seems conducive to the building of airships or the transport of troops. Our retaliatory measures are slight in the extreme. But with these machines— Sir, this ride of ours will count among the historical rides of the world!'

He came near to striking an attitude.

'We shan't get to him tonight?' asked Bert.

'No, sir!' said Laurier. 'We shall have to ride some days, sure!'

'I suppose we can't get a lift on a train – or anything?'

'No, sir! There's been no transit by Tanooda for three days. It is no good waiting. We shall have to get on as well as we can.'

'Startin' now?'

'Starting now!'

'But 'ow about— We shan't be able to do much tonight.'

'May as well ride till we're fagged and sleep then. So much clear gain. Our road is eastward.'

'Of course—' began Bert, with memories of the dawn upon Goat Island, and left his sentence unfinished.

He gave his attention to the more scientific packing of the chest-protector, for several of the plans flapped beyond his vest.

§ 5

For a week Bert led a life of mixed sensations. Amidst these fatigue in the legs predominated. Mostly he rode, rode with Laurier's back inexorably ahead, through a land like a larger England, with bigger hills and wider valleys, larger fields, wider roads, fewer hedges and wooden houses with commodious piazzas. He rode. Laurier made inquiries, Laurier chose the turnings, Laurier doubted, Laurier decided. Now it seemed they were in telephonic touch with the President; now something had happened and he was lost again. But always they had to go on, and always Bert rode. A tyre was deflated. Still he rode. He grew saddle sore. Laurier declared that unimportant. Asiatic flying-ships passed overhead, the two cyclists made a dash for cover until the sky was clear. Once a red Asiatic flying machine came fluttering after them, so low they could distinguish the aeronaut's head. He followed them for a mile. Now they came to regions of panic, now to regions of destruction, here people were fighting for food, here they seemed hardly stirred from the countryside routine. They spent a day in a deserted and damaged Albany. The Asiatics had descended and cut every wire and made a cinder-heap of the Junction, and our travellers pushed on eastward. They passed a hundred half-heeded incidents, and always Bert was toiling after Laurier's indefatigable back. . . .

Things struck upon Bert's attention and perplexed him, and then he passed on with unanswered questionings fading from his mind.

He saw a large house on fire on a hillside to the right, and no man heeding it. . . .

They came to a narrow railroad bridge and presently to a monorail train standing in the track on its safety feet. It was a remarkably sumptuous train, the Last Word Trans-Continental Express, and the passengers were all playing cards or sleeping or preparing a picnic meal on a grassy slope near at hand. They had been there six days. . . .

At one point ten dark-complexioned men were hanging in a string from the trees along the roadside. Bert wondered why. . . .

At one peaceful-looking village where they stopped off to get Bert's tyre mended and found beer and biscuits, they were approached by an extremely dirty little boy without boots, who spoke as follows:

'Deyse[13] been hanging a Chink in dose woods!'

'Hanging a Chinaman?' said Laurier.

'Sure. Der sleuths got him rubberin' der railroad sheds!'

'Oh!'

'Dose guys done wase cartridges. Deyse hung him and dey pulled his legs. Deyse doin' all der Chinks dey can fine dat weh! Dey ain't takin' no risks. All der Chinks dey can fine.'

Neither Bert nor Laurier made any reply, and presently, after a little skilful expectoration, the young gentleman was attracted by the appearance of two of his friends down the road, and shuffled off, whooping weirdly. . . .

That afternoon they almost ran over a man shot through the body and partly decomposed, lying near the middle of the road, just outside Albany. He must have been lying there for some days. . . .

Beyond Albany they came upon a motor-car with a tyre burst and a young woman sitting absolutely passive beside the driver's seat. An old man was under the car trying to effect some impossible repairs. Beyond, sitting with a rifle across his knees, with his back to the car, and staring into the woods, was a young man. The old man crawled out at their approach and still on all fours accosted Bert and Laurier. The car had broken down overnight. The old man said he could not understand what was wrong, but he was trying to puzzle it out. Neither he nor his son-in-law had any mechanical aptitude. They had been assured this was a foolproof car. It was dangerous to have to stop in this place. His party had been attacked by tramps and had had to fight. It was known they had provisions. He mentioned a great name in the world of finance. Would Laurier and Bert stop and help him? He proposed it first hopefully, then urgently, at last in tears and terror.

'No!' said Laurier inexorably. 'We must go on! We have something more than a woman to save. We have to save America!'

The girl never stirred. . . .

Once they passed a madman singing. . . .

At last they found the President hiding in a small saloon upon the outskirts of a place called Pinkerville[14] on the Hudson, and gave the plans of the Butteridge machine into his hands.

THE GREAT COLLAPSE

§ 1

And now the whole fabric of civilization was bending and giving, and dropping to pieces and melting in the furnace of the war.

The stages of the swift and universal collapse of the financial and scientific civilization with which the twentieth century opened followed each other very swiftly, so swiftly that upon the foreshortened page of history they seem altogether to overlap. To begin with, one sees the world nearly at a maximum of wealth and prosperity. To its inhabitants indeed it seemed also at a maximum of security. When now in retrospect the thoughtful observer surveys the intellectual history of this time, when one reads its surviving fragments of literature, its scraps of political oratory, the few small voices that chance has selected out of a thousand million utterances to speak to later days, the most striking thing of all this web of wisdom and error is surely that hallucination of security. To men living in our present world state, orderly, scientific and secured, nothing seems so precarious, so giddily dangerous, as the fabric of the social order with which the men of the opening of the twentieth century were content. To us it seems that every institution and relationship was the fruit of haphazard and tradition and the manifest sport of chance, their laws each made for some separate occasion and having no relation to any future needs, their customs illogical, their education aimless and wasteful. Their method of economic exploitation indeed impresses a trained and informed mind as the most frantic and destructive scramble it is possible to conceive; their credit and monetary system resting on an unsubstantial tradition of the worthiness of gold, seems a thing almost fantastically unstable. And they lived in planless cities, for the most part dangerously congested, their rails and roads and population were distributed over the earth in the wanton confusion ten thousand irrelevant considerations had made. Yet they thought confidently that this was a secure and permanent progressive system, and on the strength of some three hundred years of chance and irregular improvement answered the doubter with, 'Things always *have* gone well. We'll worry through!'

But when we contrast the state of man in the opening of the twentieth century with the condition of any previous period in his history, then perhaps we may begin to understand something of that blind confidence. It was not so much a reasoned confidence as the inevitable consequence of sustained good fortune. By such standards as they possessed, things *had* gone amazingly well for them. It is scarcely an exaggeration to say that for the first time in history whole populations found themselves regularly supplied with more than enough to eat, and the vital statistics of the time witness to an amelioration of hygienic conditions rapid beyond all precedent, and to a vast development of intelligence and ability in all the arts that make life wholesome. The level and quality of the average education had risen tremendously; and at the dawn of the twentieth century comparatively few people in Western Europe or America were unable to read or write. Never before had there been such reading masses. There was wide social security. A common man might travel safely over three-quarters of the habitable globe, could go round the earth at a cost of less than the annual earnings of a skilled artisan. Compared with the liberality and comfort of the ordinary life of the time, the order of the Roman Empire under the Antonines[1] was local and limited. And every year, every month, came some new increment to human achievement, a new country opened up, new mines, new scientific discoveries, a new machine!

For those three hundred years the movement of the world seemed wholly beneficial to mankind. Men said, indeed, that moral organization was not keeping pace with physical progress, but few attached any meaning to these phrases, the understanding of which lies at the basis of our present safety. Sustaining and constructive forces did indeed for a time more than balance the malign drift of chance and the natural ignorance, prejudice, blind passion and wasteful self-seeking of mankind.

The accidental balance on the side of Progress was far slighter and infinitely more complex and delicate in its adjustments than the people of that time suspected; but that did not alter the fact that it was an effective balance. They did not realize that this age of relative good fortune was an age of immense but temporary opportunity for their kind. They complacently assumed a necessary progress towards which they had no moral responsibility. They did not realize that this security of progress was a thing still to be won or lost, and that the time to win it was a time that passed. They went about their affairs energetically enough, and yet with a curious idleness towards those threatening things. No one troubled over the real dangers of mankind. They saw their armies and navies grow larger and more portentous; some of their ironclads at the last cost as much as their whole annual expenditure upon advanced education; they accumulated explosives and the machinery of destruction; they allowed their national traditions and jealousies to accumulate; they contemplated without concern or understanding a steady enhancement of race hostility as the races drew closer, and they permitted the growth in their midst of an evil-spirited press, mercenary and unscrupulous, incapable of good and powerful for evil. Their State had practically no control over the press at all. Quite heedlessly they allowed this touchpaper to lie at the door of their war magazine for any spark to fire. The precedents of history were all one tale of the collapse of civilizations, the dangers of the time were manifest. One is incredulous now to believe they could not see.

Could mankind have prevented this disaster of the War in the Air? An idle question that, as idle as to ask could mankind have prevented the decay that turned Assyria and Babylon to empty deserts or the slow decline and fall, the gradual social disorganization, phase by phase, that closed the chapter of the

Empire of the West. They could not, because they did not, they had not the will to arrest it. What mankind could achieve with a different will is a speculation as idle as it is magnificent. And this was no slow decadence that came to the Europeanized world; those other civilizations rotted and crumbled down, the Europeanized civilization was, as it were, blown up. Within the space of five years it was altogether disintegrated and destroyed. Up to the very eve of the War in the Air one sees a spacious spectacle of incessant advance, a worldwide security, enormous areas with highly organized industry and settled populations, gigantic cities spreading gigantically, the seas and oceans dotted with shipping, the land netted with rails and open ways. Then suddenly the German air-fleets sweep across the scene, and we are in the beginning of the end.

§ 2

This story has already told of the swift rush upon New York of the first German air-fleet and of the wild, inevitable orgy of inconclusive destruction that ensued. Behind it a second air-fleet was already swelling at its gasometers when England and France and Spain and Italy showed their hands. None of these countries had prepared for aeronautic warfare on the magnificent scale of the Germans, but each guarded secrets, each in a measure was making ready, and a common dread of German vigour and that aggressive spirit Prince Karl Albert embodied had long been drawing these powers together in secret anticipation of some such attack. This rendered their prompt co-operation possible, and they certainly co-operated promptly. The second aerial power in Europe at this time was France; the British, nervous for their Asiatic empire, and sensible of the immense moral effect of the airship upon half-educated populations, had placed their aeronautic parks in North India, and were able to play but a subordinate part in the European conflict. Still, even in England they had nine or ten big navigables, twenty or thirty smaller ones and a variety of experimental aeroplanes. Before the fleet of Prince Karl Albert had crossed England, while Bert was still surveying Manchester in bird's-eye view, the diplomatic exchanges were going on that led to an attack upon Germany. A heterogeneous collection of navigable balloons of all sizes and types gathered over the Bernese Oberland, crushed and burnt in the battle of the Alps the twenty-five Swiss airships that unexpectedly resisted this concentration, and then, leaving the Alpine glaciers and valleys strewn with strange wreckage, divided into two fleets and set itself to terrorize Berlin and destroy the Franconian Park, seeking to do this before the second air-fleet could be inflated.

Both over Berlin and Franconia the assailants with their modern explosives effected great damage before they were driven off. In Franconia twelve fully distended and five partially filled and manned giants were able to make head against, and at last, with the help of a squadron of *Drachenflieger* from Hamburg, defeat and pursue the attack and to relieve Berlin, and the Germans were straining every nerve to get an overwhelming fleet in the air, and were already raiding London and Paris when the advance fleets from the Asiatic air-parks, the first intimation of a new factor in the conflict, were reported from Burmah and Armenia.

Already, when that occurred, the whole financial fabric of the world was staggering. With the destruction of the American fleet in the North Atlantic, and the smashing conflict that ended the naval existence of Germany in the North Sea, with the burning and wrecking of billions of pounds' worth of property in the four cardinal cities of the world, the fact of the hopeless costliness of war came home for the first time, came like a blow in the face, to the consciousness of mankind. Credit went down in a wild whirl of selling. Everywhere appeared a phenomenon that had already in a mild degree manifested itself in preceding periods of panic; a desire to *secure and hoard gold* before prices reached bottom. But now it spread like wildfire, it became universal. Above was visible conflict and destruction; below something was happening far more deadly and incurable to the flimsy fabric of finance and commercialism in which men had so blindly put their trust. As the airships fought above, the visible gold supply of the world vanished below. An epidemic of private cornering and universal distrust swept the world. In a few weeks, money, except for depreciated paper, vanished into vaults, into holes, into the walls of houses, into ten million hiding-places. Money vanished, and at its disappearance trade and industry came to an end. The economic world staggered and fell dead. It was like the stroke of some disease; it was like the water vanishing out of the blood of a living creature; it was a sudden, universal coagulation of intercourse . . . .

And as the credit system, that had been the living fortress of the scientific civilization, reeled and fell upon the millions it had held together in economic relationship, as these people, perplexed and helpless, faced this marvel of credit utterly destroyed, the airships of Asia, countless and relentless, poured across the heavens, swooped eastward to America and westward to Europe. The page of history becomes a long crescendo of battle. The main body of the British-Indian air-fleet perished upon a pyre of blazing antagonists in Burma; the Germans were scattered in the great battle of the Carpathians; the vast peninsula of India burst into insurrection and civil war from end to end, and from Gobi to Morocco rose the standards of the 'Jehad'.[2] For some weeks of warfare and destruction it seemed as though the Confederation of Eastern Asia must needs conquer the world, and then the jerry-built 'modern' civilization of China too gave way under the strain. The teeming and peaceful population of China had been 'westernized' during the opening years of the twentieth century with the deepest resentment and reluctance; they had been dragooned and disciplined under Japanese and European influence into an acquiescence with sanitary methods, police controls, military service and a wholesale process of exploitation against which their whole tradition rebelled. Under the stresses of the war their endurance reached the breaking point. China rose in incoherent revolt, and the practical destruction of the central government at Peking by a handful of British and German airships that had escaped from the main battles rendered that revolt invincible. Japan followed suit. In Yokohama appeared barricades, the black flag and the social revolution. With that the whole world became a welter of conflict.

So that a universal social collapse followed, as it were a

logical consequence, upon worldwide war. Wherever there were
great populations, great masses of people found themselves
without work, without money and unable to get food. Famine
was in every working-class quarter in the world within three
weeks of the beginning of the war. Within a month there was
not a city anywhere in which the ordinary law and social pro-
cedure had not been replaced by some form of emergency
control, in which firearms and military executions were not
being used to keep order and prevent violence. And still in the
poorer quarters, and in the populous districts, and even here
and there already among those who had been wealthy, famine
spread.

§ 3

So what historians have come to call the Phase of the Emergency
Committees sprang from the opening phase and from the
phase of social collapse. Then followed a period of vehement
and passionate conflict against disintegration; everywhere the
struggle to keep order and to keep fighting went on. And at
the same time the character of the war altered through the
replacement of the huge gas-filled airships by flying-machines
as the instruments of war. So soon as the big fleet engagements
were over, the Asiatics endeavoured to establish in close proximity to the more vulnerable points of the countries against
which they were acting, fortified centres from which flying-
machine raids could be made. For a time they had everything
their own way in this, and then, as this story has told, the lost
secret of the Butteridge machine came to light, and the conflict
became equalized and less conclusive than ever. For these small
flying machines, ineffectual for any large expedition or conclusive attack, were horribly convenient for guerilla warfare,
rapidly and cheaply made, easily used, easily hidden. The design
of them was hastily copied and printed in Pinkerville, and
scattered broadcast over the United States, and copies were sent
to Europe, and there reproduced. Every man, every town, every
parish that could, was exhorted to make and use them. In a little
while they were being constructed not only by governments and

local authorities, but by robber bands, by insurgent committees, by every type of private person. The peculiar social destructiveness of the Butteridge machine lay in its complete simplicity. It was nearly as simple as a motor-bicycle. The broad outlines of the earlier stages of the war disappeared under its influence, the spacious antagonism of nations and empires and races vanished in a seething mass of detailed conflict. The world passed at a stride from a unity and simplicity broader than that of the Roman Empire at its best, to a social fragmentation as complete as the robber-baron period of the Middle Ages. But this time, for a long descent down gradual slopes of disintegration, comes a fall like a fall over a cliff. Everywhere were men and women perceiving this, and struggling desperately to keep, as it were, a hold upon the edge of the cliff.

A fourth phase follows. Through the struggle against Chaos, in the wake of the Famine, came now another old enemy of humanity – the Pestilence, the Purple Death.[3] But the war does not pause. The flags still fly. Fresh air-fleets rise, new forms of airship, and beneath their swooping struggles the world darkens – scarcely heeded by history.

It is not within the design of this book to tell that further story, to tell how the War in the Air kept on through the sheer inability of any authorities to meet and agree and end it, until every organized government in the world was as shattered and broken as a heap of china beaten with a stick. With every week of those terrible years history becomes more detailed and confused, more crowded and uncertain. Not without great and heroic resistance was civilization borne down. Out of the bitter social conflict below rose patriotic associations, brotherhoods of order, city mayors, princes, provisional committees, trying to establish an order below and to keep the sky above. The double effort destroyed them. And as the exhaustion of the mechanical resources of civilization clears the heavens of airships at last altogether, Anarchy, Famine and Pestilence are discovered triumphant below. The great nations and empires have become but names in the mouths of men. Everywhere there are ruins and unburied dead, and shrunken, yellow-faced survivors, in a mortal apathy. Here there are robbers, here vigilance committees, and here guerilla bands ruling patches of exhausted territory, strange federations and brotherhoods form and dissolve, and religious fanaticisms begotten of despair gleam in famine-bright eyes. It is a universal dissolution. The fine order and welfare of the earth have crumpled like an exploded bladder. In five short years the world and the scope of human life have undergone a retrogressive change as great as that between the age of the Antonines and the Europe of the ninth century. . . .

§ 4

Across this sombre spectacle of disaster goes a minute and insignificant person for whom perhaps the readers of this story have now some slight solicitude. Of him there remains to be told just one single miraculous thing. Through a world darkened and lost, through a civilization in its death-agony, our little Cockney errant went and found his Edna! He found his Edna!

He got back across the Atlantic partly by means of an order from the President and partly through his own good luck. He contrived to get himself aboard a British brig in the timber trade that put out from Boston without cargo, chiefly, it would seem, because its captain had a vague idea of 'getting home' to South Shields.[4] Bert was able to ship himself upon her mainly because of the seamanlike appearance of his rubber boots. They had a long, eventful voyage, they were chased, or imagined themselves to be chased, for some hours by an Asiatic ironclad, which was presently engaged by a British cruiser. The two ships fought for three hours, circling and driving southward as they fought, until the twilight and the cloud-drift of a rising gale swallowed them up. A few days later Bert's ship lost her rudder and mainmast in a gale. The crew ran out of food and subsisted on fish. They saw strange airships going eastward near the Azores, and landed to get provisions and repair the rudder at Tenerife.[5] There they found the town destroyed, and two big liners, with dead still aboard, sunken in the harbour. From these they got canned food and material for repairs, but their operations were greatly impeded by the hostility of a band of men amidst the ruins of the town, who sniped them and tried to drive them away.

At Mogador[6] they stayed and sent a boat ashore for water, and were nearly captured by an Arab ruse. Here, too, they got the Purple Death aboard, and sailed with it incubating in their blood. The cook sickened first, and then the mate, and presently everyone was down and three in the forecastle were dead. It chanced to be calm weather, and they drifted helplessly and indeed careless of their fate backwards towards the Equator. The captain doctored them all with rum. Nine died altogether, and of the four survivors none understood navigation; when at last they took heart again and could handle a sail they made a course by the stars roughly northward, and were already short of food once more when they fell in with a petrol-driven ship from Rio to Cardiff, short-handed by reason of the Purple Death and glad to take them aboard. So at last after a year of wandering Bert reached England. He landed in bright June weather, and found the Purple Death was there just beginning its ravages.

The people were in a state of panic in Cardiff and many had fled to the hills, and directly the steamer came to the harbour she was boarded and her residue of food impounded by some unauthenticated Provisional Committee. Bert tramped through a country disorganized by pestilence, foodless, and shaken to the very base of its immemorial order. He came near death and starvation many times, and once he was drawn into scenes of violence that might have ended his career. But the Bert Smallways who tramped from Cardiff to London vaguely 'going home', vaguely seeking something of his own that had no tangible form but Edna, was a very different person from the Desert Dervish who was swept out of England in Mr Butteridge's balloon a year before. He was brown and lean and enduring, steady-eyed and pestilence-salted, and his mouth, which had once hung open, shut now like a steel trap. Across his brow ran a white scar that he had got in a fight on the brig. In Cardiff he had felt the need of new clothes and a weapon, and had, by means that would have shocked him a year ago, secured a flannel shirt, a corduroy suit and a revolver and fifty

cartridges from an abandoned pawnbroker's. He also got some
soap and had his first real wash for thirteen months in a stream
outside the town. The Vigilance bands that had at first shot
plunderers very freely were now either entirely dispersed by the
plague, or busy between town and cemetery in a vain attempt
to keep pace with it. He prowled on the outskirts of the town
for three or four days, starving, and then went back to join the
Hospital Corps for a week, and so fortified himself with a few
square meals before he started eastward.

The Welsh and English countryside at that time presented the
strangest mingling of the assurance and wealth of the opening
twentieth century with a sort of Düreresque[7] mediaevalism. All
the gear, the houses and monorails, the farm hedges and power
cables, the roads and pavements, the signposts and advertisements of the former order were still for the most part intact.
Bankruptcy, social collapse, famine and pestilence had done
nothing to damage these; it was only to the great capitals and
ganglionic centres, as it were, of the State that positive destruction had come. Anyone dropped suddenly into the country
would have noticed very little difference. He would have
remarked first, perhaps, that all the hedges needed clipping,
that the roadside grass grew rank, that the road tracks were
unusually rainworn, and that the cottages by the wayside
seemed in many cases shut up, that a telephone wire had
dropped here, and that a cart stood abandoned by the wayside.
But he would still find his hunger whetted by the bright assurance that Wilder's Canned Peaches were excellent, or that there
was nothing so good for the breakfast table as Gobble's Saus-
ages. And then suddenly would come the Düreresque element;
the skeleton of a horse, or some crumpled mass of rags in the
ditch, with gaunt extended feet and a yellow, purple-blotched
skin and face, or what had been a face, gaunt and glaring and
devastated. Then here would be a field that had been ploughed
and not sown, and here a field of corn carelessly trampled
by beasts, and here a hoarding torn down across the road to
make a fire.

Then presently he would meet a man or a woman, yellow-
faced and probably negligently dressed and armed – prowling

for food. These people would have the complexions and eyes and expressions of tramps or criminals, and often the clothing of prosperous middle-class or upper-class people. Many of these would be eager for news, and willing to give help and even scraps of queer meat, or crusts of grey and doughy bread in return for it. They would listen to Bert's story with avidity, and attempt to keep him with them for a day or so. The virtual cessation of postal distribution and the collapse of all newspaper enterprise had left an immense and aching gap in the mental life of this time. Men had suddenly lost sight of the ends of the earth and had still to recover the rumour-spreading habits of the Middle Ages. In their eyes, in their bearing, in their talk, was the quality of lost and deoriented souls.

As Bert travelled from parish to parish and from district to district, avoiding as far as possible those festering centres of violence and despair, the larger towns, he found the condition of affairs varying widely. In one parish he would find the large house burnt, the vicarage wrecked, evidently in violent conflict for some suspected and perhaps imaginary store of food, unburied dead everywhere, and the whole mechanism of the community at a standstill. In another he would find organizing forces stoutly at work, newly painted noticeboards warning off vagrants, the roads and still cultivated fields policed by armed men, the pestilence under control, even nursing going on, a store of food husbanded, the cattle and sheep well guarded, and a group of two or three justices, the village doctor or a farmer, dominating the whole place; a reversion, in fact, to the autonomous community of the fifteenth century. But at any time such a village would be liable to a raid of Asiatics or Africans or suchlike air-pirates, demanding petrol and alcohol or provisions. The price of its order was an almost intolerable watchfulness and tension. Then the approach to the confused problems of some larger centre of population and the presence of a more intricate conflict would be marked by roughly smeared notices of 'Quarantine' or 'Strangers Shot', or by a string of decaying plunderers dangling from the telephone poles at the roadside. About Oxford big boards were put on the roofs warning all air wanderers off with the single word, 'Guns'.

Taking their risks amidst these things, cyclists still kept abroad, and once or twice during Bert's long tramp powerful motor-cars containing masked and goggled figures went tearing past him. There were few police in evidence, but ever and again squads of gaunt and tattered soldier-cyclists would come drifting along, and such encounters became more frequent as he got out of Wales into England. Amidst all this wreckage they were still campaigning. He had had some idea of resorting to the workhouses for the night if hunger pressed him too closely, but some of these were closed and others converted into temporary hospitals, and one he came up to at twilight near a village in Gloucestershire stood with all its doors and windows open, silent as the grave, and, as he found to his horror by stumbling along evil-smelling corridors, full of unburied dead.

From Gloucestershire Bert went northward to the British aeronautic park outside Birmingham, in the hope that he might be taken on and given food, for there the Government, or at any rate the War Office, still existed as an energetic fact, concentrated amidst collapse and social disaster upon the effort to keep the British flag still flying in the air, and trying to brisk up mayor and mayor and magistrate and magistrate in a new effort of organization. They had brought together all the best of the surviving artisans from that region, they had provisioned the park for a siege, and they were urgently building a larger type of Butteridge machine. Bert could get no footing at this work: he was not sufficiently skilled, and he had drifted to Oxford when the great fight occurred in which these works were finally wrecked. He saw something, but not very much, of the battle from a place called Boar's Hill.[8] He saw the Asiatic squadron coming up across the hills to the south-west, and he saw one of their airships circling southward again chased by two aeroplanes, the one that was ultimately overtaken, wrecked and burnt at Edge Hill. But he never learnt the issue of the combat as a whole.

He crossed the Thames from Eton to Windsor and made his way round the south of London to Bun Hill; and there he found his brother Tom, looking like some dark, defensive animal in the old shop, just recovering from the Purple Death, and Jessica upstairs delirious, and, as it seemed to him, dying grimly. She raved of sending out orders to customers, and scolded Tom perpetually lest he should be late with Mrs Thompson's potatoes and Mrs Hopkins' cauliflower, though all business had long since ceased and Tom had developed a quite uncanny skill in the snaring of rats and sparrows and the concealment of certain stores of cereals and biscuits from plundered grocers' shops. Tom received his brother with a sort of guarded warmth.

'Lor!' he said, 'it's Bert. I thought you'd be coming back some day, and I'm glad to see you. But I carn't arst you to eat anything, because I 'aven't got anything to eat. . . . Where you been, Bert, all this time?'

Bert reassured his brother by a glimpse of a partly eaten swede, and was still telling his story in fragments and parentheses, when he discovered behind the counter a yellow and forgotten note addressed to himself, 'What's this?' he said, and found it was a year-old note from Edna. 'She came 'ere,' said Tom, like one who recalls a trivial thing, 'arstin' for you and arstin' us to take 'er in. That was after the battle and settin' Clapham Rise afire. I was for takin' 'er in, but Jessica wouldn't 'ave it – and so she borrowed five shillings of me quiet like and went on. I dessay she's tole you—'

She had, Bert found. She had gone on, she said in her note, to an aunt and uncle who had a brickfield near Horsham. And there at last, after another fortnight of adventurous journeying, Bert found her.

§ 5

When Bert and Edna set eyes on one another they stared and laughed foolishly, so changed they were, and so ragged and surprised. And then they both fell weeping.

'Oh! Bertie, boy!' she cried. 'You've come – you've come!' and put out her arms and staggered. 'I told 'im. He said he'd kill me if I didn't marry him.'

But Edna was not married, and when presently Bert could get talk from her she explained the task before him. That little patch of lonely agricultural country had fallen under the power of a band of bullies led by a chief called Bill Gore, who had begun life as a butcher boy and developed into a prize-fighter and a professional 'sport'. They had been organized by a local nobleman of former eminence upon the turf, but after a time he had disappeared, no one quite knew how, and Bill had succeeded to the leadership of the countryside, and had developed his teacher's methods with considerable vigour. There had been a strain of advanced philosophy about the local nobleman, and his mind ran to 'improving the race' and producing the Over-Man,[9] which in practice took the form of himself especially and his little band in moderation marrying with some frequency. Bill followed up this idea with an enthusiasm that even trenched upon his popularity with his followers. One day he had happened upon Edna tending her pigs, and had at once fallen a-wooing with great urgency among the troughs of slush. Edna had made a gallant resistance, but he was still vigorously about and extraordinarily impatient. He might, she said, come at any time; and she looked Bert in the eyes. They were back already in the barbaric stage when a man must fight for his love.

And here one deplores the conflicts of truth with the chivalrous tradition. One would like to tell of Bert sallying forth to challenge his rival, of a ring formed and a spirited encounter, and Bert by some miracle of pluck and love and good fortune winning. But indeed nothing of the sort occurred. Instead, he reloaded his revolver very carefully, and then sat in the best room of the cottage by the derelict brickfield, looking anxious and perplexed, and listening to talk about Bill and his ways, and thinking, thinking. Then suddenly Edna's aunt, with a thrill in her voice, announced the appearance of that individual. He was coming with two others of his gang through the garden gate. Bert got up, put the women aside and looked out. They presented remarkable figures. They wore a sort of uniform of red golfing jackets and white sweaters, football singlets and stockings and boots, and each had let his fancy play about his headdress. Bill had a woman's hat full of cocks' feathers, and all had wild, slouching cowboy brims.

Bert sighed and stood up, deeply thoughtful, and Edna

watched him, marvelling. The women stood quite still. He left the window, and went out into the passage rather slowly, and with the careworn expression of a man who gives his mind to a complex and uncertain business. 'Edna!' he called, and when she came he opened the front door.

He asked very simply, and pointing to the foremost of the three, 'That 'im? . . . Sure?' . . . and being told that it was, shot his rival instantly and very accurately through the chest. He then shot Bill's best man much less tidily in the head, and then shot at and winged the third man as he fled. The third gentleman yelped, and continued running with a comical end-on twist.

Then Bert stood still meditating with the pistol in his hand, and quite regardless of the women behind him.

So far things had gone well.

It became evident to him that if he did not go into politics at once he would be hanged as an assassin, and accordingly, and without a word to the women, he went down to the village public-house he had passed an hour before on his way to Edna, entered it from the rear, and confronted the little band of ambiguous roughs, who were drinking in the taproom[10] and discussing matrimony and Bill's affections in a facetious but envious manner, with a casually held but carefully reloaded revolver, and an invitation to join what he called, I regret to say, a 'Vigilance Committee' under his direction. 'It's wanted about 'ere, and some of us are gettin' it up.' He presented himself as one having friends outside, though indeed he had no friends at all in the world but Edna and her aunt and two female cousins.

There was a quick but entirely respectful discussion of the situation. They thought him a lunatic who had tramped into this neighbourhood ignorant of Bill. They desired to temporize until their leader came. Bill would settle him. Someone spoke of Bill.

'Bill's dead,' said Bert. 'I jest shot 'im. We don't need reckon with '*im*. 'E's shot, and a red-'aired chap with a squint, '*e's* shot. We've settled up all that. There ain't going to be no more Bill, ever. 'E'd got wrong ideas about marriage and things. It's 'is sort of chap we're after.'

That carried the meeting.

Bill was perfunctorily buried, and Bert's Vigilance Committee (for so it continued to be called) reigned in his stead.

That is the end of this story so far as Bert Smallways is concerned. We leave him with his Edna to become squatters among the clay and oak thickets of the Weald, far away from the stream of events. From that time forth life became a succession of peasant's encounters, an affair of pigs and hens and small needs and little economies and children, until Clapham and Bun Hill and all the life of the Scientific Age became to Bert no more than the fading memory of a dream. He never knew how the War in the Air went on, nor whether it still went on. There were rumours of airships going and coming, and of happenings Londonward. Once or twice their shadows fell on him as he worked, but whence they came or whither they went he could not tell. Even his desire to tell died out for want of food. At times came robbers and thieves, at times came diseases among the beasts and shortness of food, once the country was worried by a pack of boar-hounds he helped to kill; he went through many inconsecutive, irrelevant adventures. He survived them all.

Accident and death came near them both ever and again, and passed them by; and they loved and suffered and were happy, and she bore him many children – eleven children – one after the other, of whom only four succumbed to the necessary hardships of their simple life. They lived and did well, as well was understood in those days. They went the way of all flesh, year by year.

THE EPILOGUE

It happened that one bright summer's morning exactly thirty years after the launching of the first German air-fleet, an old man took a small boy to look for a missing hen through the ruins of Bun Hill and out towards the splintered pinnacles of the Crystal Palace. He was not a very old man; he was, as a matter of fact, still within a few weeks of sixty-three, but constant stooping over spades and forks and the carrying of roots and manure, and exposure to the damps of life in the open air without a change of clothing, had bent him into the form of a sickle. Moreover, he had lost most of his teeth, and that had affected his digestion and through that his skin and temper. In face and expression he was curiously like that old Thomas Smallways who had once been coachman to Sir Peter Bone, and this was just as it should be, for he was Tom Smallways the son, who formerly kept the little greengrocer's shop under the straddle of the monorail viaduct in the High Street of Bun Hill. But now there were no greengrocers' shops, and Tom was living in one of the derelict villas hard by that unoccupied building site that had been and was still the scene of his daily horticulture. He and his wife lived upstairs, and in the drawing and dining rooms, which had each French windows opening on the lawn, and all about the ground floor generally, Jessica, who was now a lean and lined and baldish but still very efficient and energetic old woman, kept her three cows and a multitude of gawky hens.

These two were part of a little community of stragglers and returned fugitives, perhaps a hundred and fifty souls of them altogether, that had settled down to the new condition of things

after the Panic and Famine and Pestilence that followed in the
wake of the War. They had come back from strange refuges
and hiding-places and had squatted down among the familiar
houses and begun that hard struggle against nature for food
which was now the chief interest of their lives. They were by
sheer preoccupation with that a peaceful people, more particularly after Wilkes, the house agent, driven by some obsolete
dream of acquisition, had been drowned in the pool by the
ruined gasworks for making inquiries into title and displaying
a litigious turn of mind. (He had not been murdered, you
understand, but the people had carried an exemplary ducking
ten minutes or so beyond its healthy limits.)

This little community had returned from its original habits
of suburban parasitism to what no doubt had been the normal
life of humanity for nearly immemorial years, a life of homely
economies in the most intimate contact with cows and hens
and patches of ground, a life that breathes and exhales the scent
of cows and finds the need for stimulants satisfied by the activity
of the bacteria and vermin it engenders. Such had been the
life of the European peasant from the dawn of history to the
beginning of the Scientific Era, so it was the large majority of
the people of Asia and Africa had always been wont to live. For
a time it had seemed that by virtue of machines and scientific
civilization, Europe was to be lifted out of this perpetual round
of animal drudgery, and that America was to evade it very
largely from the outset. And with the smash of the high and
dangerous and splendid edifice of mechanical civilization that
had arisen so marvellously, back to the land came the common
man, back to the manure.

The little communities, still haunted by ten thousand memories of a greater state, gathered and developed almost tacitly
a customary law and fell under the guidance of a medicine-man
or a priest. The world rediscovered religion and the need of
something to hold its communities together. At Bun Hill this
function was entrusted to an old Baptist minister. He taught a
simple but adequate faith. In his teaching a good principle
called the Word fought perpetually against a diabolical female
influence called the Scarlet Woman[1] and an evil being called

Alcohol. This alcohol had long since become a purely spir-
itualized conception deprived of any element of material application; it had no relation to the occasional finds of whisky and
wine in Londoners' cellars that gave Bun Hill its only holidays.
He taught this doctrine on Sundays, and on weekdays he was
an amiable and kindly old man, distinguished by his quaint
disposition to wash his hands, and if possible his face, daily,
and with a wonderful genius for cutting up pigs. He held his
Sunday services in the old church in the Beckenham Road, and
then the countryside came out in a curious reminiscence of the
urban dress of Edwardian times. All the men without exception
wore frock coats, top hats and white shirts, though many
had no boots. Tom was particularly distinguished on these
occasions because he wore a top hat with gold lace about it and
a green coat and trousers that he had found upon a skeleton in
the basement of the Urban and District Bank. The women,
even Jessica, came in jackets and immense hats extravagantly
trimmed with artificial flowers and exotic birds' feathers – of
which there were abundant supplies in the shops to the north
– and the children (there were not many children, because a
large proportion of the babies born in Bun Hill died in a few
days' time of inexplicable maladies) had similar clothes cut
down to accommodate them; even Stringer's little grandson of
four wore a large top hat.

That was the Sunday costume of the Bun Hill district, a
curious and interesting survival of the genteel traditions of the
Scientific Age. On a weekday the folk were dingily and curiously
hung about with dirty rags of housecloth and scarlet flannel,
sacking, curtain serge and patches of old carpet, and went either
barefooted or on rude wooden sandals. These people, the reader
must understand, were an urban population sunken back to
the state of a barbaric peasantry, and so without any of the
simple arts a barbaric peasantry would possess. In many ways
they were curiously degenerate and incompetent. They had lost
any idea of making textiles, they could hardly make up clothes
when they had material, and they were forced to plunder the
continually dwindling supplies of the ruins about them for
cover. All the simple arts they had ever known they had lost,

and with the breakdown of modern drainage, modern water supply, shopping and the like, their civilized methods were useless. Their cooking was worse than primitive. It was a feeble muddling with food over wood fires in rusty drawing-room fireplaces; for the kitcheners[2] burnt too much fuel. Among them all no sense of baking or brewing or metal-working was to be found.

Their employment of sacking and suchlike coarse material for workaday clothing, and their habit of tying it on with string and of thrusting wadding and straw inside it for warmth, gave these people an odd, 'packed' appearance, and as it was a weekday when Tom took his little nephew for the hen-seeking excursion, so it was they were attired.

'So you've really got to Bun Hill at last, Teddy,' said old Tom, beginning to talk and slackening his pace so soon as they were out of range of old Jessica. 'You're the last of Bert's boys for me to see. Wat I've seen, young Bert I've seen, Sissie and Matt, Tom what's called after me, and Peter. The traveller people brought you along all right, eh?'

'I managed,' said Teddy, who was a dry little boy.

'Didn't want to eat you on the way?'

'They was all right,' said Teddy. 'And on the way near Leatherhead we saw a man riding on a bicycle.'

'My word!' said Tom, 'there ain't many of those about nowadays. Where was he going?'

'Said he was going to Dorking if the High Road was good enough. But I doubt if he got there. All about Burford it was flooded. We came over the hill, uncle – what they call the Roman Road. That's high and safe.'

'Don't know it,' said old Tom. 'But a bicycle! You're sure it was a bicycle? Had two wheels?'

'It was a bicycle right enough.'

'Why! I remember a time, Teddy, when there was bicycles no end, when you could stand just here – the road was as smooth as a board then – and see twenty or thirty coming and going at the same time, bicycles and moty bicycles, moty cars, all sorts of whirly things.'

'No!' said Teddy.

'I do. They'd keep on going by all day – 'undreds and 'undreds.'

'But where was they all going?' asked Teddy.

'Tearin' off to Brighton – you never seen Brighton, I expect – it's down by the sea, used to be a moce 'mazing place – and coming and going from London.'

'Why?'

'They did.'

'But why?'

'Lord knows why, Teddy. They did. Then you see that great thing there like a great big rusty nail sticking up higher than all the houses, and that one yonder, and that, and how something's fell in between 'em among the houses. They was parts of the monorail. They went down to Brighton too, and all day and night there was people going, great cars as big as 'ouses full of people.'

The little boy regarded the rusty evidences across the narrow muddy ditch of cow-droppings that had once been a High Street. He was clearly disposed to be sceptical, and yet there the ruins were! He grappled with ideas beyond the strength of his imagination.

'What did they go for?' he asked; 'all of 'em?'

'They 'ad to. Everything was on the go those days – everything.'

'Yes, but where did they come from?'

'All round 'ere, Teddy, there was people living in those 'ouses, and up the road more 'ouses and more people. You'd hardly believe me, Teddy, but it's Bible truth. You can go on that way for ever and ever, and keep on coming on 'ouses, more 'ouses, and more. There's no end to 'em. No end. They get bigger and bigger.' His voice dropped as though he named strange names. 'It's _London_,' he said.

'And it's all empty now and left alone. All day it's left alone. You don't find 'ardly a man, you won't find nothing but dogs and cats after the rats until you get round by Bromley and Beckenham, and there you find the Kentish men[3] herding swine.

(Nice rough lot they are too!) I tell you that so long as the sun is up it's as still as the grave. I been about by day – orfen and orfen.' He paused.

'And all those 'ouses and streets and ways used to be full of people before the War in the Air and the Famine and the Purple Death. They used to be full of people, Teddy, and then came a time when they was full of corpses, when you couldn't go a mile that way before the stink of 'em drove you back. It was the Purple Death 'ad killed 'em every one. The cats and dogs and 'ens and vermin caught it. Everything and everyone 'ad it. Jest a few of us 'appened to live. I pulled through and your aunt, though it made 'er lose 'er 'air. Why, you find the skeletons in the 'ouses now. This way we been into all the 'ouses and took what we wanted and buried moce of the people, but up that way, Norwood way, there's 'ouses with the glass in the windows still, and the furniture not touched – all dusty and falling to pieces – and the bones of the people lying, some in bed, some about the 'ouse, jest as the Purple Death left 'em five-and-twenty years ago. I went into one – me and old Higgins las' year – and there was a room with books, Teddy – you know what I mean by books, Teddy?'

'I seen 'em. I seen 'em with pictures.'

'Well, books all round, Teddy, 'undreds of books, beyond rhyme or reason, as the saying goes, green-mouldy and dry. I was for leavin' 'em alone – I was never much for reading – but ole Higgins he must touch 'em. "I believe I could read one of 'em *now*," 'e says.

'"Not it," I says.

'"I could," 'e says, laughing, and takes one out and opens it.

'I looked, and there, Teddy, was a cullud[4] picture, oh, so lovely! It was a picture of women and serpents in a garden. I never see anything like it.

'"This suits me," said old Higgins, "to rights."

'And then kind of friendly he gave the book a pat—'

Old Tom Smallways paused impressively.

'And then?' said Teddy.

'It all fell to dus'. White dus'!' . . . He became still more impressive. 'We didn't touch no more of them books that day. Not after that.'

For a long time both were silent. Then Tom, playing with a subject that attracted him with a fatal fascination, repeated. 'All day long they lie – still as the grave.'

Teddy took the point at last. 'Don't they lie o' nights?' he asked.

Old Tom shook his head. 'Nobody knows, boy, nobody knows.'

'But what could they do?'

'Nobody knows. Nobody ain't seen to tell – not nobody.'

'Nobody?'

'They tell tales,' said old Tom. 'They tell tales, but there ain't no believing 'em. I gets 'ome about sundown, and keeps indoors, so I can't say nothing, can I? But there's them that thinks some things and them as thinks others. I've 'eard it's unlucky to take clo'es off of 'em unless they got white bones. There's stories —'

The boy watched his uncle sharply. '*Wot* stories?' he said.

'Stories of moonlight nights and things walking about. But I take no stock in 'em. I keeps in bed. If you listen to stories – Lord! You'll get afraid of yourself in a field at midday.'

The little boy looked round and ceased his questions for a space.

'They say there's a 'og man in Beck'n'am what was lost in London three days and three nights. 'E went up after whisky to Cheapside,[5] and lorst 'is way among the ruins and wandered. Three days and three nights 'e wandered about and the streets kep' changing so's 'e couldn't get 'ome. If 'e 'adn't remembered some words out of the Bible 'e might 'ave been there now. All day 'e went and all night – and all day long it was still. It was as still as death all day long, until the sunset came and the twilight thickened, and then it began to rustle and whisper and go pit-a-pat with a sound like 'urrying feet.'

He paused.

'Yes,' said the little boy breathlessly. 'Go on. What then?'

'A sound of carts and 'orses there was, and a sound of cabs and omnibuses, and then a lot of whistling, shrill whistles,

whistles that froze 'is marrer. And directly the whistles began things begun to show, people in the streets 'urrying, people in the 'ouses and shops busying themselves, moty cars in the streets, a sort of moonlight in all the lamps and winders. People, I say, Teddy, but they wasn't people. They was the ghosts of them that was overtook, the ghosts of them that used to crowd those streets. And they went past 'im and through 'im and never 'eeded 'im, went by like fogs and vapours, Teddy. And sometimes they was cheerful and sometimes they was 'orrible, 'orrible beyond words. And once 'e come to a place called Piccadilly,[6] Teddy, and there was lights blazing like daylight and ladies and gentlemen in splendid clo'es crowding the pavement, and taxicabs follering along the road. And as 'e looked, they all went evil – evil in the face, Teddy. And it seemed to 'im suddenly *they saw'im*, and the women began to look at 'im and say things to 'im[7] – 'orrible – wicked things. One come very near 'im, Teddy, right up to 'im, and looked into 'is face – close. And she 'adn't got a face to look with, only a painted skull, and then 'e see they was all painted skulls. And one after another they crowded on 'im saying 'orrible things, and catchin' at 'im and threatenin' and coaxing 'im, so that 'is 'eart near left 'is body for fear.' . . .

'Yes,' gasped Teddy in an unendurable pause.

'Then it was he remembered the words of Scripture and saved himself alive. "The Lord is my 'Elper," 'e says, "therefore I will fear nothing," and straightaway there came a cock-crowing and the street was empty from end to end. And after that the Lord was good to 'im and guided 'im 'ome.'

Teddy stared and caught at another question. 'But who was the people,' he asked, 'who lived in all these 'ouses? What was they?'

'Gent'men in business, people with money – leastways we thought it was money till everything smashed up, and then seemingly it was jes' paper – all sorts. Why, there was 'undreds of thousands of them. There was millions. I've seen that 'I Street there regular so's you couldn't walk along the pavements, shoppin' time, with women and people shoppin'.'

'But where'd they get their food and things?'

'Bort 'em in shops like I used to 'ave. I'll show you the place, Teddy, 's we go back. People nowadays 'aven't no idee of a shop – no idee. Plate-glass winders – it's all Greek to them. Why, I've 'ad as much as a ton and a 'arf of petaties to 'andle all at one time. You'd open your eyes till they dropped out to see jest what I used to 'ave in my shop. Baskets of pears 'eaped up, marrers, apples and pears, d'licious great nuts.' His voice became luscious – 'Benanas, oranges.'

'What's Benanas?' asked the boy, 'and Oranges?'

'Fruits they was. Sweet, juicy, d'licious fruits. Foreign fruits. They brought 'em from Spain and N' York and places. In ships and things. They brought 'em to me from all over the world, and I sold 'em in my shop. *I* sold 'em, Teddy! Me what goes about now with you, dressed up in old sacks and looking for lost 'ens. People used to come into my shop, great beautiful ladies like you'd 'ardly dream of now, dressed up to the nines, and say, "Well, Mr Smallways, what you got 'smorning?" and I'd say, "Well, I got some very nice C'nadian apples," or p'raps I got custed marrers.[8] See? And they'd buy 'em. Right off they'd say, "Send me some up." Lord! what a life that was. The business of it, the bussel, the smart things you saw, moty cars going by, kerridges,[9] people, organ-grinders, German bands. Always something going past – always. If it wasn't for those empty 'ouses I'd think it all a dream.'

'But what killed all the people, uncle?' asked Teddy.

'It was a smash-up,' said old Tom. 'Everything was going right until they started that War. Everything was going like clockwork. Everybody was busy and everybody was 'appy and everybody got a good square meal every day.' He met incredulous eyes. 'Everybody,' he said firmly. 'If you couldn't get it anywhere else, you could get it in the workhuss, a nice 'ot bowl of soup called skilly,[10] and bread better'n anyone knows 'ow to make now, reg'lar *white* bread, gov'ment bread.'

Teddy marvelled, but said nothing. It made him feel deep longings that he found it wisest to fight down.

For a time the old man resigned himself to the pleasures of

gustatory reminiscence. His lips moved. 'Pickled Sammin!'[11] he whispered, 'an' vinegar. . . . Dutch cheese, *Beer*! A pipe of terbakker.'

'But '*ow* did the people get killed?' asked Teddy presently.

'There was the War. The War was the beginning of it. The War banged and flummocked about, but it didn't really *kill* many people. But it upset things. They came and set fire to London and burnt and sank all the ships there used to be in the Thames – we could see the smoke and steam for weeks – and they threw a bomb into the Crystal Palace and made a bust-up, and broke down the rail lines and things like that. But as for killin' people, it was just accidental if they did. They killed each other more. There was a great fight all hereabout one day, Teddy – up in the air. Great things bigger than fifty 'ouses, bigger than the Crystal Palace – bigger, bigger than anything, flying about up in the air and whacking at each other and dead men fallin' off 'em. T'riffic! But it wasn't so much the people they killed as the business they stopped. There wasn't any business doin', Teddy, there wasn't any money about, and nothin' to buy if you 'ad it.'

'But 'ow did the people get *killed*?' said the little boy in the pause.

'I'm tellin' you, Teddy,' said the old man. 'It was the stoppin' of business come nex'. Sudden, some'ow, there didn't seem to be any money. There was cheques – they was a bit of paper written on, and they was jes' as good as money – jes' as good if they come from customers you knew. Then all of a sudden they wasn't. I was lef' with three of 'em and two I'd given change. Then it got about that five-pun' notes were no good, and then the silver sort of went off. Gold you couldn't get for love or – anything.[12] The banks in London 'ad got it, and the banks was all smashed up. Everybody went bankrup'. Everybody was thrown out of work. Everybody!'

He paused, and scrutinized his hearer. The small boy's intelligent face expressed hopeless perplexity.

'That's 'ow it 'appened,' said old Tom. He sought for some means of expression. 'It was like stoppin' a clock,' he said. 'Things were quiet for a bit, deadly quiet, except for the airships fighting about in the sky, and then people begun to get excited. I remember my lars' customer, the very lars' customer that ever I 'ad. He was a Mr Moses Gluckstein,[13] a city gent and very pleasant and fond of sparrowgrass and chokes,[14] and 'e cut in – there 'adn't been no customers for days – and began to talk very fast, offerin' me for anything I 'ad, anything, petaties or anything, its weight in gold. 'E said it was a little speculation 'e wanted to try. 'E said it was a sort of bet reely, and very likely 'e'd lose; but never mind that, 'e wanted to try. 'E always 'ad been a gambler, 'e said. 'E said I'd only got to weigh it out and 'e'd give me 'is cheque right away. Well, that led to a bit of a argument, perfectly respectful it was, but a argument about whether a cheque was still good, and while 'e was explaining there come by a lot of these here unemployed with a great banner they 'ad for everyone to read – everyone could read those days – "We want Food." Three or four of 'em suddenly turns and comes into my shop.

' "Got any food?" says one.

' "No," I says, "not to sell. I wish I 'ad. But if I 'ad I'm afraid I couldn't let you have it. This gent, 'e's been offerin' me—"

'Mr Gluckstein 'e tried to stop me, but it was too late.

' "What's 'e been offerin' you?" says a great big chap with a 'atchet; "what's 'e been offerin' you?" I 'ad to tell.

' "Boys," 'e said, " 'ere's another feenancier!" and they took 'im out there and then, and 'ung 'im on a lam'pose down the street. 'E never lifted a finger to resist. After I tole on 'im 'e never said a word. . . .'

Tom meditated for a space. 'First chap I ever sin 'ung!' he said.

' 'Ow old was you?' asked Teddy.

' 'Bout thirty,' said old Tom.

'Why! I saw free pig-stealers 'ung before I was six,' said Teddy. 'Father took me because of my birfday being near. Said I ought to be blooded. . . .'

'Well, you never saw no one killed by a moty car, any'ow,' said old Tom after a moment of chagrin. 'And you never saw no dead men carried into a chemis' shop.'

Teddy's momentary triumph faded. 'No,' he said, 'I'aven't.'

'Nor won't. Nor won't. You'll never see the things I've seen, never. Not if you live to be a 'undred. . . . Well, as I was saying, that's how the Famine and Riotin' began. Then there was strikes and Socialism, things I never did 'old with, worse and worse. There was fightin' and shootin' down, and burnin' and plunderin'. They broke up the banks up in London and got the gold. But they couldn't make food out of gold. 'Ow did *we* get on? Well, we kep' quiet. We didn't interfere with no one and no one didn't interfere with us. We 'ad some old 'tatoes about, but mocely we lived on rats. Ours was a old 'ouse, full of rats, and the famine never seemed to bother 'em. Orfen we got a rat. Orfen. But mose of the people who lived hereabouts was too tender stummicked for rats. Didn't seem to fancy 'em. They'd been used to all sorts of fallals,[15] and they didn't take to 'onest feeding, not till it was too late. Died rather.

'It was the famine began to kill people. Even before the Purple Death come along they was dying like flies at the end of the summer. 'Ow I remember it all! I was one of the first to 'ave it. I was out seein' if I mightn't get 'old of a cat or somethin', and then I went round to my bit of ground to see whether I couldn't get up some young turnips I'd forgot, and I was took something awful. You've no idee the pain, Teddy – it doubled me up pretty near. I jes' lay down by that there corner, and your aunt come along to look for me and dragged me 'ome like a sack.

'I'd never 'ave got better if it 'adn't been for your aunt. "Tom," she says to me, "you got to get well," and I 'ad to. Then *she* sickened. She sickened, but there ain't much dyin' about your aunt. "Lor!" she says, "as if I'd leave you to go muddlin' along alone!" That's what she says. She's got a tongue 'as your aunt. But it took 'er 'air off – and arst though I might, she's never cared for the wig I got 'er – orf the old lady what was in the vicarage garden.

'Well, this 'ere Purple Death – it jes' wiped people out, Teddy. You couldn't bury 'em. And it took the dogs and the cats too, and the rats and 'orses. At last every 'ouse and garden was full of dead bodies. London way you couldn't go for the smell of them, and we 'ad to move out of the 'I Street into that villa we got. And all the water run short that way. The drains and underground tunnels took it. Gor' knows where the Purple Death come from; some say one thing and some another. Some said it come from eatin' rats and some from eatin' nothin'. Some say the Asiatics brought it from some 'I place, Thibet, I think, where it never did nobody much 'arm. All I know is it come after the Famine. And the Famine come after the Penic, and the Penic come after the War.'

Teddy thought. 'What made the Purple Death?' he asked.

''Aven't I tole you!'

'But why did they 'ave a penic?'

'They 'ad it.'

'But why did they start the War?'

'They couldn't stop theirselves. 'Aving them airships made 'em.'

'And 'ow did the War end?'

'Lord knows if it's ended, boy,' said old Tom. 'Lord knows if it's ended. There's been travellers through 'ere – there was a chap only two summers ago – say it's goin' on still. They say there's bands of people up north who keep on with it, and people in Germany and China and 'Merica and places. 'E said they still got flying machines and gas and things. But we 'aven't seen nothin' in the air now for seven years, and nobody 'asn't come nigh of us. Last we saw was a crumpled sort of airship going away – over there. It was a littleish-sized thing and lopsided, as though it 'ad something the matter with it.'

He pointed, and came to a stop at a gap in the fence, the vestiges of the old fence from which, in the company of his neighbour, Mr Stringer the milkman, he had once watched the South of England Aero Club's Saturday-afternoon ascents. Dim memories, it may be, of that particular afternoon returned to him.

'There, down there, where all that rus' looks so red and bright, that's the gasworks.'

'What's gas?' asked the little boy.

'Oh a hairy sort of nothin' what you put in balloons to make 'em go up. And you used to burn it till the 'lectricity come.'

The little boy tried vainly to imagine gas on the basis of these particulars. Then his thoughts reverted to a previous topic.

'But why didn't they stop the War?'

'Obstinacy. Everybody was getting 'urt, but everybody was 'urtin' and everybody was 'igh-spirited and patriotic, and so they smeshed up things instead. They jes' went on smeshin'. And afterwards they jes' got desp'rite and savige.'

'It ought to 'ave ended,' said the little boy.

'It didn't ought to 'ave begun,' said old Tom. 'But people was proud. People was la-dy-da-ish and uppish and proud. Too much meat and drink they 'ad. Give in – not them! And after a bit nobody arst 'em to give in. Nobody arst 'em. . . .'

He sucked his old gums thoughtfully, and his gaze strayed away across the valley to where the shattered glass of the Crystal Palace glittered in the sun. A dim large sense of waste and irrevocable lost opportunities pervaded his mind. He repeated his ultimate judgement upon all these things, obstinately, slowly and conclusively, his final saying upon the matter.

'You can say what you like,' he said: 'It didn't ought ever to 'ave begun.'

He said it simply – somebody somewhere ought to have stopped something, but who or how or why were all beyond his ken.

Appendix: Wells's Prefaces to the 1941 Penguin Edition

When *The War in the Air* was reprinted by Collins in 1921, Wells added a preface to introduce it to a new generation of readers who had grown up during the First World War. A similar but much briefer explanation forms the first paragraph of his preface to Volume 20 of the Atlantic edition of his works in 1926. The 1941 Penguin edition of the novel, the last to be produced during his lifetime, reprints the 1921 preface together with a new preface containing his much-discussed 'epitaph'.

Preface to the 1921 Edition

A short preface to *The War in the Air* has become necessary if the reader is to do justice to that book. It is one of a series of stories I have written at different times; *The World Set Free* is another, and *When the Sleeper Wakes* a third; which are usually spoken of as 'scientific romances' or 'futurist romances', but which it would be far better to call 'fantasias of possibility'. They take some developing possibility in human affairs and work it out so as to develop the broad consequences of that possibility. This *War in the Air* was written, the reader should note, in 1907, and it began to appear as a serial story in the *Pall Mall Magazine* in January, 1908. This was before the days of the flying machine; Blériot did not cross the Channel until July, 1909; and the Zeppelin airship was still in its infancy. The reader will find it amusing now to compare the guesses and notions of the author with the achieved realities of today.

But the book, I venture to think, has not been altogether superseded. The main idea is not that men will fly, or to show how they will fly; the main idea is a thesis that the experiences of the intervening years strengthen rather than supersede. The thesis is this: that with the flying machine war alters in its character; it ceases to be an affair of 'fronts' and becomes an affair of 'areas'; neither side, victor or loser, remains immune from the gravest injuries, and while there is a vast increase in the destructiveness of war, there is also an increased indecisiveness. Consequently 'War in the Air' means social destruction instead of victory as the end of war. It not only alters the methods of war but the consequences of war. After all that has happened since this fantasia of possibility was written, I do not think that there is much wrong with that thesis. And after a recent journey to Russia, of which I have given an account in *Russia in the Shadows*, I am inclined to think very well of myself as I reread the entirely imaginary account of the collapse of civilization under the strain of modern war which forms the Epilogue of this story. In 1907 this chapter was read with hearty laughter as the production of an 'imaginative novelist's' distempered brain. Is it quite so wildly funny today?

And I ask the reader to remember that date of 1907 also when he reads of Prince Karl Albert and the Graf von Win-terfeld. Seven years before the Great War, its shadow stood out upon our sunny world as plainly as all that, for the 'imaginative novelist' – or anyone else with ordinary common sense – to see. The great catastrophe marched upon us in the daylight. But everybody thought that somebody else would stop it before it really arrived. Behind that great catastrophe march others today. The steady deterioration of currency, the shrinkage of production, the ebb of educational energy in Europe, work out to consequences that are obvious to every clear-headed man. National and imperialist rivalries march whole nations at the quickstep towards social collapse. The process goes on as plainly as the militarist process was going on in the years when *The War in the Air* was written.

Do we still trust to somebody else?

H. G. WELLS

EASTON GLEBE, 1921

Preface to the 1941 Edition

Here in 1941 *The War in the Air* is being reprinted once again. It was written in 1907 and first published in 1908. It was reprinted in 1921, and then I wrote a preface which also I am reprinting. Again I ask the reader to note the warnings I gave in that year, twenty years ago. Is there anything to add to that preface now? Nothing except my epitaph. That, when the time comes, will manifestly have to be: 'I told you so. You *damned* fools.' (The italics are mine.)

H. G. Wells

Notes

CHAPTER I
OF PROGRESS AND THE SMALLWAYS FAMILY

1. *Smallways*: Wells chooses the name to emphasize the 'small ways' of the lower middle class from which he himself escaped. Significantly, his young hero, educated only enough to start him dreaming of escape, is 'Bert'. Herbert George Wells was 'Bertie' to his family.

2. *Bun Hill*: Fictional village resembling Bromley, Kent, twelve miles from London, although Wells might have remembered *Biggin* Hill, eight miles from Bromley, which following the First World War was an important Royal Air Force airfield; or even *Box* Hill near Dorking in Surrey. Wells was born in Bromley and spent much of his childhood there. (See also n.5.)

3. *balloons*: The history of ballooning goes back to the 1783 ascent directed by the Montgolfier brothers. Both balloons and powered airships were developed in the late nineteenth century, and an Aero Club of France was founded in 1898. The British Royal Aero Club was founded in 1901.

4. *ballase*: Ballast.

5. *Sir Peter Bone*: The fictional 'squire' of Bun Hill, which is presumably a corruption of 'Bone Hill'.

6. *Crystal Palace*: Constructed in Hyde Park for the Great Exhibition of 1851 and re-erected at Sydenham Hill in South London in 1854. Ironically, it was destroyed by fire in 1936.

7. *Carnegie library*: The Scottish-American industrialist Andrew Carnegie (1835–1919) founded many public libraries in the United States and Great Britain. Bromley's Carnegie Library was opened 28 May 1906.

8. *motor-bicycle*: Gottlieb Daimler (1834–1900) developed a

motorbike in 1885 and they became popular during the 1890s.

9. *out of short frocks*: In the early nineteenth century it was still customary for small children to be dressed alike and boys to be 'breeched' around the age of five, although Bert's 'frocks' are not necessarily to be meant literally.

10. *a real pistol*: Possession of firearms was legal until the 1903 Pistols Act, although a policeman would have taken a dim view of a ten-year-old having one.

11. *Boys of England American cigarettes*: A fictional brand of cigarettes, probably alluding to the periodical *Boys of England* (1866–99) which was frequently criticized for its 'corrupting' effect on youth.

12. *Chips, Comic Cuts, Alley Sloper's Half-holiday*: Popular illustrated periodicals for young people. *Chips* (1890–1952), *Comic Cuts* (1890–1953), and *Ally Sloper's Half-Holiday* (1884–1916) were immensely popular, and Ally Sloper has claims to be the first comic-book hero.

13. *seventh standard*: The highest class in the state school system. Pupils left school at 14, but progression through the 'standards' was by ability rather than age.

14. *forte*: Strong point.

15. *Brighton*: In Sussex, on the south coast; a popular holiday resort.

16. *Crawley*: On the road from London 22 miles north of Brighton.

17. *teuf-teuffed*: Imitation of the sound of a motor-cycle's engine.

18. *George Griffith*: George Chetwynd Griffith-Jones (1857–1906), one of the most popular scientific romance writers of the 1890s and a serious rival to Wells. His *The Angel of the Revolution* and *Olga Romanoff*, serialized in *Pearson's Weekly* during 1893, contained many scenes of apocalyptic aerial warfare, and *The Outlaws of the Air* the following year continued the theme.

19. *like a brisk little terrier*: The first in a series of imagery in which the aerial machines are likened to fish and animals as well as the more obvious birds and insects. In his short story 'The Land Iron-clads' (1904) Wells likens the first appearance of the tanks to monstrous animals.

20. *strange phenomena in the heavens*: The late nineteenth and early twentieth centuries were a time of experiments with flight: many of the early trials may even have found their way into records of unidentified flying objects. By the time Wells wrote *The War in the Air* there was a lively debate in the press about the potential of powered airships and heavier-than-air aeroplanes in warfare.

21. *aluminium*: Although aluminium was first produced in 1825, it was expensive to produce until electrolysis was perfected in 1886.

22. *cinematograph records*: *Pathé's Animated Gazette*, shown weekly, in 1910 was the first British cinema newsreel in a 'magazine' format, but short films of newsworthy interest were shown earlier.

23. *monorails*: Single-track railway systems, frequently with suspended carriages, were designed in Europe and the United States during the late nineteenth century. The 13-kilometre monorail in Wuppertal, Germany opened in 1901 and is still operating today.

24. *gyroscopic*: A gyroscope is 'a solid rotating wheel mounted in a ring, and having its axis free to turn in any direction' (*Oxford English Dictionary*) and among its uses is stabilizing vehicles like monorails or ships. A gyroscopically balanced monorail locomotive was patented by Louis Brennan (1852–1932) in 1903 and demonstrated in Gillingham, England in 1909.

25. *leading Zionists*: The term for supporters of a Jewish return to Israel (Zion) became common in the 1890s.

26. *Home Counties Power Distribution Company*: Fictional.

27. *English Channel was bridged*: Plans for a bridge across the English Channel were drawn up by the French engineer J. A. Thom de Gamond (1807–76) and further plans were presented at the Paris Exhibition of 1889. None was attempted.

28. *Eiffel Tower*: Designed by Gustave Eiffel (1832–1923), the Eiffel Tower was built for the Paris Exhibition of 1889 and after much controversy became the most popular landmark in Paris.

29. *submarine crawler*: Numerous attempts at developing submarines were made throughout the nineteenth century, and by 1906, when the first German U-boat was launched, submarines were operational in the British and French navies. The fictional Alberto Cassini's 'crawler', however, may owe something to earlier prototypes of wheeled submarines which would travel along the seabed, designed by the American Simon Lake (1866–1945).

30. *Aldershot*: In Hampshire, is a garrison town for the British army. The HM Balloon Factory founded in nearby Farnborough in 1908 became the Royal Aircraft Establishment in 1918.

31. *Wright Brothers*: Orville and Wilbur Wright. On 17 December 1903 Orville Wright made the first successful flight (120 feet) in a powered aeroplane.

32. *people in Ireland*: Fictional: Wells is extrapolating from the (real) Wright brothers and their (fictional) disappearance to invent a scenario of fictional aeronautical pioneers being apparently taken up by secret War Departments.

33. *De Booley*: Apparently Wells's own invention, but there may be an echo of French aviation pioneer Louis Blériot (1872–1936), who was later (1909) to be the first man to fly across the English Channel.

34. *Lydd*: In Romney Marsh in Kent was the site of an artillery practice camp before the First World War.

35. *Galway*: In the west of Ireland.

36. *Alfred Butteridge*: Invented name.

37. *megatherium*: Extinct giant sloth which flourished in South America into prehistoric times.

38. *Steinhart's account*: The shop is in a difficult financial situation which even Grubb's closer attention may not overcome if a large account from one of their customers fails to take them out of their troubles.

39. *dissepiments*: Partitions (a term taken from botany).

40. *viscus*: Internal organ (i.e. his heart).

41. *Daily Requiem*: The newspaper is fictional, but there may be a joke involving the idea of a Requiem Mass for the souls of the dead, although Wells was not a Roman Catholic.

CHAPTER 2

HOW BERT SMALLWAYS GOT INTO DIFFICULTIES

1. *stokers from Gravesend*: On the Thames estuary east of London, in the county of Kent, Gravesend was a major port for coal-powered steamships whether for trade or passenger services and a gateway to the London docks further upstream. The stokers would have shovelled coal into the steamships' furnaces.

2. *Whitsuntide*: The seventh Sunday after Easter.

3. *High Road from London to Brighton*: The current A23 runs from London to Brighton, far enough west of Bromley not to identify 'Bun Hill' directly with Wells's birthplace.

4. *spatchcocked*: Killed and cooked hurriedly. The position of the property would seem to encourage accidents: the joke is that they could make a living from compensation paid by motorists for hens they have run over.

5. *beano*: A festive day out, from the slang term 'bean-feast', often used for a 'works outing' paid for by an employer.

6. *Monroe Doctrine*: The principle of opposition by the United States to European intervention in the Western Hemisphere, put forward in 1823 by President James Monroe (1758–1831).

7. *Boer War*: 1899–1902. The colonial war against the Boers, of Dutch and German ancestry, settled in the Orange Free State and the Transvaal, resulted in victory for the Empire but sharply divided opinion in Britain.

8. *Nineveh*: A city on the river Tigris, near Mosul in modern Iraq. It was an important city from the third millennium BC onwards, and was the capital of the Assyrian Empire, in which capacity it was mentioned in the Bible: 'Yet forty days, and Nineveh shall be overthrown!' (Jonah 3:4). It was destroyed in 612 BC.

9. *lit . . . his lamps*: the headlights of his motorcycle. There were a number of possible ways of lighting, including carbide lamps similar to those used in mines. These were sometimes difficult to operate.

10. *Austrian blanket*: A high-quality patchwork rug manufactured by Wormald & Walker of England.

11. *Oxford intonation*: The drawl of someone educated at Oxford University, and hence a gentleman of a higher social class than Bert.

12. *tarpaulin*: Waterproofed sheet of canvas.

13. *by way of Clapham*: They are near West Kingsdown on the North Downs, north-west Kent, 23 miles by road from Clapham, in South London. Surbiton is 12 miles south-west of Clapham. It would be a different route, but the distance is not significant.

14. *Promethean*: In Greek mythology, Prometheus stole the secret of fire from the gods and gave it to mankind. He was punished by being chained to a rock where each day a vulture tore out his liver, which regenerated overnight.

15. *masked Twareg*: The Touareg were originally a nomadic group living in the Sahara desert region of North Africa.

16. *O.R.P.H.*: Off (slang): emphasizing the word by spelling it out (as pronounced).

17. *into a cocked hat*: Utterly defeated.

18. *breakdown*: An instrumental dance tune often finishing off a performance, associated with the fashion for American folk music, especially 'minstrel' music.

19. *The Bitter Cry of the Middle Class*: A reference to the Reverend Andrew Mearns's famous pamphlet *The Bitter Cry of Outcast London* (1883), which exposed the lives of the London poor.

20. *dominoes*: Loose cloaks are worn with a mask covering the upper part of the face.

21. *those popular ditties*: Mock comic songs of the type sung in music halls or seaside entertainments.

22. *Littlestone in Kent*: A small seaside resort in Kent, between Dungeness and Dymchurch.

23. *Eng*: 'Hang (it)' was a common expression of frustration. Grubb's dropped 'h' and changed vowel-sound are signs of his lower-class origins.

24. *tow beard*: False beard made of flax or hemp fibres.

CHAPTER 3
THE BALLOON

1. '*on the dibs*': On the money (slang term).

2. *aneroid*: A barometer, in which air pressure is measured without using fluids such as mercury or alcohol.

3. *Kodak*: The 'Kodak' camera was marketed from 1888 by George Eastman (1854–1932). Its simple operation gave the power to take snapshots to ordinary people.

4. *Roman pie*: A pie containing layers of chicken, other meats, anchovies and pasta.

5. *ordnance maps*: The accurate mapping of Britain became the responsibility of the Board of Ordnance in 1791 as part of the preparation for defence against possible invasion from revolutionary France. Ordnance Survey is still a government agency producing maps.

6. *Je suis Anglais . . .*: 'I am English. It's a mistake. I arrived here by chance.'

7. *Apportez moi . . .*: Something like: 'Bring me to the British Consul-o, please.' (Bert is making almost but not quite correct guesses at the right vocabulary and grammar.)

8. *Drachenfleiger*: Literally 'Dragon-flyer': coined word for 'aircraft'.

9. *Monte Rosas*: Monte Rosa (4,634 metres/15,199 feet) is the highest mountain in Switzerland.

10. *Voici Mossoo . . .*: More pidgin French. 'Here, Mister! I am an English inventor. My name is Butteridge. B.U.T.T.E.R.I.D.G.E. I have here to sell the secret of the *flying machine*. Understand? To sell for cash quickly, cash in hand. Understand? It's the machine to play in the air. Understand? It's the machine to make

like a bird. Understand? To balance. Yes, exactly! Beats the bird, in fact, at its own game. I desire to sell this to your national government. Would you direct me there?'

11. *prolate moon*: A full moon which because of atmospheric distortion seems drawn out at the poles, like the shape of an egg.

12. *old invention*: One of Wells's science-fictional speculations, a self-heating can. Such a can, enabling instant hot coffee, went on sale in Britain in 2001, although a self-heating can using the burning of cordite was in use in the British armed forces in 1939.

13. *Höhenweg*: A hiking trail in the mountains near Wildbad in the Black Forest.

14. *Têtes*: 'Heads!' as Bert would call in English to warn people of something being dropped or propelled towards them.

15. *G. P. R. James*: (1799–1860). Author of historical romances, which were the subject of parody. The presence of a 'solitary horseman' in them became something of a literary joke. *Darnley* (1830) begins, 'On the morning of the 24th day of March, 1520, a traveller was seen riding in the small rigged cross-road which, traversing the eastern part of Kent, formed the immediate communication between Wye and Canterbury.'

16. *Franconia*: A former Duchy in southern Germany, now the northern part of Bavaria.

17. *Zeppelin airship*: Ferdinand von Zeppelin (1838–1917) created a propeller-driven airship which made its first flight on 2 July 1900. In 1906 an improved model flew at thirty miles per hour.

18. *Lebaudy*: Extrapolated from the 1903 37-mile flight to Paris by Paul Lebaudy (1858–1937) and his brother Pierre, the first fully powered air journey. Ironically, in 1908, a Lebaudy airship crashed killing its crew.

19. *hydrogen*: The lightest gas. The main problem is that it is inflammable.

20. *aerostat*: Unpowered balloon.

21. *Pforzheim type*: Pforzheim is a German city on the edge of the Black Forest. As with many other instances in this and subsequent chapters, Wells is inventing technologies, individuals or places to suit his story.

CHAPTER 4

THE GERMAN AIR-FLEET

1. *the 'Yellow Peril'*: The European fear of the potential power of the Asiatic nations, was documented in much fiction of the time, such as *The Yellow Danger* (1898), a novel by M. P. Shiel (1865–1947).

2. *White Man's Burthen*: 'The White Man's Burden' is a poem by Rudyard Kipling (1865–1936).

3. *Buluwayo*: City in Zimbabwe (then Southern Rhodesia, which became a British colony in 1888).

4. *East is east*: From 'The Ballad of East and West'.

5. *Burns at them and Mill and Darwin*: All are associated with ideas of Liberty. The Scottish poet Robert Burns (1759–96) wrote the line 'A man's a man for a' that' ('For a' that and a' that'); the philosopher John Stuart Mill (1806–73) wrote *On Liberty* (1859); and the scientist Charles Darwin (1809–82) presented ideas on evolution which came to undermine conventional theories on race.

6. *Moltke*: Helmuth von Moltke (1800–91), Prussian general and chief of staff during the Franco-Prussian War of 1870–71 and the period of German unification.

7. *Prince Karl Albert*: Fictional figure embodying the suspicion of German militarism and expansion under Kaiser Wilhem II (1859–1941), under whom Germany later entered the First World War in 1914.

8. *Black Prince*: Edward, Prince of Wales (1330–76), eldest son of Edward III of England.

9. *Alcibiades*: (c. 450–404 BC) Athenian general and politician who was a pupil of Socrates.

10. *Over-man*: German 'oberman', sometimes translated 'superman'. A term from the writings of German philosopher Friedrich Wilhelm Nietzsche (1844–1900).

11. *Heligoland*: German island in the North Sea off the mouth of the River Elbe.

12. *Defender, C.C.I.*: In 1895 an American yacht called *Defender* won the America's Cup race, a sailing contest first won by (and named after) the *America* in 1851.

13. *Rudolf Martin*: (1876–1916) German civil servant. His *Berlin-Bagdad*, forecasting the coming German world empire in the age of airship travel, was published in 1907 and an extract appeared in the *Review of Reviews*.

14. *the Strand*: Main thoroughfare in London north of the Thames, leading to Trafalgar Square, site of the National Gallery and Nelson's Column.

15. *Selbst*: Himself.

16. *Besser*: Better.

17. *mitbringen*: Bring (something): the officer wants 'Butteridge' brought along to the flagship.

18. *Kopf*: Head.

19. *hals*: Neck.

20. *Vorwärts*: Forward.

21. *Woolwich Dockyard*: English naval dockyard on the south bank of the River Thames. It closed as a dockyard in 1869.

22. *shaving-strops*: Leather strips used for sharpening razors.

23. *Dummer*: Stupid.

24. *a norfis*: An office.

25. *crack on the nob*: Blow on the head.

26. *Vaterland*: Fatherland.

27. *Ra-ther*: Spoken with an aristocratic drawl.

28. *Rhodes scholar*: In his will Cecil Rhodes (1853–1902) endowed scholarships to enable international students to study at Oxford University.

29. *German Alexander*: Likened to Alexander the Great (356–323 BC.) whose conquests included Persia, Egypt and reached as far as India.

30. *Hoch*: A toast to the nobility: the equivalent of 'The Queen!' in an equivalent British gathering.

31. *Cockney*: A Londoner, literally one born 'within the sound of Bow Bells' but used as here to imply vulgarity.

32. *hochgeborene*: 'Noble', 'high-born'.

33. *eagle's nest*: The term (in German, 'Adlerhorst') was later used for Adolf Hitler's retreat in the Bavarian mountains at Berchtesgarten during the Second World War.

34. *Luftschiffe*: Airship(s).

35. *Daily Courier*: A popular name for a newspaper. There was a London *Daily Courier* in 1896.

36. *Viel besser, nicht wahr*: 'Much better, isn't it?'

37. *als Ballast*: As ballast.

38. *neural and haemal canals*: The canal in the backbone where the spinal cord passes; and the large blood-vessels.

39. *Ship Canal*: The Manchester Ship Canal, opened in 1894, runs from Eastham on the Mersey estuary six miles south of Liverpool to Manchester.

40. *Camberwell and Rotherhithe*: Originally a rural village, Camber-
     well became a residential area of South London known for its
     slums as were the docks and shipyard area of Rotherhithe. Both
     are now part of the London borough of Southwark.
41. *Siegfried Schmalz*: Invented artist. 'Schmalz' literally means
     'grease'.

CHAPTER 5

THE BATTLE OF THE NORTH ATLANTIC

1.   *Eiserne Kreuz*: Iron Cross.
2.   *Miles Standish*: (c. 1584–1656) one of the Pilgrim Fathers who
     came to New England on the *Mayflower*.
3.   *Karl der Grosse*: Charles the Great or Charlemagne (742–814)
     the founder of the Holy Roman Empire.
4.   *Barbarossa*: Frederick the Great (c. 1123–90), Holy Roman
     Emperor.
5.   *Gott im Himmel . . .*: 'God in heaven! The old *Barbarossa*! But
     what a brave warrior!'
6.   *Susquehanna*: The airships in this battle include, on the American
     side the *Susquehanna*, named after the river which flows to
     Chesapeake Bay, the *Delaware* (the state or the river), and three
     ships named after Presidents: Andrew Jackson (1767–1845),
     hero of the War of 1812 between the United States and Great
     Britain; he was President 1829–37; Abraham Lincoln (1809–
     65), President at the outbreak of the Civil War in 1861; and
     Theodore Roosevelt (1858–1919), Vice-President of the United
     States in 1900, who became President when McKinley was assas-
     sinated and was re-elected in 1905. Later in the battle we glimpse
     the *Monitor*, named after the ship built by the Union in the Civil
     War which fought the *Virginia* in 1862 in the first battle between
     ironclad battleships. On the German side, as well as the *Vater-
     land*, airships include the *Bremen* (north German city on the
     River Weser), the *Weimar* (east German city famous for literature
     and music during the eighteenth and nineteenth centuries), the
     Fürst Bismarck (Prince Otto von Bismarck (1815–98), architect
     of German unification), the *Vogel-stern* (trans. Birdstar), the
     Preussen (Prussia), the *Hermann* and the *Germanicus* (the German
     chief, c. 18 BC–AD 9, also known as Arminius, who ensured
     freedom from the Roman Empire by wiping out three legions
     in AD 9, and Germanicus Caesar, 15 BC–AD 19, who defeated

him in battle in AD 16). There is also the *Adler* (Eagle): some years after the publication of *The War in the Air* the Austrian psychiatrist Alfred Adler (1870–1937) developed a theory of psychology based upon humanity's struggle for a sense of power.

7. *Da waren Albrecht . . .*: 'Albrecht – good old Albrecht, and old Zimmermann, and von Rosen were there!'

8. *wireless telegraphy*: The use of the telegraph revolutionized nineteenth-century communications. The radio pioneer Gugliemo Marconi (1874–1937) patented a system of radio telegraphy in 1896. It was used by the British navy during the Boer War (1899–1902).

9. *barbette*: Gun turret.

10. *Crimean War*: 1854–55. England and France allied against Russia, which was attempting to gain access to the Mediterranean Sea through the Turkish straits of Bosporus and Dardanelles.

11. *Bank Holiday rag*: Bank Holidays were traditionally a time of disorder at holiday resorts.

CHAPTER 6
HOW WAR CAME TO NEW YORK

1. *black and sinister polyglot population*: Not necessarily (but including) Afro-Americans from the South. Immigrants came to the United States from all over the world, but especially Central and Eastern Europe.

2. *Alsatias*: A name given in the seventeenth century to London's Whitefriars district, where debtors could claim sanctuary; thus, a refuge for undesirables or lawbreakers.

3. *They thought America was safe*: An ironic sentence read after September 11th 2001.

4. *Farragut monument*: Erected in 1881 to commemorate the Civil War hero Admiral David G. Farragut (1801–70).

5. *Albany legislature*: Albany is the capital of New York State.

6. *Southern submarines of 1864*: During the American Civil War the Confederate States used submarines against Unionist ships, sinking the USS *Housatonic*.

7. *Cabot Sinclair*: Fictional name.

8. *Doan swivel*: Wells's fictional technological device to allow heavy guns to move on a vertical axis.

9. *Ocean Grove*: New Jersey, on the Atlantic shore.

10. *Matawan*: Town in New Jersey, facing north-east to New York bay.

11. *City Hall*: The seat of New York city government, situated in lower Manhattan.

12. *Knype group*: Named after a fictional press magnate, but possibly inspired by people like William Randolph Hearst (1863–1951).

13. *O'Hagen*: A name possibly chosen to represent the strong Irish influence in American politics in Wells's time.

14. *Monson Building*: Fictional? The late nineteenth and early twentieth centuries were the heroic age of skyscraper building in New York. Wells may have had in mind the Singer Building at 165 Broadway, near City Hall. Constructed 1906–8, it was at the time the tallest building in America.

15. *ganglia*: Nerve centres.

16. *Union Square*: Park linking Broadway and Park Avenue South.

17. *Dexter building*: The Dexter Building in Chicago was constructed in 1887. In Wells's future another has been constructed on Union Square, New York.

18. *Tiffany's*: Tiffany & Co., the celebrated jeweller's on Fifth Avenue from 1837.

19. *Tammany Hall*: A building on 14th Street which became symbolic of the corruption of New York's political administration in the late nineteenth century.

20. *Blut und Eisen . . .*: Blood and iron! . . . Ah, blood and iron!

CHAPTER 7

THE *VATERLAND* IS DISABLED

1. *jiu-jitsu*: Japanese martial art.

2. *Colt-Coburn-Langley*: Fictional weapons manufacturer, but with references to real people. Samuel Colt (1814–62) whose Colt Firearms Company was the biggest supplier of handguns for the Union army during the American Civil War and became famous for the Colt .45, used throughout the American West. Samuel Pierpont Langley (1834–96) was a pioneer in aviation who in 1896 experimented with model steam-powered aircraft.

3. *Bengal lights*: A firework producing a vivid blue light.

4. *New York was our Moscow*: The invasion of Russia by Napoleon Bonaparte (1759–1821) in 1812 was frustrated when the Russians set fire to Moscow, forcing the French to make a humiliating retreat through the bitterly cold Russian winter snows.

5.   *Ein feste Burg ist unser Gott*: A hymn by Martin Luther (1483–
     1546), 'A Mighty Castle is Our God'.
6.   *Labrador*: The mainland part of the territory, now province of
     Newfoundland and Labrador in Eastern Canada.
7.   *Innertkirchen*: Swiss resort, near Lake Engstlen.
8.   *Alexandria . . . Port Arthur . . . Casablanca*: The British occupa-
     tion of Egypt in 1882 was preceded by the bombardment of the
     fortifications of Alexandria leading to riots and a massacre. The
     Russo-Japanese War of 1904–5 began with a devastating surprise
     attack upon on the Russian fleet in Port Arthur (now Dalian in
     China) which was later occupied by the Japanese. In 1907, French
     troops landed in Casablanca, Morocco and by 1912 the country
     became a French protectorate.

CHAPTER 8

A WORLD AT WAR

1.   *Tan Ting-siang*: A fictional name for an Asiatic leader. The place
     names Chinsi-fu and Tsingyen are likewise 'generic' Chinese
     names, while the 'Niaio' as a specific or general name for the
     Asiatic flying-machine seems also to be Wells's invention, perhaps
     echoing Old French 'niais' (nestling): a hand-reared falcon.
2.   *Nova Zembla*: Novaya Zemlya, a group of islands in the Russian
     Arctic.
3.   *Communist insurrection*: The citizens of Paris declared a Com-
     mune in protest against the city's surrender in the Franco-
     Prussian War. Its brutal suppression by the National Government
     killed between 10,000 and 30,000 people.
4.   *Universal Peace Conference*: There had in fact been a Peace Confer-
     ence at The Hague, Netherlands in 1899 which reached conclusions
     on the rules of war and arbitration ('The Hague Convention') but at
     which little progress was made on issues of disarmament.
5.   *Winterhouse-Dunne*: Fictional, but again with roots in reality.
     J. W. Dunne (1875–1949) designed aircraft in the early years of
     the twentieth century and later wrote a book on precognition,
     An Experiment With Time (1927); this influenced Wells during
     the writing of *The Shape of Things to Come*.
6.   *Mohini K. Chatterjee*: A possible echo of Mohini Mohun
     Chatterjee (1858–1936), Indian theosophist guru who translated
     many Hindu spiritual writings and about whom W. B. Yeats
     (1865–1939) wrote the poem 'Mohini Chatterjee'.

7. *Battle of Lissa*: 20 July 1866, between Austrian and Italian naval fleets.
8. *Prospect Park*: In the city of Niagara Falls, New York.
9. *Goat Island*: Island in the middle of the River Niagara, separating the Horseshoe Falls from the American and Bridal Veil Falls.
10. *catspaws*: People used as tools or dupes by other people: in this case a rather unusual term for ordinary soldiers (and Wells may have had the Catskill mountains in southern New York State unconsciously in mind).

CHAPTER 9
ON GOAT ISLAND

1. *rummy*: Odd, strange.
2. *Dummer Kerl*: Stupid oaf.
3. *anent*: Concerning: an archaic word to convey a humorous tone to the passage.
4. *kid in frocks*: See Ch. 1, n. 9.

CHAPTER 10
THE WORLD UNDER THE WAR

1. *flapped disconcertingly*: This passage makes it clear that Wells's account of aeroplane flight differed from what was to happen. Since the Wright Brothers, fixed-wing aircraft rely on the balance between the thrust of the propeller and the drag of air resistance, and the pressure of airflow over the wings which creates an upward acting force. Wells is imagining 'ornithopters' which move their wings after the manner of birds or insects, which theoretically creates more lift.
2. *bowie-knife*: Knife popularized by the American adventurer Jim Bowie (1796–1836) who died at the Battle of the Alamo in Texas.
3. *New Forest*: Region in the southern English counties of Hampshire, Dorset and Wiltshire, created as a hunting reserve in 1079 by William the Conqueror (1027–87).
4. *comic, respectful niggers*: The stereotypes Bert expects from his reading of popular fiction. In the text, Wells uses the then more respectful 'Negro'.
5. *goatee*: A short tufted beard on the chin, resembling that of a goat.
6. *I suppose it is America*: The United States was and is a country of many immigrants for whom English is a second language.

7. *Tanooda*: Fictional place.

8. *Esperanto*: An artificial language designed to overcome language barriers by Ludwig L. Zamenhof (1859–1917) who published a dictionary in 1887.

9. *store*: Generally, American English uses 'store' for 'shop', but there's also the sense that a 'store' deals on a larger scale and with more variety than a mere 'shop'.

10. *diastole*: Relaxation (of a heart muscle). A *systole* is the contraction of the heart.

11. *décolletage*: Exposure of the chest and shoulders, as in a low-cut dress or blouse.

12. *Berkshire Hills*: In western Massachusetts.

13. *Deyse*: 'There's' in a strong New York accent.

14. *Pinkerville*: Fictional place.

CHAPTER 11

THE GREAT COLLAPSE

1. *Antonines*: The Emperor Antonius Pius (86–161) and his adopted son Marcus Aurelius (121–180), whose reigns were noted for good government.

2. *Jehad*: More usually spelt 'Jihad'. Islamic 'struggle' or 'Holy War'.

3. *Purple Death*: A term found several times in science fiction. A short story by W. L. Alden (1837–1908), 'The Purple Death', was published in *Cassell's* magazine in February 1895, but Wells may have been thinking of M. P. Shiel's *The Purple Cloud* (1901).

4. *South Shields*: Port at the mouth of the River Tyne in north-east England.

5. *Tenerife*: One of the Canary Islands, in the Atlantic Ocean.

6. *Mogador*: Town on the coast of Morocco, now called Essaouira.

7. *Düreresque*: After the manner of Albrecht Dürer (1471–1528), German painter and engraver known for his grotesque studies.

8. *Boar's Hill*: Just outside Oxford.

9. *Over-Man*: See Ch. 4, n. 10.

10. *taproom*: Public bar.

THE EPILOGUE

1. *Scarlet Woman*: Or the 'Whore of Babylon'. An image in popular preaching derived from Revelation 17:3: 'There I saw a woman sitting on a scarlet beast that was covered with blasphemous names and had seven heads and ten horns.'

2. *kitcheners*: Cooking ranges fitted with various appliances such as ovens, gas hobs and boilers.

3. *Kentish men*: A native of West Kent. Those born east of the River Medway, which flows through Tonbridge and Maidstone to Rochester south of the Thames estuary are 'Men of Kent'. Wells, born in Bromley, was a 'Kentish man', and the joke about 'nice rough lot' is self-directed.

4. *cullud*: Coloured.

5. *Cheapside*: Street in the City of London; the historic merchants' quarter.

6. *Piccadilly*: Fashionable street in central London noted for fine architecture, clubs and shops. Piccadilly Circus is the heart of London's West End.

7. *say things to 'im*: Piccadilly was also a haunt of prostitutes.

8. *custed marrers*: Custard marrows, a variety of squash.

9. *kerridges*: Carriages.

10. *skilly*: Watery oatmeal porridge given to inmates of workhouses or prisons.

11. *Sammin*: Salmon.

12. *love or – anything*: The saying is 'love or money' but he realizes that in context it is incongruous.

13. *Moses Gluckstein*: A stereotypical Jewish financier of the type all too common in fiction of the time.

14. *sparrowgrass and chokes*: Asparagus and artichokes.

15. *fallals*: Luxuries.

Andy Sawyer

READ MORE IN PENGUIN

In every corner of the world, on every subject under the sun, Penguin represents quality and variety – the very best in publishing today.

For complete information about books available from Penguin – including Puffins, Penguin Classics and Arkana – and how to order them, write to us at the appropriate address below. Please note that for copyright reasons the selection of books varies from country to country.

In the United Kingdom: Please write to *Dept. EP, Penguin Books Ltd, Bath Road, Harmondsworth, West Drayton, Middlesex UB7 0DA*

In the United States: Please write to *Consumer Services, Penguin Putnam Inc., 405 Murray Hill Parkway, East Rutherford, New Jersey 07073-2136.* VISA and MasterCard holders call 1-800-631-8571 to order Penguin titles

In Canada: Please write to *Penguin Books Canada Ltd, 10 Alcorn Avenue, Suite 300, Toronto, Ontario M4V 3B2*

In Australia: Please write to *Penguin Books Australia Ltd, 487 Maroondah Highway, Ringwood, Victoria 3134*

In New Zealand: Please write to *Penguin Books (NZ) Ltd, Private Bag 102902, North Shore Mail Centre, Auckland 10*

In India: Please write to *Penguin Books India Pvt Ltd, 11 Community Centre, Panchsheel Park, New Delhi 110017*

In the Netherlands: Please write to *Penguin Books Netherlands bv, Postbus 3507, NL-1001 AH Amsterdam*

In Germany: Please write to *Penguin Books Deutschland GmbH, Metzlerstrasse 26, 60594 Frankfurt am Main*

In Spain: Please write to *Penguin Books S. A., Bravo Murillo 19, 1°B, 28015 Madrid*

In Italy: Please write to *Penguin Italia s.r.l., Via Vittorio Emanuele 45/a, 20094 Corsico, Milano*

In France: Please write to *Penguin France, 12, Rue Prosper Ferradou, 31700 Blagnac*

In Japan: Please write to *Penguin Books Japan Ltd, Iidabashi KM-Bldg, 2-23-9 Koraku, Bunkyo-Ku, Tokyo 112-0004*

In South Africa: Please write to *Penguin Books South Africa (Pty) Ltd, P.O. Box 751093, Gardenview, 2047 Johannesburg*

PENGUIN CLASSICS

THE TIME MACHINE   H.G. WELLS

'I had made myself the most complicated and the most hopeless trap that ever a man devised'

When a Victorian scientist propels himself into the year 802,701 AD, he is initially delighted to find that suffering has been replaced by beauty, contentment and peace. Entranced at first by the Eloi, an elfin species descended from man, he soon realizes that this beautiful people are simply remnants of a once-great culture – now weak and childishly afraid of the dark. They have every reason to be afraid: in deep tunnels beneath their paradise lurks another race descended from humanity – the sinister Morlocks. And when the scientist's time machine vanishes, it becomes clear he must search these tunnels, if he is ever to return to his own era.

The Time Machine is the first and greatest modern portrayal of time-travel. Part of a brand-new Penguin series of H. G. Wells's works, this edition includes a newly established text, a full biographical essay on Wells, a further reading list and detailed notes. Marina Warner's introduction considers Wells's development of the 'scientific romance' and places the novel in the context of its times.

Introduced by Marina Warner
Textual Editing by Patrick Parrinder
Notes by Steven McLean

PENGUIN CLASSICS

THE FIRST MEN IN THE MOON   H.G. WELLS

'I fell and fell and fell for evermore into the abyss of the sky'

When penniless businessman Mr Bedford retreats to the Kent coast to write a play, he meets by chance the brilliant Dr Cavor, an absent-minded scientist on the brink of developing a material that blocks gravity. Cavor soon succeeds in his experiments, only to tell a stunned Bedford the invention makes possible one of the oldest dreams of humanity: a journey to the moon. With Bedford motivated by money, and Cavor by the desire for knowledge, the two embark on the expedition. But neither are prepared for what they find – a world of freezing nights, boiling days and sinister alien life, on which they may be trapped forever.

The First Men in the Moon is one of the first and greatest science fiction novels. Part of a brand-new Penguin series of H. G. Wells's works, this edition includes a newly established text, a full biographical essay on Wells, a further reading list and detailed notes. China Mieville's introduction places the novel in literary context, and reveals it as a skilled critique of Imperialism.

Introduced by China Mieville
Textual Editing by Patrick Parrinder
Notes by Steven McLean

PENGUIN CLASSICS

THE ISLAND OF DR MOREAU   H.G. WELLS

'The study of Nature makes a man at last as remorseless as Nature'

Adrift in a dinghy, Edward Prendick, the single survivor from the good ship *Lady Vain*, is rescued by a vessel carrying a profoundly unusual cargo – a menagerie of savage animals. Tended to recovery by their keeper Montgomery, who gives him dark medicine that tastes of blood, Prendick soon finds himself stranded upon an uncharted island in the Pacific with his rescuer and the beasts. Here, he meets Montgomery's master, the sinister Dr Moreau – a brilliant scientist whose notorious experiments in vivisection have caused him to abandon the civilized world. It soon becomes clear he has been developing these experiments – with truly horrific results.

A parable on Darwinian theory, and a biting social satire, *The Island of Dr Moreau* is a fascinating exploration of what it is to be human. Part of a brand-new Penguin series of H. G. Wells's works, this edition includes a newly established text, a full biographical essay on Wells, a further reading list and detailed notes. Margaret Atwood's introduction explores the social and scientific relevance of this influential work.

Introduced by Margaret Atwood
Textual Editing by Patrick Parrinder
Notes by Steven McLean

PENGUIN CLASSICS

A MODERN UTOPIA   H.G. WELLS

'There is no justice in Nature perhaps, but the idea of justice must be sacred'

While walking in the Swiss Alps, two English travellers fall into a space-warp, and suddenly find themselves in another world. In many ways the same as our own – even down to the characters that inhabit it – this new planet is still radically different, for the two walkers are now upon a Utopian Earth controlled by a single World Government. Here, as they soon learn, all share a common language, there is sexual, economic and racial equality, and society is ruled by socialist ideals enforced by an austere, voluntary elite: the 'Samurai'. But what will the Utopians make of these new visitors from a less perfect world?.

A compelling blend of philosophical discussion and imaginative narrative, *A Modern Utopia* is one of Wells's most positive visions of a possible world. Part of a brand-new Penguin series of H. G. Wells's works, this edition includes a newly established text, a full biographical reading list and detailed notes. The introduction, by Francis Wheen, considers the virtues and flaws of Wells's ideal society.

Introduced by Francis Wheen
Textual Editing by Gregory Claeys
Notes by Gregory Claeys